The Brides' Fair

By

Hal Fleming

PublishAmerica
Baltimore

© 2008 by Hal Fleming.
All rights reserved. No part of this book may be reproduced, stored in a retrieval system or transmitted in any form or by any means without the prior written permission of the publishers, except by a reviewer who may quote brief passages in a review to be printed in a newspaper, magazine or journal.

First printing

PublishAmerica has allowed this work to remain exactly as the author intended, verbatim, without editorial input.

All characters in this book are fictitious, and any resemblance to real persons, living or dead, is coincidental.

ISBN: 1-60563-706-8
PUBLISHED BY PUBLISHAMERICA, LLLP
www.publishamerica.com
Baltimore

Printed in the United States of America

The annual Brides' Fair among the Ait Hadidou Berbers of the Mid Atlas mountains is a unique tradition in that it is the young virgin brides who presumably select their husbands by circling men who have declared themselves available. Importantly, and counter to customs throughout most of North Africa and the Middle East, older, married women can, of their own free will, return to the Brides' Fair to divorce and select a new husband in this communal event.

To Rosalind

Hope you enjoy this.

Ant Thms

9/20/08

Dedicated to the brides of the Mid Atlas, and to my wife, Arlene, who encouraged me to keep trying.

Chapter I

On the morning before the Brides' Fair, Other Mother Itto called her through the enveloping rose caftan of dawn, an oddly soft call, cool and caressing like the summer winds on the high plateau. Most mornings Itto was all snap and growl, marshaling them to a quick gulp of heavily sugared tea and a piece of flat barley bread and then off to a long day's work. But this morning Kachou did not have to hurry down the trail to gather brush for the bread oven and the tea braziers. Nor would she have to lead the sheep and goats to search out scarce new patches of esparto and sage grasses over the steep slopes and among the mountain's crevices. All routines were to be changed during these dreaded several days, and so Kachou wiggled further down under the crudely knotted carpet that she and half sister, Izza, used as a blanket on their narrow wooden couch. How Kachou had wailed and shivered against her last night, but Izza, only eleven, had few words of comfort and could only cry along with her.

Now Other Mother Itto and Aunt Rabha stood over the couch in the stone and mud mortared sleeping hut. "Up, up Kachou, and you too Izza. Cousin Ben Kaddour will be through soon with his truck and you must prepare." Peeking from the corner of the carpet, she saw that the two were already in their best skirts and striped wool hondoros shawls. They had patterned their faces and hands with henna and applied kohl blackening around their eyes. Little could mask Other Mother Itto's trough-lined face nor the liverish color of her eyes. She had only forty-two or three years, but already moved with an old granny's stoop and shuffle. Aunt Rabha, ten years younger still could carry herself erect. She had the fine, sharp nose of a field hawk and the color of sun-browned straw, yet with the birthing of children almost every winter, she would wither like the grasses and most every growing thing in the high mountains.

"No more of your stubbornness, daughter." Other Mother Itto's voice turned familiarly stern, and she ripped back the cover, but then paused to stroke the long luxuriant black hair of her step-daughter.

Aunt Rabha supervised her bath in the stone hut that served as a hamam for all the six households of inter-related families in the ksar of El Husein, Kachou's own father. Granny Melouda and the full grown boy cousin, Haddou, with the chest muscles of a caid's horse but the brain of a bed flea had been keeping the fire going since long before dawn. To conserve precious water all the girls of the ksar including Itto's own daughters Anissa and Jamila, Aunt Rabha's Rachida and Safia and four other cousins, one of whom, Zora, being also a new bride, were rounded up to soak in the stone and plaster pool of steaming water.

"But you are a strong, healthy girl, Kachou, more blessed with *baraka* than most. And never forget you are the great grand daughter of a marabout saint," Aunt Rabha had counseled her over and over these past days until the eyes wandered in the head. Descended from a great one? Where in what shadow or cave did he exist? She had tried to call him in the night; she had sent out prayers of urgency for her salvation, but only the stiff mountain winds answered back.

"You will suffer all the trials of your marriage bed well. You will give cousin Ben Moha many fine, strong children."

"And be old and wrinkled up too soon or die too young like my mother," Kachou said.

"What's so bad about it cousin?" Zora who was also 15 had told her. "You will have your own hut and a warm man besides you most nights. You will no longer have to tend sheep and goats like a mere girl. You will do woman's work."

"But you are marrying a young boy, Ben Kaddour's son. And who do I get but old Ben Moha." And why could she not choose, why must she accept what had been decided barely hours after they pulled her from her mother's thighs, decided before she could distinguish the shapes and sounds hovering overhead? They, Zora, Izza, Anissa, Rachida, whispered by the night fires, by the wells, in the pastures, spoke of what the old ways and constant rhythms would bring; how they would be taken up to a big special souk before the snows closed the trails and passes; how they would be hennaed and prettied up so they could parade smart and sure; how they would circle twice he who exchanged their eyes' flash, their nod, their quick tap of hands. They whispered the secrets of how with the man they would be changed from girl to woman, and how the young men of their choosing would not soon leave them for their wanderings, but would take them off to the cities on the coast or even to France.

"But why must I get old Ben Moha?"

THE BRIDES' FAIR

"Who brings in 700 quintals of corn and barley. Who gets much fine wool from his sheep and whose brother sends money orders from Belgium on all the feast days," Aunt Rabha informed Kachou.

"Who cares about such things? I will throw myself onto the pointed rocks of the deepest gorge before I let him climb on me," Kachou cried as Granny Melouda and Aunt Rabha worked a solution of henna into her waist long hair.

"But you won't dare do that. You will not bring shame to Baba El Husein's house." Aunt Rabha called for the idiot boy, Haddou, to bring more cold water for the rinsing pool. Haddou had little thought for the nakedness of his girl cousins for he brought water to the hamam in great clay jugs most every morning. Also, Baba El Husein had made Haddou's father call the sheep doctor from the big village down on the lower plateau. The sheep doctor took his knife to the boy's bad seed that sprouted from time to time when blood cousins married blood cousins up in the isolated high plateau.

"This Ben Moha is of your father El Husein's own clan," Aunt Rabha explained. "A contract was made for you many years ago before you could walk or talk."

"And you my own Aunt would let me just go to his ksar, be abused by his other women, be used at whim like some serving girl?"

"Listen to me fine one," Granny Melouda said splashing handfuls of ice cold water over the girl who stood in her nakedness a full two hands taller than the old woman. "You have the swollen head of a wild city girl." The woman roughly scoured the girl's backside with dried leaves dipped in powdered pumice. Kachou whined and squirmed. "You think this is bad, spoiled daughter? Ben Moha will have you screaming all right soon enough. They may need to call an old granny of their own household to pry you open for him."

"Stop that talk, Granny Melouda," Aunt Rabha said.

Kachou still refused to accept it. She had been promised in infancy to Ben Moha, the patriarch of the ksar at two hour walk up the west trail, near the well favored for its tea water. Baba El Husein and Other Mother Itto had spared her this knowledge until several months ago, when, at the time of her fifteenth birthday, ten sacks of sugar came down the trail by donkey as the first of many bridal gifts. "But why me? Certainly others, cousin Zora, would bring more status, would better bind the clans together."

"We finalized the agreement at a tea ceremony after your mother's internment," Baba El Husein had explained over and over by the night fires. "You were only a few days old, and my cousin twice removed, then a young man in his early twenties was touched by the circumstances. Your strong *baraka* had caused you to survive. And thus we mad a compact from which no one can now retreat."

Aunt Rabha patterned Kachou's high cheek bones and broad forehead with henna, saying that the array of tightly clustered circles and stars would give her protection against her worries. Kachou thought of the last time, the happy time she had been so elaborately done up. Last year the Caid's agents came through to choose her and Zora to go to the grand fair at Zemmara for Independence Day. It had to be the most important time of her fourteen years to be among that great assembly of young people drawn from all the plateaus and valleys of the province. When their chaperones were not looking they played at dipping their eyes at boys, the soldiers mostly, not those boys who sat idle in the tea houses among the old grey beards. It was a joyful time and she and Zora wore their distinctive hondoros shawls, their spangled snoods and their peaked caps with pride. They caused no real trouble and brought no shame upon their ksar.

Now she lay on her back while Aunt Rabha with the quick steady hand of a master calligrapher marked the intricate henna patterns on her throat and neck down to the cleft between her breasts. No woman had ever marked her so.

"It's what I remember from your mother's clan," Aunt Rabha said. "The signs mean many things. They mean you the woman are the tent of the family, the husband the main pole, the children the stakes. They mean you will have a long life and many children."

"But I do not want many children. I do not want Ben Moha for a husband. I do not want any husband."

"Hush your shameful mouth child."

The tattoos seemed to take hours. The whole ksar had to come to inspect her as well as Zora who hardly complained at all when they had marked her up. Candle flames danced everywhere in the bath hut, and every finished tattoo received a chorus of piercing ululations. Itto, Rhaba and all the other women became in the shadows the specters that had come to her in the middle of the night, laughing and howling. Finally, she was permitted to put on the new white knickers sewn from city cloth and the black wool marriage skirt she had reluctantly woven over the summer months. Aunt Rabha colored their cheeks with rouge paste, and all those hovering around her repeated over and over that Kachou and Zora would be the most beautiful of the Zabra brides. She had heard tell of a girl at last year's fair who defied the customs, who just walked the twenty kilometers down to where the old Renault bus passes, and she was never heard from again. But how could this be done, for now Uncle ben Kaddour's truck strained and rattled up the stony piste to El Husein's ksar? The women near the gate gave out with shattering ululations of welcome that long reverberated against the rock walls of the high plateau.

***** ***** ***** ***** ***** ***** *****

That same early morning in the capital city some three hundred kilometers north, Eric Dalton prepared himself, also reluctantly, to make the long trek through the Mid Atlas mountains to the Brides' Fair. Although his office in the fortress-like embassy faced the inner court as a protection against terrorist attacks, he could still hear the muezzins calling the faithful to prayer. Through high wattage amplifiers, the sounds soared penetrating the old medina, the ancient Roman port, the Chella, and the *Nouvelle Ville*. The passion and the constancy of these voices reassured him for an instant until the phone rang and Ambassador Harlan Crane intruded rudely on the cries of Allah Akbar.

"It's still all laid on for a 0730 departure," Eric replied to the question about the trip to the Brides' Fair. Calling from the Residence, the Ambassador said that his wife, Pamela, was just about ready. Could that be a bit of anxiety in the voice, not the usual sharpness? He had apparently lost out in persuading her, as he had tried with Eric, not to go. 'It's too damn risky, Country's on the brink of disaster.'

His houseman, Larbi, dressed in his white jacket, would be serving Crane his breakfast at this very moment as he had served three American Ambassadors before him in the official residence. This morning, however, Larbi's practiced hand would tremble ever so slightly as he placed the cup and saucer. There would be no buttery croissants nor herb omelets, just plain toast made from American white bread which arrived frozen at the Embassy commissary once a month. But as a concession to the bounties of this country, the Ambassador would concede to one small glass of freshly squeezed orange juice.

"What do they want us to believe this morning?" Crane asked.

"No change. Security en route to the Fair is very tight, and we have confirmation of that. Some protests expected in the cities, but not in the countryside or mountains. We're helping out with electronic intercepts. Of course the French are as well."

Crane abruptly changed the subject and raised the issue of his meeting with the Minister of Interior this morning. "As I said last evening, I don't think it's a good idea. We've nothing really new to tell him, do we? And don't you think the excuses for the delays and the machinations of the Pentagon and the Congress are becoming rather worn?" The issue which had ballooned into a dark cloud over usually cordial bilateral relations, had to do with high tech surveillance equipment, bought and paid for months ago, but still not delivered.

Eric wanted to punctuate his counsel with "Mr. Ambassador" and "Sir" to keep his distance with formality, but the man for some egalitarian reason which did not ring true, insisted on first names. The Ambassador roared back his disagreement. They had been over this already last evening as well when Crane stormed into his office hovering over his desk, tall, avuncular, ready to pounce like a mantis.

"No, I don't need you with me. And you needn' t be worried that I'll break a lot of crockery, get us PNG'd or give you all heart failure," Crane had fumed last evening when all in the front office and most other staff had sensibly gone home. "I've been on this earth 64 years, made millions in business, been elected state governor twice, so I don't need you or anyone with me to wipe my rear end. You go on that damn culture trip. Pam insists on going too, although I don't know how she'll tolerate the flies and the dirt. But you will keep your eye on her, even for my sake."

The confrontations with Crane more embarrassed than intimidated him, and since the man lashed out at most everyone who dared disagree, Eric did not consider himself a victim. That's how he survived: *illigetimus non carbarundum est*, and he had worked with one or two real bastards in his twenty year career with the Department; the first Ambassador during that tour in Rome, also political, also a FOP, Friend of the President, also deluded by the supposed grandeur of his office; also intimidated by the pros on his staff. And that short-lived Assistant Secretary back in Washington who relished keeping everyone around till ten in the evening redrafting, and redrafting urgent memos to the White House, losing all the precision and most of the meaning. None of them though were as bad as Crane, however, who even the sticklers for protocol in the other Embassies and the host government tended to shun. The officials paused for only for the briefest salutation, the barest handshake, and then circled back to Eric or other old pros for the latest on the Middle East Peace Process, the Iraq insurgency, the War on Terrorism and all the much studied issues he dealt with evasively or with candor as his instructions from Washington so dictated. The Embassy senior staff meetings the Ambassador chaired were cold, even hostile. There were few 'good mornings' for anyone, not even for the over-worked secretaries, and Eric had to stroke the bruised egos, wipe the tear-stained face of Dina Johnson, the front office major domo, more than once. And there were those midnight phone calls and another pretext or compulsion for calling an emergency meeting.

THE BRIDES' FAIR

"That's right, Eric, Washington's asked for my personal views on the host country's military readiness, and ASAP"

"But Harlan, we sent that report just last week. You signed off on it, don't you remember?"

"Not that mealy-mouth crap. 'On the one hand this, and on the other that.' No, I'm going to give them the down-and-dirty, unwashed story. So get the right people for 8 am, before you all get lost in your typical routines."

The man never stopped, driven by either contempt for them all or by fear of the subtleties, shadows and long, labyrinthian threads of diplomacy, of which the foreign affairs in-crowd, made too much of at times, Eric had to admit. "Yes, Harlan," he said and calmly replaced the receiver, pausing with his paperwork, his moving commas around on paper as he described his job, to make a record of the conversation on his PC, scrolling into his files and entering his security code for the confidential drawer. No matter how brief or inconclusive the discussion, he was precise in noting time, date, statements, points and digressions as close to verbatim as possible just in case Crane did real damage to U.S. interests, sounded off to the press without clearance, or demanded Eric's recall to Washington, not an unacceptable idea; he would be a hero to the old guard having stood his ground against an erratic political appointee.. He didn't believe Crane would go that far. Eric was both resented and needed. The balance could be tolerated. . But regardless, neither of them would change, and for better or worse, he, not Crane, would endure this mission.

Outside, the much amplified morning call to prayer had ended. The Embassy began to come to life. The elaborate electronics and air conditioning systems shivered through the building duct work. He heard the sucking clunk of a nearby two inch steel security door; the clicking of a woman's heels in the corridor outside. That would be his secretary Elsie Tedesco, faithfully arriving early to help him clear out the last flood of staff memos, intelligence reports and cables. He had only a few minutes to finish his reading before he had to leave, and he set about it with his customary, meticulousness, ink pen, not ball point, at the ready.

He ordered and reordered the stacks before him, discarding half the circular cables, the long winded reports on international trade meetings, the redundant and mostly outdated "top secrets" on enemies real or potential. He did not measure his increasingly solitary life in coffee spoons as T.S. Eliot's man, but in memoranda.

One message from the Ministry of Interior to all diplomatic missions troubled him but was so damn obvious that he almost managed a smile. The message with its long-outdated stylistic flourishes assured Embassies and other accredited missions that reports of incidents along the eastern and southern borders of the country were completely unfounded. 'The Government assures you of its highest esteem and begs to inform Your Excellency that travel to the Imichil Fair in the Mid Atlas mountains or to any touristic destination whatsoever can be made in complete safety.'

The Ministry spin doctors were at it again, and he could picture some of his colleagues at the other foreign embassies doubling up with laughter. Outposts attacked? Infiltrators running amuck? The fantasies of under-employed diplomats and journalists? The senior political counselor at the French Embassy, Alain de la Batie, couldn't have been more certain of the raid below Zagora last week. "But of course it was the Mouvememnt Populaire pour la Liberation Mahgrebian. Several guerrillas and border guards killed. You will never know the exact body count in this country. The dead are taken away and buried *rapidment*."

"*Mais, Msieu Dalton, Cher Ami,*" Mohamed Bennani, the Minister of Interior had said. "How one can turn an arrest of Tuareg *counterbandistes* running high grade Burmese heroin through the Sahara for the Nigerian syndicate, into a bloody confrontation with the MPLM is much beyond my comprehension. We have all in check, M'sieu Dalton, all under control."

Was the car bomb in Casablanca last month which killed seven innocent pedestrians and got big play in the often censored local press, some devious French plot? Or a strike by an obscure fundamentalist faction? Or other radical factions backed by Al Qaeda or Iran ? Of course the Government urged all of them to go to the Brides' Fair or roam the countryside at will. The city was plastered with posters. Flyers flowed into the Embassy every day. Because of the current crisis up the line in the Middle East, tourism was in its worst slump since the Arab-Israeli War years ago. For the Diplomatic Corps not to make its annual pilgrimage would be a devastating blow.

His main reason for joining the annual Embassy trip to the mountain *fête* had nothing to do with shoring up the host country's tourism industry, nor in wanting to take a breather from the Ambassador, however. He had promised an old friend, Cynthia Dennis, the Embassy "Visa Lady" and the trip organizer, that he would go. He had been at post two years already and could never find the time even for a long weekend. His wife, Hillary, in the months before she left for the States, had given up suggesting outings far removed from the pressures of the Embassy. There were no more offers of treks to historic Roman and Arab sites, of escapes to remote beaches. Yes, it would be good to finally get away he repeated over and over until he became at last convinced; it would good to purge himself, to drink in the mountain air deeply, to reacquaint himself with Cynthia Dennis, to make new friends.

"Very much a must-do thing during one's tour here, Eric," Giles Whitcomb, his British counterpart said. "Now the young bride thing is not to every one's taste, not PC you know, but the folklore and spectacle are quite a good show. And the trip up through those gorges and ravines? You wont ever forget it."

He scanned through another stack of cables without reading more than the first tag line of most. Another bleat for an overdue trade report. The Embassy was down two officers in the ECON section; Washington would just have to wait; A report on more trench war fare with the Congress and the White House over the primary responsibility for managing the country's foreign policy apparatus, the State Department or the Pentagon. Jan Hessburgh in ADMIN had lost her father. He had gotten an advance from the communications duty officer last evening and called Jan. She was prepared for the news; had her bags packed and everything. She thanked him for his concern.

And there was an out going cable designated "immediate" and "secret" drafted by Peter Younger, the new junior officer in Political. The Iranian People's Delegate was seen at the Brazilian reception cozying up to the Pakistani Ambassador, Mohammad Sharif. The Sudanese, El Hassan, hovered about. Snatches of conversation were overheard by the Brits, the French. Lips read by someone clever. You had to believe they were up to something. Cocktails were all business no matter the polite, tinkling inanities. There was a communications intercept hinting of it. Was Fortress America being targeted again? Did it have to do with weapons or drugs? Or did it have to do with funds for the local liberation movement? Peter had taken it as far as he could in his straightforward, unembellished report. How Eric envied Peter. As a junior officer he too was full of it, alert to the warnings, to ferreting out the real players. He had been acutely on top of those pairing off for *tête-a-têtes*, those stepping out for strolls in the garden; the Cubans imploring the Russians; the Swedes and the other Nordics ganging up on the U.S. over a vote on the environment or children's rights in the UN. He once had rooted about in diplomatic garbage for evidence of danger to the Embassy, to U.S. interests. He had been a thorough, diligent officer in the fierce competition with other bright, rising stars. But "immediate?" Should they want to rouse Washington from its bed? Pry the new, desk officer, Karen McDougal, from the arms of her lover? Get the boys at the National Security Council and the CIA all astir? "A good job of work, Peter," he wrote. "But I wouldn't send it "immediate:" "Secret," of course, but routine and slugged for the attention of the Assistant Secretary. 'Immediates' have away of overly exciting folks back in beautiful, downtown Washington."

Buried in the stack of incoming overnights was an urgent message from the Department announcing the visit of a five person Congressional Delegation the end of next week. Congressman Joe Farrell, the young and feisty Chairman of the Subcommittee on Human Rights and an evangelical believer in his cause, had his long list of imponderable questions. "Does the country assure the free exchange of ideas at all levels of the society?" "Have MPLM prisoners reportedly being held by the Government been seen by members of the International Red Cross?" The Congressman of course wanted an audience with the King with the usual photo ops. This would not be possible, for the Palace regarded Farrell as the enemy, but the Congressman's young staff would burn up the fax machines and clog the E-mail accusing the Embassy of not really trying to get that meeting for their man

He asked Elsie to red flag this one and make sure the Ambassador sees it, which she would have done anyway. "This could be trouble," he said. "We don't want word to get outside the Embassy about this. The Congressman could be targeted by our friends here as well as our friends' enemies. Talk to Security, and I'll write a note to the Ambassador." He paused, frozen for a long second, and then noticed Elsie pursing her lips and clenching her teeth. After two years together during long days and too many weekends, she could sense his moods, predict his next words.

"No, you're not going to cancel because of Congressman Farrell or any of it. And you've got just 15 minutes to get yourself down to the van," she said.

"But I'll never forgive myself if things blow," he said.

"They'll blow whether you're here or not. None of us, not God Himself can control these things anymore," she said.

She was the wisest one. She read all the mounds of stuff that flew in and out of the office. She massaged the reports, heard the talk yet never let herself get lost in the weeds like too many of them. "Fifteens minutes, you say?" They returned to writing instructions, including one to the Political Section on the Farrell visit.

"Bad timing as always. Planning on the QT as best you can. This is an American VIP security issue as you know, and advise Farrell's office not to talk to the press, to deny, to set up a ruse trip with Embassy Kuwait. Try to fill every minute of their schedule without confirming or naming names. They wont get near the palace or the political prisoners, of course, but don't forget a spot of tourism to take the edge off. Ye will be so judged by the those brown paper parcels stuffed with mountain carpets, brass trays, and silver hands of Fatima, not by your reputed diplomatic brilliance."

Eric wrote several more notes and reminders to staff, and asked Elsie to go edit and final copy the talking points the Ambassador hopefully would use in his meeting this morning with the Minister of Interior. After locking up his safe, he took one look around his office as he always did before taking a trip, preparing himself for the remote possibility of never coming back to this place which with its framed photos, mementoes, books and *objets d'art*. This had been the center of his life, his anchor. There once was an order and routine to it which could be packed up in boxes as it was every three or four years and shipped off to the next foreign outpost or back to Washington where the drill would be very much the same even though the environment could vary, could be dangerous, dull or demanding. . He could be reassigned in the middle of the night, given some new priority assignment and never return. He could be blown up or assassinated as had several close friends out on missions to remote corners of the world few back in the States knew or cared about.

His office and his life no longer seemed that transportable, if it ever was. There was never a 'just beam me up, Scotty' to the next horizon where he would be instantly acclimated. One always left something behind at the previous post no matter how routine the challenges had been, how mundane the daily living. There was always at least one colleague in one host government office who could give you a fair game of tennis on those early mornings when the red clay courts were still freshly rolled and unscarred by sneakers. And even in the most drab countries there endured at least one vision of some landscape with its ancient ruins where the herders and their charges moved slowly without sound through the historic rubble. And perhaps for some there was always a sweet encounter with a grateful local lover in an inn somewhere well off the beaten diplomatic path.

On his office walls hung the meritorious award plaques; the signed photos of several of his former Ambassadors with whom he had served on his steady climb upwards to the senior ranks; the few handicraft souvenirs, including his favorite from the Senofou tribe of West Africa; mystical creatures half human, half antelope and caiman, a ritualistic bonding of man and animal. Inked thickly on home spun cloth, it represented nature in balance, the hunter and the hunted in harmony. If only with a few simple strokes of a brush his world could be so ordered. He still kept on his desk the photo portrait of Hillary and the two children, Peter and Susan, taken several years back when the kids, ten and twelve, had begun to reveal in their faces something of their individuality, and when

Hillary, with her lovely dimply beam, appeared to be resigned to the life of a diplomatic nomad. Shouldn't he now confine the portrait to the lower desk drawer along with the must-read articles and the yet-to-be answered correspondence from old friends? Three months ago Hillary abruptly, without warning left for the States with Susan in tow, Peter being at his boarding school in Massachusetts, thankfully far removed from this painful coming apart.

The note was too text book, too familiar. "I need a real life, Eric, with roots, parents and family only an hour or two away. Yours is not the real world anymore, not for me at least. Take care of yourself. Love, Hilary." Was it longing for the shopping malls, the beltways, the pampering of one's very own garden that drove her back to the States? Hillary wasn't really like that. No, he was mostly to blame. He had been overly preoccupied with his future in the service, with the specter of being selected out like so many at 50, only six years hence; with those mid-forty anxieties about why he was here doing what he did and not on the other, greener side of some illusionary fence making mega bucks in the private sector like most from his law school class.

He remained standing before the African cloth with its immutable figures and sifted over and over what had gone wrong. Had he been too obtuse, too absorbed to notice the deterioration of a 20 year old partnership that had seemed so steady and sure since his law school days?

"Oh, Exalted one, I have come for my instructions," Stu Connors, the rumpled and somewhat portly senior political officer poked through the office door. He would be acting for Eric during the next three days ."You needn't give me the key to the executive washroom, nor the codes for the doomsday button, I couldn't possibly deal with that level of responsibility." The man, older than Eric by ten years and looking all of it or more, was only half facetious. He would never be promoted beyond his current rank, and it seemed obvious, although the personnel people would never tell, that there was something in his record. Bouts of alcoholism? Crossing swords with an unforgiving Ambassador somewhere along the way? But the man was a brilliant analyst and a dogged worker, and if Eric could enjoy the luxury of friendship with any on staff here at post, it was with this physical wreck of a man. On hearing about Hillary's sudden departure, Stu had come by the house to get him stinking drunk on what he called martinis but proved to be straight gin, without the whisper of anything but ice. The man had lost a wife as well the year before, but with finality, with no hope for a reconciliation, nor a civil meeting in some restaurant to be mature about it for the sake of the children . Adrian Connors had died in great pain from bone cancer, "two weeks after her fiftieth, and before this terrible thing, never sick a day, and unlike me doing all the right things, exercise, tennis, vitamins. We were college friends too. Never really knew another woman."

"I did pick up a few things at the Canadian dinner last evening, " Stu Connor said settling himself on the office couch, a familiar resting place for the many private *tête-a-têtes* with the DCM in sorting out fact from myth in this country and on making certain their reporting to Washington was forceful without being alarmist. "It's about that UN Refugee camp down below Zagora. The Government wants to move it inland 200 kilometers, and the UN High Commission is refusing, saying it would be inaccessible to those coming across the border. Is it a matter of who blinks first? No, I don't think so. The UN director down there, the Swede, Erickson, is going by the official manual and seeing no evil and hearing no evil as those humanitarians are wont to do. But it's a juicy target. Raise a little hell down there among 20,000 destitute but ever photogenic Mauritanian and Tuareg women and children and you bet the MPLM will get its story on the BBC, CNN, and Antenne 3."

Eric had to take the threat of the MPLM seriously, even though it still remained tepid stuff when he compared it to being the last American official air lifted out of Mogadishu ten years ago, not after three months temporary duty in Sarjevo during the worst of it, when the Serbs and the Bosnians were hard at obliterating each other. For every crisis these days there was a discernible beginning but really never any closure as the UN, the Pentagon and the White House talked and back pedaled and talked some more. And so Eric viewed all levels of civil disorder as equally dangerous and equally without end. "Better recheck our evacuation plan and see if any Americans are working in that camp. They'd be the hostages of choice, wouldn't they?" That was the standard drill, to go beyond it would start a panic, would get Ambassador Crane more roiled up than usual.

"Eric, you're losing it, my friend. How could you forget our own Mother Teresa? The much younger American version; our Karen Gunderson? She was honey drawing flies at the Ambassador's Fourth of July bash."

He did recall talking to the attractive nurse for a few minutes. She had never before left the state of Minnesota, except for several high school band trips to Ohio and Indiana, and now she was 5,000 miles away living on the flat plains before the Sahara desert, coping with the destitute and dying. "It's really not so bad," she told him. "After too many nights in ER at City Hospital back in Minneapolis coping with the gun shot victims, car smashed bodies and the drug ODs, there's a certain peace out there working with those refugees."

Cynthia Dennis had taken the nurse in tow, believing, correctly of course, that he needed relief from such captivity, knowing he needed to keep circulating. He could never pause for more than a minute. He had his tried and true routine typically starting off in one corner of the reception, of the cocktail and munchy horde, chatting up every last guest, side-stepping always to the right, never lingering too long no matter how fascinating, important or attractive the guest. "Remain engaged with the Cuban Ambassador, or a good looking woman, and how the rumors will fly, Buddy Boy about a U.S. *rapprochement* with Castro or about a new mistress."

"Yes, I remember the nurse, now that you mention her. Rather special, wasn't she? Try to get the Ambassador's attention on this for the meeting this morning with Mohammed Bennani." The Ambassador would waste little time over the danger to the UN camp. 'Refugees? Just more welfare cases on the big UN teat.'

Eric handed Stu Connors several cables he had pulled out of the stack, including the one on the Congressman Farell visit. Then they quickly reviewed the Ambassador's schedule for the next three days, and Eric scanned his office one last time, gave his secretary Elsie further instructions and a quick hug. "You know how to reach me on the van radio. We'll check in regularly."

"May the road be smooth, your companions entertaining, and may you find the bride of your choice at the Imichil fair," Stu Connor said walking him to the outer room shared with the Ambassador and cut off from the rest of the Embassy by heavy stainless steel, blast proof doors.

Eric, as was his way, arrived exactly on time outside in the rear, walled compound which served as parking lot for the staff and for the official vehicles of the Embassy. The blue North African sky had no clouds or limit, often startling those not used to such clarity. It was a sky well known to artists and cinematographers, and he always remarked that it should somehow be bottled and sold for hard foreign exchange to those countries with depressing weather, in perpetual grayness. Gulls and storks wheeled, cried and clacked their long bills above the forests of radio masts and satellite communication dishes on the Embassy roof as if trapped by the electronic web, unable to break free to the open spaces on the river delta and the bay beyond.

Ahmed, an Embassy watchman, released the bolt locks on the black iron gate. His companion, a local policeman assigned to diplomatic protection, uncoiled himself from his stool in the rear gate house and snapped to attention with the barrel of his automatic weapon pointed down. Another security guard passed a reflective, spatula-like affair under the frame of each vehicle checking for explosives. The travelers to the Brides' Fair, led by Karen, Eric Dalton's God daughter, and her mother Cynthia Dennis, began to arrive. He kissed them on both cheeks in the international fashion. "I had this gnawing feeling you wouldn't show." At not even 7:30 am, Cynthia was fresh and glowing with anticipation for the trip, the brilliant morning light playing on her eyes and hair. "I thought you'd send down a note with your secretary, not willing to face me in person, telling me about some crisis that had just come up, like the ending of the world."

They were old friends, and it wasn't like her to be impish, to ridicule. But having at last freed himself from his desk, he manage a smile. "No, only a minor revolution in some god-forsaken country which doesn't need my attention for the next 72 hours at least." How the North African sun clung to her and to Karen, illuminating and framing them like a Vermeer painting, but they needed no such enhancements. Cynthia seemed as young and vital as when they were first together on mission in the Philippines, was it 17 year ago? She could easily pass as Karen's older sister, certainly not her mother. He always could find those adulatory words, studied opinions on this and that, clever summations in his kit bag, but this morning he couldn't even manage a 'How great you both look. How really lovely.' Hillary had left him high and dry, and all women, even one as close as Cynthia seemed to mock him.

"Well, take care of Pam for me," the Ambassador said directly to Eric, disregarding Cynthia and the others, not pausing to greet the local employees in the rear courtyard. It would have been so much appreciated, if Crane had stopped a minute to congratulate the head auto mechanic, Benabdessalam, for his daughter's scholarship to Brown University; to have inquired after, Ben Moussa, the Embassy gardener's new baby. But Crane paid no attention to any of those streaming through the Embassy gate into the now bustling rear court yard. He had what appeared to be sleep-deprived puffiness about the eyes, a face too florid. Something pulled at any semblance of vigor and command. "She's not to get any special treatment from you or anyone else. Just don't let her get married off to some old camel herder."

"Only a young sheik will do," Mrs. Crane said with a wry smile and a pose from an old Betty Davis movie. She was over twenty years her husband's junior and had a well-groomed sleekness that even the least generous in their community would call attractive. With her unscuffed hiking boots, factory faded jeans, and a many-pocketed field jacket she was the very catalog model of one off for a romp in the mountains.

Jerry Donatelli, the Gunny Sergeant of the Marine Guard unit arrived with his wife, Mai. He would share the driving of the big boxy passenger van with the Marine Lance Corporal, Jess Williams. Doug Baker, the new public affairs officer, his wife Edna; Dr. Jonathan McMannus, an agricultural advisor, and Monique Addleman, a teacher of English as a foreign language filled the other seats . "We could have squeezed in one or two more in the very back I suppose, but then we would have had very little room for luggage and things. But everyone who signed is here and on time too, "Cynthia said. "A very good beginning, don't you think?"

They left the Embassy compound only twenty minutes behind schedule, after Benabdelssalam probed around the motor one more time, and after the Marines did their checkout on the satellite radio gear. Taking a short cut to the Meknes road, they wove through the slow morning rush hour traffic, through the old city's horse shoe gates and walls formed centuries ago from rose colored puddled clay and capped with medieval crenellations. Outside the walls again they were in to the world of glass, steel and ferro-concrete and the thousands in western and traditional dress rushing to jobs in offices and shops. At the crowded street corners, the bright morning sun silhouetted the legs and torsos of clerks and secretaries in thin, slipless long dresses and caftans, violating all modesty, causing the most voyeuristic among them to avert their eyes. For those who refused to see this modernity, who avoided the starkly revealed office workers, there were always the donkey carts slowing traffic, and the veiled women in billowing black djelabas, pushing their way through sidewalk crowds like dark creatures battering through the high seas.

***** ***** ***** ***** ***** ***** *****

Four hundred kilometers south of El Husein's ksar in the Mid Atlas mountains, a man who called himself Moustapha wheeled a Land Rover across the desert plate toward the *piste* road which led to the oasis town of El Mamid. Two other young men, called Ali and Rachid were curled up asleep in the back two rows of the vehicle for they both had shared the driving throughout the night. Up front in the passenger bucket seat sat a young woman, Maleka, who was wide awake. Like the driver, Moustapha, she wore a scarf over her nose and mouth and a cloth cap against the powdery sand which coated everything in the interior, and rendered the upper, unprotected half of their faces ghostly yellow. Moustapha had taken the wheel from Rachid only an hour ago at dawn when the great orange sun rose out of the sea of dunes that the faint tracks skirted.

"There will certainly be a check point before the town," the young woman said.

"Yes, but we'll get through it. We have all the right papers, but most of the local police down in this region can't read them anyway. We'll get through," he repeated to reassure her. Rachid had said it was wrong to let the girl come with them on the mission, but Moustapha had persisted and their leader, El Surugi backed him saying again that women were equal in their cause. Besides a young bourgeois couple and their driver and cousin would be less suspicious at the Brides' Fair mixing in with the tourists, the journalists, the film makers and the officials than four young men, clearly not of the mountain Berber clans. But now, to get through the first check points, they were a party of hydraulic engineers out on ground water surveys. Such a group would not include a woman . Even with her hair up under cap, with an oversized jacket and the dust's thick coating, her fine features and pencil-thin eyebrows could betray her to anyone who stopped to scrutinize carefully, but local constabulary would only wave them through, would not even look at their papers.

They left the jarring and thudding caused by the gouged and rutted desert tracks and climbed onto a graded dirt road that ran north towards Ain Medrissa. The Land Rover with a *Service Hydraulique* ´ emblem stenciled on its front doors towed a drilling rig which danced and rattled noisily. The red Arabic lettering in the upper quadrant of the matriculation plates designated it an official government vehicle. The chain strung across the road and the red and white signs marked *ARRET* came up too soon. "They're supposed to be right before the village, not this far out in the middle of nowhere." He could have easily crashed through the flimsy barrier, but downshifted and braked. They must have been the very first vehicle this morning, for the three man detail in the short wheel based police Land Rover scrambled sleepily from the canvas covered rear. Moustapha readied his false *ordre de mission* and the four forged government identity cards.

Only a nuisance; surely they would be waved on by a semi-literate local militia man who never questioned the business of traveling officials, but the man who stepped down from the vehicle and approached wore the epaulets of a *chef de brigade* and the gray uniform of the National police. "*Salam alakum*," the man said.

"*Alakum salam*," Moustapha replied and shook a cigarette from his pack to offer the head of the patrol. He explained calmly yawning now and then, feigning fatigue from hard duty, that they had been on mission doing test bores along the southern slopes of the Jebal al Jafra.

"But that is far from here, two hundred kilometers or so northeast. And you are coming up the piste from the south. You perhaps had other duties.?"

"No, we simply got turned around, took a wrong track. It's our first time in the region. And we're just out of engineering school and this is our first real mission. But no catastrophe. We did get some positive test bores."

"Got lost?" The man studied the three other passengers, and if he paused a second more at Maleka, Moustapha did not notice. "Yes, I can see you're not from this region, but it is odd to me that your service would send you out on your first mission without an experienced person, a chauffeur who knows every desert track. Those here in the south can navigate the dunes and the desert plate, read the stars if necessary like the best sea captain."

Moustapha remained calm. "They were short handed in Zemmara. Water's become such a priority with the drought persisting."

"Based in Zemmara are you? I take a glass of tea now and then with the Water Service Director, Ahmed Ben Omar. I am temporarily based there myself, but I've never heard tell of any new young engineers being assigned to Ben Omar's cadre." He threw the bogus identity papers back at Moustapha after scanning them with a bemused smile, and signaled to his men to approach.

Knowing they were trapped Moustapha had no choice but to knee his questioner in the groin and then chop him hard at the neck as he had been instructed to do over and over until he finally got it right. Rachid, coiled and apprehensive, ripped the crouching policeman nearest the vehicle with the AK 47 he had wrapped up in a djelaba. The other policeman sitting in the cab returned the fire, and the brown and desolate land cracked with splintering glass and the screech of metal penetrating metal. It was over in seconds. The dead man by the police vehicle stared up at the cloudless sky as if startled by its brilliance. Rachid had rushed forward and now held his gun on the second policeman who sat moaning about Allah's mercy while he spit out rivers of blood. Maleka had been hit in the shoulder and rocked with pain on the sand.

"We must kill them," Rachid yelled his weapon steady at the policeman's bloody head. The adrenalin surged and Moustapha struggled to clear his mind. None of them had ever killed. He had made his reputation in the movement by calmly wiring and blowing the telephone and telegraph station at Souk El Khemis as the Panhard armored cars raced in to retake the town. In their camp they talked always with bravado about sacrifice, martyrdom, killing, but few had witnessed it like this.

'Avoid harming your own brothers and sisters,' they repeatedly told them in the encampment. 'They are not the enemy. They are all connected one to the other and indeed to you by blood or by tradition. Harming them will only stir up the furies against us.' "We will leave them here to be found or to die, but we will not...." Moustapha trailed off.

"This one will not live the hour out. Look at the blood he's losing. And the Chief, what do you think he'll do if survives? Do you think he'll thank us for sparing him, and go about his business? And look at Maleka. She'll slow us down. Our mission's over before it has really begun."

Moustapha ignored him and went over to Maleka. He could feel her pain and wanted to reach out to comfort her, but he could not touch her especially in front of the others. They had forbidden all such contact, even a simple gesture of commiseration, of kindness. Ali had pulled off her jacket and now was cutting away her pullover shirt with his clasp knife. He did this with some skill for before joining their group he had been in a school for paramedics. "Not too serious, I think. The bullets splintered coming through the truck door. She has the splinters, one or two deep in her back. Should be cut out, but I can't do it, not without antiseptics and anti-biotics.'" Ali probed around the several wounds to the upper back and left forearm, gingerly with his knife.

"She'll be worse than useless now," Rachid said. "I knew we shouldn't have brought a woman along. It's another curse on us."

"Leave me here. Some truck will come soon headed for the desert trails. I'll make my way back to camp," Maleka said trying to rise to her feet.

"No, that's impossible. We'll get you patched up, and you will continue with us," Moustapha said. He told Ali to go look after the bleeding police man, and he stood for those few minutes scanning the horizon where the morning sun sat just above the flat scrub land. He masked his own doubts and despair from Ali and Rachid. He must continue to lead regardless of these setbacks. He looked then to the foothills of the mountains where their journey must take them. As empty and as desolate as the land appeared there were herders of camels and goats out in the scrub land. Others up in the crags and rocks followed narrow paths down to the source of their favorite tea water. The gun fire had reverberated about for some kilometers, and those that normally would be absorbed in their respective morning tasks would stop, change course and begin to converge cautiously. Moustapha knew the back, desert side of these hills and mountains. His Uncle Ahmed, his mother's middle brother, had a rose and almond farm not too far away. As a boy only a decade ago he used to help with the goats and sometimes was allowed to ride out on one of the fine roan stallions. On such a clear morning as this, he could see down to where the vegetation gave way to scrub and sand, where the one road shimmered from the sun's heat, where all movement was clearly framed, the sole truck churning up a long spume of dust, the rib-thin jackal scurrying after scant prey.

As soon as Ali reported that the bleeding policeman was beyond hope, they pulled the two vehicles far off the road to where the sand dunes hid them from the road's view. They scooped out two shallow graves and dragged the dead policeman into the first. This is not what they came to do. They had an officer of the national police groaning in pain, one man dead and the other dying. They hauled the second bloody mess into the sand grave. He still breathed with difficulty and they could not bury him alive. It had to be Moustapha who would send him to oblivion, for Rachid had his kill, and, he,. Moustapha, could not give him a second opportunity. He had the pistol of the doubled-up officer in his hand. As a socialist and an agnostic he spurned the religion of his father's house, but as the close range shot to the back of the man's head erupted in a shower of bone and matter, he murmured Allah's name, Allah the merciful and compassionate. Rachid indifferently shovel sand over the two corpses, while Ali raced the engine of the police vehicle forward and reverse a score of times until the tires dug themselves into the soft sand and the vehicle was mostly buried .

Maleka lay stretched out on the middle seat of the Service Hydraulique Land Rover. The officer of the national police lay gagged and bound on the rear deck covered from view by a canvas ground sheet. Moustapha climbed into the middle seat of the Land Rover to be both close to their hostage and to be near his wounded companion. They had no one but each other and the movement. Each of their own fathers had renounced them. Their uncles followed suit. Perhaps their mothers remembered them in their silent prayers, thought of them as they went about their daily chores. He toyed with his Glock machine pistol. One brief burst and the moaning policemen would be finished. Rachid up front fumed on that they had failed before they even began, that they would bring much shame upon their cause, that they must split up as soon as possible.

Ali brought the Land Rover to life, and with a constricted voice murmured 'Allah Akbar' as they headed north towards the foothills and to the village which served those occasional travelers coming in from the scrub land and the desert as well as those venturing up into the mountains, the high plateaus and beyond.

Chapter II

Including the Marines up front negotiating the road, there were eleven of them, all more or less from the official American community. Eric Dalton sat uncomfortably in the back row of the van with Mai Donnatelli and Pam Crane on either side. He had graciously insisted they take the window seats, but all three were right over the rear wheels and truck-like springs which hit every rut and pot hole. The city would soon give way to cork trees, to open fields and to long rows of the ubiquitous eucalyptus trees planted every where by the French during the colonial era. They were only in the near suburbs where chaotic streets calmed, and white walled villas replaced rundown tenements. There was still time to ask the Marines up front to let him off and call for his driver, Maphoud. He could never face Cynthia or Karen again if he pulled that stunt. The Ambassador would be furious that he had abandoned his wife, Pam Crane.

Did Cynthia say count on seven hours minimum, seven hours cooped up in this steel box? Finally as he would at a dinner party, he turned to the person on his right, Mrs. Donatelli, to begin the small talk. He gently asked about her time growing up in Laos, and how she escaped. Would it be the all-too-typical tale of forced separation from her family, of starvation, butchery and rape? Somewhere before that brutality, there was a French grandfather, obvious in her more angular nose, the fuller sensuality of her lips. But she did not hint at the horrors she must have witnessed, but told of a happy, bourgeois world complete with a large teak wood house, an amah for her brothers and sisters, a cook, a grounds man, and all the other frills and embellishments. "Father and mother both professors at the *lycée,* you know. I smell the jasmine still, hear our laughter, see parents close together on verandah couch."

Pam Crane to whom he next turned, so used to being the center of attention as the Ambassador's wife, had been listening with interest to Mai Donatelli. "Is it your first trip to the Atlas mountains?"

"Marrakech, I've been to Marrakech where you can sweat in your little suit by the pool and look up over the palms to the mountains with snow on their peaks. Yes, Marrakech was interesting, but it was a bit much for Harlan, you know that big square with all the beggars and flies."

Eric could visualize her showing off her trim, mid forties body in her bikini, the pool surrounded by high foliage and stucco walls so the broiling 'Europeans' wouldn't offend local sensibilities; the Ambassador nearby in his lounge chair, glued to his cell phone. Like Mai, Pam Crane would gloss over her girlhood past, not dwell on the teenage beauty contests in hard scrabble Sandusky, was it? Nor would there be confessionals about making out in the back seat of Chevies, about the runway fashion modeling, about the well-heeled New York escorts. Things well past would not now intrude.

But Eric had it mostly wrong. At least Sandusky was not exactly hard scrabble, but situated nicely on Lake Erie. It had a rich history; Commodore Perry and all that. How many booster talks had she given as Miss Ohio, as the Governor's wife? 'Besides, Eric, nice Catholic girls didn't go all the way parked out at Cedar Point; feared God and the P word they did.'

The other voyagers sitting in the three rows forward seemed mostly absorbed with the city scenes, more familiar to some than to others who preferred the secure confines of the Embassy compound, and, as infrequently as possible, the controlled, escorted rituals of diplomatic outings. Most had wakened much too early this morning still reviewing the cinematic dreams of AK 47 wielding boys with thick black hair, angry black eyes and checkered kefiyahs masking the nose and mouth. They saw themselves as hostages being tormented and indecently abused by their captives, or they had witnessed their swift, ignominious end in some fetid, derelict place.

He knew them from their personnel files, and in some cases from a direct intervention on his part. In recent weeks there had been a matter involving the Gunny Sergeant at the wheel, and another with the teacher sitting directly in front of him, continually teasing at her long auburn hair. In the row beyond the teacher and the newly arrived Bakers, Cynthia Dennis had already captured the Ag Professor, Dr. McMannus, overwhelming him with the minutia of the Bab Roua Gate with its horse shoe arch, with the Chella and its clacking storks among the highpoints of the ruins. She could go on non-stop for hours some would say, passing out a store house of facts to those who would listen. Eric hoped she might pause for a time so they could sit down together in the high mountains and review as they never had the events 17 years back when they first confronted the impromptu nature of death.

THE BRIDES' FAIR

To all the others but Cynthia he would remain the senior guy, watchful, all-knowing, aloof. He would show them little of himself, just the light, humorous bits of a too interesting life in the service of his country. The others in the van could spin out their well-filtered fluff also, fantasies of lives that once were or should have been, slight tales such as told by the pilgrims on the road to Canterbury.

These intimate matters didn't, however, totally preoccupy him, and for a time he tuned out the chatter in the van as his traveling party became acquainted or reacquainted with one another. He focused instead on the Lance Corporal sitting in the passenger seat up front. The Marine had been looking intently in the van's side mirror for the past several minutes, oblivious to the street scenes, to the several levels of conversation and to the Gunny Sergeant at the wheel clutching it with both hands in the stranglehold of a novice or of an overly unsure driver. After a few minutes in this steady pose, the young Marine calmly turned his head to the rear as if to check out what he had been watching reflectively in the side mirror. In this brief look backwards over the passengers in the three rows of seats, he locked eyes with Eric Dalton for no more than a split second. Turning about as if to check for something in his bag behind the seat on the rear deck, Eric saw the Renault sedan, a derelict ten-year-old model, following them at about four car lengths. It slowed when they did and stopped when they did also at the one traffic light. A classic tail. It could be the police or the Sureté. They were on high alert, but wouldn't most likely play cat and mouse with an official vehicle of the U.S. Embassy, and they would be driving newer autos, washed daily in their compounds by cheap labor.

Eric held off alerting his companions, and knew the Marine would act similarly, not out of fear of causing panic, for most had been brushed by such threats and had well learned the protective drills. So as not to put a pall on the cheerful ambience in the van, he reached into his old gym bag for his camera, and looking surprised called for the Sergeant to stop at the news and notion boutique just up ahead where he could buy film for his Nikon. There wouldn't probably be another opportunity and certainly everyone could use more film on an outing such as this. Cynthia agreed and advised that it would be a good idea for all to get out and stretch a bit, for from this juncture they had about two hours on the fast Meknes road and to the turn off to the Mid Atlas mountains. As they slowed down before a row of shops, Eric noticed that the old Renault had stopped behind them before a café, its two occupants descending in all probability for their morning tea.

***** ***** ***** ***** ***** ***** *****

Achmed Abhouri, third son of Mohamed Abhouri, Customs Officer, continued on with his impassioned thoughts as he sat down at a table on the awning-shaded patio of the café. "It would be a simple matter; a short burst, a grenade, an RPG, and we would be heroes."

"To whom? For what?" asked his bearded companion, Majdi, whose disheveled shock of thick black hair had known no comb or brush in days. "Besides my mule-headed confederate, we are not here to kill or die, today at least. We are ordered explicitly to cause no incidents, to raise no suspicions."

His companion, one he had not chosen, thought himself so smart with his Sorbonne degrees and his fine way of speaking, but he was worse than the American and English infidels. Achmed, only 18, and yet, if ever, to sit for his baccalaureate exams, had witnessed Majdi drinking beer right out in the open, defying with his sharp tongue and wild manner anyone to say a word. He knew that the man never fasted during Ramadan, declaring to all who dared to listen that as a man of the mountains, a Berber, the gods of his fathers dwelt among the rocks and the woodlands and not in the heavens. Achmed had heard the man go on so until his ears rang. "Then I will assassinate them tomorrow or the next day. I will find a way."

"Ridiculous," Majdi said as the waiter brought them heavily sugared mint tea. The scalding hot glasses had unchipped gold rims and were sparkling clean for this was a better class of café then they were used to. They took the glasses between thumb and finger, and, blowing gently on the liquid at the brim, took small sips as they talked. "Our assignment is to record the vehicles from the Embassies on their way to the big mousem, the Brides' Fair; to simply take a survey. That is the limit of what we have to do today. Tomorrow may be different."

"It is a fool's task, beneath what a least I am capable of; reading off diplomatic license plates and jotting them down in a cahier like a school boy at the *medressa*." Achmed, not typically so vainglorious, had indeed become frustrated. This morning between 7 and now past 8, they had recorded 18 vehicles with official plates and with foreigners riding inside. They had to continue with this nonsense until noon, by which time almost all travelers to the Fair would have started out on the seven hour trek up into the mountains. But why wait to corner them up on the high plateaus if that was the plan? It would be so simple to attack them here in these quiet suburban streets, to just drive past and unload a clip from an

THE BRIDES' FAIR

AK 47. So simple a matter, but someone, somewhere it appeared, preferred a more complex scenario.

"And if you kill one of these Americans or all eleven and live to boast about it, will that get you a fat position with the Ministry of Make Work? Will it get you a fancy villa in this posh neighborhood, and a pretty, cream skin wife to warm your bed? And if you martyr yourself in the process like so many of the blind and misguided, do you really believe that nubile virgins will cart your blasted remains up to heaven?" Majdi ceased his harangue for a big Mercedes touring car filled with foreigners slowed at the intersection before the corner café. He dutifully wrote down in the notebook the Corps Diplomatique plate number and " Emb of Germany; 2 men, 2 women, 3 children (European); nanny and chauffeur (North African)."

Following the German Embassy vehicle at four lengths came a new tan Peugeot. Its three male occupants wore fresh white shirts not yet wilted by the heat, and stylish aviator sunglasses which hid their expressions. "The National Police," Majdi said from his perch on the outdoor patio of the café. "Without question," Achmed concurred for the men with their sleek black hair and similar dress seemed copies of one another.

"You see how difficult it will be to slaughter the infidels with all the police about?" Majdi said

"I will find a way. You don't know the hate I have in my heart," Achmed said sipping at his hot tea.

"You will only make matters worse. Your sister, isn't she on some important mission? Do you want to put her at risk?"

At the mention of his sister from the foul mouth of the Berber heretic, Achmed wished to hurl his hot tea in the man's face, but was stopped by the beeping of Majdi's pocket phone.

***** ***** ***** ***** ***** ***** *****

They had stopped for only ten minutes to shop in the upscale suburbs of the capital city, buying film, hard candy and other items, and now to the relief of the two Marines from the Embassy guard, were at last on the open road towards their destination. Except for those in the back row, most passenger sat in relative comfort as they raced through the rolling green belt of the Atlantic coastal plains towards the Mid Atlas mountains. Being still early in the morning, they shook off their bleariness by passing round several thermoses of coffee and tea and engaging in small talk about the pastoral economy, the permanency of the mortared mud brick habitation clustered helter-skelter on the landscape, and the passing of donkey carts driven by drably attired children. Deceptively cool as most coastal mornings, they kept the van windows shut tight against the road dust and noise. Where the summer wheat stubble had been plowed under, the black loam held fast streaks of ground fog which mostly shrouded the white egrets poking for grubs and bits of grain in the furrows. The mist refracted the sun light and distorted the horizon ahead of them, making on-coming trucks, cars and farm carts float abstractly. Driving these roads in the so-called Third World requires constant vigilance. Serious accidents are common and emergency services are scant. It is not akin to driving the back rural roads in America, where except for the occasional erratic teenager or menacing drunks, drivers tend to be more disciplined than most in this part of the world and even in Europe, particularly southern Europe. Some students of the issue conclude that even with their penchant for individualism, even with the car as an extension of the moods and passions of the self, Americans simply have been driving longer and at longer distances than others and are more conforming to the rules of the road. Many Europeans and North Africans as well took to the auto en masse only during the decades after World War II when inexpensive, slow moving conveyances such as the Citroen 2CV and the Fiat became widely available.

Driving in New York City is not a course for the meek of any nation. The experienced driver knows that taxis will try to cut him off for lane advantage at every opportunity, but will brake obediently at red lights and for ambling pedestrians. In North Africa, drivers will tend to cluster in great knots around traffic lights and stop signs, such as they are, jockeying for advantage, primed to roar off the split second the light clicks green. Lanes and queues become irrelevant, the tangle of autos impervious to any orderly continuation. These clusters of cars have been likened to masses of sheep trying to push through a narrow gate, for herding sheep is one of the more ubiquitous of occupations in a country where there are many more of these animals than people.

Then too in countries such as this, the curse of the French-inspired *priorité a droite* leads to donkey carts and other ponderous vehicles as well as human kind to proceed fearlessly from dirt track to high speed asphalt roads with the inevitable consequences. The drivers of these roads must also be exceedingly patient with slow-moving and often grossly over-burdened trucks that can back up traffic for a kilometer or more. Daring to dart around these vehicles on winding two lane roads has been the cause of too many smash ups as the rusty, part-stripped wrecks off in the grasses bore witness and which the passengers of the white U.S. Embassy van regarded silently, keeping their apprehensions to themselves.

Mai Donatelli, the late 30's Eurasian woman, now sat in the middle of the last row wedged between Eric Dalton and Pam Crane. She had insisted on changing since she was the smallest of the three and noting the DCM's long legs needed relief. On every jar and thud she floated up and down in cotton shorts and T shirt several sizes too large. The clothes well-disguised almost all her femaleness. Unavoidably as well on the sharp zigs and zags her olive tan leg slapped against his chinos. She remained oblivious to this closeness and went on about the lately harvested brown and ochre fields through which they passed, and about how in her country of birth, Laos, every growing thing remained green and moist for all seasons like fresh steamed snow peas.

It couldn't be some predatory or sly sexual thing he knew. He had been to those crowded cities of Indo China where people pressed closely together in households of only a few hundred square feet, and were packed solid on jitneys, streets, queues for rice and every other basic need. The body became switched off indifferent to jostles, to an unintended hand. He agreed with her about the verdancy of Asia. He recalled the Philippines where the clouds stayed gray and heavy with water, where even dead sticks stuck up as fences soon rooted in the rich decay, where even the slightest skin scrape could quickly ulcerate.

Pam Crane, sitting on the right window side, appeared to be fascinated in their talk of Laos, in the contrasts between North Africa and Asia. "I haven't been anywhere really, except to London and Paris, of course," she declaimed. She somehow sensed his discomfort when they veered around sharp curves or darted passed slow moving market trucks. She yelled out on two such occasions, as if not to be mistaken, "It's like a roller coaster, a god damn roller coaster," and each time she shoved Mai Donatelli hard against him.

But Ambassador's wives must show decorum and the flag at all times, and certainly not lose it, be mischievous, play silly school girl games. They must be interested in everything and everyone, but for no more than a few minutes at a time, mind you. Circulate, circulate, and never talk politics or religion. The weather, of course, is always a safe bet. Hillary tried to train herself so, to be fully prepared for the day Eric would be named Ambassador, a real probability, or so it once seemed. But by her own admission she never got beyond C minus, liking to linger and gossip, speaking her mind on everything from abortion rights to the latest follies of Washington.

A roller coaster ride, indeed. They, Mai and he, became riveted hip to hip, Siamese twins, Ying and Yang, and he could scrunch his six one frame no further against the left-most door. He discovered, at any rate, that Mrs. Donatelli was no mere bag of bones, but of soft, yielding flesh.

But he had been forced into her life before, been already obscenely intimate. It was after 3am a month ago when Jess Williams, the Marine on night duty, woke him on the emergency radio by his bed. It was a distant, distorted voice. Was it a car bomb, a protest at the Embassy gates, the assassination of a colleague? No, it was closer to home, a domestic altercation involving the Donatelli family who lived in the married NCO apartment on the second floor of the Marine Guard House. "Sounds pretty serious, Sir, and I could use some back up. I just can't go knocking on their door. The Sarge is my CO, you know, Sir."

There had been a violent argument over the 16 year old son, Greg, who had come home at two in the morning from some get together. The boy, who had the soft exotic looks and long eye lashes of his mother, had been in trouble before. He ran around with a rowdy bunch of locals and other diplomatic kids, those some labeled the spoiled embassy brats. The Security Officer, Art Meacham, had made a report. The kids were heavy into kif, the local pot, into porno movies, the local party girls who hung around the Marine House, and into each other it appeared. "They'll nail the boy. You know how it's going to read: 'US. Marine's son a dope smoking flit.' You know how they like to embarrass Uncle Sam."

The shattered pieces of bone china littered the white shag rug like confetti on a bridal veil. Sergeant Jerry Donatelli, who had been drinking heavily, "Sir-ed" him too often as he tried to explain. Although a year shy of fifty, he had a hard weight room body which could do considerable damage. The wife, Mai, sobbed against the brightly striped cushions of her sofa. Her hands covered her tears and most of her bruises. The human devastation and the apartment's government issue drabness contrasted sharply with the array of pictures on almost every inch of wall space; line drawings of hopeful old and young faces; subdued impressionistic oils of the old yellow and rose-hued structures that rimmed the mouth of the delta. The boy remained behind the locked door of his room, hysterically cursing his father. Eric eked out with difficulty the wife's version, ignoring the husband's interruptions and counter claims. He was that evening the 911 responder, the judge and the shrink. He placed the Sergeant on report and asked to see his personnel file. There was no prior record of spousal abuse, although that could be deceptive, the family liaison officer, or the FLO, Alice Weber, explained. There were, however, photo copies of old cryptic memoranda from the Navy Department and several reclamas from Lance Corporal J. Donatelli all relating to the request to marry an alien woman claiming to be 18 and of no fixed address other than a United Nations camp for refugees outside of chaotic Bangkok.

"But they could be alive." He returned to Mai Donatelli's past, to her parents. He did not intend to press her, only to help her look for hope. "They may have made it to a camp in Thailand. They may have thought all these years there was no point in searching, that you had been killed."

"No, all gone, long ago now. Pathet Lao kill them all. Mother and father both intellectuals, both teachers and members of the RLG, Royal Lao, you know. We live in big house in Vientiane, have servants, and lovely garden with flowers. Everywhere you smell jasmine. Everywhere so calm. Now I think burned to ground Nothing left."

Parents educated professionals? An idyllic, want-for-nothing childhood? Did she mostly embellish, construct for herself a fairy tale life? Or had she been sold off at 14 by a poor father to the soldiers' brothels of Bangkok like so many? Mai Donatelli returned to pointing out the terraced agriculture, the vineyards, the olive groves. Her long, thin fingers arched and wove passed him towards the car window.

'Sorry you so uncomfortable, M'sieu Dalton,' Mai Donatelli would like to have said. 'Some men afraid of Asian girls, think we're going to eat them alive, poison them with strange things, dope them up, give them big disease. Jerry never like that. Never afraid. He call me his Asian pearl, and used to love me much. Now all changed. All mixed up about having to go, to retire, to leave Marines. He want to hurt me now. I can't help leg and butt against you, M'sieu Dalton. We adult, well passed thirty. We have to endure for it's a long, long trip. And you only half right. I not sold off to be whore in bar like so many. I sold as bride from refugee camp by Thai man with UN cap. He arranged everything, factory jobs, maid's work, brides to rich Americans and Australians. He the arranger while the others, the whites with UN hats look the other way and fill out their papers and their forms.'

She knew. She didn't harbor false hopes, dream about her former life, her parents or listen to the rumors brought by all the travelers. Civil wars in Indo China, Africa, the Middle East had gone beyond mere avenging brutality. They spared few and violated many, deeply interring under the jungle thicket that which was human, that which was supposed to be of enduring beauty. It seemed inevitable to him at least, that such barbaric blood letting would reach here sooner or later, spilling over the borders from the east, storming up from the

Sahara desert. But Eric and the rest of them in this Embassy van would not witness the worst of it. Quickly and efficiently they would all be transferred out to some other garden spot where they would, for a time at least, barely sense the chaos bubbling up from below.

The van continued to thud and swerve on the poor, narrow road. "And you say this is the easy part," Edna Baker, already determined to relish her discomfort, said to the driver, Sergeant Donatelli. "Are you sure you've got the air on high?" She, early fifties, sat in the middle along with her husband, Doug, and the teacher, Monique Addleman, who had insisted they take the window seat to get the best view of a countryside she knew like the back of her hand. The Bakers had arrived in the summer rotation of Foreign Service staff, only six weeks ago now. After their last tours in plush posts like Paris and Geneva, Edna was convinced her husband had fallen from grace, and, having been assigned to fly blown North Africa, his career in jeopardy.

"First time out of the city what with all the unpacking, getting the house in order, learning the drill in my job, and His Nibs wanting speeches and press releases every hour or so.," Doug Baker said gregariously being no Grinch like his wife, but being too much of an old pro to forget that His Nib's wife was sitting right behind him.

"This is our 10th move with this outfit, and the worst," Edna added. "We've had the Embassy workman out every day it seems and they never seem to get it right."

They classified her as a whiner. The locals at the Embassy, those who did all the dirty jobs, hated those work orders assigning them to the Baker house. Eric tolerated the Edna Bakers of his world as long as she did not become truly abusive. She had dutifully followed her husband from post to post for more than thirty years, been uprooted just when she felt she had settled in. She had some rights to bitch and complain. For younger officers just starting out he had a less charitable message. 'Remember back in the States you'd be doing it yourself or complaining about some outrageous plumbing bill.'

"Bet you've seen quite a bit of the country in your two years here, Eric," Doug Baker said to abruptly change the subject.

"Not really. I sometimes rush to Casa, Tangier, Marrakech with visiting delegations, but I rarely have time to stop and absorb what I see, " he said. Nor would he hardly stop to notice whether it was Easter or Aid El Kebir. In the grind of law school years back, they, his friends said he never saw the seasons change. "Is it spring so soon? Happy Easter, Bunny Rabbit! "

THE BRIDES' FAIR

"Well, Eric," Cynthia Dennis said. "We're going to see to it that our favorite Deputy Chief has a wonderful relaxing time, takes in everything, forgets all his urgent cables, his dip notes and his *demarches*."

"Yes, I second that, "Pam Crane said. "And His Nibs can't bother us, can he?"

"I wouldn't be so sure, Mrs. Crane," Doug Baker shot back. "'They've got a big, bad radio up front."

"Please call me Pam, not Mrs. Crane," she asked sweetly.

Eric watched Monique Addleman tease her long auburn hair up and down a longish Mondigliani neck marred only by a pin head size mole, dead center at the apex of her spine. Kimberly Mayhew in his tenth grade home room at Falmouth High, sat only a foot or so in front of him slowly riding tawny bright hair up and down her neck with forever the same motion by fingers too well manicured for a 16 year old. He struggled to concentrate: Hardy's Shropshire lad being compared by Miss Edna Bromley, the teacher, to Keat's Ode on a Grecian urn. Same message: youth frozen in immortality. It had little meaning for kids at that age, for even with the occasional teen age smash ups on Route 6, they already believed themselves to be immortal. The elixirs from Kimberly's morning shower made him spin and dream, but when the bell shook all of them to attention and they filed off to algebra or science lab, he could only nod his recognition of her with appropriate 16 year old indifference. Eric occasionally passed Monique in the Embassy halls where she offered a pleasantly crisp *"Bonjour, Msieu Dalton"* He knew from her file she was half French on her mother's side and in addition to teaching English to Moroccan students and businessmen, she gave refresher lessons in French to Embassy officers as well as beginning French for spouses. 'Very competent as a teacher, attractive, but a bit shy,' it said somewhere in her file.

That had not been his only contact, for he did have to intrude on her life, plunge directly into her world as well. The very new Language School Director, Alan Jenkins, a fussy school masterly bachelor, a throw back to another era, wanted to get rid of her and another woman teacher, a British girl, Fiona 'Something.' Christopher Reilly, a co-worker of Monique's, persisted on seeing Eric in person and as soon as possible. The matter couldn't be discussed on the phone. Eric tried to patiently explain to the young man that the Embassy didn't interfere in the management of other agencies like Drug Enforcement, CIA, USAID and the Peace Corps, and the Language School fell squarely in that category. It wasn't really true. Eric had to sift through all the dirt and reports on every U.S. agency out here, had to be all-knowing or suffer the consequences. "We just don't get into the weeds on personnel matters, on budgets and accounts," he waffled straight out. No need for the young man to know their messy ways. Couldn't there be something below the surface? Some indiscretion? Some complaint coming from the host government perhaps, he asked?

Reilly, not put off, had managed an audience with the Ambassador himself, been given that rare access when the Embassy staff sought such at their own peril. There were the abrupt, terse phone calls, and Chris Reilly was escorted across the outer office to that of DCM Dalton.

He couldn't sit calmly in the chair before Eric's desk, but paced the room. He was a strapping early thirties, with a broad face, which except for this occasion, was usually affable and welcoming. He seemed more like a college athlete, a football quarter back, than a teacher of English as a foreign language. He had a certain commanding manner which translated to being a bit too sure of himself, but perhaps like so many hangers on overseas, he was either a romantic, rich, or apprehensive about returning to the States and beginning a conventional career and family. Skillfully, Christopher made his case and held his ground well, convincing Eric to go round to the school on a get-acquainted visit, to confront the owlish Dr. Jenkins in his impeccably neat office. Yes, the Embassy should be making more inspection visits to show its support of these programs, to take nothing for granted. And yes, Christopher Reilly wasn't only concerned with fair treatment for Monique; there had to be something more between them. It seemed so obvious, but he shouldn't measure everything in old-fashion boy-girl terms.

"But Mr. Dalton-may I call you Eric?—shouldn't we be more concerned with prevention? Just think of these two young women, attractive young women at that one might add, teaching mostly young Moslem males. Something unfortunate could occur, don't you see?"

But he did see. The man had fantasies about Islamic fundamentalists, thought someone would bomb his school, blow him and his brand new Renault car to smithereens. This was Jenkins' first overseas assignment. Washington had fallen down on its screening for such personnel. It claimed that overseas assignments no longer carried that special cachet, that Americans were becoming, again, more and more insular. "Be thankful, that we found anyone at all for the school.' Eric explained that if indeed there were any anti-American terrorist plots they would be directed at more newsworthy targets than the Language School. "You provide a needed service, Dr. Jenkins. Even would-be terrorists feel they need to learn English. You probably have a few among your students." Not mincing words with the man, nor wasting too much time, he told Jenkins to look about town and find the women professors at the local University and in the Med

School; told him that as a matter of policy the Embassy could not accept an all-male teaching staff.

That was it, except for reading Ms Addleman's file to reassure himself that he had made the right decision. Christopher and he agreed that they would tell no one about the matter, but in the small American community, rumors circulated like hawks above prey darting in an open field. She had to know. It was the way she had said *'bon jour'* when this early morning she climbed into the van, the last arrival and out of breath. She nodded to the other passengers, but for him she had a smile of more than recognition . As for himself, he too smiled at the irony of it all. His arcane preoccupations with diplomacy, with projecting and protecting the interests of the United States, had not totally neutered his humanity. Going off to a remote, mountain Brides' Fair, vulnerable, practically divorced, he could not help but notice the women close to him.

"Doesn't this road follow the old Roman one from Volubilis to the coast?" Dr. McMannus asked Cynthia Dennis, speaking for the first time since he entered the van with one perfunctory 'good morning.' But he had thoroughly read the notes and pamphlets that Cynthia had spent hours putting together in a blue folder with each traveler's name in bold computer graphic print .

"Yes, in part. You can still see some of the original cobble stones marked off by the side of the road. They've found a few of those stone *bornes routieres*, the Roman numerals all but eroded here and there through the wheat fields, for the road ran straighter than this. Roman engineers wouldn't have tolerated these twists and curves. Isn't a shame we wont have time to stop in Volubilis, to see the very start of the road north where it takes off straight and sure from the arched gateway?" For Cynthia everything wherever she lived in the world was to be soaked up, thoroughly infused, become part of one's altered state, not just sorted away for occasional reminiscences at dinner parties. To her captive audience she went on about pottery shards; the trade in fish paste and olive oil; the difference between second century mosaics and 13th century Arabic zelig; the dolphin motif in intricately laid tile floors ; the faces of sea gods with seaweed hair and startled, bulging eyes; Roman city planning; Islamic architecture; the Marabout shrines All this minutia was not to be hoarded, used to elevate one above the indifferent and misinformed, but as precious gifts meant to be shared with acquaintances, with new arrivals, with visiting VIPs as a challenge for them to learn more, to become as informed as she. Knowing Cynthia since their very first posting in the Philippines, she would indeed want to stop every few minutes, take them all on mini expeditions, mindless of time, the imperatives of reaching a destination.

"Have you been to Volubilis yet, Dr. McManus?" she asked.

"Not really. I zip all over the country for field trials, soil samples, that sort of thing. Like Mr. Dalton, I never seem to be able to stop and smell the roses, but I do hear things from my Moroccan counterparts. Don't you find the connection between the ruler Juba II and one of Cleopatra's daughters fascinating? It ties everything together, doesn't it, Greek, Egyptian, Roman, Berber? I'm sure you can fill in all the details, Mrs. Dennis." In spite of his Van Dyke beard and heavy rimmed sun glasses, he was a youngish, scholarly looking mid-thirties. Something about McMannus came up two or three months ago. It was at Ahmed El Fassi's reception at the Agricultural Ministry. There was McMannus a horticulture expert from Cal State going on in perfect French, past subjunctives and all, throwing in a few Arabic phrases for good measure. They said he had mastered Spanish as well. Yet, he seemed to live for his varieties of citrus, melons and aubergines and nothing else, and buried himself in grafting species, in breeding seeds. A loner in a country where friends were readily made, where the American community was close knit and accommodating to all.

"Well, Eric, I can assure you he's not one of ours," Bob Steiner, the CIA station chief had said, but poor Bob was just a processor of forms and paper like most in the Embassy and wouldn't know half the muck his agency wallowed in out here.

"Look at his CV. He's spent seven years in French-speaking Africa, working closely with the natives, not holed up in Fortress America like the rest of us, Andy Kimball, the Economic Counselor, explained. And perhaps you could put a positive spin on it: Highly competent American advisor with excellent French and passable Arabic, who didn't just pal around with the same old ex-pat crowd, but took an interest in the country's people and history. You could believe all that if it made you more secure at night, but the American intelligence wizards like the Brits before them recruit archaeologists, missionaries, teachers and the more obvious aid workers to be not only their eyes and ears in remote places but to be prepared for more hazardous duties. "Things are seldom as they seem; skim milk masquerades as cream;" a Gilbert and Sullivan round useful in his skeptical regard for most everything these days. "And don't forget the obvious, boys and girls. The man went through a messy divorce a few years back. He's off to lick his wounds in the Foreign Legion and get his revenge."

"Don't you just find an abundance of baths and brothels in these old Roman towns?" Edna Baker asked.

"I wonder if one had anything to do with the other," Pam Crane said stifling a laugh.

"And I read in your notes, Cynthia," Doug Baker said, "That Juba got himself assassinated by old Little Boots Caligula for daring to wear the imperial purple during an unwise visit to Rome."

"It goes to show, doesn't it?" Dr McMannus said. "That it's sometimes wiser to keep one's light under a bushel."

They went on the three of them describing all that remained of the Westernmost city of the Roman empire, about the earthquake that had finally after 1800 years shaken apart the empty, marble temples and villas, leaving standing a few columns and archways, and as well most of the fanciful mosaic tile floors. Cynthia kept turning to the passengers behind her so as not to exclude them in the discussion. Dr. McMannus too turned once after asking Cynthia a question to see if the others, particularly, Monique Addleman, who also knew the country, had anything to contribute.

Eric couldn't keep up with Cynthia's enthusiasm. "There's going to be this absolutely fascinating lecture and demonstration tonight on Arab and Berber music chez mois. You and Hillary just have to tear yourselves away from that Swedish reception early.' If it wasn't recitals and lectures, she would be off Saturday afternoons leading queasy new arrivals and visitors into the exotic back alleys of the Sale medina. She was always full of adventure, taking those rusty old ferries across Manila Bay; six months pregnant with Karen, riding those jammed Jeepney taxis all over Manila, outings few Americans dared take for fear of being mugged or worse. But for all that independent spirit, all that wonderment of new places, when Tom was killed she proved to be like most any twenty-two year old widow, lost and overwhelmed. "Don't worry so about me, Eric, I'm really pretty tough," she said over and over as if not really convinced. They were sitting on a hot, sticky sand beach at the Ambassador's Club, an hour's drive from Quezon City on Manila Bay. A few raggedy kids had managed to slip by the drowsy guards through the wood and wire enclosure. Some sifted through last weekend's trash. Others kept begging them for coins and cigarettes. She had lavished herself with sun oil in the hope that the stretch marks from Karen's birth would somehow be bubbled away by the sun. Tom Dennis had been dead a month now, his body still not identified. She did not look forward to returning to the States with his remains, with facing his parents and his friends at that devastating funeral that would have to be held. She remained quite still even with the kids circling about crying "You got dime? You got Malboro?" The breeze off the flat, unruffled bay, the tall, stately palms just behind them provided little relief from the heat, but she declined a cooling swim in the Club's big, fresh water pool or in the inviting Bay. He did her back and shoulders with the oil as he had often done for Hillary. How alike the two women were from this vantage point, the evenly spaced ridges of the spine, the taut tanned skin which whitened momentarily with the impression of the fingers; the light colored hair neatly bound in a pony tail by a ring of frilly elastic cloth; the body radiating health even with the mind's depression. Slathering on the prescribed sun blocker, he believed himself to have remained coolly analytical, marveling at how smoothly the spine dipped into the seat of the bathing suit where through the cloth he could see it join the pelvis to provide structure for the body's mobility; how the lower torso could uniquely move to walk, jog, to offer as well as to receive pleasure; how its engineering could bring forth life with a minimum of pain, or so Hillary and Cynthia, both equally stoical about such matters would have him think.

"That's ridiculous, Eric. Wild horses couldn't stop him from going on that mission. He was in that way like me., always ready to volunteer, to try something new, "she had told him when he came all stammering with his condolences, grief and guilt

And Tom had jumped at the opportunity to be liaison officer to a US counter-insurgency team going down to Mindanao with Filipino counterparts to do yet another assessment of the protracted conflict in that region. The Philippine Air Force C130 blew up shortly after take off from Cebu on its return leg. It was a bomb, of course. All were killed, and they had to dig scraps and body parts from the thick tropical vegetation. The Army forensic team finally sent in its report: 'Positive identification of dental work.' A mid twenties Yale law grad, in perfect condition, all polish and no warts, did have a cavity or two. But also he had the drive, the ambition, certainly; wanted to make Ambassador by his 40s, maybe get into politics after that. Eric, Chief of Section, and senior to Tom by only a few years, had been the one to sign the papers, to push through the orders, to encourage him to go for it. And all these years it still gnawed at him, a sharp claw pulling, scraping inside at a heart otherwise strong and healthy. Yes, he saw his name still there in black and white as the approving officer on the last of J. Thomas Dennis Jr.'s travel orders.

Cynthia continued to hold the attention of most in the van. Even the bemused, bored Pam Crane, the cranky Edna Baker, and the self-absorbed Monique Addleman seemed to listen. She painted an elaborate trans-Saharan camel train, 10,000 long, steadfast against the heat, the imponderable dunes, leaving from the 'port' of Sijilmasa, or perhaps from Marrakech, going to the salt mines at Tagharza, and on, one thousand kilometers on, to the Sahelian terminals of Gao, Timbuktu and Jenne. "They carried to the Mende people of

Africa as well, Islamic scholars, the Koran, and other than salt, they brought back gold to the merchants of Fez and Marrakech."

"And slaves, they brought back African slaves," Dr. McMannus added with some emphasis.

Cynthia conjured up a column of mounted soldiers of the Third Augusta Legion, describing in some detail the uniforms, the leather breast plate, the short broad swords, the harness. They were a day's journey out of Juba's city collecting harvest taxes, launching punitive strikes against marauding foothill tribes, parading their invincibility through the scattered mud walled hamlets. They accepted for tribute and in kind for tax, black eyed boys and girls. They took no sickly wretches, only the straight limbed and healthy for the baths and brothels. The troopers of two thousand years ago assured the flow of hard wheat, olive oil, red wine and fish sauce to the ports of Tingis and Sallaca. Out in this country side little had changed except for the telephone wires, the asphalt road and the gasoline powered vehicles. The women in these rich coastal plains threw leather and clay buckets down wells that had been redug and relined often over the many years. Donkeys still trudged with the same great clay water jugs lashed to their flanks. And everywhere as for centuries sheep and long legged birds fed on the wheat stubble. "The ancestors of the Third Augusta remain still up in the hills above the ruins, and even with inevitable intermarriage with the local tribes, they keep producing throwbacks with blonde hair and blue eyes." Cynthia relished her special knowledge and looked about the van to note the perplexity of most of the passengers, except for her daughter, and of course Eric, who were in the know, had heard the story many times being offered to the VIPs on rushed tours of the ancient ruins. 'But they couldn't be blonde. The Romans had to be dark like the Italians, or like some of these North Africans.' 'But you see,' Cynthia said beaming as she answered her riddle. "They weren't from Rome, but mercenaries from York, England.' And if they had the time she would have marched them all down below the crumbling city to where the grave markers of the legionnaires stood all these 1800 years, the Latin inscriptions still legible to the knowing eye.

The immutability of this place amazed Eric as it must have Cynthia; the site not picked clean of all its quarried stone and marble, the graves undesecrated, the history largely intact. And, yes, being Roman could mean being from York or from the Levant, from Gaul or Nubia. How similarly blended they in the American van were, Italian, African, Asian, Jew, French, Scots Irish, English and combinations thereof; how similar except for the difficult question what of the American experiment, what of their particular humanity would endure for the many centuries, let alone remain in tact on this uncomfortably jostling trip to the Mid Atlas?

They passed through the first town of any size. Great stork nests overwhelmed the sagging roof of a 1930's French colonial farm house. For half a century French farmers had prospered in the rich soil of this region on the Country's Atlantic Plains, extracting from it an abundance as had the Roman many centuries before them. Neither had conducted elaborate agronomic studies, for they could simply feel the dark brown alluvial earth crumbling just so in their hands, and could measure the amplitude of the rains through the inevitably changing seasons.

"Any good carpets in this place?" Edna Baker asked. "I gather half the natives are employed weaving carpets, the other half selling them."

"You have to travel farther out, up into the mountains where we're going to find real quality, good bargains." Cynthia replied. She pointed to a building of the Merinid influence with its zilig tile and fresco facade.

"I sketch old buildings, arches, mosques back in the city, "Mai Donatelli said. Yes, Eric had been struck by her work, the fine Durer-like lines of her drawings, the subtle use of color in her oils. He was astonished at first, but surmised that this incongruously fine talent was somehow an outpouring of the chaos in her life both now in the Marine Guard House and in the past when she fled the terror and brutality of Laos. From this anguish came this mastery and perception.

Idle men sat about on the terrace of a tea and coffee house, the young in jeans and cheap Italian shoes; the old in heavy djellabas and yellow leather slippers. They pretended to ignore the slow passing of the big white American van through the jam of trucks stacked to tottering with sacks of wheat and wool. Such strangers came this way often to the fetes and the fantasias being held everywhere in the harvest season.

They broke free of the town and sped again towards the foothills of the Mid Atlas. Along the side of the road, a donkey ladened with great clay water jugs strained to move. A girl of ten or so twitched the donkey on with her stick. She wore a head scarf and an ankle length robe that had lost all color through endless beatings out of dirt and washings out of sweat. They expected her to wave exuberantly at the passing vehicle, but Karen Dennis asked Jess Williams to slow down just for a few seconds. As the van crept up besides her, the young girl suddenly realized that this would not be the usual salutation to strangers rushing on to their own worlds down the road. She had heard tales of souls and even persons being snatched away. Before the cameras could poke through the rolled down windows, she pulled the donkey to her, the muzzle nudging into her belly, and turned the beast's head as well as her own away from the rude, lingering assault. She moved the animal off into a grove of cork trees, at about the moment the radio crackled alive, "Post 1 to Post 8. Message for Mr. Dalton at his convenience."

"Anyone for a pit stop?" Corporal Williams asked.

Chapter III

Traveling southeast from the capital, the narrow belt of rich alluvial soil on the coastal plains gives way to wooded foothills and grassy plateaus. These evolve into a conglomeration of escarpments, gullies and precipitous gorges which form the fingers and arms of the mountains. Some say the extensive Atlas mountain range sits as a spinal column dividing the country almost in half with these fertile Atlantic Plains on one side and mostly semi-arid grassland and desert on the other. Beginning westward as ganglia of old mountains, the range finds its summit in Jebal Toubkal near the great oasis city of Marrakech. In all the vast continent this peak is second only to Mount Kilimanjaro in East Africa two thousand miles to the south east. The High Atlas graduates down at the extreme western end to the Anti-Atlas group passed Agadir, the last major city on the Atlantic coast. These mountains protect the valleys of the Sous and the Maas from the corrosive Sahara winds. The Anti-Atlas slope into the Atlantic Ocean, and geologists theorize that before the continental drift these mountains ended in the Appalachians in the eastern United States. Moroccans often use this fact or theory to trumpet their connection with America if not by blood then by rock and stone. Also, it is not by linguistic accident that the mountains and the Ocean have the same root. In the ancient tales, Atlas held up the world astride the waters of the Mediterranean and the Atlantic at Tangier where the cave of the giant god is found.

But the American Embassy van went eastward towards the younger part of the range by several millions of years. The passengers could see the cedar forest up ahead where Romans, Moors from ancient Fez, Arab Caids, and French colonials took refuge over the centuries from the boiling summers of the Atlantic Plains. In contrast to the open, clear blue world of these plains, the cedar forests of the foot hills plunged them into shadows caused by the thick growth on either side of the meandering road. Having gotten accustomed to the openness, to the vast, rolling wheat fields and the terraced vineyards, the forest now closed off most vistas to the travelers.

"All's well at Watch 1. He's off too see the Wizard with Dad in tow. They have your Bible, but will they take to prayer?" They had pulled off the road into a cedar groove on the first rise above the plains. Eric sat in the front seat with the Gunny Sergeant listening to Stu Connors go on, amused by his own gibberish. They had no secure channel on the vehicle's two way radio. How many others would be listening? The French, perhaps. The Russians no longer, the intelligence people assured them; too broke these days. The Moroccan internal security boys? In deciphering Stu, the Ambassador had left for his scheduled meeting with Minister Bennani, and the Defense Attaché, "Dad", had gone along, not Stu himself, for he had to Chair the 'Prayer Breakfast' or Senior Staff meeting this morning, and right after meet with the local employees' grievance committee over the planned 5% cuts in personnel this year. The Ambassador had his talking points but would he stick to the script? "Sorry you won't be able to go to the big party at Rick's Place tomorrow. Clowns and jugglers galore." Rick, of course was Bogart in the movie *Casablanca*, and the Embassy had met yesterday on the probability of big demonstrations by the Union de Travailleurs in Casa and Meknes. The MPLM might try to make some show of solidarity over the government's new austerity measures and the 20% unemployment rate. There would certainly be a scattering of anti-American posters blaming Uncle Sam for poverty; blaming him for the venal Saudis and Kuwaitis; blaming him for the mess in the Middle East, but the focus most likely would be on local economic issues, not on America. "I read you loud and clear, "Eric replied.

"One more thing, Old Friend, he wants to paint the place orange, but through all the usual noise, I said yellow's the preferred color. Said I would get your input."

"Yes, stay with the yellow," Eric said. The cryptic message meant that the Ambassador wanted to put the Embassy on orange alert, high readiness. That would send shock waves all over the capital. "The Americans must know something we don't," all would say, and the media would surely pick it up, meaning all hell would break out with the Prime Minister's office and even with beautiful, downtown Washington. They were under no imminent danger, and the MPLM had yet to specifically target the U.S. in any of its rather pedestrian 'down-with-the-oppressors' rhetoric. Stu had stood his ground, advising against sending out false alarms, and had gotten his head chewed off. Most other Embassy officers, knowing all the ground rules for readiness alerts, would be more worried about their performance report, their promotion and their pension and would have scurried away with obsequious 'yes sirs.'

Half of Eric's career was consumed with damage control, undoing the flubs of others, and a few of his own. The other half was devoted to process, meetings, reports, policy papers, reading in on intelligence, learning a new language. Some of this was complex, tied up in the constraints, mandates and other fine print of government lawyers and U.S. Congressional oversight committees. There were the mines and bobby traps some set by his own duplicitous colleagues, as well as by inveigling host government 'fixers.' He had to be always persuasive, yet correct; patient, yet mindful of deadlines; courageous if not nervy. It all sounded so interesting, yet for all of the visibility, being on the center stage in crises like Somalia and Bosnia, being able to immerse himself, if he could find the time, in this culturally rich country, making new friends, however ephemeral, in every corner of the planet, something indeed was missing. Was it only the typical mid-forties thing? He did not ascribe to life having such exact rhythms; it had more to do with having something to show, having some documented proof of one's existence. Back in the States there were those stock traders and businessmen who could look at their monthly bank accounts and have testament to their worth. A university professor had all the books he had to publish. A sculptor could transform a piece of marble into something at least a few would admire.

"It's only been two hours. Old Friend, but you're already sorely missed," the senior political officer said signing off.

With two thermoses of coffee and one of tea all consumed, the need to go preoccupied them. They all went off, some of the women together, others separately searching for some privacy in the woods and thickets. After Eric had finished he found a flat shelf of rock near the van which served as a perfect bench. From the wooded area behind him, he heard the muffled voices of his companions as they returned from their ablutions and began to rejoin one another. Someone, Doug Baker, laughed with deep bass gusto. Dry brush crackled and hissed under the crunch of sneakers, boots and walking shoes. Off to his right the road continued its upward course, disappearing into the dark evergreens. Reassuringly, several cars bound for the Fair passed by. There were waves, rolled down windows, greetings from familiar colleagues of the capital's diplomatic corps before the vehicles became lost in the darkness of the tree-shrouded road. Sergeant Donatelli paced about the parked van, smoking a cigarette in quick, agitated drags. He did not wave back at the passing cars, as Eric did, and as did the others from the edge of the wood.

THE BRIDES' FAIR

From his perch, Eric had a fine view of the rolling land six hundred meters below. The golden brown wheat stubble from the recent harvest and the green pastures stretched unbroken to the horizon except for the black, sinuous asphalt main road and the dirt tracks spidering as entryways into the rich, productive land. Here and there white egrets rose in bevies from the fields like startled moths. Just at the horizon's end gray smudges cloaked the two old royal cities, Meknes and Fez, and all in between remained still and undisturbed except for the rising birds and the glint of vehicles on the main road caught by the full, mid-morning sun. These lands had given up their harvests continuously since the time of the Romans and undoubtedly before; since the French in the 1920s and 30s; during the brief occupation of German and then Allied military in the 1940s, and during the struggle for independence in the late 1950s. In other regions of the country, periodic drought played havoc with the food supply, but here on these rain fed Atlantic Plains the rhythm of farming remained more constant, rarely interrupted even in the worst of times.

From this high vantage, Eric found it difficult to imagine a country on the brink of civil unrest, or even, for that matter, ordinary people caught up in the normal strife of daily life. He could hear no gruff, harsh voices as men and women out in the farming villages, in the old medinas, in the secure walled villas, and even in the modern apartment flats confronted one another over the mundane as well as the all-important. Here above these calm, unchanging plains he had found a temporary respite. He did not look forward to returning to the confining van and being again trapped by the problems of his fellow passengers.

Cynthia soon joined him on his rocky shelf. "Nothing new, I suppose?" she asked.

It was personal, not about demonstrations and terrorists. "Another phone call from Peter late last night. He's still taking it badly."

"Well, he's up at that school, way up in Massachusetts. The place he comes to in Christmas and in the summer is suddenly no longer the same. Does he come to you, to Hillary, stay at school during his holidays with the other abandoned kids?"

After Hillary had left, she invited him to dinner several times at her house in Agdal right across from the park and the university campus, but he could only find the time to accept once. They sat out on the terrace drinking after-dinner port. He told her about Susan's long, confused letter, blaming him for always working late, going off on long official trips without them. "When have we last had a real family vacation, all together with no phones, deadlines, major crises in the world?" And then finally Hillary's letter last week after two months of silence, of not returning phone calls. She had gotten the renters out of their house in McLean. She mentioned briefly a dinner with Jack O'Connel. "He was with us two tours ago in Rome. In his early 50;s, I believe. His wife too had left him about two years ago, and he reacted to it by taking early retirement. He landed a job teaching international affairs at George Washington, and he's consulting as well. You see Hillary's going after community, stability, roots. The old story."

"I think she'll quickly get bored with even the idea of that and come back. I know I would with the same old familiarity, with no new roads to travel."

"But you're a professional nomad like me. Hilary really tried to be one too. I would bet she's gone to see our lawyer, Larry Weintraub, about formalizing the separation, about moving towards divorce."

Doug and Edna Baker returned from the woods, waved, and went right off again to get photo shots of a great field of grazing sheep on the field just below them. Sergeant Donatelli still paced about the van, looking at his watch to signal that they were losing time.

"Well, dear friend, you know Karen and I are always here for you," Cynthia said.

They had become close immediately after Tom's death. And when the identification of the remains was conclusive, he and the Ambassador, Ambassador Phil Orlando, wasn't it ?, went together to tell her, the sparkling young wife who had captivated everyone with her zest to learn Tugaleg and her venturing all over Manila and Luzon with her baby strapped to her back papoose style. In the month long wait for the news she had largely repressed her grief, anger and confusion. They sat on her cement patio in the diplomatic compound with its high walls and razor wire. To accommodate a muggy Manila evening pungent with bougainvillea and jasmine, she wore a lose cotton shift; he the short sleeve Hispano-Filipino shirt. The thin cotton apparel was blotched with sweat although they hardly moved as they gulped their St. Miguel beers. She was at her most vulnerable. He wanted Hillary with him for support, but she had to attend another painfully boring American School board meeting. She wasn't failing her duty to a friend. She had already managed between classes, correcting papers and more meetings to organize a farewell coffee for Cynthia and the baby.

"Did I love him? He just wouldn't stop calling, inviting me to parties, introducing me to all his friends. I was hardly out of college, wanting to do Paris and Greece, do all the things my buddies were doing. I didn't just want to plunge into marriage. That was so old fashioned, right? Sure there was the sexual thing, the chemistry and all. I would have grown to understand him better, to be comfortably in love. but then his mother looked down her nose at me, wanted

Tom, to go places in the State Department, become Ambassador at 40 and run for Congress. She had it all planned, and for that he needed one of those trophy wives not some claims adjuster's daughter from suburban Hartford. She never had more than five words for me."

She had a couple of gin and tonics, doubles. And now some beer. With all that Chinese food he insisted they eat. "No, I'm not the slightest bit drunk, and you've been such a real good buddy, a good old buddy." She pressed against him as they sat on the bamboo settee, and kissed him full and hard. "Hillary would understand. Good buddy Hillary would understand. Everybody needs to be human, needs to touch another somebody, another buddy somebody."

Did she finally pass out after more ramblings? She needed to get all the weeks of grief and confusion out, and with the drinking and all he had encouraged her. She was sick. It flowed out in rivers, she being too out of it to wretch. He remembered having to clean up the mess and get her to bed. He looked in on the sleeping baby, and thought of writing a note for the maid, Conchita, who would come at 7 AM, only a few hours away. A note would only confuse things more, he must have concluded.

They now looked down on the rolling fields with all the cultivated plots, the fallow vegetation, the scattered hamlets all like a great patch work quilt. From their perch they had a moment of reverent silence, thinking similar thoughts about how distant the Embassy and their personal problems had become." We should talk more, Eric. I think it does us both some good."

Monique Addleman wandered off alone for her needs, not chumming up with the older women, Pam Crane, Cynthia Dennis and Mrs. Baker and declining to go for a quick jog with restless Karen Dennis who then bolted back down the road towards a patch of meadow thick with sheep and a few fine young stallions and mares which were her particular interest. No false modesty caused Monique to seek an independent path. She had lived two years in a country where all, men and women alike, used the outdoors, the narrow medina alleys and the miles of beaches. She herself had been forced to squat down often in open fields spreading her skirt out like a tent. Most in observance of a code of privacy would turn from these awkward sights, but occasionally she would catch someone bemused to see a 'European' stooping to their rough level. She went up an incline and into the thickets and undergrowth, holding back springy branches and feeling each step on blankets of bark and needles with the waffle sole of her running shoes. Even as a Californian and an above-average tennis player she did not thrill to back packing and mountain climbing like Chris and most of her crowd of ex pat teachers. Nevertheless, the woods seemed peaceful enough, and it was good to get away from the others and have her own private space.

Further on and near the banks of a stream, the taller cedars formed canopies of interlacing branches, emitting only narrow shafts of light. She recalled being taken as a small girl to the cathedral at Reims by her mother who had grown up nearby in a farming community in the Rhone valley. The light from the stained glass windows on high struck the altar, the archways and the stone floor in much the same way as now it came down like numerous spot lights, catching her up in the sun's serenity and warmth. She found a fallen log on which she placed her canvas bag, and retrieving her package of tissues she set about gathering her ankle length skirt about her waist. She had gained a pound or two fretting and eating too many almond pastries these past weeks. His scratches still showed on her legs and butt. The North African men she knew kept their fingernails long to identify their place in society far removed from the laborers and fellaheen. It had been ten days ago when he had banged at her door in the medina where she lived in a treasure of an apartment, a renovated 17th century fort over looking the river delta. They had vowed it over and done with. The thought of a Moslem from one of the old Fez families ever marrying an American Jewess—and being half Catholic French compounded the problem—was just not going to happen in spite of all his talk and her fantasies. But then she had to let him in, for he was making such a fuss, talking all his political stuff in the hall with her three neighbors on the landing certainly all ears. He kept on in French, Arabic and the English she had taught him, making no sense at all to her at this late hour. Without so much as pausing to ask how she had been, he grabbed for the crotch of the jeans she had just slipped on. He took her first against the bed holding her head down on the thick, old style feather mattress. She hated doing it this way so removed from his face, his quickened breathing, the reverberation of his heart. But some like him couldn't deal with it, preferred this distant anonymity, feared the closeness of their lover's eyes on their momentary excitement. Here, they said some boys learned screwing this way out in the fields with the sheep, which is what some of them thought of their women anyway. Through her bleariness she studied the deep carvings on the oak head board intently for the first time. The Moorish geometric patterns, the dentils, the intertwined squiggles of old Arabic letters were suppose to bring good baraka to those who slept and loved in it, that's what the old guy in the medina who sold it to her said. After her pleading, she now had him close above thrusting her down hard into the feather stuffed mattress, causing the stout bed to heave and rattle, causing her to give him the satisfaction of her cries which must have penetrated the heavy masonry walls of her lovely flat, which must have echoed howling out over her balcony and across the wide river delta.

So stupid and helpless. In class she was all stern and cold, black rimmed glasses, hair bound up tightly, long loose dress revealing nothing; but let some guy like him touch her, wrench her about right into morning, wring out every gram of emotion. Her father, Max, told her over and over to leave her 'chicken shit' little job, in North Africa. 'You deserve better, Babe. You've got looks, you've got a Masters; you're trilingual so you must have some brains. Come home, do the marriage thing, and give me some grand children before it's too late for both of us."

The woods her cathedral, she would in the manner of her mother's faith make confession. She would divulge her shame, all her messy affairs. She would ask for a sign, for guidance. 'Father, how many Hail Mary's need I make for atonement? I feel alone out here and afraid, not of bombs, but of myself. I'm alone with myself, empty, but, yes, there is someone who looks over me. He is not God, but a colleague, Chris Reily. He looks out for us all at the school, the students too. He comforts us in his big bear arms, but no I have not lain with him or enticed him with my ways. He belongs to Fiona, my British friend, and I do have some principles, Father. I do not poach guys from my friends. And there's the Professor. He wants to take care of me too. He calls me all the time, but I do not think he is for me. The clock is ticking, Father, and I fear ending up alone with my hair pulled tight into a frumpish bun, my dry, empty hips widened, my pointer continuously on the blackboard parsing English sentences.'

In the North African woods, the light radiated down through a profusion of arched branches above her. This brought her peace, enabling her to expiate her anxiety and inhale deeply of the forest's verdancy. She could and would get her life on track, make enduring friendships instead of punishing herself for something she couldn't quite define, wasting herself on guys who took her nowhere, added nothing new but their own hang-ups. At the Brides' Fair she would be the normal person and seek out new, normal people. She would try as hard as their awkward relationship would permit, to discuss these things with Max during his visit next week. She would agree with him that at almost thirty it was time to shake the bushes for a husband, or at least have a child or two. As unsettled as she was and as unfashionable as it had become, she did want kids; she at least deserved that more enduring pleasure.

As she squatted down to let the coffee and orange juiced primed urine stream onto the absorbent mat of dead brown needles, she saw an encrusted piece of metal, which for an instant she mistook for some oddly bent twig. A metal cap of some sort held an elongated spike. It could be left over from some forestry enterprise, but recognizing it was more than some abandoned piece of hardware she reached for it, and then something cracked in the thicket behind her. She turned and saw a wild thing's eyes boring at her, caught by a shaft of sunlight. She managed in one quick swoop to pull down her skirt, grab her pack and run yelling through the forest.

***** ***** ***** ***** ***** ***** *****

In the capital, Ahmed ben Alami Bennani prepared to meet the American Ambassador. His secretary had passed the message that the bulky black sedan, flags flying from its hood and the accompanying chase car had just left the front gate of the Embassy compound and would arrive at the old, colonial era Ministerial block in approximately 10 minutes. The city was small. One could, except during the worse morning traffic, reach any point of importance in twenty minutes. Also, one could get to know rather quickly anybody of note. Disconcerting to some, few in public or diplomatic life could effectively conceal even the most innocently mundane comings and goings from scrutiny, and his Ministry, in the interests of the state, managed such scrutiny. His buzzer sounded again. His assistants had left for their stations in the downstairs foyer Ahmed Bennani would have preferred to hold this important *séance du travail* in the more decorously appointed offices of state at the palace, not here in this dank, old French-built *bureau d'administration* with its paint-flaking walls and chaotic warren of offices and rooms. Perhaps though, it would be more appropriate to appear a bit scruffy and down-at-the-heels when discussing military assistance.

Even though the palace so sanctioned it, he should not really be the one discussing matters of military hardware. As Minister of the Interior and National Security, he preferred to stay in the operational shadows, not out in public view, even though some believed he commanded more power and trust than almost anyone else in the civil government. Certainly, the Prime Minister, Mohammed Boulassri, and the chairman of the defense committee, General Abdlemalek Guessous, his wife's second cousin, had more real, wide-ranging power.

He rose from his desk with its richly carved panels and footings. The mountain oak carved in the old Arabic script told of the Seventeenth Century battle of the Sultans, the outcome of which had unified the country. The desk had been presented to him by the woodcraft guild of his district. The fine wood and the intricate turnings recalled his responsibility in preserving that hard won unity, in preserving civil order.

THE BRIDES' FAIR

The delegation entered. The Ambassador appeared an aging Atlas to the youthful, diminutive Minister who was small even by the norms of his generation and ethnicity, a defect he had long compensated for, not by Napoleonic swagger, but through a well-honed mind and an articulate, deep throated voice. The Ambassador held out a surprisingly flaccid hand, and a mid-forties woman who appeared to be of European and North African mixture introduced herself as Madame Tijani, the interpreter. A florid faced man with an American hair style the Minister thought had long gone from fashion, called himself Colonel Henry Garvey, the Defense Attaché.

"It is fortuitous, Your Excellency, that you are not conversant in French, for it will give me a welcomed opportunity to use my feeble English," the Minister said. "Madame Tijani can assist me through my difficulties which I'm certain will be many."

"You speak very well, sir," the American Ambassador said. "But where did you learn it?"

"It was your government which sent me to Harvard for my MBA more than 20 years ago."

"Fine school, but I want to get right to business, Mr. Minister, to bring you up to date with where we are with your request, to let you know it's getting my personal attention."

No time for a few pleasantries. Plunge right in. Some American were like that, others like the Deputy, Msieu Dalton, asked after family, brought news about the American political scene, digressed on reports of more flooding in Bangladesh, to the Russian economic crisis, didn't try to rush matters. And why hadn't he come to help this Ambassador? Oh, yes, off to that Mid-Atlas fair. He had checked the lists last evening. "I do appreciate your personal interest, Excellency. I had hoped to have the Deputy Foreign Minister here as well, but he has been called to Paris, the Quai d'Orsay on this business. Some rumors of a radical French element involved with the workers' union rallies this weekend, and perhaps Iranian backing as well." Ahmed threw his little bombs on the table to obviously see if the Americans knew anything, or would admit to knowing anything of these rumors.

"Iranians? Do we have that information, Colonel?"

"I don't believe so, Sir." Colonel Garvey appeared flustered, and not sure of his response scanned the talking points in his folder. "I'll have to check on that, Sir."

The exasperated Ambassador said. "Well, we can give you an update on your request for the night vision goggles and the electronic detection gear, can't we Colonel?"

Certainly, the equipment still was of some priority, but Ahmed Bennani had covered his bets. He would meet this afternoon with Jacque Deauville, an operative at the French Embassy. The French had offered similar material, but it was wise to play all cards, to keep encouraging the American to participate, to not offend the great colossus of the West. "As soon as this upcoming weekend of rallies and fairs is done with, I'll have my Deputy Chief of Security meet with the Colonel here to help finalize matters. We of course want to proceed with some urgency. "

"We've been pushing our lawyers, and I've made several calls to the White House to get those people to come to closure."

"We have another matter holding things back, Sir," Colonel Garvey dared to interject and pointed to the Deputy Chief of Mission's paper.

"Oh, yes, it's that Congressional Oversight Committee, you know Congressman Joe Farrell," the Ambassador said.

"It is he who is planning a visit next week, " Ahmed Bennani said. "And has sent us a list of complicated questions on our treatment of MPLM prisoners, of whom we have none, of course."

"Unfortunately, he'll have to be dealt with," the Ambassador said. "He's asked that a hold be put on the equipment. He really doesn't know the issues here. A flaming liberal you know. Can't tell the good guys from the bad ones. We will work very hard to open his eye."

Bemused by the candor of the Americans he asked Madame Tijani to translate to make certain he understood the Ambassador's regard for the Congressman.

"You have a very serious security problem here, Mr. Minister, and I'm not going to stand by and let some prima donna like Farrell and our squabbling lawyers let our good friends down."

"I very much appreciate your strong support, Excellency, but "very serious?" That is somewhat apocryphal. We are certainly not falling over the brink as some of your journalists and others would have it. When I lived in your Boston two decades ago I was seized with the trouble in your big cities, with some rioting in your African American quarters, with student protests, with the bombings by your white militia. On your television fear, confusion, murder in the streets seemed to be everywhere present. Except for a few noisy rallies on Harvard Square, I did not witness such calamities; I did not see America on the brink. We have dissident voices here as well, and we have many students ourselves who have passionate ideas. I was a student in Paris in the 1960's with passionate ideas. Some might have falsely labeled me a communist. So, this is to say Excellency, that we may have a few security problems, yes, but we need to also give our restless young outlets for their passion and ideas." Ahmed Bennani half believed his own words and knew it was not that simple controlling the fires of the young.

"Sir, I'm a businessman and a politician," the Ambassador said cutting the air with his hand for emphasis. "I appreciate your talk about the problems in America with student hot heads, but you've got something different here. You've got infiltrators coming across your borders to cause real trouble."

"Yes, we have had a few incidents with smugglers and the like." Ahmed Bennani reverted to the official line. The Ambassador had missed the point about the young, however, and it was just as well. If the government were to admit to the presence of the MPLM in several camps across the border in the near Sahara, then one would find among these four or five hundred at the most, former students from the country's three main universities which had become cauldrons of religious and political dissent. He would not apprise the man of the actions they had taken in the past 72 hours; the arrest of known leaders, including the fire brand, Achmed Benslimane and his entire family. These were quiet, night time operations, but the rumors would soon spread with some pleased by the pro-activeness and others decrying that civil rights were being violated. No one ever kept clean hands in these matters and Ahmed Bennani himself would be haunted by these decisions.

He had learned nothing new from the visit of the American Ambassador. The delays with the equipment the Americans had offered weeks ago, the visit of that Congressman, these had been all reported to him in great detail by his cousin Ali Alaoui, Ambassador in Washington. So why had this man Crane come with hat in hand? He would find the occasion to ask M'sieu Dalton about any hidden agenda, any message not fully communicated.

The sugared mint tea arrived with the almond filled pastries. "I'm sure you've tasted these many times, Excellency," he said passing the platter. "They are called horns of the gazelle, from the time in my father's own youth when those animals used to roam our rain fed plains. But the gazelles are all gone now, the desert has encroached, and we have only these delicious reminders."

"Interesting, Sir." The Ambassador nibbled at one thinking of his restrictive diet, thinking of the irrelevancy of such tea ceremonies in a crowded business day, thinking that if this smug little man didn't get some fire under his butt, he'd be as extinct as those gazelles of his.

***** ***** ***** ***** ***** ***** *****

Moustapha who had led his small unit across the border only a few hours ago sat alone in the middle seat, turning occasionally to nod encouragingly at Maleka, slumped in the seat behind him, but fully conscious, her eyes with sorrow in them, meeting his. The police officer bound and gagged on the back deck appeared still, and Moustapha removed the canvas cover periodically to determine his status. Ali drove the *Service Hydraulique* Land Rover down the piste road toward the oasis town of El Mamid. He had stopped a kilometer back at a dry gulch formed by mountain run off in the winter months. Probing down in the dirt he found enough mud and smeared it over the half dozen bullet holes on the passenger side door. How far would these disguises carry them.? There would be other check points, other patrols like the one 60 kilometers back. Someone soon would realize that radio contact with the Chef de Brigade had been lost and would send out a search detail. Perhaps riding boldly into the small town would not be wise. The fellaheen on the edge of the desert did not keep things to themselves. The arrival of every truck, car, every camel train was an omen good or bad to be studied, analyzed from all perspectives. Speculation moved through the tea houses, the family compounds, at the water wells like noisy swarms of locust. Conformity, familiarity would be the rule and all strangers suspect, but according to the traditions, to be greeted face to face with charity.

"We should split up. I will go on by bus and grand taxi. What is it, two hundred kilometers more? Five, six hours at the most." Rachid said. The fine road dust deepened the few faint lines of his face, grayed his bushy eyebrows, making him appear much older, more haggard than his twenty-six years.

"They will be checking the taxis and buses as they always do looking for smugglers and aliens," Moustapha said, but Rachid persisted and reminded him that he had traveled these roads before, that he could handle himself very well and needed none of Moustapha's counsel.

"You must finish off the one in back. He has probably heard and seen enough already. You must get rid of Maleka as well. She will slow you down, ruin all your chances. We should have left her back there with the others."

"Abandon a colleague? Dispatch her like some unwanted dog?" Moustapha found himself shouting and restrained himself. They had to talk in whispers for the police officer may hear their plans. Rachid played at being ruthless and unfeeling. He would butcher all "symbols of oppression," bankers, rich land owners, those who owned the carpet and textile mills where girls of ten and twelve with gnarled old hands worked hours on end at the looms. He would slaughter the high officials who rode about in their long black Mercedes and who managed somehow to stuff their bank accounts in Geneva and Paris with twice the per annum stipend of even a well off bureaucrat. He would disembowel their wives and ravage their precious, spoiled daughters. "All of them, wives, children, infants as well; slit their throats like sheep and then, maybe then, they'll come to our table, then, maybe then things will change. And above all I'll terminate those who have kept them in power, have looked the other way at the corruption and the human abuse: the French and the Americans, not just a few token targets, but as many as possible; make those who have so much power and who know so little suffering bleed."

They argued in the training camp where they encouraged such free thought, such venting of hatred, that this approach would certainly backfire, that even the decrepit poor in the fetid *bidonvilles* would be against them, would be repulsed. But Rachid closed his ears to such arguments, and claimed he, would murder, or 'assassinate'—the term he used—those in his own great family, those of his own blood. He would willingly strap explosive charges to his body and rain havoc on the seats of power and bring glorious martyrdom to himself. Moustapha did not believe the extreme words of Rachid, but he remained wary of the man. They both, and many others in the still-nascent *Mouvement Populaire* were the sons, of the so-called elite. Almost all of them, even those from unimportant backgrounds, such as Maleka and Ali, had some university training. Wasn't it then presumptuous, if not arrogant of them who had never really suffered, scratched for food, lived mean, brutish lives, to be at the forefront of the revolution, to presume to speak for the millions of the less fortunate? Was it out of idleness or guilt that they found structure, employment and passion in the Movement? Into the night they would argue on the cooling desert floor, huddled about small fires in the shielding circle made by their tents. Are the poor too cowed, too intimidated, too without resources to help themselves or stand with us? Don't we need them totally with us, not cringing from our bloody acts?

"No, we will get Maleka attended to, at a *Poste de Santé* in the next town. Moustapha fought back at the waves of desperation which tried to pull him under. They would go on, succeed. The other units of the movement now infiltrating the cities depended on it. He had little choice. They had killed a man in the brief fire fight and shot another in cold blood. They would become the hunted assassins not the hunters they were meant to be. He recalled how honored he had been to be selected as a unit chief by the Commander, the one they called El Suguri after the desert wind storm; how thoroughly they had planned for days, how it would all fit together, the disturbances in the cities, the power plants, the

TV stations and at the big mountain marriage fetes. "You will change from being a party of water engineers, to film makers come to shoot the marriage market and the spectacle. You will have expensive camera gear in your bags masking the weapons. There will be others we can not name along the way and at the Fair who will help you reach your objective."

Disguise, false identities, slipping through the shadows, it had seemed so possible. But here on the open plain they stood out like a great sultan's harka of richly draped baggage trains. He slowed down and stopped before a grove of king palms and small, well-irrigated parcels of broad beans, corn and citrus. At four kilometers distant they could see the rose hued walls of El Mamid .

Moustapha took his map from its protective plastic sleeve. His route to the Mid-Atlas had been marked off in red pencil,and they had not so far deviated from it. Yes, the map indicated a health post in El Mamid, but news would be out in a flash that a person, a stranger with superficial gun shot had been treated. No, here at Zagora they would find help. "We will go to this UN refugee camp, above Zagora. They will have foreign doctors there who may not ask too many questions. It is only 60 kilometers out of the way and we can take a back way around the town ahead. Perhaps, you should go on alone, as you suggest." As determined and as ruthless as Rachid was, he just might make it. There would be many vehicles on the roads to the three day event. A young camera man whose car had broken down might just be believed "We will meet as planned late tonight. We should be there no later than 10 in the evening when the last fires are fading." Moustapha well realized that they all should break up and go separately to the fair if they had any chance of succeeding. But he could not leave Maleka until it was certain she would be well, that she would not be cornered and trapped like a rat in a dead end medina alley. The administering of anti-biotics, cleaning the wounds, tweezering out the few fragments, putting in a few stitches couldn't take more than an hour. Then he would demand that she leave them, go on to Casa, not to the house of her parents, for she would not be welcomed by her father who had renounced her, but to that of her older sister, Shafika who would gladly take her in, keep her safe, see to her proper recuperation.

Several donkey carts from the nearby ksar plodded up the dirt road towards the town, as Rachid took his old university back pack and an equipment packed duffel bag, barely nodded his good-byes and walked unhurriedly towards one of the carts to ask the boy driver for a ride, as if he were back in Casablanca hailing a Renault taxi. Ali turned the vehicle about and returned down the road. Moustapha looked under the canvas. The police officer's eyes met his and they were full of hate. Moustapha fingered the trigger of the automatic pistol but

THE BRIDES' FAIR

quickly tossed it down on the seat, angry at the thoughts that pricked his skin. At a nearby oasis of palms and flowering bushes fed by the underground water from the mountains, he signaled they should stop. He would with Ali's help drag the policeman from the rear deck, take him behind the clutch of vegetation, and quickly, without much thought, put a shot to his head, making him a martyr, giving him his glorious eternity and his virgins of paradise. Before they opened the door of the vehicle's back deck, Ali pointed down the road to a slowly moving Saviem truck piled with bales of wool, with women in festival garb seated comfortably between the bales and engaged in animated conversation and with the men in the cab of the truck looking down the road to where two men in uniform stood at the rear of a dirt streaked Land Rover.

Chapter IV

Some concluded that Monique Addleman who came tearing through the cedar forest, through thickets, thorn bushes and back-lashing branches had been frightened by a wild animal, a wild boar most likely which were known to browse and rut in these Mid Atlas foothills. Others first thoughts were of an attack from rebels or from bandits gunning for an American hostage prize, possibly mistaking the teacher for Pamela Crane, the Ambassador's wife, possibly after all of them until frightened away. Eric also believed at first they might be under attack. The cedar forest's underbrush crackled and echoed like small arms fire. Even the human screams seemed familiar. They were exposed and vulnerable, for he had become too used to having a cocoon of security about him. In this era of terrorists and assassinations, the armor-plated sedans, the thick fortress American Embassy walls, the massive blast proof doors, the armored vests, and the circle of body guards with those infernal radio buttons conspicuously in their ears, had become too intrusively common place, too much a part of the diplomatic landscape wherever in the world. While this tight ring of protection could be easily punctured at any time by a determined assailant, Eric, nevertheless was rarely free to step outside, to roam unattended in the country side, or like Cynthia to leisurely explore the broken stones and tiles of ancient settlements. Any sight seeing excursions or trips to cultural shrines these days had always been with phalanxes of Washington VIPs and host country officials, and always locked in tight by the security men.

The young woman broke through the wall of brush and hurtled towards him and in a moment found the security of his arms. To some it may have seemed awkward, embarrassing even with her torn blouse, her frayed skirt half about her. He felt the sweat, the rivulets of blood, the several welts at her back. It seemed she had been whipped sharply for some offense and now pressed tight for protection against a further assault. They often him sought him out to relieve their distress and pain. Often he seemed to play the father, the big brother, the comforter. A loss of a parent, spouse, sibling, child, an unplanned departure from post, the medical report of one's irreversible demise, caused women young and old of whatever color or condition to come to his office, to telephone him at his residence, to make an appointment with his secretary He admitted to a recurring fantasy. He saw himself leading them away from their anguish, through the destruction, the blackened cities of a foolish war, far from the stench of death to a new beginning in a remote, untouched corner of the world. They would start again to raise children; they would insulate themselves against the horrors of their past.

Possibly he proved more accessible now during these uncertain times. As the boss, *patron*, senior colleague, he, in the confines of an office or an Embassy provided the structure, the order for all of their pedestrian routines, but was not as imperiously set apart as an Ambassador, an Assistant Secretary, or the ultimate *grand patron*. Perhaps, he unavoidably looked too much the part at 6 foot one, broad shouldered, still trim at 43, visage unjudgemental, benign. It wasn't some power he had over others to draw them magnetically to his side. Taciturn Yankees didn't not give themselves to such pretensions. Nor did he play some perfunctory role like a priest parceling out forgiveness, wine and wafers. These brief, hopefully soothing embraces spoke mainly to an essential universal humanity of which he gratefully had a part.

She continued to press tight, wanting to be engulfed as a child or pet during a clamorous thunderstorm. She was his daughter Susan with a bloody mouth after her first attempt down hill on a two wheeler; she was Hilary clinging in nested spoon fashion after their loving in the early morning, or when coming apart after the sudden death of her father she clung to him for solace. Monique gasped out apologies for being a nuisance, for causing all this trouble, blaming herself, now flagellating herself verbally. He found a calming voice. Did she want to go on; the trip would become more difficult? Finally, Cynthia and Mai Donatelli eased the young woman away. Her hard grip had become too sustained. They guided her to the vehicle where they removed her torn blouse and skirt, dabbed the cuts with antiseptic pads from the medical kit. Karen who was Monique size offered a T shirt from her back pack, as Monique still confused, had difficulty remembering whether she had another skirt or a pair of jeans in her bag.

All the others gathered around Eric by the side of the road. He sent the young Marine and the Ag Professor back in the thicket one more time to search, to thrash about and try to come up with something reassuring. Some like Edna

Baker glanced back to the dark green conifers and thick tangle of undergrowth as if they heard noises however faint. Eric said this was an isolated incident for there were no signs of anything or persons lurking in the forest. Very possibly a wild animal, a boar perhaps had been rummaging around in the woods but had been frightened off. He proposed, however, that some including Monique might wish to return to the capital. They could call the Embassy for a vehicle and it could be here within two hours. He would ask the Marine Corporal to accompany her back to the Embassy and the nurse, and he and perhaps Dr. McMannus could help the Sergeant with the driving.

Edna Baker thought that what happened in the woods might be an omen of some kind, and with all that was going on in the country now, they had been not been too smart to travel out like going on some Sunday picnic back in the States. She would gladly go back with Ms Addleman and any others. With little discussion, no one else including her husband, Doug Baker, wished to return. "We need a little high adventure, and who's afraid of a big bad wild pig?" he said

Monique, somewhat recovered, and having found her jeans and bag, approached the group and was clued in on DCM Dalton's proposal. "But I'm not going back. I've looked forward to the Brides' Fair for almost a year now. I'm sorry I made such a fuss, but you all can see I'm all right now. Just a few little cuts and scratches." She held out her scratched up arm and steady hand for all to witness that she had regained her wits.

Hearing this, Edna Baker demurred. "I won't be the only one. No way."

Three young boys, none more than ten, who had been tending sheep and goats in the lower pasture came slowly up the road towards the big white American van, their curiosity aroused but still too wary or timid to approach closely. The ever-prepared Cynthia tried to win them over with hard candy and M and Ms, but still they remained across the road from the van, pointing excitedly at the forest and attempting to communicate in broken French.

"What was that all about?" Eric asked as they finally, after almost an hour's delay prepared to get underway.

"It's just amazing. You won't believe this." Cynthia retrieved a document from her thick folder and flipping through it stopped on a brief passage. "Look, this is the El Kariba Forest and those boys were trying to tell me it's a bad place, a place haunted by djins. Read this. I got it from your friend, Giles Whitcomb at the UK Mission who's quite a scholar, you know."

Henri Belier, a French historian writing in the 1890's described an incident that occurred late in the 16th Century in the El Kariba Forest at the rise above the plains where the grassy pasture land gives way to cedars and other conifers. The

THE BRIDES' FAIR

Sultan Moulay Achmed Ben Slimane with his great harka, his tattered parasol, his two hundred horsemen, his servants, slaves and concubines stopped to make camp after several months of campaigning in the mountains. He had inflicted much devastation among the rebellious hill tribes and took many as slaves, mostly young boys and girls for his several palaces. But on his last night in the forest before descending towards the royal city of Fez, the Berber warrior, Sidi Ben Yassi, now canonized as a marabou saint, rode in with a horde of avenging horsemen. The Sultan and some meager few of his guard managed to escape the vicious scything down of men and women alike. It is said that almost every tree in the forest hung with a head, even those of the captured young from their tribal federation for they had already been soiled by the Sultan and his camp.

Monique frightened half to death by the ghost of a Berber slave girl? Cynthia didn't believe this, but, then, like so many she sought answers for the cruelties of nature in old myths, superstitions and folk lore richly embellished by each passing generation. In this Moslem country, she attended the one Protestant service in the capital, a Sunday haven for ex pats and others of the diplomatic community. "It's not so much to save my soul or wash way my many sins, but for stability's sake. Yes, stability. It's like having a bit of a familiar old, crusty anchor in our rootless and stormy profession."

Eric, a lapsed Episcopalian, an anachronistic sect itself in these times, found himself voluntarily in church only during Christmas. He admitted begrudgingly to a thorough enjoyment of the old noels, the soaring Handel oratorios with their brass and timpani, the fanciful decorations of the large cathedrals.

A remarkable coincident they agreed sitting on their rock bench while some, notably Dr McMannus, still thrashed about in the woods looking for the wild boar or whatever. So uncanny, they said, to have chosen this very spot to interrupt their journey and relieve themselves. "We bumped against the past," Cynthia said. "There must be some connection to us here and now and to our present journey to the Brides' Fair. I can tell by your look you think I'm batty, just going off the edge over old bones, pottery shards and fanciful tales."

"You know I don't think that. I'm a friend, right? Sometimes we do need such stories to take the hard edge off of events we do not understand. It's only that a living thing frightened Monique, a living animal or a human."

"This is Base 1, requesting Sit Rep per our last communication. Anything new, Old Buddy?" Walt Schultz in the Embassy Com Center came in loud and clear.

"Had a run in with something wild, animal that is," Jess Williams responded. " One of our party involved. Not to worry, wasn't the First Lady. You know the teacher from the language school? Fine drink of water with red-brown locks? She got some minor cuts and stuff escaping from that critter. Doing O.K. now. Everybody's O.K, but we've lost almost an hour here at point E on our route, and the DCM says we've got to get on down the road now. Catch you later."

When they finally got under way, the group shifted their seating arrangements, and Eric, still in the rear pew, found himself next to Monique with Karen on the other side. Over the road noise he ventured innocuous queries. How long had she been in country? Didn't he have that information in the files as he had on every American in the official community? Did she enjoy teaching, living in North Africa?

The reply, "I do, very much" was a bit diffident. "My father's coming out next week. And I have the trimester tests for my advanced students next week too. Well, he's not coming all the way from LA just to see me. He makes films. Coming to take a look around." She wanted to add 'and to persuade me to leave, to get real and come back to the States.' Knowing Max, he had lot up his sleeve, like marriage to his camera man friend, Phil Stokes, who just got divorced. "Not yet forty-five, Babes." That would be really desperate.

Max's film making sparked the interest of Doug Baker who pressed for more specifics. Did her father need Embassy assistance? Had he found a local agent to work with? Did he know about the perfect light here, the low production costs, the ease of dealing with the authorities, the lack of hassle with permits?

"Repeat after me one time again. *Repetez un fois encore*," Eric Dalton could see her before the tongue-tied, the earnest, the tone deaf, giving meaning to phrases, nuances to words, breaking down the barriers. Her file said she had been three years at Embassy Abidjan before Rabat, six years in all as a teacher in Francophone Africa . Bilingual. Brought up in California; product of a French mother, a textile designer, and a Jewish-American father, a minor league film maker from LA. Parents divorced. Father did get an award a couple of years ago for a film he did on Bosnia, "Where have all the Young Men Gone?" 'She gets high marks as a teacher. Good success rates with her students. Poised, attractive as you must have noticed. Good image for the Embassy, for the good old USA. Nothing on drugs or booze. Appears to be clean. Appears to have a discrete thing going with someone, most likely Christopher Reily, another language teacher at the Cultural Center.'

And weren't some of her students pressing her? She taught mostly 23 to 30 year old men going to the States for graduate degrees, and a few older businessmen and government officials. "Can't we meet for a *thé a la menthe* after class? Just a half hour of conversation to perfect my poor English. I would be so ever grateful." Darkly handsome, young men as well as those older had a talent for laying it on thick, talking the pants off any 'euro' ice maiden. How many secretaries and young officers had been too willingly overwhelmed, regardless of the gentle hints in the orientation lectures, warnings about the old let-me-show-you-the-Kasbah routine? "Let me invite you for couscous, a tagine, bastilla. Let me intoxicate you with saffron, cumin and coriander, get your blood raging on heavily sugared tea."

No, she did not know what exact project her father had in mind. He didn't go into those details with her, but he had asked her to make some appointments including one at the Embassy where Mr. Baker's kind offer of help could be realized. She sat stiffly on the seat beside Mr. Dalton. Her cuts and bruises must have been uncomfortable with the van's swaying and the shuddering caused by the many ruptures in the asphalt road. Yes, she would be meeting some of her language school friends at the fair. She didn't make up her mind about going until the last minute, and then all the places in Chris's jeep were spoken for. "It's really just fine coming on the trip with you instead. You've all been so very kind, and I really needed to meet new people, not hang out with the same old crowd." She abruptly handed the object she had picked up in the woods to Cynthia Dennis. "It's a pin, one for a caftan, isn't it?"

Cynthia turned it over and over with intense interest, rubbed it hard with tissues retrieved from her cornucopian leather sack, and pronounced after several minutes of silent deliberation that it was indeed a caftan pin, a fibula of a style she had seen in the fine boutiques of the city. A triangular pendant, of richly worked metal served to hold a three and a half inch miniature sword-like spike which with a semi-circular rod formed a clasp. "The fibula, you know, was basically a Roman device to hold the toga together around the upper torso. It's the same principle with the caftan."

"But isn't it rather big for a dress pin?" Pam Crane asked.

"I believe women also used them to defend themselves. It looks rather like a small dagger doesn't it?" Cynthia replied.

Dr. McMannus asked to examine it. "The long tine is certainly silver plated over brass for hardness, and the head is silver also with several stones set in it. It's still encrusted with dirt, but I would guess opals, bluish white opals." He admitted that he collected *objets d'art* here and there on his assignments, gold filigree jewelry from West Africa, a few tribal masks, a 19th century rose water salver. "All old stuff, not the tourist junk you find everywhere. It's a very modest collection. I'd take this pin to Dr. Majid Tahar at the antiquities museum near the

Bab Rouah gate. He'll tell you if it dates from the time of Mrs. Dennis's sultan, or was dropped in the woods more recently by a person or a bird or whatever. I'd be happy to go with you if you'd like," he said to Monique, who nodded to acknowledge the offer.

Yes, the pin was unique as the young woman herself, Cynthia believed the pendant's design, the raised crenellations, the triangular shape were probably of Moorish Andulsian roots, a product of the Fez medina two or three hundred years back, but not more recently. As Dr. McMannus had just explained, only a true expert could tell. But she was not so preoccupied with the pin's origins, with dredging up facts on the Roman, Almohad and Merinid dynasties that she didn't observe what was going on about her in the present. Some thought her overbearing, and she could go on too long about the differences between lambrequin and polylobe arches, appear to be more concerned with dusty old things than with people. She avoided sitting around with the Embassy 'girls' gossiping about some Ambassador's peccadilloes and who was doing what to whom. She'd rather read a book at her desk during lunch, absorb herself in new, challenging things. They thought her a stickler for good manners, decorum, and the proper Embassy image. 'Hey guys, it comes with the job,' she had to remind them. But she was definitely no prude, despite what they all thought. Having just hit the big 4 0 last May, she hardly felt old, or resigned to perpetual widowhood. She was still youngish, with healthy appetites and all, but she was more prudent than most. Avoid the local men. As the guardian of the gates to the US, consular officers could get themselves into compromising messes over visas, with careers ruined, abrupt, tearful departures from post. And then, you had to be careful with the few bachelors at the Embassy, who were mostly junior officers, mostly too young. And the wider diplomatic community? Embassy secrets spilled out in love-mussed beds? At least her current male friend, Lars, had no interest in the plotting and counter-plotting of her country. It was inevitable they should get together, after the introductions by Stu Connors. They both were unattached, still vital and not yet middle age. They were thoughtful of one another and filled each other's good old basic human needs. It wasn't love, yet it possibly could grow that way. But unfortunately he was back at his Ministry in Copenhagen over a thousand miles away, and that meant the problems of working out a weekend here and there in Madrid or Paris. They had tentatively planned a ski trip for the Christmas holidays. Karen would come too, although she thought him too old- he was 49 only, and truly divorced. Karen thought Cynthia's counterpart at the Ministry of Foreign Affairs had real blood, not Nordic ice water running in his veins. But that was impossible, even though the man persisted in inviting her to dinner. "Not even lunch, Mrs. Dennis? We invite all our diplomatic associates to lunch. It is also a custom in your country as well I understand." She was certainly tempted, and saw in a dream once his handsome face over her and close as in love making, but it was impossible. Yes, she could certainly tell these younger women something about the company of men on assignments overseas and how after these 17 years she had learned well to disguise her feelings behind the pottery shards and the minutia of antiquity.

Monique, on the other hand was too obvious, provocative even. Back in the cedar forest after that frightening incident, Cynthia had given the young woman all her attention and kindness without thought, damping down her hysteria, bathing the dozen or so scratches, washing out the thin rivulets of blood with the alcohol pads from the van's medical kit. Mai Donatelli helped as well getting her into a T shirt and jeans, cooing to calm her, brushing her rich auburn hair, thinking her almost anorexically thin with a waist line some would die for. " Look, you'll have something to tell your friends, your grand children. On the way to a mountain fair in the Mid Atlas of North Africa, I was chased through the woods by a wild boar. They'll laugh, thinking it so absurd."

And yes, she had seen the look Monique gave Eric as she slipped in beside him in the rear seat, displacing Mai Donatelli, causing musical chairs which in and of itself wasn't a bad idea on a long trip. And to be perfectly objective, it was very possible the girl was only reaching out to a father figure, and Eric filled that role very well, in spite of himself. It was Psych 101, fear, protection, sex all mixed up in the hormonal surge of the incident back in the forest. She should be understanding, amused even. Hadn't it been like that in Manila? She saw a drunk, frightened young woman with a three month old baby, and a dead husband blown to splinters, and she was falling all over this same man.

Cynthia returned momentarily to playing the part of guide and pointed out the steep roof Swiss-like chalets sitting back among the tall dark pines, incongruously out of place in these Berber mountain woodlands. The French built them along this road in the 1930's and 1940's. "Yes, it certainly snows at this elevation. Yes, they use them as summer cottages to escape the heat of Fez and Meknes."

She couldn't let Eric be taken in so. For someone so cool and controlled, how could he make himself so vulnerable? Without a wife for four months, the familiar warmth in the bed gone, the easy groping towards one another in the night or early morning, the well-practiced fulfillment. Cynthia envied married couples and their easy familiarity, and it was hard to conceive of Eric and Hillary ending all of that in some head strong rush to the divorce courts. So embarrassed by that drunken night in Manila, it had taken Cynthia four or five years before she could reestablish contact. The thought of being at the same official reception or luncheon with either of the Daltons made her panic. But they kept after her, showed real concern for how she was coping with a young daughter, how the new overseas assignment was going. Finally, she was able to put that muggy night away in a box on a high shelf in the closet, and wrapped up in it was some immature, drunken girl of not even 23, someone she hardly knew. They, Eric and Hilary, became her family. Their house on Cape Cod was hers whenever; they celebrated each others birthdays, and for most of these years they found themselves together for Thanksgiving and some Christmases, even though it could mean two days of flying steerage each way. But something had changed this past year at post. Hillary had become more distant; there were few why don't you drop by after work for a few drink invitations. Eric pulled 12 hour days and went out to diplomatic 'dos' three or four times a week, and except for meetings she rarely saw him. But she was determined to do what she could. She would call Hillary in the States, at the house in McLean as soon as they got back from this trip, have a real heart to heart like they used to when they would divulge the hopes and dreams for their children, when she was bursting to tell someone close, someone like Hillary about her latest affair, about what she should do about Lars or even Ahmed Laloui ? Yes, she would definitely call Hillary, snap her out of this foolishnes, get her good friends back together.

Just outside the last town of any size before the gorges, ravines and mountain passes of the Mid Atlas range, they came upon a hundred black, goat hair tents lined up in perfect military bivouac order as well as a more chaotic out door market. On the far side of the tents, hoof-agitated clouds of dust veiled a charging file of magnificent horses bearing turbaned riders who held long-barreled rifles aloft with one hand. At the end of the hundred meter charge, the horsemen reigned into a perfect abreast halt simultaneously firing off their guns. Almost immediately with the reports still echoing through the hills, another file of horsemen began their charge from the far end of the field.

" We must stop, Eric". Cynthia said. " It's a moussem, an important moussem from the number of tents and the size of the crowds.

"There are fairs everywhere this weekend. Aren't they like harvest fairs back in the States? " Dr. McMannus asked.

"Please, Uncle Eric," Karen said, "Just look at those horses. I bet they have some really terrific bridles and saddles. "

Karen being an accomplished equestrian was passionate about horses, and the others, their cameras out at the ready were thrilled by the first real spectacle

THE BRIDES' FAIR

they had chanced upon since setting out from the capital almost four hours ago. Monique said that she really needed to buy a caftan. She didn't think it proper to walk around the Brides' Fair in jeans. Cynthia rather boldly suggested to Mai Donatelli that she too might wish to look for something 'more formal and more anonymous' than her shorts and T shirt, emblazoned "U.S. Marine Corps," anchor and all.

Eric knew it useless to make the case against stopping due to the unknown, the possibility of unruly, hostile crowds. The fair didn't appear on the list of approved tourist events and was an event for the area's locals who may not abide the intrusion of outsiders. Cynthia countered that tradition everywhere welcomed the stranger. Bread and salt were offered, and no host would question the why and wherefore of one's passing. Eric instead mentioned the loss of more time, more diversions which the Brides' Fair would make redundant, arriving at their destination on dangerous roads well after dark. After more pleadings he signaled the Lance Corporal to stop, and advised everyone as authoritatively as he was able that they could pause no more than 15 minutes.

Jess Williams had to back up having passed the place, albeit at a slow speed until the DCM finally came to a decision. He parked between a pair of goat chewed trees, and everyone piled out, assuring Mr. Dalton that they'd watch the time. The group split in three with the teenager, the Ambassador's wife, and the new man, Mr. Baker, going off towards the upper field where the horsemen were having a rodeo of some kind. The red headed teacher, the Sergeant's wife and Mrs. Baker headed off in the other direction into the big outdoor market. The DCM, the Visa Lady, and the guy with the fancy beard, the Professor, also headed into the market and seemed to be going towards a stage of some kind where musicians and dancers were doing their stuff. The Gunny didn't want to do anything much but smoke his unfiltered coffin nails by the van, so Jess took off after Mrs. Crane and her group. "Watch the Ambassador's Lady like a hawk," they had told him. "You never know who's out their waiting to be a hero or a martyr.

Those damn rifles blasting off every few minutes made him edgy. Good cover for other fire, not that he knew much about it other than punching his ticket at the firing range and watching old war movies. Like many of his generation his only time near anything remotely resembling action was sitting in the Gulf in an assault ship with 600 other grunts, sweating his balls off doing drills on a steaming deck, showing the flag which is about all the pols back in Washington had them doing these days. But the Corps had been good to him, and he had stayed far away from trouble during his four years, and got rewarded for it by being shipped off to Embassy Guard unit duty, not bad for a 23 year old two striper from the funky row houses of North Philly. He wasn't fooled by 'the man' though. His selection to go to North Africa had as much to do with him having a brown face, and 'the man' needing to show these folks overseas how democratic he was than with his record. He hadn't wanted to come on this trip. Being cooped up for three straight days with these Embassy 'bees', people he still couldn't dig, was hardship duty without the extra pay. He could be taking care of business, getting it on with Zoubida, taking her to the beach and stuff. And then he had to deal with the Gunny, Donatelli, nodding off back there in the van; you had stay far away from that grunt today. Had another fight with his old lady, Mai, and got blasted at the Marine House last night. Jess couldn't understand why these guys with fine, foxy wives always had so much trouble.

And Miss Long Tall Sally, the English teacher? Now there was more trouble. He had just gone in the woods, minding his business, looking forward to a good long piss like everyone else, when he heard all this yelling and carrying on. "Mrs. Crane?' He went flying like he was back doing the 100 yard dash at Lincoln High, his regulation boots tearing up the weeds, and there she is all caught up in the thicket, her blouse torn and half off. 'O K., Ma'm .You're O.K.' He had her free in a few seconds, but the bitch kept on hitting at him and scratching him with those nails. 'What the hell did she think was going down? That he was trying to jump on her bones?'

Now back in the States he was used to white women clutching at their hand bags most every time he passed by on the sidewalk or sucking in their breath when he went into a crowded store. Here the locals and the European chicks too walking around in the city, never tensed up like that when he passed by, didn't think he was out to rob or rape them. And she, the scrawny bitch, could plainly see what was going down, that he was trying his best to help her. Maybe her mind was blown and he should just forget it. He rarely carried any big chips on his shoulders like some dudes, just small splinters.

It was all timing like most everything else. He stood right behind Mrs. Crane in the crowd, so close he could tell she had shampooed her hair this morning and had doused herself with some perfume that must have cost a bundle, seeing that her old man, the head honcho himself, was made of money. The guys on the horses held the reins with one hand and their old fashioned rifles with the other. The object was to pull up sharp to a dead stop, the row of ten or more riders neat and even, and at the same time fire off the guns. It was called a fantasia, Karen Dennis explained, and Jess thought fantasia had to do with some old Disney flick.

THE BRIDES' FAIR

"Isn't this great, Corporal," Mrs. Crane said, turning to him, lightly touching his hand. "I'm so glad you're here." She gushed in that phony way some of them did when they thought they should make you feel at ease.

They pushed on through the crowds at the end of the field to get a better look at the horsemen. After each team discharged their long rifles, the field hung choked with gun powder like ground fog on a cool morning until the stiff winds coursing down from the mountains dispersed all readying the field for the succeeding team. Doug Baker, his broad fleshy face beaming with affability tried hard to disguise his uneasiness. He had lived on assignment in mainly European cities with their familiar rhythms and street scenes. Here the pungent smells of animals and rank human sweat mixed with gun powder got to him as did the press of rough hewn, rural men and boys wearing dark heavy hooded robes in the fashion of medieval monks and friars.

A man of a different caste pushed towards the Americans. He wore the soft leather riding boots, the white pantaloons and tunic of one of the fantasia cavaliers. He beckoned them to follow him to the VIP viewing tent which Doug Baker feared was some sort of ruse to trap and rob them. Karen and Jess, however, advised that this was only the usual offer of hospitality to passing strangers. And indeed they were seated around a large gleaming brass platter while fuming black teas was poured into another pitcher stuffed to the full with a cone of sugar and clumps of fresh mint leaves. Mrs. Crane savored it all, beamed and profusely expressed her thanks in her few words of Arabic. Mr. Baker only took a wary sip, while Karen pointed admiringly at the silver embossed and tapestry-like bridles which were hung decoratively about the tent.

While the four drank their mint tea, Eric, Cynthia and Jonathan McMannus pushed through a maze of lanes and byways. To the outside observer the jumble of merchandise, crafts and food stuff could seem chaotic, but there was an order to it all Those who offered gold and silver jewelry clustered together as did those who sold plastic and metal house wares. Everything had an assigned place and those who came to shop or browse found the logic and layout little different than that in the great covered bazaars of the cities. With live sheep corralled everywhere behind the merchants and bales of raw and dyed wool piled up in great mounds, the rain fed grazing lands of the foot hills, Dr. McMannus explained, were among the most productive in the country. He pointed out the sacks of walnuts, the plump peaches and apples, noting that these were the products of the cooler, temperate hill country, while the many displays of dates, almonds and olives were carted up from the semi-arid low lands to the south.

Eric observed how the Professor engaged the rural farm merchants with an easy bon homie, in his serviceable Arabic. "From where do these nuts of the argon tree come?" "Have the rains been good to you this year?" "Are the prices for your wheat and barley better than before?" In his mid 30s, McMannus still found joy in the things the earth could yield with practiced and caring attention. Both Eric and Cynthia paused to hear the Professor and his interlocutors, buying some of the fine fruit and nuts he recommended, and due to the time, not pressing on through the crowds to hear the folk music. " I may have been wrong about him," Eric said to Cynthia. "He's really into his plants, his horticulture, not just another contract expert who couldn't make it elsewhere and who sneaks around like a demented school boy looking up girls' skirts."

"You're too quick to judge people, Eric. That's not like the Eric I knew. Jonathan is really a nice young man, a bit on the shy, serious side, but nice." She went on to tell him about the time the Professor joined her group for a tour of an ancient Roman fish paste factory near Tangier, and how informative and really helpful he had been.

He wanted to say 'so are they all nice and honorable men,' but it was time to go and he had to set the example.

In starting back to the van, they came upon Monique Addleman being followed by a stream of kids, veiled women in black robes, and men in their heavy wool djellabas. She wore a brilliantly white caftan, her found fibula pin spiked into the cloth just above her breasts, and her long red hair flying about wildly in the stiff breezes coming down from the mountains. The Professor rushed forward through the crowd believing she needed assistance and show of male support.

"I don't know what it is about her. She's like a magnet the way trouble follows her around, "Cynthia said.

"Aren't they just curious? She is certainly different looking, wouldn't you say?" Eric said. He should not give excuses for her It should be 'here we go again .' Monique set upon by phantoms in the woods, and now causing a riot at a rural fair? He should escort her to one of those grand taxis parked under the row of eucalyptus trees, and send her quickly back to the capital before something disastrous happened.

"Well, as Karen would say, she's sending out a whole bunch of messages," Cynthia said

"Messages?" He didn't quite get the implication, but before he could pursue it with Cynthia, a young, clean shaven soldier of the national guard wearing a pressed, new uniform saluted him, asking him if he was *le responsable*. He did not

THE BRIDES' FAIR

wish to be responsible for Monique or anyone, he just wanted only to be an anonymous member of the traveling party; no Canterbury Friar leading his flock to the fair, hearing the long tales and intimate confessions. But it couldn't be. He was the senior man, the flack catcher, the buck stopper. He explained to the young civil guard who watched the commotion across the road with some apprehension, that they were with the diplomatic corps.

"Yes, I can see that, Excellency. Your matriculation plates. *Ambassade Americaine, n'est-ce pas?* You are *en route* to the big fair up in the mountains. That is where they all go this morning."

Monique crossed the road at a slow, determined pace, a score or so of the curious trailing her but at a measured distance. At a comment from someone, she answered back sharply in the Maghrebi dialect. Harsh, guttural words spit out on distorted, angry lips.

"You should have heard her bargaining for our caftans. The old vendors were stunned, ready to give her any price she asked, "Edna Baker said.

"She is of your Embassy as well?" the visibly nervous soldier asked.

He explained that she taught languages at the Embassy cultural center and carried an official passport.

"But these herders, farmers, woodsmen will not see it that way, Excellency. A woman in a caftan, with hair like fire, speaking our tongue like one of us. Some have already run to the fable tellers in the tents there for an explanation."

An apparition among them on the first day of their celebration, sent to spoil their sanctified ground? Eric with his best diplomatic embroidery apologized for any disturbance their brief visit had caused and assured the young keeper of civil order that Ms Addleman was all flesh and blood and could be seen any day of the week in her classrooms back in Rabat. "I trust you will reassure these good people that we only wish them well and that no harm will come to them." Their tea water will not spoil; their women and ewes will not abort; they will not be struck down dead in their sleep tonight. "And now we must be on our way."

"Yes," the young guardsman said with relief. "And yes, Excellency, we're advising all who pass by today, do not pick up strangers, hitch hikers."

"Is there some trouble?"

"No, there is not trouble, but one should always be prudent, is that not right, Excellency?"

"You caused quite a stir," Cynthia said to Monique as they piled into the van.

"It's the hair, I think. They believe I'm a djin, a witch, Aiycha Kandisha herself. That's the way it is sometimes, isn't it Mrs. Dennis? You're either an air head, a dumb Fatima or a witch."

They finally got underway, the crowd near the van silent, sullen. At the edge of the fair grounds, they passed the white domed shrine of the marabout saint, the Berber famed in this region, the same who had reeked havoc upon the Sultan's harka back in the cedar forest. In the nearby town they gassed up, unwrapped their sandwiches, and listened as Karen described the war horses and the Arabian breeds, the ornate reins and bridles she had seen at the fantasia, and the present of one tightly woven wool bridle, embroidered with silk, that their host at tea had presented to her. Edna Baker carped that the carpets she had been shown at the fair were no match for Turkish or Persian, while Mai Donatelli showed off the rose caftan she had purchased. "Not white like Monique's. White is for brides or the dead," she said matter-of-factly.

After a half hour, they arrive at a spot where the road forked and the asphalt abruptly ended. The Tourist Board had erected a large, billboard sized sign pointing the way. A line drawn lithograph depicted three faces with pronounced, hawk-like noses, deep-set kohl-lined eyes and suggestions of tribal tattoos on foreheads and cheeks. Pointed caps rose from the heads in stepped progression like the range of mountains before them. The dirt road ahead edged a dry gulch, snaked through one of the last stands of evergreens at this elevation, then began to steeply rise through a pass dynamited from formations of metamorphosed schist and basaltic lava.

At his gruff insistence, Sergeant Donatelli had taken over the wheel from the young Lance Corporal, and with the progression of switch backs, the chance of meeting a truck or bus on a blind curve and the jarring of the dirt road, his T shirt stained quickly with sweat even as the air on their ascent became cooler.

"Want some water, honey," Mai Donatelli offered up a bottle of Evian.

"What's this " honey" shit?" the Sergeant said, causing all other conversation in the van to abruptly cease.

So stunned were they all, that even the sharp eyed Lance Corporal didn't notice the old model Renault parked off the road and mostly hidden by the large mounted posters of the Mid Atlas brides. Nor could he suspect that this was the vehicle that had been following the big, white American van since the city, catching up with it finally during the long pause the passengers took at the local fair about 50 kilometers down in the foot hills.

Achmed more determined to strike out, than his colleague Magdi, had feigned going to relieve himself in those clean, scented rooms at the back of the well-appointed tea room. He had completely tricked the man, the heretic who craved pig flesh and who drank alcohol openly defying all custom. While they had watched the white van parked up ahead and noted as their instructions dictated the passing of other diplomatic traffic, paying a modicum of attention to their mundane task, Magdi continued to lecture him, more in ranting than instructional tones. He would try to shock and offend anyone who dared to listen, any captive audience. Christianity and Judaism had been brewed in a fetid cauldron for the masses of brainless sheep who clung to such superstitions and fantasies. He would go on with words and about times past Achmed half understood for he had left his studies at the *lycée* too soon. He did have to agree with Magdi that the Romans missed a great opportunity to save civilization from its inevitable demise. Rather than crucifying rebellious Jewish and Christian prophets they should have plowed Jerusalem into the earth and salted the land to make it unfertile as they had done in Carthage, wherever that was. Yes, the American Jews and Christians who were always together and who were most likely together riding in that van should be done away with, for they caused nothing but trouble and hardship in the world of today let alone in time past. Achmed saw that more and more clearly as his mission, a more meaningful mission than writing notes on passing vehicles.

But Magdi wouldn't stop there. He went on to say that the Prophet Mohammed was a fraud and an opportunist, and that Islam should have been buried in the sand as well. How could he believe that? One could not simply eliminate Allah. He was everywhere, in the fields, the sky, in the sinews and blood. To do such would mean the elimination of man himself and all other living things. No, Magdi was a raving mad man whose studies in Paris had forever damaged his brain. He would have then and there thrown the hot tea at the man, but the waiters hovered near and the white van, now reloaded with its passengers, moved off from the curb.

He had quickly fled the tea room through the back alley, and come around to the street and the car. As he sped off Magdi rushed out to the patio and stood there shaking his fist in confusion.

Now hidden behind the sign of the virgin brides and having proved to himself that he could lay in wait for the American van, Achmed thought of what he could do next within reason but with finality. He had no weapons, not even a pocket knife. He never driven the roads ahead, but had heard tell of the precipitous drops and the twists and turns, which caused many accidents of speeding drivers and of trucks with poor braking systems. He again would get ahead when, it stopped somewhere as it most likely would to allow the occupants to view the gorges and ravines Then would he have his chance. The old Renault would be his weapon. His sister Maleka, whom Magdi had defiled by calling her name, his older sister, who had raised him after the passing of their mother, would praise him for his initiative as would all jihadists everywhere.

***** ***** ***** ***** ***** ***** *****

Minister Mohammed Bennani's third floor wing remained abuzz with activity during the long luncheon period that most everyone in the complex of government offices used to see to their personal affairs, to lunch leisurely with colleagues or visiting dignitaries, or to meet their mistresses for afternoon trysts. Not one who believed in over-working his staff, allowing the routine to become urgent as did some administrators, he, nevertheless, under these unusual circumstances had kept his two secretaries and several of his more resourceful assistants at peak effort for well over a week now. Madame Sebti put through another call about the missing patrol at the El Mahmid check point. Although this could be as serious as the raid three months ago below Erfoud, he wouldn't permit the sounding of alarms until they had more facts in hand. "How could a patrol of regular, experienced national police just disappear? Only a few shards of auto glass? Were they just spirited away by the djins? By invisible-to-radar MPLM helicopters? Wasn't there someone out in the *bled* who possessed a modicum of logic and initiative? Inconceivable that they have not yet made an exhaustive search of the sands around the road where the bits of glass were found. Yes, we have those special dogs the Germans gave us growing fat and idle in the Meknes barracks. Use them. Fly them down immediately. Get them in the dunes." "Idiots," he muttered slamming down the receiver.

Then on the phone from the Prime Minister's office it was Ahmed Lahlou, his father's brother's second son. "Why, Sidi, don't you think I'm more needed at my desk trying to hold together my network of incompetent baksheesh takers and lay-abouts together? Oh, certainly there are exceptions, many exceptions. Some dedicated and ingenious men. I only speak from fatigue, Cousin. A good manager should not blame others, but astutely engineer the remedial repairs, make the necessary adjustments. But to go to that Fair in the Mid Atlas even for two hours?" The decision had been made, and his cousin who as a boy had sat at his table many times was only the messenger. All available high ranking officials would visit the rural fairs, the city fetes as well, to demonstrate the country's power and unity. "A sagacious policy without question. Lead a delegation? Two deputies from Tourism and Handicrafts?" Well, they were from important families. He knew them well. "A foreign dignitary or two? Wasn't that the province of Foreign Affairs, not Interior. Yes, the American Ambassador is a possibility. I met with him for the first time this morning, only a few hours ago. Praise to our fathers that your office should invite him not mine. His Excellency believes we should be more concerned about the MPLM than we appear to be. It might be very informative for him to spend an hour or two with us in the remote region of the Mid Atlas.

Yet another call His wife, Khadija, informed him that she would be out late this evening at Madame Benjeloun's. Yes, the children would be home in their rear wing apartment, presumably studying. Yes, Jamila would certainly be there. She so far respected her curfew and no longer tried to sneak off with that Alaoui boy to the empty beach cottage at Sable d'Or. No, the meeting wasn't going to be more troublesome discussion on changing the divorce and inheritance laws. It was about her petition to the Foreign Affairs Ministry to head the delegation to New York again this year. Yes, one month at the UN for the World Women's Council. She was the only one who knew the issues, who was qualified to project a forward-thinking image of her country on women's rights .

And how could he go off to the marriage fair in the mountains at a time like this, she asked? No, it wasn't the terrorists. They were mostly irrelevant to her concerns. But couldn't he understand that the primitive Berber festival represented a throw-back, a slap in the face to women and all that she had worked for these past dozen years? Girls at 14 and 15 being forced to pick a mate before the snows closed the passes, before their own parents could no longer feed them. "To sanction that barbaric custom by your presence would only embarrass your wife, would cast the House of Bennani in a duplicitous mold." She became strident in the manner she reserved for the so-called scholars of the country's laws and customs, for the councils of reluctant men who guarded the status quo, who talked progress and reform and did nothing.

He once supported his wife's social advocacy work. They had forged a productive union devoted to the public good. They were from among the oldest and most closely knit of those families who were the last to evacuate Andalusian Grenada before the Christian hordes of King Ferdinan desecrated the bright tiled courts and flourishing gardens of Moorish Spain. His and Khadija's blood co-mingled for they both were closely related through all the inter-marriages over six hundred years, and so too should their mind and passion be the same, but wasn't. She had lost her circumspection and balance, had gone too far. It had been their cousin Ahmed Lahlou, the same who had passed him the instructions to attend the moussem of the mountain Ait Haddidou tribe, who had mentioned it over cards last week in their exclusive club by the rear gate of the palace "Another one of Madame's interviews is circulating our offices. She goes too far this time; makes subtle accusations against the Palace itself. She would have our laws abruptly changed, our women rush to embrace all these Western notions. There was a time when we thought ourselves backward, but now our respected advisors looking at the many problems of the West, particularly of America, believe we must more carefully control the pace of change or we will become quickly unraveled, our very structure, our families and clans blown asunder."

It had been difficult to discuss these matters with Khadija, for her head was now ruled by foreign elements, by all the tracts and rhetoric she carried back from meetings in New York and Geneva. It would be difficult, however, to turn down her request to head the delegation She was clearly the most qualified. President of the National Women's League, a *license* from the *Faculté de Droit*, Paris. Who could take her place? They could only stack the delegation with more conservative women like Fatima Benchekroun, and he would have to advise her that all her actions were now under close scrutiny, a task which would cause more unpleasantness in their marriage.

The buzzer sounded and he cut Khadija off, suggesting once more it might be fitting if she went with him to the Brides' Fair, but not waiting for her screeching response. "Infiltrators in Casa, in Dar Bida? We expected as much." No, we cannot force a cancellation of the Transportation Workers march, the *Union des Syndicalistes* rally. The National Students' Assembly will have its rally as well. We have undercover people in all those groups, and they must remain resolutely invisible. No arrests unless approved by this office. I appreciate that the governor is anxious. We are all anxious. But we should not only be concerned about the rallies and the speeches. It's the power plants, the TV stations, the bridges and the rural fairs where they will want to make their biggest splash.

"Will you go directly home this evening or to the club, Sidi? They want to know where you can be reached," Madame Sebti, his chief secretary said. Her ebony hair had cascaded from the silver barrettes which customarily kept it neatly in place. Though she was usually a very presentable thirty-eight—it was imprudent to assign younger women, no matter how skilled to a Minister's office—she showed the strain of too many long days.

"We will not stay late tonight. Have the second chauffeur drive you home promptly at six. I will go to the club for a short while. A few hands of bridge and a light supper. And has Madame Rakki called this morning?"

She responded 'yes' that there was a message while he was on the phone. She revealed little in those fatigue-reddened eyes, but she knew by her patron's question that rather than cards he might pass the remainder of the evening with the youngish widow who was installed in the new Dar es Salaam apartments on the *Corniche*. Madame Sebti, whose position demanded the utmost confidentiality, also knew by the question that she was to leave Madame Rakki's telephone number with the night duty officer. She had never given out that particular number before, but with all the recent problems, coming up every hour it seemed, she knew the Minister wished it so. Few in the inner circles of the government would think it particularly odd to find the Minister with his mistress. Most of them had such women, hadn't they? A few of his peers, not progressive men like the Minister, still took second and even third wives. And the woman after all was no peasant or opportunist who might upset balances, cause a scandal. Hadn't Madame Rakki been more fortunate than most to be released from a bad marriage with her social standing and inheritance intact? Hadn't her husband's foolish driving on the Casablanca auto route one rainy evening made separation very final and without recriminations? She, then, was a fitting second companion for Minister Benanni, one who could respond intelligently to the man's outpourings, one who could appropriately service the over-taxed man's needs. Madame Sebti, herself separated for ten years from a doltish officer of military transport, had to admit to tinges of envy. After all Madame Sebti did spend more time with the man than any other woman, could fathom all his moods, anticipate his instructions, but then the thought of offering him her dry, long unused body brought such shame, and she long realized that she must be content to be close to him vicariously through Madame Rakki as well as through his official wife, Khadija, who was to be greatly admired in her own right as well.

***** ***** ***** ***** ***** ***** *****

At the end of the long morning and before heading off to a solitary lunch to be prefaced by a large, ice cold gin martini, Stu Connors, sitting in for DCM Dalton, had managed to chair two in-house meetings without blowing it and clear out the few routine cables that had so far that day percolated up from the various sections of the U.S. Embassy. When the Ambassador buzzed for him to come at once, he was on the phone to Freddy Parker-White, the BBC's man in country. "No, Old Boy, we don't have the Marines up on the roof in their flack jackets. We're not evacuating non-essential personnel, and the Ambassador isn't packing his bags. In an hour exactly he'll be hosting a lunch for a U.S. agricultural machinery trade delegation. That's right, Freddy, non-lethal farm tractors and reapers. A Special Forces unit? That's really far out, Old Boy. I thought you'd stopped sloshing down Scotch for breakfast."

Miss Ellen Whitaker, pulled in from the Economic Affairs section when the Ambassador's regular secretary, Dina Johnson, had called in sick as she had been doing most Fridays lately, had that tell-tail wounded look. Her first run-in with the Ambassador over something she couldn't be expected to know: where had Dina filed the numbers for his all-important net-work back in the States, including the U.S. Congress, and the right offices in the White House itself. Stu Connors dared to lift her chin up out of her papers, smile, and then grimace with exaggeration as he walked through the door to the Ambassador's office.

Harlan Crane sat ram-rod erect at his desk, offering no greeting, no let's move to the couch to be more comfortable. Even an old veteran, steeped in prima donnas, wonder boys, hard chargers, FOPs, or Friends of the President, had to be just a little apprehensive, not because the man mastered the art of humiliation and belittlement, but out of worry that he'd really muck things up with the host government. "The PM's office just called. Some guy named Lahlou. They want me to go with that wimp Bennani to the Brides' Fair where Mrs Crane, Dalton and the rest of them have gone. You tell me, Connors, why the devil should I even take the request seriously?"

He let the man spout on. Going by VIP helicopter for even two or three hours would send the wrong message. "Because of the women's rights angle?"

"What the hell's that about? No, they want me there to show how secure everything is. That they have things under control, which they don't of course. All hell's going to break loose this weekend, and everyone in this country's acting like its business as usual. Someone's got to make them take this MPLM seriously."

"Another thing as well, Sir," Stu sallied forth again. "There's an unwritten rule that both the DCM and you shouldn't be away and hard to reach at the same time."

" I don't give a you-know-what about your fussy little rules," Crane snapped. "It would only be for two or three hours, and I'm sure they've got radios. They're not totally incompetent."

The Ambassador obviously hadn't made his mind up about going. He had already reported at the ten o'clock senior staff about his earlier meeting with Mohammed Bennani, calling him among other things " a pompous little twerp." Stu, as some others in the bug-proof Plexiglas conference room with its stale, conditioned air, thought what was Bennani expected to do but dissemble. He wasn't going to spill it out to the American Ambassador, reveal the details of the informers, the special units, the beefed up patrols.

THE BRIDES' FAIR

"So you don't think I should go? Let me think about it." Ellen Whitaker managed to get a call through to Washington, and the Ambassador waved Stu Connors out of the room.

"A fun morning?" Stu asked the secretary.

"Thank God he has to go host that luncheon," she whispered. "He has me calling all over Washington where it's only six in the morning, getting people out of bed, or barking at me because they won't come to the phone. How can a human being behave so?" She wore little make up, but in her state the flush of color combined with the soft artificial light to soften the angularity of her chin and nose. "Not even to say 'good morning' when I hurried up here leaving a pile of deadlines behind. Not even to know my name after two months on board."

"It's not you, my dear. He treats us all equally rotten. At least he doesn't have favorites or pets."

" Oh, I know. I heard about him the minute I stepped off the plane. And the way he treats poor Mr. Dalton, who's such a nice man, always stopping at your desk for a cheery word, He gets the worst of it, I hear."

"That's what deputies are for, to be kicked and blamed for everything that goes wrong." Stu had worked with a number of foreign service secretaries over the years, but this one had some spark to her, didn't just revere and excuse the behavior of Ambassadors and other high potentates for whom they worked. For some it was almost a convent-like devotion. "My husband is the Ambassador; I am married to the Service." Most of them never married, for how could you work those hours and pack up every two or three years for another assignment in Helsinki, Yerevan, Jakarta or wherever and cope with the egos and intimacy of a husband? Some of them, his secretary back in Paris, Mary Jane O'Donnel, became the daughter he never had. He just received one of her newsy letters about how she was making the most of Islamabad and how Critter, her old half-breed Persian had survived the trip from Washington. Ellen Whitaker after 15 years of roaming the globe undoubtedly churned out such letters to uncle-like former bosses. Had there been lovers? Of course. She was no Plain Jane. Did she keep a cat like Mary Jane O'Donnel so she could empathize with its indifference to enduring attachments?

They heard the full heel precision paced gate of the Defense Attaché, Colonel Andrew Garvey out in the corridor, coming through the high security inner cube of offices. Ellen Whitaker smiled appreciatively at Stu Connors for stopping to chat and got back to her PC and the latest change in schedule for the Farrell CODEL.

"I've a call already this morning from my desk at the Pentagon, Stu. They're pretty damn upset." The man off to a luncheon at the South Koreans wore his dress whites and a chest load of service ribbons, a Mondrian of primary colors. They had moved to Eric Dalton's office just across from the Ambassador's. Both men were about the same age, facing the same prospects and uncertainties about retirement next year, but Garvey still projected the vigor of a thirty year old, while Stu Connors struggled against a swift deterioration exacerbated by his wife's death eighteen months ago. "The Ambassador's only making things worse, making everybody in Washington dig in their heels."

"I hear they're already dug in up to their shin bones," Stu said dryly.

"But he's accusing my people of sitting on their butts, of being obstructionists, when the fingers point to your State Department lawyers and the Congressional Oversight Committee."

Stu didn't want to argue with the man, but hadn't Eric surmised that as soon as the Pentagon sensed which way the wind was blowing they jumped right in the middle of the mess saying they didn't have all the stuff in stock, crying crocodile tears and telling the Committee they'd have to take from active units, which was a crock in and of itself since most of the gear you could get right off the shelves of several high tech retail outlets. "O.K. Andy. I'll make some calls after lunch and tell my boys and girls to cool things down with your boys and girls. But first I'll run this by Eric during our radio check at three. I'm sure he'll agree we should stick together on this, even if we can't convince His Nibs to cool it."

The Colonel thanked Stu for his understanding, his collegiality, saying that they had to cover their backsides, advise everyone that they had tried to counsel Crane not to interfere with Washington's "go slow" policy on the equipment. He wheeled and was off down a hallway lined with 'on-loan' Wyeths, Rockwells and a Remington, showing off America to the privileged few allowed this far within the Embassy. At the South Korean luncheon, the South Asian food would be abundant and familiar to the Colonel, and with some of the other military attachés he could re-live that time far back in his career when war fighting was more straightforward, not so over-laid with murky politics and insipid diplomacy.

The Ambassador soon followed to his farm machinery luncheon after rattling off to a less intimidated Ellen Whitaker all the calls to Washington she needed to put through when he returned. Stu found himself back at her desk, as she prepared to lock up her hard drive and the classified traffic. "You're the type who enjoys good food, good wine and good company, I know."

THE BRIDES' FAIR

"I really don't know about wine at lunch today with him going to keep me on my toes till six or seven." Flustered at the invitation, she ruffled once more through the stack of papers.

"Well, we might grab a light something-or-other down at the Alhambra. They serve a very nice fish salad, a *fruits de mer*, or if you prefer, a vegetable couscous." She met him promptly in three minutes by the ladies. They walked together through the maze of corridors and security doors. She had a smart bounce to her step, and was at once soft and feminine, not all angles, arms and hands shuffling papers, stroking keyboards. He sucked in his drinkers gut, thinking he too would forgo wine at lunch, and they talked on and on about the friends they had in common from their posts in Washington and abroad.

***** ***** ***** ***** ***** ***** *****

The UN refugee camp east of Zagora, had the look and feel of most of the many camps on the African continent; the military-style tents rowed up neatly along regulation grid lines; the thousands of mostly women, children and the elderly motionless in the tents' shade, conserving energy, resigned to their confinement; the odors of slake lime, disinfectant and human waste blending into a nauseating brew in the mid morning heat. The women, mostly Tuaregs from the semi-arid regions along the edges of the Sahara, were slight, the color of almond skins, and swaddled from head to foot in black. They were nearly lost in the shadows of the tents, and their black eyes peered blankly over their veils. Only the toddlers moved jerkily between the long avenues formed by the tents. They were naked from the waist down, with the girls wearing bright necklaces of trade beads and amber. The older boys of ten and eleven, still too young to fight for their clan over water, grazing rights and the purity of their religion, were also robed in black, but unlike the resigned, accepting women, held themselves proud and haughty.

Oddly among these 20,000 camped on the Zagora plains, no child cried, no mother shouted harsh reprimands. Hands appeared instantly from the robes of older sisters to retrieve those who stumbled or lost their way among the maze of canvas and poles.

Near midday, the Service Hydaulique Land Rover approached the UN camp in a swirl of yellow dust. The thousand or more tents arrayed along the flat plain appeared like ruptures in the ochre earth itself, like outcroppings or dunes stabilized by grasses. Those not familiar with the land and the heat-distorted air might assume as they approached closer and perceived the shape of things more clearly, that this was nothing but some mirage, that such a vast orderly city of human beings could not possibly exist in this place.

Carl Erick Ericksson, the camp director, wore a floppy cap and dark glasses to counter the effects of the North African sun on his pale blue Nordic eyes. Greeting the man from the water exploration service courteously, welcoming the interruption from dealing with miseries of 20,000 souls, he was ever-mindful of the importance of staying on friendly terms with the functionaries of the host government, no matter how minor in rank . With the tent walls of his 'office' rolled up, several score of curious children and robed Tuareg boys watched on in silence. Someone behind a canvas partition chatted away on a radio, reading out figures of death this month from dysentery, malarial fever, child birth, and measles. Seated around a metal table, water and orange drink offered, the director heard how the young 'man', the 'geologist' of the team, who wore a cap and whose face was coated with fine yellow ochre sand, had come by his wounds. "Yes, we were set upon by bandits, smugglers. They were apparently after our vehicle." The young man appeared obviously city bred and educated like his wounded partner. Carl Erick was more suspicious of this fact than of the gun shot wound. The rural services attracted a rougher breed of men. Few *universitaires* of the middle class would voluntarily work out here in the isolated towns and hamlets, unless they were truly doing their two year *service civil* in lieu of being conscripted into the military, and even those usually could work their family connections to be posted in the coastal cities. He thought it was best not to probe too deeply. They could be who they said they were, or drug runners up from the desert, or an undercover military unit. Regardless, they had not come to do harm, and his only business was caring for the destitute, the sick and the wounded without exception or prejudice.

"We must see to your wounds," he said as he moved behind the partition to speak to his assistant. He then led them through the "streets" of his city, as he called it, to a four tent complex which served as the central clinic of the camp. Near the entrance, several Tuareg women robed in black hovered silently over a child's corpse, preparing it for burial in the designated ground on the eastern periphery of the camp. Inside, a midwife and a UN nurse had just completed a difficult delivery, the desert woman accepting her pain in stoic silence, the infant boy held up for her view still coated in blood and afterbirth.

In the emergency section of the central clinic tent, Carl Erick found Doctor Basri, a Ministry of Health secondee from Casablanca, and a nurse, Ms Gunderson, from the American state of Minnesota Maleka tried to remain silent, fearing her voice would give her away. But she put up a fuss when they needed to remove her jacket and pull over. It was no use though. She could hardly play the devout and the modest woman dressed as she was as a man. She took off her cap, shook out her short cropped hair, pretending to be perplexed by any suggestion that she had disguised her sex. She became at once more animated than she been since early this morning when there was noise and screeching metal all at once around her. As they removed her clothing and probed her shoulder, she denied she felt much pain. She told the doctor and the American nurse that she had wanted to go straight to their home base in Zemmera, but that the chief of mission, Moustapha, insisted that they take this detour, and that she was so happy with his decision and with the kind attention she was about to receive.

Moustapha and Carl Erick stepped outside the headquarters tent. "The staff has lunch about one and we'd be most pleased if you could join us," the camp director said. "Also, we're expecting a government team out from Zagora as well. They come every month or so to go through the camp, check our records, look for smugglers. For some reason they always get here at lunch time."

Moustapha calmly replied that they were long overdue at their post in Zemmera, and that he wanted to get his geologist back to where 'he' could recuperate. It took a half hour for the doctor and the American nurse to remove the metal splinters in Maleka's shoulder, to suture the wound, give her a shot of anti-biotics and an envelop of pills. "You're running a slight fever. You came just in time. The wound was septic, but very treatable." The team appeared pleased with their work and the opportunity to handle something out of the routine. Maleka dressed, replacing her field cap. A line of sallow, feverish women and children had formed at the emergency medical tent, and Dr. Basri and Ms Gunderson plunged back into the routine of their long 16 hour day, rewarding in that it made every effort to preserve life while respecting the dignity of the human spirit, observing as called for by their profession the necessary confidentiality.

Moustapha waited outside the 'front office' tent hearing with some apprehension the well-muffled voices of the staff inside as well as the ebbing and surging of humanity in the densely packed camp. He smoked a cigarette, which he rarely did. He had gotten it from Ali. The strong Turkish blend was harsh in his throat, but he continued with it, inhaling deeply in anticipation of some narcotic effect. They took so long with her. Were there complications, her wounds too festered, her fever too rampant? He couldn't go on if her life were to seep away in this desolate place, her purpose unfulfilled. The Swedish director had been summoned to deal with some emergency far down an alley of the tents.

Moustapha had watched him recede, suspicious it might be some ruse to double back to his headquarters area and to summon the authorities on his radio.

The mid-morning heat rose quickly and mercilessly, even with the stiff breeze from the south which flapped the Red Crescent and blue UN flags. A nurse and three of her aids recruited from among the hale and able refugee women, set up a folding table nearby and fetched Styrofoam containers of supplies. Women with infants and young children began to slowly, hesitantly emerge from the alleys and from the dark hollows of the tents. Gaunt and haggard, wearing black caftans, black head scarves but no veils, it would take an experienced eye to discern that many of the women were teenagers as young as 15. Some clutched an infant to the folds of their caftan while dragging a toddler with the free hand. The nurses' aids harangued them with sharp words, relishing their new position of power in the camp's hierarchy. The vaccinations began slowly, but soon established a rhythm and order. Numb with fright, neither the children nor the girls cried out or winced at the prick of the syringes.

What was the point of such protection, such insurance against measles, diphtheria, tetanus, polio? The UN would compile its hopeful statistics on deaths averted, but few would be available to provide such hope when these children grew older and needed school and work. Could he and Maleka through their actions provide them with a better life? So many others had tried through their revolutions and their martyrdom, but little seemed to change. The despair of those such as these in this refugee tent city remained intractable.

Maleka walked unaided from the hospital tent down the long alley and soon stood beside him. Color had returned to her face, and she told him she felt fine and could go on. "They know. They had to remove my shirt, you see. They may not say anything about it, but we must now hurry from here."

They heard some commotion over from where they had parked the Land Rover and walked quickly towards it, not running, not wanting to attract attention. Ali who had just filled a jerry can of water from the camp's main pump, shouted, gesticulated and pointed to the rear deck of the vehicle. A group of boys, a few with the long curved knives of their absent fathers under their djellabas, stood by silent, expressionless as if they failed to understand. "He's escaped. I know they helped him. I was only away for a few minutes."

Moutapha motioned to Ali to calm himself. He could see the bunched up tarp and the cut ropes on the back deck of the Land Rover. Their prisoner must have banged the rear door with his booted feet to call attention. The camp had guards somewhere to be sure, and the Chef de Brigade would have his story out in minutes. A crowd of refugee women now gathered about them, and they would soon be trapped, needing to brandish their weapons. How utterly weak of him not to have done away with the man back at the oasis, or back at the first encounter as Rachid had strongly urged.

They piled into the vehicle as the Director, Carl Erick, appeared. "I would ask you to stay for lunch as meager as it is, but I see you're in a hurry." He apparently hadn't yet heard of the police man's escape, or feigned ignorance of the fact.

Moustapha with the traditional flourishes of his culture thanked the Director for all his help with his wounded colleague as well as for the water which they had taken without first asking permission.

"But you know well it is the custom, that water belongs to everyone, the stranger, the traveler, everyone, and there is never need to ask permission."

Chapter V

Now began the most difficult phase of their journey, and most in the van tried not to focus on the Sergeant's tense labor at the wheel. The ravines and gorges became more precipitous, rising up too close to the edge of the narrow tracks and dynamited passages which constituted the road. Scattered on the plateaus below or as if pasted against the vaults of rock, were clusters of squat, rectangular habitation fashioned of stone and *pisé*, a blend of mortared mud and barley straw binder. The lodges and compounds clinging to these surfaces and almost lost in the shadows of the deep valleys, were colored rose like much of the mountains and, thus, difficult to detect at a casual glance. Some of the dwellings stood behind crenellated walls of stone and *pisé*. Some of the compounds thrust up tapered towers and parapets of an almost medieval design and European character except for the bands of geometric symbols unique to this remote corner of the earth.

How many centuries ago had they come through these mountains, following the winter run off stream beds through difficult passageways up to the hidden valleys of the high plateaus? And hadn't they created a secret kingdom, a veritable Shangri-La where for centuries the cycle of life unrolled without fear of contaminating elements from foreign invaders? These walls of rose and gray rock had provided formidable protection against the world until some 60 or 70 years ago when French military engineers blasted through the rock to form these roadways, or, where such shelves proved unfeasible and where gorges needed to be spanned, had pinioned concrete supports and bridge ways deep into the rock.

Cynthia Dennis consulted with Sergeant Donatelli and determined that an average speed of 15 miles an hour through the high pass and the tortuous switch backs, it would take them about two and a half hours to cover the remaining 40 miles to their destination. They might pick up some time when the road descended into the high plateau and valley. This would put them at the fair at 6 PM or just about dusk.

"I'm looking forward to a nice long hot shower," Pam Crane said. Her face streaked with road dust for the air conditioner had been turned off to conserve fuel and to not strain an engine starved for oxygen at these elevations. She and others put on head scarves against the dirt. Mai Donatelli had fashioned one from a T shirt. The men donned baseball caps and army field hats. Eric unfolded from his pack his old fishing hat which with its wide brim could be squashed about to resemble a bush hat worn to contend with the sun and flies in a Kenya or an Australia. The clouds of road dust kicked up by the slow-moving van coated everything inside a fine yellowish-gray. Dr. McMannus's bushy black eyebrows became those of an old man. Only Monique Addleman seemed impervious to the pervasive dust as she teased her long red hair up and down her neck, revealing at the measured intervals red welts from where branches had whipped against an otherwise unblemished skin.

"Speaking of getting cleaned up," Cynthia said. "We could all take a swim. Just before Imichil are two deep mountain lakes; a man's lake and a woman's. There's a story, but of course, about a Romeo and Juliet-like suicide that keeps the lake forever filled and warm with the tears of the young lovers."

"Who would want to swim in a suicide lake?" Edna Baker asked.

"Oh, I would love a brisk swim, but it will have to be *au naturel*. Did anyone bring a swim suit?" Pam Crane asked.

They came to a small settlement marked by a concrete obelisk dedicated to the engineers and builders of the high pass. Also, a ubiquitous fire engine red sign read 'Kooka Koola' in white Arabic letters. Rock vendors and their rickety, legs-akimbo tables perched themselves precariously at the road's edge. The tables sagged under arrays of amethyst, polished onyx and fossilized crustaceans. On the other side of the road a dozen dwellings of mud-mortared stone, some with rough lime stucco surfacing, were stacked up a step of rock so that the buildings seemed as one multi-storied unit.

"We're overdue to call in, Sir," Jess Williams advised Eric Dalton.

The Sergeant, after an arduous hour through the mountain pass said he desperately needed a cigarette, ignoring his wife's admonishments about restarting bad habits. The others headed for the rock vendors or to photograph the dramatic view of the deep gorges and the mountain peaks.

"If the Ambassador finds out we've gone around him, he'll have our balls fried on a platter." Stu Connor came in clearly as if he were right next to Eric Dalton who had moved up to the front of the van displacing the two Marines.

"It's always best to stay in the huddle," Eric said. They must remain loyal to Crane in spite of everything; he was, after all, the representative of the President of the United States. "But, and a big but too," Eric added. "You need to signal the coach on the sidelines that he needs to send in a winning play, for the guards on the line are getting beat up something bad." And Crane was constantly on the phone to Washington. "Calling all his old girl friends still I suppose? Mitsy? Monica? Myra? Shame on him." Stu would telephone Washington on the scrambler, rather than send a cable which the whole world would read regardless of any 'secret' classification. They needed a clear, unambiguous instruction to keep Crane in check, as well as to get the Pentagon, upset that it was being blamed for the equipment delays, off their backs. They needed to know from the secretaries and the communications' office, who other than the usual suspects, he was telephoning day and night. Could Stu finesse that without causing the Ambassador to go ballistic? Eric had talked to their Desk Officer back in Washington only two days ago about sending instructions on the 'go slow' policy. The message, if indeed it had been written, was undoubtedly being cleared by every possible office in State and in the Pentagon. Eric feared that given any differences between staff and a political Ambassador, Washington would try to stay on the fence, opt to do nothing. "We must try everything possible to get the coach to send us a play."

Eric learned from Stu Connor that the Ambassador might show up at the Brides' Fair with the Minister of the Interior, Bennani, in the early afternoon tomorrow for the fantasia and the communal marriage ceremony. "It's not a good idea. He shouldn't go flying off to Disney Land while I'm up on this Ferris Wheel. I'm sure you told him that. And besides haven't you noticed that he hasn't looked well lately? But we can't stop him, can we?"

Edna Baker haggled with the rock vendors who had her surrounded, and were thrusting objects at her in an increasingly demanding manner. Doug Baker tried to wade into the tight circle around his wife, but then Monique who had gone off with others to photograph the deep gorges appeared, uttered a few words in Mahgrebi Arabic and the vendors gave way and at once were sheepishly silent. "Well, I'll be damned," Edna Baker said. "You saved me. I really thought they were either going to beat me to death with those rocks or push me off the cliff." Together as if they were old friends, the two women selected several egg shaped polished onyx stones that Edna wanted for paper weights.

Cynthia thought a group picture would be nice set against the Grand Canyon-like view and the cloudless blue sky. Pam Crane complained about being wind blown and dirty, but finally Cynthia prevailed, lining up even a surprisingly shy

THE BRIDES' FAIR

Dr. McMannus who fussed with his beard and wind-whipped hair. At Cynthia's instruction to get closer, Monique draped an arm on Eric Dalton's shoulder, and Pam Crane found herself close by the muscular Marine corporal and did the same. With some negotiation by Cynthia and Monique, however, Cynthia turned her camera over to a willing rock vendor and joined the picture, standing on the other side of Eric, her arm joining that of Monique's.

The photo session and the buying of fossilized rocks delayed them another 20 minutes, and they soon were held up again. Motoring on for about four kilometers in a downward descent from the high pass, they came upon a Peugeot station wagon that had apparently skidded off the road only moments before. At some thirty feet down an embankment, it had been blocked from tumbling further into the ravine by an outcropping rock and now rested at a forty-five degree tilt. The passengers were beginning to struggle from the vehicle through the two, left-most doors.

"Man, would you believe it?" Jess Williams said as he followed the DCM out of the van and down the rocky slope. "Back up there in the pass, it would have been *fini, wallou*, all she wrote."

The driver, Pierre Deschamps, whom Eric knew as the cultural affairs officer of the French Embassy appeared only slightly shaken. *"J'ai crevé le pneu la, et je ne roulais que vingt. Quelle pagaille."* He held close a sob-wracked wife, and one of the two children, a boy of eight whose nose and mouth streamed with blood.

Jess Williams cut the engine of the fuming car, and Cynthia convinced the young boy to tilt his head back to catch the blood while she probed for any broken cartilage or loose teeth. The other passenger, a Moroccan man of twenty-six or seven appeared stonily calm, in shock perhaps, or accepting the accident as the will of Allah.

"What do I care? The car was our old one. Never take a new car on these roads," Pierre Deschamps muttered while still hugging and soothing his wife.

The Marines and the Moroccan salvaged the luggage and then with Ed Baker and Eric Dalton formed a human chain to guide all of the victims up to the road. Two other vehicles bearing travelers to the Brides' Fair stopped.

"You'd have to call a tow truck all the way from Kasba Talda. It wouldn't be worth it at all," Gunther Stohlman from the German Embassy said to the Frenchman. "You should write it off."

"Yes, I've decided that. I will leave it for the two legged vultures. They'll have it stripped to its bones for parts in a week."

"But we must get you back to the capital," Eric Dalton said, noting that Cynthia seemed to have the boy's bleeding under control.

"No going back. We've been planning to come to this fair for two years, and this is our last chance, you see. I'm being reassigned to New Delhi next month. We must continue." The mid-thirties woman, Christine Deschamps, still ashen and bleary-eyed nodded in agreement.

The big Mercedes van was crammed to capacity, but Hans van Luyten from the Dutch Embassy offered to squeeze two in his Volvo wagon. Eric asked the Marines to place some of the luggage from the rear deck of the American van on the roof rack, and by doing so, they freed up the jump seats. After some negotiation, it was decided that Christine Deschamps, her son Phillipe, who hadn't once complained or cried, and the Moroccan man would go with the Americans. The Frenchman and his daughter, Marie-Ange would ride with the Dutch. The Moroccan, introduced himself in good English as Ali Kadiri a film technician contracted to the Ministry of Culture and Tourism. He climbed into the rear deck jump seats with Corporal Williams, while Monique and Karen Dennis moved up to the front passenger seat, making room in the middle row for Christine and Phillipe Deschamps.

Now in a caravan with the two other vehicles, all boiling up road dust in the descent down into the valley of the Ait Haddidou, they saw in the distance an old French observation post, its ferro-concrete supports pinioned to the rock face, rose some 20 meters above the road. The tower atop the structure looked down on the gorges and passes to the south as well as the valley below.

"They built it in the late 1930's to look out against marauders and as an early warning against the possibility of a German-Italian invasion sweeping in from Tripolitania through the desert," Cynthia explained after leafing through her notes.

"But it's been long-abandoned, or so it appears," Dr. McMannus said.

"Yes, who would want to be cooped up there in the harsh winters with the winds howling day and night?" Doug Baker asked.

The passengers, however, failed to notice as they approached the tower Lieutenant Mohammed Berrada of the Pioneer Scouts, peering at them through his Zeiss binoculars and then turning to rapidly descend the winding metal stairs.

********** ********** ********** ********** **********

"Yes, it was here in this very spot," The Chef de Brigade told those who had come out from Zagora within an hour of his call from his pocket phone. "Such amateurs they were, not bothering to look for the phone." The hot arid winds churned in from the great desert just beyond them. The Chef de Brigade was unable to stoop down to examine the shards of auto glass and the sun-glistening brass shells. He had much pain in his neck and abdomen. The young assassin who chopped him down in this very place in the early morning, had not the power to crack the vertebrae only bruise them badly. At the United Nations refugee camp, where he had first hid in an empty tent, fearing that the killers would search for him, the foreign nurse and the doctor had trussed him up and fit a foam rubber collar on his neck.

"You did not see or hear what they did with the others?" The older man who had been flown in from headquarters said. In the back of a Land Cruiser, three dogs of the European tracking hound breed barked incessantly and slammed their agitated bodies against the wire cage on the rear deck.

"No, as I said, I was barely conscious then. But later, perhaps an hour later, I heard their voices, but couldn't hear them well. One of them had been wounded by our guns, and they talked about seeking treatment. Two men argued in whispers, and one of these men left the vehicle saying he would go alone, and that they would meet up at their destination later. They did not specify where that was. They drove to a place with trees and bushes and were about to pull me from the vehicle, to kill me I was certain, but then something stopped them, an approaching truck. I could see little, trussed up like a sheep in the back. An hour later we came to the refugee camp, and I was left with one of the assassins. I convinced the stupid fool to find me water, and by knocking repeatedly on the back door with my feet, I was able to get the attention of some brave boys who had knives to cut me loose."

'They will not penetrate the nets we have out everywhere, but first we must see to the dead," the director had said when he arrived with the dogs by helicopter.

"We will finally put these dogs to use after two years. They were a gift you know from the Germans, and we said what do we need them for? Few ever disappear or are lost. We have many watchful eyes, and the news passes quickly through the tea houses. We sent the handler here, Habib three months to Germany, to have a fine holiday and to learn about these dogs. He and the dogs have grown fat on all the fine meats they are fed, and from doing little these two years. But now they all will have their chance." Indeed, the handler of the ugly, fleshy faced dogs had grown too portly sitting around the kennels. He had as well suffered the abuse of his colleagues, who thought his task as keeper of these creased and threatening creatures something of the devil's work.

"You will release your dogs. We have much to do before night fall," the Director of Special Investigations said. Yes, he and the Chef de Brigade, as in pain as he was, would have to get on, up into the mountains to join in the search for the murderers.

Habib leashed the three over-heated animals, cooing to them softly like to an adored one. One of the Director's team from headquarters, Achmed, who thought most dogs, let alone those with the faces of old men, creatures from below the earth itself, danced back nervously as the first grateful animal was released from the cage and handed off to him.

"The scent has to be here near the broken glass," the Chef de Brigade said, thinking of the many glasses of tea shared with these brothers, being invited to their simple homes for end-of-Ramadan feasts, to the circumcision rituals of their sons. The dog held by Habib, found something and shoveled its fleshy muzzle into the sand. With its powerful front paws it begin to dig furiously, flinging sand back over the encircling men which stung them as if from a desert storm.

Habib pulled the dog off and in seconds, the spades of the two probationary police detail from the Zemmara barracks struck the metal cab of the police Land Rover. The infiltrators had let the vehicle dig its own grave by revving it in high gear, racing it in reverse and forward until it sank into the fine desert sand. They had shoveled more sand over it and piled some dead sage brush about. Except for the shattered windshield, some sand which had hour glassed in through several bullet holes, and the dried blood splattered about in the front cab, the vehicle seemed basically recoverable. One of the probationaries turned the key, still in the ignition and with in minutes they managed to race the engine forwards and backwards and get it back on the road.

"Will the State give us all decorations for salvaging this material?" the Chef de Brigade shouted angrily. "We did not come here to please the accountants in headquarters."

The three dogs started in their furious digging and barking a few meters from where the vehicle had been hidden. Soon one of them had a gentle mouth on the stiff brown hand of his senior Sergeant, Salim. The body of Abdelatif, the three chevron non commissioned officer, lay inches away. He had a gaping wound in the back of his head.

"Allah, Akbar. Oh, compassionate and merciful one, forgive us this terrible cruelty, the loss of these fine sons and fathers." The Chef de Brigade's words echoed through the empty dunes, and he regretted that his bandaged neck and lower body pains, kept him from helping wash the bodies in the water from the Jerry cans and to dress them in the fresh white djellabas they had brought for this awful purpose.

***** ***** ***** ***** ***** ***** *****

THE BRIDES' FAIR

They raced away from the UN refuge camp, the orderly array of white tents receding into paper scraps in the road dust and refractory of the late morning sun. They abandoned the drilling rig they had been towing, not only to give the underpowered Land Rover more speed, but with the realization that their disguises and masquerades so far had brought them little useful gain and had been too easily uncovered. In less troubled times the road skirting the mountain and its foothills to the south saw only little traffic, but today in the time of harvest and marriage fairs there would be those who dared to travel even in the face of rebel alerts and heightened militia presence. An easier route than crossing the mountains from the north and the cities of the Atlantic plains, one might miss the spectacular ravines and gorges, but welcome fewer S curves, switchbacks, and hair-raising roads chiseled into the walls of mountains. Many of the local farmers, shepherds and festival participants preferred the southern route as well, driving down the rocky tracks from their mountain hamlets to join the mostly straight paved road.

Approximately 20 kilometers from the cross road town which joined the easier southern route up to the Imichil plateau, they stopped at a fairly modern gas station complete with a refreshment room. In the foot hills five kilometers above the station stood a tourist hotel designed to resemble a large, traditional ksar with crenellated walls and square watch towers. Its rose colored stucco walls glowed iridescently in the late morning sun, transforming the structure into an unreal fantasy castle floating in space. At the gas station, a line of vehicles waited while a lone attendant serviced all four pumps. Several shaggy 'European' back packers walked about the waiting cars, vans and trucks begging rides. An old truck piled with bales of wool and holding in its wood sided break as well a number of costumed women, had stopped in front of the service garage. Three men squatted on the ground by the truck's open hood waiting for the mechanic who appeared indifferent to their needs, but more solicitous of others in fancier conveyances who begged his services.

Moustapha and Maleka removed their baggage from the Land Rover and quickly disappeared into the tea room. Ali would continue directly on towards the cross roads town, abandoning the vehicle in a gulley or behind a clump of vegetation. He would hitch a ride alone as would Moustapha and Maleka as well. They had to succeed, had to reach the mountain fair this evening where at their designated rendezvous they would review their plans for tomorrow.

There were a fair number of customers in the tea room taking midday refreshments before the last leg of their journey, the four hour ascent up into the mountains. Moustapha had changed from his dusty, gray public servant uniform into more suitable clothing, and alone at a small corner table he waited for Maleka to do the same. A turbaned waiter, his mouth full of gold teeth, brought a plate of beignets and steaming hot minted tea. The glasses which had seen no real wash soap this day were smudged with previous use. Moustapha had long ago eschewed the sanitary finickiness of his father's house where a servant girl would be tongue-lashed for setting out a spoon with one water spot. He sipped his tea slowly, his thumb and forefinger clamped tight on the cooler rim. He felt the sugary concoction course through his weary body, not relieving him, only reawakening his apprehensiveness.

'We will get there, do not worry so. We have managed to get this far through the road blocks, through that business at the refugee camp.' He had tried to reassure Ali who complained as he never had they would never reach the mountain fair unless they turned into great hawks and flew. Moustapha cajoled and commanded as a leader must do, but the doubts tortured him as well. Weren't they just spoiled, soft hand youth playing at the age old game of rebellion? Champions of the poor; out with the old order, in with something new that was abstract, hard to define, but spoke of justice, equality, opportunity for all. Shouldn't they stop this pretense, get themselves back to the cities, and go work in the banks and the businesses of their families? Yet, it was a miracle that they had gotten this far and were so near, only a hundred twenty kilometers away by his map, a few hours if the roads were fast. " Rachid is most likely there already," he had said to Ali. "You know how cleverly he can slip through the shadows like a phantom. Yes, Rachid will be waiting for us." He would get through as sly and as slippery as he was, but would he make a mess of things with his brash, head strong ways?

The men they had to kill in the early morning kept reappearing like a television image that could not be zapped away with a device. He saw over and over the eruption at the back of the police man's head, the shattering of bone and flesh. Moustapha feared that more blood would be spilled before their mission ended, but prayed for distance and anonymity in this necessity.

Maleka joined him at the corner table, after having changed in the wash room. With her luminous raven hair free from her cap, with a modicum of make up, and wearing a long skirt and wind breaker, she became again an attractive young woman who could pass for Spanish or Italian. He had not seen her like this since back at the University and at the language school. She smiled at his sign of admiration. They would take these exchanges but so far, for here in this far region, even with all the passing tourists from foreign lands, the mixing of men and women in public places could bring stares of disapproval. But they were used to being silent in their thoughts for one another. In their desert training camp men and the few women had been counseled on celibacy, discipline and the seriousness of their purpose.

This was not enough for some like Rachid and even Ali who argued. "We should not have women in this business. It is unnatural for them to take up arms. They will only bring bad *baraka*." They labeled them camp followers, for only unmarried and unescorted women would come to live among fighting men. Had not it always been so with Roman legionnaires, infidel Crusaders, spit and polish armies, guerilla bands? Women flocked about like scavenging birds to earn a few scraps of food for the use of their bodies. El Surugi, their leader, had a different perspective. They must cut through the web of convention that held trapped all those who were poor, were women, were of the wrong class, and give them the freedom to earn their equal place in the world. The cynical ones of the political science faculty said that these were hollow phrases and that everything that moved the world came down to money and power, which went hand in glove with of course, sex..

He and Maleka had met in the secret MPLM cell at the university. Unlike himself who had been had been raised in one of those old villas of infinite rooms hidden behind scabrous mortared walls where entry ways were Minotaur mazes to confound intruders, Maleka had grown up in one of the newer, non-descript, poured concrete apartment blocks. Most of his friends, those with modern beach houses at Sable D'Or and perhaps *pied a terres* in Paris or Seville, did not usually associate with those of Maleka's class. He found her unusual, alert to more than house parties and the collection of gold jewelry. Besides she was hauntingly attractive. They vowed they could no longer be blind to the squalor and ignorance around them. Although the Soviet Union had collapsed and communism had been discredited, the movement's leader, El Surugi, described in his manifesto, "The New Beginning," a society somewhere between Karl Marx and Swedish socialism. "It's no good just to continue pushing the same wheel round and round again like dumb donkeys, marrying our cousins only to horde more wealth in Switzerland and France; having more smart, spoiled children who will grow up to do the same; putting walls around the squalid *bidonvilles* and pretending they don't exist."

They talked often over coffee about how they would change the status quo without making the mistakes of Stalin and Mao; how they wished for a peaceful revolution after Ghandi and Mandela, but knew it was not feasible, that violence had to be part of it, that the entrenched lethargy of the society had to be shaken awake by thunder and fire. They vowed their love for one another as well, but stopped short of consummating it. That would complicate matters and besides El Surugi had strict rules. Even touching, an encouraging hug or buss on the cheek was forbidden. "You will remain as neuters here, celibates with one purpose and one passion." Now as they contemplated their next move, each thought to themselves about the ultimate irony, of death and never having the chance to know each other to the full.

Maleka sipped her tea taking pleasure in its warmth and its soothing qualities. He pleaded with her again to return to the city, to disappear quietly into the street scene. Certainly her cousin, Shafika, would take her in. She was not a suspect, not under surveillance. "We will do this together as we have planned for some time," she said. "I am in little pain now, and my arms are strong enough again to control my weapon. I will do this with you and will not hear otherwise."

It would be of no avail to argue with her, nor, looking at the time, to miss their opportunities for transportation. They now went their separate ways and parted with the barest brushing of the hands. He did not look back to see the moisture welling in her dark eyes, nor to reveal his own distress. She would go out soon and have little difficulty finding the vehicle that would take her on to the fair. He went over to the broken down truck by the service garage. While many of his class would not deign to dirty their hands working with the tools and machines of *bricoleurs*, he had enjoyed tinkering with the workings of motor cycles and autos behind the walls of his family compound. He had proven helpful in El Surugi's camp when drivers of disabled trucks and jeeps sat idly by while he quickly discovered a clogged air filter or a brake fluid leak. At the truck, three men continued to squat patiently on the ground, while the costumed women sitting in the break complained and chastised. It was the will of Allah, the oldest man, the truck's owner said. They would not be able to continue to the fair. It had been so destined. Moustapha politely differed, and set about his work, borrowing tools from the garage mechanic, too awed to refuse a young stranger, a likely descendent of the venerable Moors, who knew precisely what he was about.

***** ***** ***** ***** ***** ***** *****

The radio call confirmed his suspicions. Praising him for his quick action, his superior officer, Captain Naisiri, ordered him down from the watch tower and on to an urgent assignment. Lieutenant Mohamed Berrada felt renewed, for three days and nights in this aerie above the high pass road had been, until the very last, tortuously dull. The incident at the span less than an hour ago focused it all at once, and coming at the end of the mission, was its capstone.

THE BRIDES' FAIR

    The vehicle moving on the road below had appeared out of place. Scanning with his powerful German binoculars those advancing up the road and following them the two kilometers until they crossed the span, he had become an expert in the types and conditions of vehicles that moved up the mountain road to the high plateau and to the fair grounds. Most were of the diplomatic missions, for few foreigners but these ventured this far. Some sturdy farm trucks with their cargoes of animals and hill people also passed, but most of the locals used the roads south of the mountains that were both less arduous and spectacular. Then too there had been many fast moving sedans of officials, performers and police. But the one he had .watched most intently during this last hour of his mission was an old, slow-moving Renault, its small engine starved for oxygen. Strange too that the Renault crossed the 50 meter span formed of arched steel trusses and concrete, crossed over, halted and turned around a full 180 degrees, its chassis still mostly in the road.

    Believing at first it had broken down or stood waiting for someone, he looked down the road in the other direction, seeing clearly at about two kilometers distance a column of several vehicles, all with diplomatic matriculation plates. The Lieutenant and his corporal, Aboukar, hurried down the winding metal stairs to the fastest of their vehicles. It took them only ten minutes to reach the span for they had grown to master these roads during their three days. Yet, before they actually crossed, the Renault started up from the far side of the span towards them. They drew their weapons and signaled it to stop, but it had come on its engine revving up to a sickly whine. Suddenly it swerved breaking through the flimsy wire guard rail and hurtling down a 100 meters where it imploded into a smear of broken metal and body parts that were barely distinguishable among the rock and ruble of the gorge.

    Lieutenant Berrada and the corporal spent the next minutes repairing the guard rail with items from their vehicle's tool kit and testing the integrity of the span before they permitted any traffic to cross. Those they finally waved on included a white American-made van bearing plates of the U.S. Embassy..

    Returning to the watch tower they learned by radio that the Renault appeared to have been stolen yesterday in Rabat, and from the Lieutenant's detailed account, his superiors concluded that the driver had been most likely up to no good. A team would be sent to recover and identify the remains, but the Lieutenant should now move on with dispatch.

    It was mid afternoon, and his driver had returned already with the main meal of the day prepared by the women from one of the stone and mud brick hovels that were fastened to the side of a rocky slope. The corporal and Ahmed, the radio operator, attended to their prayers, their rugs together on the small concrete terrace facing east. The Sergeant, Ali ben Alami, returned up the winding metal staircase from the hole in the concrete two floors below which served as the toilet. In preparation to leave, the Lieutenant began washing himself with the cold water from the metal bucket displaying bravado indifference both to its temperature and that of the cool mountain air. It had been a good team, he acknowledged, well disciplined, each man knowing his job. He would write them good reports.

"I am ordered down for a special mission. I must leave now for there is a *rendez vous* to make," he said to the approaching driver. "The corporal will go with us as well."

They didn't wait for the others to gather, but sat on the cold concrete floor of the old French observation post eating their sugared couscous and tagine of lamb and almonds. They swept some pieces of their barley bread into the food, and others into a plate of honey. They ate silently and quickly while the others in the detail joined them one by one. "You will remain here with Ahmed and watch the road," he said to the sergeant to whom he handed his special infra red binoculars. "You must be especially vigilant for they say that several MPLM rebels have gotten through the screen. That one in the Renault could have been a collaborator, but I think not. He wished to martyr himself before accomplishing anything at all. "

The Lieutenant, the Corporal and the driver, Malek, gathered their haversacks and bedrolls in the cavernous guard tower that had been long stripped of its wood partitions and doors for firewood. The driver bumped the vehicle down the steep trail from the aerie to the piste road. Not a poetic or intellectual man, the Lieutenant had missed his morning heart pumping work out with his squad back at the barracks, and had grown restless with the isolation and monotony of these three days in the great concrete tower. Still he had been awed by the grandeur of these mountains. The great and only Allah surely had labored long and hard to shape these massifs, these steps and balconies to his paradise. How unfortunate that some as he had just witnessed would be driven to violate this grandeur by terror and violence. He knew well the stupidity of war, of random slaughter. He was a soldier as was his father and his father's father. His grand father had fought with General Le Clerk and the Free French against the last remnants of Rommel's Afrika Corps. Not many years later, he had stood with his company against the conniving of those very French, and had marched them under guard from their barracks down the wide boulevards of Casablanca to their awaiting ships. His father still told of rushing off with the Pioneer Scouts, being flown cold and cramped in a rattling DC3 all the way to Cairo, there to fight along with a wider clan of brothers against the Zionist invaders. The Pioneers had proven themselves. Their cousins of less mettle and discipline fled across the Sinai, dropping their rifles and their very boots. But as Allah bore witness, they of the Maghreb stood their ground. The Israelis did not choose to confront them and skirted their great battle tanks around their positions. Certainly a great moment and of much meaning to his father, but to glorify such contests and the mass leaching of blood in foreign sands could puff one up with false pride. The soldiers of his barracks all coming into this life after the great battles in the Sinai, still continued to sing raucously and boastfully of their unit's triumphal stand.

It was the way with all armies, and, in spite of his distaste for the glorification of war, he himself had hoped he would see more action, would be sent down to the desert's edge to search out those bandits, who loftily labeled themselves a liberation front. Instead he had mostly checked off tourist cars like the lowliest of policemen. But he had obeyed his superiors without questioning, without scheming to go off on the desert patrols as some would. Such strict obedience would assure him his Captaincy next spring, and that would mean a bigger house, and his own car and driver. This would please his wife and return her to some of the status she had enjoyed in her own father's house. This would please his own father as well, for the cycle of three generations of Berradas as officers in the same unit would remain unbroken.

The driver, Malek, begged his permission to stop a moment in the stone and *pisé* brick cluster of huts which with its one general store and one incongruous Coca Cola sign constituted a hamlet. From one of the huts he produced a stooped old woman in a wash-grayed caftan. An erect but frail daughter stood behind the mother, with two young children clinging to her. These had been the cooks and the laundresses for the five soldiers who camped in the old French watch post. The women wailed their farewells. The coins given to them for their enterprise had been a boon. It appeared clear as well that the driver had taken his dividend on the thin daughter's mat, the men of the household being long absent and mostly forgotten. The driver took a few more coins from his field jacket pocket as they turned to leave. At least the driver had gotten his heartier seed into those thin loins, and perhaps there would be some benefit in that.

The driver pushed the Japanese made jeep to its limits on the downward run, swerving out to scrape a guard rail on one of the many curves and cut backs. He could sense the young corporal's fear, but the Lieutenant remained impassive, imbued with the fatalism of his people, balanced against the belief that it was not his time to die. Half way down, the road straightened and the last frontier of oak and cedar braved the elevation providing a refreshing welcome. They continued down and after an hour of hard fast driving arrived at the wide paved road which ran between the foothills to the north and the scrub land and desert plate to the south. A new Peugeot sedan waited for them at the junction. It bore no government matriculation plates, but inside the men had the aspect of officials. Included among them was a man in his mid-forties with a rubber collar around his neck and an arm trussed up in a sling.

On being instructed to take the disabled man with him, Lieutenant Berrada protested. His mission would be much handicapped, necessitating much attention and delay. But before he could speak further, the older man uncoiled himself easily from the sedan and saluted. "He is the only witness to these terrible killings. He is the only one who can identify the assassins," the Lieutenant was so advised. Without much further discussion, they headed east towards the cross road town which straddled the alternate route up to the mountain fair. The assassins had to be somewhere in the area, the Chef de Brigade advised. Nearby they had discarded some equipment from their flimsy, amateur ruse. "We will find them, Inchalla."

In the high noon heat, the traffic proved considerable by rural back country standards where during the midday when even the Saharan winds conspired to do their worst. Most with any sense paused in shade, found time to pray, to rest, to take cooling water and light sustenance. Therefore, as they raced in and out of the lane of east-bound traffic, they were shocked to be nearly over-taken by a large safari-like utility truck going at even higher speeds. Malek, the chauffeur, alertly pulled sharply in front of the offending vehicle forcing it to brake, swerve and skid off the road to avoid a collision.

A tall, large-framed 'European' stepped down from his cab. Late twenties or early thirties, he wore jeans and expensive-looking hiking boots. His vehicle, festooned with fog lamps, a side search light, and over-sized rear view mirrors appeared new and in top condition although coated with road dust. The young man apologized in good French, but there was an accent.

"I would have more respect for these roads," Lieutenant Berrada said. He should leave the foreign motorists to their fate. He was a military man not a policeman concerned with driving infractions. He noticed that all in the vehicle were about the same age, including a young woman, Spanish or North African, who sat in the driver's cab and had the refined features of one who has not known the hard labors of the fields. Another woman, a blond with a rosy cheerful demeanor also sat up front in the jump seat. In the back two rows of seats, there were others; several more women, one chubby, spilling half out of her sloganed T shirt, another passably attractive except for stringy, unkempt hair; and there were men as well including an aesthetic-looking bearded one with old-style metal framed glasses and a dark skinned, fine featured one dressed more neatly whose lineage at least in part came from Sub-Saharan Africa he assumed.

Having recorded over three hundred license plates in his three day duty, the Lieutenant focused on the TT preface to the vehicle number designating that the owner had been officially sanctioned as a technical advisor to the government. Nevertheless, while accepting the driver's apologies, he asked to see the registration and identity cards. American, of course, even the part African, the Lieutenant should have guessed. The *cartes d'identité* confirmed it. The group indeed was going to the mountain fair, but they had lost time by taking a side trip down past Zemmara to see the desert. They claimed to have been on the road for more than 8 hours. And Zemmara? The incident at the check point was in the Zemmara region. But except for this Mediterranean-looking woman, these were typical young Americans, casually attired, many poorly groomed like those who came to Marrakech looking all the time for cheap kif in the Jemma El F'na square. Those who attacked the national police were reported to be four North African men in their mid to late 20's.

"And where do you come from? Not America?" he asked the young woman in Arabic. Of light tan complexion, her thick black hair was cut short in a stylish Western fashion.

She answered back in correct Arabic that she was from the capital, born and raised there, and began calmly searching for her papers in her camping sack as if she was well-accustomed to showing such proof. She had not missed the man sitting in the back seat of the Lieutenant's jeep. He was indeed the police man at the check point, the one who had escaped at the refugee camp. Her heart stopped and she felt no breath come.

"And she's my very good friend," the tall man they called Chris said, putting his arm around her and pulling her close.

A ruse to throw him off? Regardless, the Lieutenant was not pleased by the sight of this obviously well-off American claiming possession of this Moroccan woman, one of his own country. He sensed her defiance of him, she who should be back in her proper household under the protection of her father and brothers and not running about camping and sleeping with corrupting foreigners. He kept his disgust to himself. He could not waste his time with these Americans and this slut of a woman. He pointed down the road, informing them it was only a few kilometers more to the cross roads and a hundred more to where they would find the horse shoe gate of the Brides' Fair.

The expensive, well-outfitted vehicle climbed back on the road. "You didn't have to go that far, to imply we were more than just friends," Maleka said perhaps more curtly than called for. Nevertheless, she breathed easier realizing that neither the doctor nor the helpful American nurse at the UN facility had betrayed her identity. "But, thank you."

"Whatever works," Chris said. " Anything for an old student."

***** ***** ***** ***** ***** ***** *****

Not more than a half hour further right at the cross road junction, Ali did not fare as well with the scrutiny of Lieutenant Berrada's patrol. He had fulfilled his instructions and now waited to first compose himself and then seek transportation. Weary, the mid day heat, a heat he was not used to, conspired to further discourage him. Ali thought fleetingly of ending this misadventure, of returning to his life in the city 500 kilometers over the mountains to the north; of completing his paramedical training and taking up a normal life. But they had taken oaths and had exchanged the blood of their slashed forearms. Nor could he walk away from Moustapha, an older brother to him, and a good and decent man unlike Rachid and some of the others in the movement. Also, he alone had the special weapons skills they needed.

Three kilometers back he had gone off the paved road and found a dry gully formed by the seasonal mountain run off. He had pushed the Land Rover into it, being satisfied that it could not be seen from the main road unless someone came up this path to relieve themselves.

Now he sat on his gear, tired from his exertions and sweating profusely from the heat. Vehicles passed by every minute or so, some slowing so their occupants might determine whether he needed assistance. He waved them by, and this would prove unwise. Grand taxis too, it was said, would soon be up the road, and he would prefer to pay his way rather than be offered the charity of strangers. After a time, a large jeep type vehicle passed, but stopped and reversed itself. Ali knew at once by the official matriculation plates that the odds again were against him. A tall man in a crisp military uniform descended from the jeep and walked towards him. He wore sun glasses and had the epaulets of an officer on the shoulders of his tunic.

Ali tried not to panic, responding to the officer's questions steadily and as they had rehearsed several times. The identity card he proffered designated him a

THE BRIDES' FAIR

technician of the cinema. "Only a lowly one, Sir. Sound, you see? One of the unseen many behind the camera. Yes, we're making a film of the folk lore at the big fair. Look my equipment is all here with me," and opening his duffel bags he displayed microphones of various types, telescoping booms, meters and gauges, electronic amplifiers, all neatly wrapped in cloth and plastic.

None of this did any good, for the driver came forward to inform the officer of something. Then, Ali was pushed roughly towards the jeep, where the Chef de Brigade in the middle seat pulled down the hood of his cloak. "Without doubt he is one of them, Lieutenant. "It was he who made the mistake of leaving me alone while he went to find me water. Such kindness by a son of Satan is now repaid."

Chapter VI

Hundreds of charcoal fires smudged the rose caftan of the sun which now went to disrobe, went to find a modest place behind the ring of mountains. Kachou, her half-sister Izza and four girl cousins from the ksar of El Husein hurried through the rows of black goat hair tents to the place by the horse shoe arch where all the trucks were parked. Considering she had resisted with all her power coming to the souk, Kachou had a joyful day, had made every moment count, waving at people by the road and in the towns as her Uncle's truck made its way up to the high plateau; making silly faces for the cameras of the 'Europeans;' arching her eyebrows ever so slightly at some boys she recognized, and relishing every swallow of almond and honey pastries that some vendors gave free to the young fiancées. So far she had only one regret. She had not got the attention of the handsome city man who, magically it seemed, fixed her Uncle's truck. The man had stayed in the honored seat up in the cab and had with too much of the customary respect avoided the sight of the women. "But he is old, no?" Izza had whispered.

"He is younger than my Ben Moha, and has a finer way about him."

"Stop your dreams, Kachou. He's not of our people."

"That makes no difference to me. None at all."

Kachou, Izza and others of her clan had already paraded up and down the center ground, through the press of so many people, thinking themselves better turned out, smarter in their carriage than the girls of all the other ksars of their great mountain clan. Many would be married for the first time tomorrow in the big ceremony, but others, older girls and women who wore the flat caps had come to find new husbands having suffered indignities and abuse in the households of their in-laws and having elected as their right the chance to find someone new and more compatible. If she had to marry tomorrow, she would certainly be back next year seeking someone more to her liking. But now with

THE BRIDES' FAIR

the fading of the light, she led the others through the maze of tents, through the milling crowds back to her Uncle's truck.

They had pitched an awning off the side of the truck, and Other Mother, Itto, already had the evening tea brazier going. This would be the women's shelter, for the men would be off late haggling over rams, donkeys, horses and camels, and then spinning long tales through the night with relatives they saw only once a year at this fair. Itto and Aunt Rabah squatted on the carpets of the shelter, talking animatedly to several women from her Uncle's ksar. Each wore heavy, egg-sized amber beads and many bracelets of coin silver. The bracelets clattered with the gesticulation of intricately tattooed hands, the weaving fingers giving grace to throaty voices.

"Look at these worthless daughters," Itto bellowed. "Gadding about the whole day like Fassi Arab princesses. Well, there still work to do, water to fetch from the standpipe, and bread and goat cheese to buy from the vendors. You were expecting a feast of stew and sweets? Oh, the men will bring mutton soon. I'm sure they'll kill a fat, old ram in celebration of a good trading day, and to give thanks to Allah who sent the fine young man to our aid." She handed Kachou a few coins, and softening her voice said to the others, "She's come along since the last harvest, you see? Pretty enough and so healthy. Never sick a day last winter when the fever took two children and some of the old. Yes, you should see her in the baths. She's getting a fine woman's body. She will please Ben Moha who has over three hundred sheep as you know, and a brother in France who sends back postal money orders."

"Yes, she is a fine daughter," a woman known as Aunt Lamia said. "You have done well by raising the daughter of your husband's dead wife, may her memory be blessed. But will she be obedient when she goes to her new husband's lodge? You know how some of these girls think today. And do I see some spirit bedeviling those eyes? What do you say to that, daughter?"

But Kachou had heard all this before and darted away. She ran past the great corals of horses, mules, donkeys and camels, many of which would be sold off to those from the low lands since fodder in the high plateaus would be scarce during the long winter. Sell off your abundance, your unwanted before the snows close everything in. The young brides were nothing more than such abundances, more mouths to feed.

The sun was now all smudged over with the smoky fires of night, and the propane gas lanterns hanging on the ridge poles hissed and glowed a fierce white. She easily followed the strong, good odors that overwhelmed the stink of a thousand tethered animals, to the line of tents where flat barley bread baked on the sides of concave clay ovens, where brochettes of mutton heart, kidney and gigot crackled on charcoal braziers. She studied everything, seeing who were the favorites among the bread sellers. There was no hurry to get back for the women would take their time this evening organizing the meal. Much gossip remained about who had died of poisoned tea, who in their clan had shamed her husband, and who had more silver caftan fibulas and more bracelets of pure gold. The crowds surged through the lanes to buy items for their meal. If you weren't determined and stood your ground, they would bump you from the lines before the stalls. And Kachou who would be sixteen soon after the longest winter night would not let herself be pushed about by rude women and turbaned graybeards.

She saw him come round into the lane of commissary tents, his ceremonial djellaba almost hiding his city-made pants and fine, brass-studded sandals. His white turban covered his approaching baldness and his chin beard showed flecks of gray. But the man she was supposed to wed did not notice her, just another rouged and hennaed bride elbowing her way towards the baker's counter. How would she address him if by chance he did see her? 'My great and future benefactor, I am so eager to come into your lodge and be your second or third worthless woman.' Baba El Husein and Other Mother, Itto, would rage to hear her scandalous thoughts. But Baba recognized that she was different, that the baraka from her mother was strong. Wasn't that why he sent her in spite of all the jealousy in the compound down to school for five years, freeing her from most of her chores? She had learned to write the undulating Arabic script, French as well, and to do the hardest sums. It had cost Baba one good ram a year to the teacher for a place for her and her half-sister Izza. Now she and Izza were the only ones in the ksar who could do her father's tallies and read the letters from the men working in the cities on the coast or in France. And because she had been infused with the vaccines brought by the government people to the school, and because of her strong baraka she had survived all the winters, had not suffered a withered leg or clouded eyes and was already taller than Itto, Aunt Rabah, and every girl or woman in the compound. And all of this was to be discarded, handed over to Ben Moha who strolled on with his male kinsmen passing her by without notice.

"I want ten from the top of that pile, the freshest ones, please," she shouted over the cries of the others at the bread stall. She fingered each encrusted and bubbled up piece for oven warmth. Old Granny made better bread in the compound, but this was the best of the vendors.

"Oh, Kachou, I thought you'd be here. Did they cheat you on the bread?" Her half-sister Izza ran up to the stall clutching a paper parcel of goat cheese.

"Don't be silly. I can keep my wits about me. And besides these vendors wouldn't dare cheat us who belong to this place. They would have spells put upon them if they did."

Izza as all of Itto's children was darker than she. They told by the night fire that Itto's grandmother had come from *Afarika*, down below the great desert in a place called Senegal. Yet, the mixture of these darker bloods into El Husein's clan had been welcomed. To bring new, far off seed into the close, inter-clan matings was favored for its special baraka. Izza, who shared her bed, giving her warmth on those cold nights when the djins rode the death hawk up the fierce drafts from the lower valleys, would not marry until after two more harvests. But she already fancied a boy from the school whose father had beside the usual sheep and goats, twelve cattle and a truck newer than Uncle ben Kadour's. He even ran a boutique in the village at the end of the West Trail that sold seed, fertilizer, iron back hoe blades and other tools.

"You are a silly one to always dream about something that will not happen," she had chided her sister once. "They will not pay the bride price for one such as you, even with five year's schooling and from a clan that has the finest ksar up the high plateau trail. You will not marry a fine man of the city who works miracles with trucks. We are still nothing but peasants, and Majdi's father is a rich store keeper." For days Kachou felt much shame. She should not have been so bitter about Izza's prospects, only angry at her own bad fortune.

"We must get back to the truck," Izza said. "You know Mother Itto's anger when we fool around like this."

"There's no hurry. The women are having a fine time gossiping." Kachou tucked the stack of flat bread under her thick, wide shawl and started towards the sounds of the drums and the three string lutes. Izza tagged behind complaining that they would be scolded and that all the other costumed girls had gone back to their respective shelters. "We do not have to be like all the others, Izza, always like obedient sheep. This is a fair. There are many things to see and do"

In the flat, center field the authorities had erected ceremonial tents with black appliqué symbols of old style lamps. These were like the tents the old caids from the lower valleys employed when they made their potent emissaries to pacify the unaligned, hostile tribes. Now the important men of the region wearing their white djellabas and soft leather slippers sat with the uniformed government men on the pillows and the banquettes under these great tents. They sipped their evening tea and watched the dancers and the musicians performing on the wooden platforms before them. It was an hour before the evening meal, and the commissary ovens of the caids and of the Tourist Board emitted rich smells of roasting lamb and stewing chicken. Hundreds of foreigners were gathered around the stage where women dancers in white caftans and blue sashes alternated their movements with turbaned men shod in fine riding boots. A singer cried about her man going off from her lodge to a battle in the lower valleys. The women's chorus echoed the chant. The men stiffly swayed and lightly stamped their booted feet. The women swayed also to the chant, their hips drove the men on either side to keep the rhythm.

Before this day, Kachou had never seen these foreigners, these Europeans in the flesh. They wore none of the fine gowns and suits of the people in the magazines that circulated through the compound. They were dressed for camping in jeans, slacks, pullovers and an assortment of field jackets. The procession of foreigners entered through the horse shoe arch gate, the lights of their vehicles searching a path to the several rows of city-made tents which served as their hotel. After only two more sunsets all would be gone and the great plateau would once more hold nothing but the old abandoned ksar, the new mosque, and the white domed shrine of the marabout saint from her real mother's blood line. The place would remain deserted, with only the stiff winds and the rare visitor bringing eggs or dried herbs and flowers tied in bunches to the shrine.

One of the vehicles that crawled passed Kachou and Izza, poking its way through the crowded lanes, following the Tourist Board signs, bore the diplomatic license plates of the American mission. The passengers in the van, road-weary after nine hours travel, regarded in numbed quiescence the mass of people moving everywhere at once, the corrals of animals, the entertainers in the distance on spot lit stages; dancers, musicians, jugglers, fire eaters. It was as if a great, three ring circus had found its way to this remote place and crowds were rushing about the midway to see everything before the main performance. And indeed there were tents of many types and sizes scattered across the front lot of The Greatest Show On Earth.

Eric Dalton caught the darting glance of a costumed bride who hurried passed carrying a stack of flat bread. She wore the peaked cap of a virgin bride, and even though heavily made up with kohl darkened eye brows and lashes, rouged cheeks and hennaed forehead and hands, Eric saw through the traditional veneer that she was young, his daughter Susan's age. Startled less by this than by their sudden brief intimacy, she too feared that this foreign man in the white van had plunged swiftly into her, like a djin who came in the night to rut down between the legs. Somewhere among Cynthia's notes he read last evening at home before nodding off to sleep 'They have their conventions of modest behavior, but they can size a man up in a flash, and then dip their eyes away in mock shyness. That intense flash of anticipation of the bridal bed, of the pain, the joy, their coming womanhood.'

They were efficient at the Tourist Board reception, with their accommodations awaiting them and their dining table assigned. Even Edna Baker seemed impressed as they were led down the row of large VIP tents in the 'hotel' section. To one of two tents bearing the French tricolor, they led Christine Deschamps and her son Phillipe to a reunion with her husband and daughter who had arrived only moments before. Pierre Deschamps, effusive with thanks, invited his *chers amis* American friends to come for a nightcap after dinner and the folk dancing. They found the dirt floor of the American Mission tent layered with mountain carpets patterned in tendrils and squiggles of deep blues and reds. Eighteen cots with cotton sheets and thick wool blankets were arrayed in three rows.

"But we're only eleven," Edna Baker said, and Cynthia explained as she had in her orientation packet that Bill Baxter, the Consul General up in Tangier, his wife, Amy, their two kids, and his secretary, Nancy Schluger, had been signed up but they had to cancel due to a unplanned goodwill visit of two U.S. Navy frigates. "That still makes only sixteen."

"It's the symmetry of the thing," Dr. McManus said to Edna with a tinge of impatience. "Can't you see all the tents are set up for 18?"

"And no double beds. What's a cold, lonely person to do?" Pam Crane quipped.

Eric thought of their other passenger who was helping the Marines unload the baggage and drink coolers. "That's very kind of you, Monsieur," the well-spoken man said. "But I have to find my colleagues. We're here to shoot footage of the folk lore, you know, the dancing, the brides' ceremony, the fantasia. And we must get started."

Dr. McMannus offered to help the man with his gear, and both Cynthia and Pam went on with how interested they would be in seeing the film. The man replied that he would be happy to give them all the information once he knew the plans of the Tourist Board. He was only a lowly sound and light technician, and not in on all the big decisions. He declined Dr, McMannus's *tres gentile* offer, and, apparently embarrassed by all the attention, he moved off through the car park, the two rows of 'hotel' tents and into the milling crowd.

Would it be an hour before the gongs rang for dinner? The smells of stewing and roasting meats, dark, invasive cumin, more heady but equally permeating saffron reminded them they had not eaten anything all day except a sandwich, most having little breakfast as well, only grabbing a juice and a quick gulp of coffee as they raced to meet the 7 am departure schedule. Some thought there would be only enough time to wash, change and have a 'real drink of something,' as Pam put it. Monique wanted to search for her friends at the *camping sauvage*, the place for the back backers up behind the 'hotel,' but reconsidering, thought she would stay with the group at least through dinner. Dr. McMannus was eager to try out his new camera, but was convinced by Pam to stay and have a much needed drink. Karen, thought it absolutely a big fat waste to sit around the tent 'catching flies and stuff' when they had come all this way to see things. First they had to wash off the road dust in the two *salles de bains* tents, then change into fresh clothes. Some knew the art of changing under the blankets, squirming, contorting. Others simply went in the shadows of the tent and stripped knowing that they were in civilized, non-threatening company, or accepting that a patch of bare flesh could offend or arouse only the perverted.

After quickly changing, and using his 'wash and dries', rather than face the lines in the bath house, Eric first went back to the van to call up Stu Connor at the Embassy some 300 kilometers northeast of this Mid Atlas plateau. The Ambassador when he at last left his office for a World Bank reception, still sputtered on about wasting his valuable time, about all the phony folk lore. "I'll bet my pension he'll decide to come at the very last minute when he has to get himself to the air base. He'll leave us all hanging until then, of course, as is his way."

Eric asked Stu to check on several matters, and as well to verify with Washington whether Congressman Farrell's trip was on as scheduled. "I'll check with you tomorrow to see if you've learned anything new." He took the backpack from the pile of remaining luggage outside the van. He had bought it as a birthday present for Peter a couple of years ago for that camping trip they planned to take up in Maine, but never did. Their home leave had become just too rushed, relatives, old friends demanding time, Washington pulling him in on two occasions for urgent meetings that only inched some minor policy decision forward if that. Hillary who had made the plans, who had put together a schedule by consensus, she reminded him, could no longer play the stoic and wept. In the senior ranks of the Department these last several years all had been rushed, a blur of deadlines and showing up at meetings of questionable outcome. At least these past nine, ten hours had given him some change of venue, some totally new set of worries As hard as he tried, he couldn't get that incident in the Kariba Forest out of his mind, the crackling of branches like gunfire; a frightened woman pressing desperately close. A young woman pressing against him was confusing

THE BRIDES' FAIR

enough. He had been disgusted by his own fear as well as the flush of his sensations. He admitted, however, to being thankful that all had not atrophied from overwork and several months of an empty marriage bed. But he had sorted out the feelings for what they were, and while most men would find Monique striking, he was certainly not taken in by her as Cynthia probably feared. The language teacher was, as son Peter would put it, a bit of a flake.

"Back there in that forest, Corporal, was it you or Dr. McManus who first reached Monique Addleman?" he asked Jess Williams who completed shutting down the radio and locking the van up for the night.

"I believe I did, Sir," Jess Williams said. "Man, was she frantic. She got herself all caught up in that bush and she was fighting it. She even scratched me." He pointed to a few small cuts in the deep tan skin of his neck, cuts probably made by her fingernails as she grasped at him.

"Whatever frightened her was back up in the woods, did she say?"

"Yes, Sir. She had been running away from something, that wild pig."

"And where was Dr. McMannus?"

"He came up right after I did to help. He was right near by."

"And theothers? Doug Baker, for instance?"

"I didn't notice, Sir. But I was flying, you know, making tracks."

When compared with the sullen, grumpy Sergeant Jerry Donatelli, who should have retired last year on his eligibility date, the considerably younger Jess Williams had extended himself, kept alert and never complained. "We both have to continue to keep a sharp eye out for any trouble. I just heard on the radio, the Ambassador may be coming for a short visit tomorrow . I'll have to tell Mrs. Crane, but we shouldn't get the others all worked up."

"I'll keep it to myself, Sir," the Corporal said, and Eric had confidence that he would.

They joined the small circle of drinkers in the center of the American tent. The Sergeant lay back on his bunk with two "dead soldier" beer cans already propped on his broad chest. Pam Crane, looked her sleek and elegant best, even though she, in spite of Cynthia's advice about the effects of the altitude, was quickly into her second scotch whiskey on the rocks. Doug Baker regaled the group with stories of his hard travels years back in East Africa when an enraged elephant got his tusks into the Land Rover just inches away from the family jewels. Edna Baker smoldered and nudged her husband several times to tone it down not that she hadn't heard these same stories a hundred times at least in twenty-five years of marriage, but because of the presence of the Ambassador's wife and the DCM. Also, she and her husband had never been to Africa before now. Eric wanted to take Pam Crane aside to inform her about her husband's probable visit, but she sat on the edge of a bunk next to the Corporal whom she insisted join them and not stay in the shadows like some servant. Everyone, especially Pam, to Edna Baker's chagrin, seemed to be enjoying Doug Baker's stories. She was raucous and unrestrained in her laughter. "Why, you know boys and girls the Watusi in Kenya are famous for their long appendages, and when I was traveling in the Massai Mara….."

Sober or not, jokes in bad taste or not, there could be no rules. They had to let their hair down a bit after the long trip, after repressing all those thoughts of careening off the narrow, twisting road into a gorge, after all the fantasies about seat mates pressed close on every curve, about the fear of some terrorist waiting for them around the next bend in the road. Cynthia understood this as well and politely smiled at the punch lines. She suggested to Karen that she might wish to leave and go see the horses, but her daughter replied that she heard much more raunchy stuff at her *Lycée*, and in French. At first Monique stifled her amusement fearing that to enjoy herself, get fully into the spirit of things would be out of character, particularly in the presence of DCM Dalton whom she found a bit awesome.

As the affable, uncomplicated Doug Baker spun out his shaggy dog tale of the tall Watusi warriors, Eric reached back in his memory and pulled up Harlan Crane's confirmation hearing for his Ambassadorial appointment almost two years ago. It was one of those typical "gotcha" Washington events, with aggressive young staffers on the Senate Foreign Relations Committee feeding sensitive tid bits to Woodward and Bernstein 'wanna bes' on the *Post* and the *Times*. Hadn't Crane, the wealthy Governor, lost his last election when his opponent smeared his family values platform, dragging up old scandals and sleaze? There was a messy divorce from his rich high school sweetheart who had bank rolled their first computer hardware company. There were the tear jerker photos of the wife and the three beautiful children next to that of Crane and his latest 20 something bimbo. And hadn't Pam Crane emerged about then? She had been a model, with all the winks and nods that profession usually evoked, until it was proven that she had actually had had a successful, albeit brief, career in fashion and advertising. And hadn't the smear campaign gone nowhere, given shock-fatigued Washington? And weren't Harlan and his lady, while not exactly model citizens, or free from political deal making and questionable friendships, given credit for an economic resurgence in their state? It came out as well that Pamela Crane had been an attentive mother to a boy now in his first year at college, and had been out in the front lines on women's rights and racial equality, serving as more than a figure head on a dozen boards and committees.

"Now confess up, Doug," Pam said. " Have you really been on all these tough, fantastic adventures in Africa?" There as silence and then a deep roar of laughter from Doug Baker. She had got his number, and probably heard all his old shaggy dog stories before. "Oh, yes indeed," she said, " But I bet all you bold and brave people of the world felt your heart stopping just a couple of times when we were crawling around those gorges and there was nothing between us an eternity but a few inches of dirt road" She seemed to relish being a little high, being familiar with those to whom she, as the Ambassador's lady, had remained aloof. And for someone who spent much time and money keeping her face and figure youthful, she downed her whiskey with the ease of water. Looking dead at Eric, she said, "Shouldn't have any more, right? I'll be good so, please, no more looks."

Monique Addleman's long, graceful fingers slipped around the plastic glass of chardonnay offered by Corporal Williams, as if were a crystal goblet. With her wavy auburn hair brushing her shoulders, her toga-like caftan and its opal-studded fibula, she looked like someone out of a Pre-Raphaelite painting, a classic Rosetti . "Thanks," she said to the Corporal. "Thanks for all you did to help me, back there in the woods. I must have said awful things, so please forgive me."

"And how's our poor dear? Feeling better are we?" Pam said with an edge of sarcasm.

"I'll be all right, Mrs. Crane."

"I'll bet you will, sweets, but none of this Mrs. Crane business. I'm not that old. Where are your friends, I'm sure they're thrilled that you're here."

"I looked for my friend, Chris's jeep, but I guess he's still on the road."

"Well, we don't want you to feel neglected, do we Eric?" She started to pour herself another drink, but the dinner gong boomed through the encampment, and the resourceful Jess Williams scooped away her glass and all the others.

They sat all squeezed together North African fashion on the cushions that circled a large tray of glossy worked brass. There were over 300 others in the big dining tent most of whom they knew from the diplomatic corps. All, even the usually squeamish Edna Baker ate with the right hand, using piece of flat bread as a spoon to scoop into the pungent meats, vegetables and grains. Before leaving for the dining tent, Pam had redeemed herself to her companions by going to Mai Donatelli's rescue and insisting that the Sergeant get himself up from his cot, put on the shirt Mai was trying to hand him, and come to dinner with the rest of them. Pam, never a big eater, determined to keep her shape, proved as starved as everyone else, but how Cynthia had to go on and on explaining the origins of and the ingredients in every damn dish. Some things were better left a mystery, but try to tell her that without offense. And that stiff, long nose Eric Dalton sat watching their every gesture, shrewdly summing them up, cataloguing each and everyone for his damn files. Still he was sort of appealing even for a bureaucrat. Square jawed and sensitive yet with a certain aura of firm command that had Cynthia and Monique in their different ways sniffing about. Pam had to admit that she too thought about him that way once, for a minute or too in one of those day dreams everyone has all the time and no one acknowledges. At one of those interminable diplomatic soirees he danced with her with a surprising expertise, but of course he had to ask her to dance out of duty; deputy's couldn't leave the Ambassador's lady unattended. Still with a pleasant little buzz, she wondered did his reserve melt when he had a woman beneath him in bed. Would he do it with her too for duty? She laughed out loud at the thought. "Doug Baker, you're so funny," she told the group at the table, to cover up her own silliness. Every damn one of them around in her party, even Eric Dalton, even grumpy Edna Baker had their secrets about making out with old, new and imagined lovers, thought about it ten times a day at least. Oh, she could play the grand lady with real style, could be serious and effective leading meetings on social issues, health care, poverty, choice, but she never completely blanked out that which was basic to life.

Eric had told her on the walk to the dining tent that Harlan was probably coming tomorrow around noon. Poor baby thinking he had to when invited by the biggies in the palace. "Doesn't want to come, I bet. Shouldn't be racing around the country, you know?" She was having such a good time, in her way, not having to order servants about for another damn official luncheon, not having to stand in reception lines for hours at a time, not being able to kick back and be herself. She hoped she could take the slow road back to the city, so she could have time to get to know these people better, to make some real friends for a change. She feared, however, that she would have to go back with Harlan on the helicopter, and by tomorrow evening it would be back to the residence and her boring duties. Well, you were only so free when you served the public and your country. You carry that glass house everywhere like a snail.

Hans van Luyten, the Dutch *chargé d'affaires* was one of several who stopped by the table to chat, forcing them to stop their ravenous gorging, to revert to the tinkling phrases, the mostly empty words. She thought Hans different than the rest of them, and listened attentively as he told them the Deschamps family faired well and could be seen over in the corner with the large French contingent. Was he free, divorced or something? From a rich Amsterdam banking family? You saw him at all the receptions and other diplomatic do's. A tall, crisp, vigorous 50 or so and confident, with none of the constipated hang ups of these Washington 'crats. Had she told him she was Dutch on her mother's side, yes, near Delft ? Had she danced with him too long at—was it the Brazilian National Day soiree? Well, dear Harlan never reproached her any more for these "little dalliances" as some would call them. Despite all that absolutely vile gossip back in Washington and Ohio she had never done anything at all to betray him. You bet it had been tough at times, a real fidelity test when she was out all hours of the day and night campaigning for him with those cute helpful guys always around her, but she had kept her legs together, had been the loyal, supportive wife. Now Harlan's motor seemed to be winding down, and God he was only 64. She didn't want to imagine it. After twenty years you know a person pretty well. He did not want her to cover herself with ashes because of him, to throw herself on some burning wood pile. He wanted her to live her life.

"You seemed to have cornered all the truly beautiful women, Eric," the Dutch chargé said, and the American Deputy Chief looked around the table in that intense way of his, probably analyzing each mole, each chin and cheek line as if he had to have supporting evidence for Hans's kind words. Certainly she tried to look her best., to hang on as best she could to those days of kicky clothes, runway struts, photos of herself plastered everywhere. 'Midwest wholesome' they labeled it, defining a career that lasted an intense two and a half years, a lifetime in that ephemeral business. Thank God Harlan came along when he did.

You would certainly call Cynthia attractive, and she didn't appear to fuss with herself at all. She was one of those real English roses, each petal you pealed back as lovely and perfect as the previous. Now Karen reminded her of herself when she was seventeen going on twenty-one, a real princess, stuck up and too pretty for her own good. And then you had poor, precious Monique. She took all the prizes She had no trouble getting the men all hot and bothered, and a few women too she bet. And even Mai Donatelli, finally out of her shorts and T shirt and into that flattering gown was, with her exotic Eurasian features and in the shadows made by the propane lamps, very much a beauty. Why she had hooked up with that old creep of a Marine, but he had probably rescued her from some whore house or refugee camp like so many GIs had done then in the aftermath of the long Indo-China wars. And then you had Edna Baker, and you had to really be generous about the looks of that big butt grump, but the face was not that bad, better when she tried a smile. She too had had her good days and dreamed about them still. "That old European charm, won't work on us savvy Americans, will it ladies?" Pam said.

"Well, for my part," Cynthia said. "Hans can put on the charm any time."

Eric and Hans inevitably got right down to business, exchanging the latest news on tomorrow's rallies, on speculation on what the MPLM was planning." It would have been a bore sitting around the capital, contributing to all the hysteria as only we diplomats can do, and not come to Imichil."

"But you men are going on too much as always about revolutions and rumors of revolutions." Pam Crane said.

"You are absolutely right, my dear. Please forgive me." Hans would join them down by the folk dancing after dinner. Everyone would gravitate there. It would be the last event of a very long day.

After stuffing himself on four courses, including a sort of pie of almonds and pigeons of all things, Jess Williams sat alone on one of the benches watching the painted up mountain ladies on the stage sway back and forth. Nearby were the Bakers, and just off to the right he could see Mrs. Crane and that Dutchman. The DCM and Mrs. Dennis were back behind him in the shadows made by a semi circle of tents. The drummers and those lute players on the stage had a different, faster rhythm than the ladies who kept it cool. They rode the music slow, sometimes letting out with a chant, more like a cry of being hurt only a little, not real bad. One all rouged and thickly mascarared lady seem to keep her eyes dead on him. When the crying chant came, her eyes rolled up in her head and her mouth would get all funny like she was coming or something. And then she and the others would do a quick hop and slide, and one of them would raise a tambourine and pump it real fast with the flat of her hand. It all meant something, about love and humping most likely. Back in the city, Jess and some of the guys had seen those shake dancers, mostly Egyptian gals, and there was no problem figuring them out. They could grind their bellies and butts like nothing else. They could get it on, but this mountain dance was just too cool. But there had to be something there, something far out. They came all this way, over all those bad roads, so something great must be going down up there on the stage. He missed his little friend, Zoubida, but he did feel a little better about being here with all these civilians. Mrs. Crane, Mrs. Dennis and the DCM, too, were being real nice, making him feel like one of them. You had to get out and see things. Most of the guys in the contingent just hung around the Marine House shooting pool, drinking beer and watching porno flicks on the VCR.

Karen Dennis found him sitting on the bench watching the dancers and the musicians go on with that repetitive, hypnotic routine for the several hundred or so huddled around in the cool night air. "Jess, there you are. I've been looking all over for you," she said nudging his shoulder with her hand as if they were long lost buddies. "Some French and German kids are getting a party going up in the *Camping Sauvage*, and we're trying to round up some of the younger set, and I've been looking for you and Monique. Come on, Marine, we need to represent America."

She seemed as nice as her mom, who sent cookies and stuff to the Marine House, and always invited them on those excursions of hers to the museums and markets. Yeah, Karen seemed OK; she didn't want to go alone to that European set and needed some company. She was like one of those officer kids back at Quantico or out there in Okinawa when he did 14 months in a ready assault unit. They could be so friendly and color blind on the beaches and at the barbecues. But you didn't dare touch any of that stuff, especially the teen age stuff like Karen Dennis.

"I'm always ready to party, but tonight I'm so wiped out from that drive and all. Right after the dancers, I'm heading to that nice warm bunk," he lied for he had to keep his eye on the DCM and Mrs. Crane . He hoped they wouldn't stay up half the night for he could use a good night's sleep, having gotten up at five after having had to pull duty until midnight so he could go on this trip.

"We came all this way to have a good time, and you just can't go off to bed so early." She gave him one of those little girl pouts. Being so pretty and all she was probably used to getting her way.

He needed to let loose and party, but not here with these people, not with Miss Jail Bait. He told her he had to check around with the DCM, and then he might try to catch up with her in the camping area. "It's right behind the car park, isn't it? Monique should be around here someplace. Hope you can find her." Now there was someone ready for some good hard loving, weird but ready, but not with this Marine, no way. He joined the Marines to stay out of trouble, to not get sucked down by the street like most of the black dudes he knew back in Philly. If he got his Sergeant's stripe next month as expected, he definitely would stay in for the long haul, and he would try to marry Zoubida, which would be possible but complicated. Her family was nice every time he came by, making him feel real welcome, stuffing him with those almond cookies, and her mother must have known they were not just holding hands. How nine of them lived in those three small rooms he never knew, but they had it all neat when he came by, all the cushions and banquettes up against the walls. He gave her a couple of cartoons of cigarettes once a week from the commissary. You weren't supposed to give stuff like that to the locals but everybody did, and Zoubida's brothers could sell them for a good price. There was none of this color business with them like all those uptight folk back in Philly. They were almost as dark as he was, anyhow. But would he have to become a Moslem to marry her? That wouldn't be so bad, but it might get "the Man" all upset, and, either way, you had to go through all that red tape to marry a foreigner especially an Arab one.. The 'Man' could be really up tight about that if he wanted to.

"Hey, Corporal, you see Mai anywhere? It was the Sergeant himself, looking like he had gotten into more beer.

"No, Sarge. She's got to be around here watching the dancing or shopping up in one of the tents still doing business."

"I've been looking all over the damn place." He muttered something about hoping she stayed lost, but Jess didn't think he meant it. These guys marry these Asian women thinking they're going to be obedient little slaves forever, worshipping their masters. But Mai after twenty years and two kids-one had died of the big C when only five—had gotten wise, wasn't taking any more of his shit. And what made it all worse, the Sarge was getting smashed all the time lately, and you could hear him taking out after Mai from their apartment in the Marine House like he didn't care who heard him. He was no head shrinker, but Jerry was having it bad knowing he had to check out next year, leave the Corps, the only world he knew. When Jess got up there, ready to go he would have his shit together, bought one of those fast food franchises, maybe found a job teaching and coaching track; he would have another life all planned. That was a long, long way off, and for now, he wished this dancing would stop and all these good folks would hit the sack.

From where they sat far in the back on carpets that were scattered about in lieu of benches, Eric and Cynthia could see Corporal Williams, the Bakers, Pam Crane and Hans van Luyten. They noticed that Karen had stopped to chat a few minutes with the Marine; guessed correctly that after remaining quiet all day, a feat for a teenager, she was restless for company. Different groups of dancers and musicians rotated up to the stage every twenty minutes or so, conveying the costumes and traditions of their particular sub clan. The cool night air prickled and stiff mountain breezes diffused the heavy odors of a thousand corralled animals as well as those more pleasant aromas from the many dinner fires which still flickered in the distance. An old stooped man passed through the audience offering steaming hot minted tea from a silver pot with a long, beak-like spout.

She traced the dippers among the profusion of stars and thought she detected Lupus and Centaraus in the southern sky. Eric rocketed up to the sky with her bumping off those points of light like a ball bearing in an old pin ball game. She caught up to him, understanding all of his worries. Yes, there would be some disturbances at the rallies in Casa tomorrow, not on the scale of Cairo or Istanbul. Mild by comparison to Belfast or Israel. But they would try to shake up the power structure, rupture the complex compacts of order and privilege. No, they wouldn't try to burn or sack the Embassy. "It's one of the few times when we're not the enemy, not the Great Satan for the majority here at least." And yes, he was worried that the Ambassador was trying to meddle with Washington on this electronic equipment business, getting the thousand pound gorillas in the Pentagon all riled up. And State was playing its usual equivocal games, when everyone knew the hold up on the equipment had little to do with a well-considered policy decision and everything to do with kowtowing to a popular young Congressman, Joe Farrell. "It never changes. We're so good at groping and stumbling, playing the blind man."

He told her the Ambassador would probably come up tomorrow by helicopter for the main ceremony. They talked about his illness. Heart condition, wasn't it? Didn't he suffer a mild stroke after that awful Senate confirmation business. And he was 64 or so, and she mid forties. Not that big a difference for tycoons, movie stars and other shakers and movers.

"Well, she's not waiting for her widow's weeds, is she?" Cynthia said. "She's over there snuggled all up to Hans van Luyten. I guess I shouldn't be so harsh on prospective widows." She laughed. She hardly felt widow-like herself. She had been married to Tom Dennis not even two years, and seventeen years of ups and downs, heartbreaks, a few love affairs had intervened since his death.

They concluded that Pam had her wits about her. She wasn't going to jump in the sack with Hans, or do anything else foolish. "Underneath all the expensive cosmetics, she's a canny one."

And Monique? She was a bit strange and needed to be watched. Eric swore that she hadn't gotten under his skin. Cynthia teased him: "And if you were left all alone with her? If I and the others weren't here? Come on Eric, give me a break."

They did agree that she had acted a bit odd with their passenger, that Ali Kadiri, the nice young man up to work on a film. She was the only one not to introduce herself. And did you see how she moved to the very front on the van with Sergeant Donatelli, how she scrunched down in the seat like a child trying to hide?

"More important than Pamela and Monique and the murkiness of US foreign policy, there's you Eric Dalton, my good friend." The dancers mesmerized. The chanting spoke of the ageless themes of love, war, abandonment and death. "I'm concerned about you, and Hillary of course. And shouldn't I have a vested interest? Aren't I an ex-lover of sorts?"

He nearly let the hot tea glass slip from his hand. She spoke of Manila, recalled that muggy Philippine night which should have remained forgotten.

"Haven't we been so properly adult, so European in saying nothing? I think we both, at least I did, began to feel something when we were on that hot beach out passed Makatoi. I rubbed on lotion and you did my back and shoulders. It had been six weeks since Tom was killed. They still hadn't made the identification, and of course I was all mixed up, not knowing what to do next, waiting around in Manila for the forensic people to finish. You were so kind. And Hillary so understanding of your attention. When it was all resolved, and I had to leave with what was left of him, go home to face his parents who kept accusing me, saying 'What did you do to our son?' You came by that house in Forbes Park. I remember we drank an ocean of G and Ts. But we didn't scheme and plot. It was just an accident, wasn't it? Just a small, one time accident with no dents or scrapes."

He had to tell her his version of that night, but hesitated, for he was less and less sure of what really happened in Manila, and more bothered by the Cynthia of the now and present. Sure, he had found her attractive. They all did. When she first arrived in Manila, they all thought she was a real original, not the typical nervous young wife out in a steamy Third World country for the first time. He remembered how she stood out at the grand event of the year, the Ambassador's Fourth of July lawn party The Dennises had just arrived in the Philippines that June, during the big summer rotation of staff. She was so fresh and lovely in her floral pattern summer dress and her broad brim hat. She had a clutch of young naval officers from Subic Bay around her, telling them how she had started a course in Tugaleg, and about her first ride in one of those gaudy Jeepney taxis. She didn't keep to herself in the residential compound complaining about the government issue furniture, the heat and the monstrous cockroaches. She was clearly different.

"It was one of those hot, soupy nights. You wore one of those sheer barong shirts. You were usually so proper with your shirt, ties, and sear sucker suits."

Hillary would have come too, but she had some long, protracted board meeting at the American School where she had finally landed a job teaching sixth grade math and science. Cynthia had already started into the gin and tonics before he arrived. She hugged him and thanked him over and over again for stopping by. They sat out on the red clay terrace of the small, non-descript concrete and

THE BRIDES' FAIR

stucco house, very much like his own, a house of regulation size for junior officers. He suggested, rather insisted that they eat something, and the housekeeper, Conchita, put the baby, Karen, to bed and heated some Chinese in the small kitchen before she left for the evening. Cynthia went on and on about Tom, and how he had overwhelmed her, rushed her into marrying him, rushed her overseas. "I could never figure whether I loved him, or this exciting new world of his, the travel, new places, new people."

They drank San Miguel beer with the great mound of Chinese food the housekeeper had managed to put together from the freezer. He could see it happening. She became bleary eyed, going on with what Conchita had told her about young widows, how they began to grow more and more hair just everywhere. She slumped against him, kissed him on the cheek, and said over and over what a real good friend he had been.

The dancers and the drumming stopped, and he could see Hans and Pam searching them out and remembered they were invited to go by the French tent for a night cap. "We really do need to talk more about that night, about Manila."

"Yes, We should talk. " he said, unsure of what resolution there would be in opening up that dust covered box. She had worn her hair long then, and it lay veiled across her face as she slept. Before he left her, he parted the hair from her eyes and mouth, and with a fresh damp wash cloth cleaned her up again . Two mornings later, Hillary organized a farewell coffee with the Embassy wives, and she was gone on the evening flight. She avoided him and Hillary as well for about five years, and then, almost totally transformed into a hard working Consular Officer and single mom, she answered their calls and letters. They never talked about it, not even after all those times they happened to be alone up at the old Dalton place near Falmouth when they would invite her up for a summer week, when all of them were just good buddies and nothing more.

They caught up with Pam Crane and Hans van Luyten and together walked towards the row of white-washed stones marking the military style tents of the hotel concession. In one of the French tents they found Mai Donatelli sitting there with the Deschamps and one of the political counselors, Henri Petard. Mai, seemed comfortable among them. There was of course a shared language, and with her father's father, a shared heritage. They turned the heavy vellum pages of her sketch book, admiring the finely drawn arches, the craggy medina faces. "Jerry not with you?" she said with some hope.

In the course of the half hour or so they spent being hosted by Pierre Deschamps with cognac and a fine brie, Eric surmised from the intensity of Mai's conversation with Petard, that their interests went beyond an admiration for her talent as an artist, or his familiarity with Laos and Southeast Asia. Between the pleasantries, the retracing of the difficult journey, the retrospective on Pierre's accident, Eric saw another marriage disintegrating and Sergeant Donatelli storming about, unable to reconnect with a woman who had grown beyond him.

When Cynthia declared that it was near midnight and she could hardly keep her eyes open, Mai rose with the others, collected her sketch book and said goodbye to her hosts and joined Eric, Cynthia and the other guests on the foot path to the American tent. "He stay mad all the time now," the Eurasian woman said, and Cynthia put her arm around her and told her she understood.

Hans van Luyten said good night to all before the Netherlands tent, bussing Pam on both cheeks in what could only be a public embrace. Pam, however, said she could never handle brandy and needed to get the cob webs out of her system or she'd be tossing all night. Seeing the Marine corporal still on duty, still following them at a measured distance, she asked him to accompany her on one more turn around the deserted fair grounds. As they hugged before the American tent, Cynthia, whispered how fantasies meld with the science of time and place, about the Kariba forest, about the Fair itself, about whether Manilla after all these years, was not just one of her fanciful myths. But she could not stay up with him. The altitude and the cognac had made her dizzy as well. "I always seem to fade on you at the wrong time."

The drumming, the chanting and the raucous hand clapping from the ceremonial tent finally ended. All the young Berber fiancées had long ago been sent to their bed rolls under the watchful eyes of mothers and aunts. Eric found himself walking down the line passed the last of the hotel tents and up the ridge above the lower field of the car park and the *camping sauvage*. Night fires still starred the field and the brisk cold wind coursed up through the deep ravines flattening his windbreaker. He felt a bit drowsy, but couldn't yet face the forced intimacy of the American sleeping tent. He hoped Jerry Donatelli would be soundly snoring, working off his six pack high, not making a scene with his wife; that Edna Baker wouldn't be tossing and cursing on her unfamiliar bed, and that Cynthia would dream about the present and leave ancient history behind

Down below in the jumble of camping tents, jeeps and safari vehicles, he could see clearly through the propane silhouetted canvas a couple preparing for bed. They slipped down together into their sleeping bag. Through the window of a van, a bare arm snaked up to extinguish a lamp. Somewhere a tape deck played, muted brasses distorted by the winds and rocks. Was it Vivaldi? He heard the rustle of whispers. "The young in one another's arms." The murmurs went on for all times, and they drove him to abandoned his watch and run down the rock shingles almost stumbling and falling twice.

Back in the main encampment, a night guard waggled a flashlight at his approach. He sat by his tea brazier next to the diplomatic car park. The craggy faced, brown toothed guard offered him a glass, not of the sweet minted variety, but of a herbal brew. Wrapped in his wool djellaba, he made out in a mixture of French and Maghrebi Arabic that he had worked at the fair for many years, his *patron* being related to the local caid. "But they do not come here as they used to. More and more the young have no need to come here to trade and to find a mate. They go off to the grand medinas on the coast and mostly never come back here. And who can blame them, I say? The grasses are less and less each year, and the wool up in this high plateau is becoming too coarse for carpets."

The man's back was turned to the vehicle park, but Eric faced it, seeing the moonlight dancing on the bright painted metal. He sipped the herbal tea as the man went on about his wives, his children's' wives and his grand children who, by Allah's goodness, filled his compound, his humble ksar. The white U.S. Embassy van parked among scores of motionless vehicles appeared to move, to come shuddering to life, to sway subtly like the Berber dancers. Fatigue? The herbal tea containing some hallucinogen? More familiar rhythms in the night? He gave the night guard a few coins for the tea and for the *baraka* of his grandchildren and rushed at last toward his bunk in the sleeping tent.

Chapter VII

Sometime in the early morning, Eric Dalton awoke to the wind flapping the sidewalls of the tent, a cool, clean wind dissipating the odors of animals and humans in the great encampment. In the darkness he wondered if Sergeant Donatelli's snoring had not shaken even the most exhausted of his other companions into a hazy half-consciousness. How many beers had the man consumed in trying to flood out his Vietnam nightmares, and his fears that Mai, his wife, had vanished away forever into the thick tangle of the Indo China jungle? Eric could not distinguish whether Mai slept easily beside her husband in the nearby bunk, or tossed fretfully with her own nightmares. Eric had struggled off to sleep, imagining the cries and murmurs of lovers, seeing the big white van rock and sway, and Monique, her dress shredded, running towards him, but then the motion slowed, and the welted and scratched legs of the girl seem to churn in place forever. But it was no longer Monique, but Hillary, a young Hillary, running to embrace him in an airport somewhere, an amalgamation of all the many airports he had ever seen. He dropped his flight bag and lingered in her softness. And there was Cynthia at the ticket counter stamping visas in a mountain of passports. She wore her hair long as when a young woman in Manila. It hid her face. She didn't look up when she informed him with bureaucratic curtness that he would have to return tomorrow for his passport, but then she recognized him and handed him the document which she had embroidered especially for him in silver filigree after a 15th Century Moorish design.

The flapping of the sidewall became that of the jib sheet of the Dalton ketch. He and his father set out fishing very early on a cool June Cape Cod morning when the ground fog blurred the wharf, and the masts of the ketches, sloops and day sailers in the boat basin bobbed and jabbed at its underbelly tearing out patches of sky. The gulls took up their watchful, sentinel positions in orderly files along the roof ridges and eaves of the old fish packing shed. They fired off the

THE BRIDES' FAIR

Ford inboard and slipped out into the swells of Nantucket Sound, heading out four, five miles to the spot in the greasy, green-black sea where they said you could always haul in a mess of sea bass. They had fifteen relatives and guests that weekend, and the Judge had promised them broiled fish for dinner, along with sweet Cape Cod corn, yeast rolls and tomato and onion salad swimming in vinegar, olive oil and fresh dill. Before the triumphant feast, there would be generous libations of gin and Indian tonic, at least enough to cut the salt heat of summer.

His father wore old khakis freshly splattered with house paint, for the two of them had just completed a week's hard work scraping, caulking and applying two coats of oil based paint to the clapboards, porch rails, spindles, window trim and all the Victorian gingerbread of the old, ten room summer cottage. Father had proven to the family, neighbors and himself that house painting could be mastered by even a district court judge without falling off ladders or having to resort to pricey contractors. He came down two weeks in the summer, leaving behind all his papers, briefs, law course lecture notes, and went at his precious vacation with gusto. The summer before, it had been auto mechanics, getting an old salt-rusted Chevy, purchased for the beach, in perfect running trim. And before that it had been mastering carpentry and electrical wiring to create two more guest rooms under the dormers of the attic. Eric and his younger brother, Walter, had to learn and do as well, becoming in their teens self-sufficient in the construction and mechanical crafts, learning along side their father, missing precious beach time with friends. Eric now flabbergasted secretaries and staff in the 8 or 9 offices in which he had set up shop in Washington and overseas. Yes, he would hang his own pictures and awards, do his own painting if necessary. It couldn't take more than an hour with a roller and trim brush. No, there was no need to bother the general services people.

'We are indeed in the golden age of America. You can't be overweening or arrogant about it, but we are the ones who will shape the future of the world for generations to come.' The chop became more difficult. They only ran on the jib now, and spiked the hooks of the trawl lines with the slippery squid bait. His father continue to thunder out his glowing, no-room-for-gloom prophecies over the waves buffeting, the sudden snap of the lines, another frantically grasping creature unhooked and secure in the ice of the center box. 'There's outer space, information technology, breakthroughs in medical science. A great deal to master and promulgate throughout the dark, forgotten corners of the world.' They struggled for balance as they tore out the three-pronged hooks. Their hands became jellied with fish blood as they piled up their easy harvest.

'Is it going to be law, medicine, finance, business? That's what fathers are supposed to ask their sons in the privacy of fishing trips together.'

Did he answer his father decisively then? Had he been so certain at seventeen or eighteen that it was to be international law with diplomacy as an objective? Had he just confidently creamed the SATs, gone off to college, expecting that everything, careers, marriage and all would fall into place?

The Judge in his mid seventies now triumphed in his garden, grafting his roses, plumbing the internet for advice on phlox, alyssum, hostas and bee balm. He still bellowed out optimistic predictions, dismissing the Kennedy assassinations, Vietnam, Watergate, the foreign policy muddles of Central America, Angola, the Middle East as mere hick-ups on the continuum of history and greatness. Eric, Hillary and the kids were on home leave. His brother Walter was there with Angie and their three boys. His mother's sister, Aunt Sue and Craig had flown in to Hyannis all the way from Frisco. Cynthia and Karen came up from Reston, Virginia. It had been a full house, and except for the jangling calls from his bureau in Washington, a warm and contented house.

'We've lost it, become too tied up in our own knots, a Prometheus bound. We fear foreigners, especially brown and yellow ones, and thus fear the world stage. We bully instead of lead, and our gold plated military has become a glorified Home Guard largely confined to barracks, spending its money in lavish PX s'

'You're over-indulging yourself in the fine print of your job, son. You need to get yourself recalibrated, see things in better perspective, take up a hobby, enjoy your family while you can, go out fishing in the old ketch with Peter and Susan too.'

Get out while the getting is good, while you're still energetic enough to try something else, before this place grinds you down to a pencil stub. He could resign from the senior service. He had his twenty years, and the pension—and everyone was obsessed with their pensions—could be deferred until he was fifty. He could teach international law at some unhurried, mid-sized New England University. And from there he could do occasional consulting in Boston and New York, taking corporate VPs through the fine print and legalistic mine fields of global trade. Or continue to stick it out, keep his neck well tucked in and his eyes on the ground, to be rewarded with an Ambassadorship to Chad, Mauritania or Slovakia, for most likely that's all that would be available at the time he made that golden list.

The waves smacked at the rising and falling prow. The tightly joined frame shook off each offense with a bare shudder. But the sidewall of the tent flapped more incessantly now, and at not even six in the morning, he rose to take care of the problem, being careful not to stumble into a neighboring bunk. Karen got up as well. She had gone to bed in a pullover that reached to her knees. Slipping on jeans and running shoes, she threw him a conspiratorial kiss—they presumably being the only ones awake-and was out the tent in seconds. He found a loose rope and secured the sidewall to the ridge line of the canvas and then to a neighboring pole. Breakfast wouldn't be for another hour at least, and he eagerly worked his way back between the sheets and the thick, engulfing blanket.

'Now Karen, she has such poise, good manners, none of that bottled up anxiety, that smoldering defiance of some of these kids.'

'They do grow up. She'll soon be eighteen, a woman in full bloom. But, believe me, she was no angel when she was 15, 16. Back in Reston those kids in the high school were into everything, and I was a nervous wreck worrying about her.'

'But her mother's genes prevailed, didn't they? Wasn't she Honor Society, Class VP, soccer co-captain? And there's more, isn't there?'

'Yes, there's more, but then there was the sweet, sickly smell of pot in her room And then the time she came back from a house party at three in the morning, screaming at me, 'No, I didn't do it with anyone, and it's none of your business anyway.'

'It's not been easy, I know, being alone, dragging her all over the world, in and out of how many schools? You should hear the groans and moans from Susan and Peter each of the dozen times we were moved, and they were yanked out of this or that school and away from their friends. And then you plunk these kids down in some alien town, and you worry about hostage taking or worse, not to mention protecting them from disease and diseased lovers.

'Do any of us really want to be protected when we're in our teens, when we think we're old enough for whatever? It may sound strange but some of us want to know what pain and being hurt is all about. It's on the check list of growing up. It's there for comparison to what's loving and decent.'

She lay beside him, and in the darkness he groped for the familiar backside, the firm, well-exercised thighs, but it wasn't Hillary. A young Berber bride, with heavily blackened eyes, lay there frozen, frightened and began yelling at him. And someone, not her, not Karen nor Hilary nor Monique, was being hurt. There were cries and screams out in the back of the tent where the Sergeant had dragged her accusing her of being out all night playing the slut, and when Eric got there, still dazed with sleep, the corporal and Cynthia had already pulled Mai back from his flailing fists, but that intriguing Eurasian mouth was bleeding. Half of Eric's diplomatic corps colleagues wearing an assortment of sleeping garb were out in the back, bemused at the sight of an American domestic brawl. And Pam Crane and the Bakers were there, but not McMannus nor Monique. He heard himself barking out, "What in hell's name is this about, Sergeant?" But Eric had seen it coming, seen the boorish, hostile behavior during the entire trip, heard the wife try to make overtures and then give up and seek out other company. You could make excuses for the man. The Vietnam nightmares still haunted him, but they still haunted half of the politicians and generals in Washington it seemed. And there was the imminent retirement, being pushed out of the secure Marine Corps nest at fifty. But the man should have sought help for all of his anxieties and not struck out against a person who had tried to love him for twenty years, who bore him two sons, who tried to understand his America, who suffered his abuses with silent, Asian stoicism. "I'm afraid, Sergeant, I'll have to report this to your CO in the States. And one more such outburst, and you're going back to the capital on the first grand taxi, and back State side on the first plane."

The Sergeant continued to boil red, "But you don't know, Sir. You don't know what she's been up to all night."

"Not true. All lies." Mai opened her balled fist revealing a palm of red henna tattoos, symbols to bring good fortune, to stave off illness, to ward away the night djins, to be happy in love. She explained how her French friends took her to the tent late last evening so she could sketch the women still applying the intricate patterns on their daughters for tomorrow's festival; how one Berber woman wanted to give her the good signs for no money, free because she cried out for the blessings; how it took over an hour under the gas light. The woman walked her back to the tent after one in the morning. "You were drunk asleep," she said to her husband. "Always drunk asleep."

"I thought I was dreaming," Cynthia said. "But it was real. I woke up in the middle of the night to the sound of women's voices just outside the tent. One was speaking French; it was Mai; the other mostly Berber."

Before breakfast, when the grim truce between the Donatelli's appeared to hold, Eric caught up with Jess Williams again. Neither Monique nor the Professor used their beds last night, and neither Jess nor anyone else had seen them. Edna Baker thought they were off together making out. Cynthia did not think that was likely. She had probably found her friend, Chris from the language school and was in the camping area behind the car park. Pam agreed with that assessment, saying that while the Professor may be interested in her, she doesn't reciprocate the feeling, 'thinks he's a bit of jerk, to put a fine point on it.'

THE BRIDES' FAIR

"We need to find them, turn this fair in side out. We need to find them soon. And one other thing, Corporal, only you have the keys to the van, isn't that right?"

"Not quite, Sir. The Gunny has a set too," the young man said, and walked a brisk, military pace toward the tent line and the camping area.

Chapter VIII

When he could distinguish in the first light of dawn the hanging white thread in the mosque tower as indeed white, the muezzin called the faithful to prayer. The voice, not transformed by electronic speakers as in the great mosques of the coastal cities, welled up, rasped, cracked in its fervor, and reverberated through the chambers and out the upper arches of the rectangular, Almorhad-style tower. "Allah akbar. He is Allah the one, Allah the eternally besought of all….."

The mosque, plaster-patched and white-washed yearly for the great mountain fair, possessed an artificial newness compared with the crumbling, mortared mud and stone habitation and crenellated walls of the abandoned 18th century mountain villa which abutted its nave at several junctures for support. The sole, functioning horse shoe arch served as the ceremonial entrance to the fair. It was festooned with strings of electric light, powered by a pulsating diesel generator. The lights still glowed a harsh yellow in the breaking dawn.

Most of the stockmen and herders stirred first at the muezzin's call, beat the straw and dust from their woolen capes and headed to their morning prayers. Others, mountain men who knew more about the deities of the streams, water wells, and the craggy openings in the rocks than the great religion of the east, took up their tea braziers and trudged directly to the stockades behind the tented city, behind the white mosque and the disintegrating villa. The animals were tethered in long rows or penned by type. Several hundred camels, including many young from the summer's increase, knelt on horn-padded knees. A few, anticipating the arrival of their masters, wobbled up on spindly legs and characteristically spit out great wads of brown mucous. Donkeys and mules strained on their tethers to sweep in the last scraps of their ration of lower plateau grasses. A battalion of horses included well-groomed Arabians, the heavy war horse breeds and sleek-coated colts stood well apart from those hopeless old nags the truckers would buy to cart down to the abattoirs on the lower plains.

Already in the gray, stippled light prospecting traders hefted the genitals of the timhadite and the beni guil rams. They probed the jaws and the vulvas of the ewes for signs of parasites. Still more sheep and long hair nubian goats streamed down the ridge lines and paths toward the animal souk, passing the parked vehicles in dust churning clouds, passing the odd assortment of tents and vans of the 'the Europeans' in their *camping sauvage*, passing the more orderly 'hotel' compound. And through these driven flocks came the first troops of the turbaned, horsemen mounting exceptional creatures wearing either leather harness studded with worked silver or those of tightly woven wool embroidered with gold thread and silk. As knights arriving to jousting meet, they located their stations and tents which had been prepared for them by their advance party of grooms.

Under the black, goat hair awning attached to the side of her Uncle's high board Berliet truck, Kachou blew kisses of life into her sleeping half-sister, Izza's ear. On a bed of old carpets and covered with a man's djellaba and their own hondora haiks, they had slept warmly intertwined. Nearby, her other-mother Itto and her two aunts snored in crazy harmony. Scattered about in deep sleep under layers of wool carpets and haiks, burrowed like dog puppies, were cousin Zora, also a virgin bride, and younger girl cousins from her ksar. Kachou, even with the comforting warmth of her sister's body, ached with envy for her peace, for she herself had not slept well. The night djins had made their visitations, had whispered their terrible stories, had rudely pulled her hair, pulled her back from sleep into prickly consciousness. It would only be worse, she knew waking next to old Ben Moha a few morning's hence after the blessings of the imams and the caids, after the ceremonies in the compound of his clan, after all the offerings of dates and milk. The night djins harped about the pain, about the blood from her parted thighs being waved on the nuptial sheet to the ululating women of his clan like the severed head of an enemy from the lower plains.

"I know what I must do," she spoke in the ear of her sister, who struggled to come around, who pressed sleep-dry lips against her cheek. "Don't I have the *baraka* of Sidi Aben Yassi? Wasn't he of my mother's blood? Should I not go to his marabout which is right here in this place? I will bring offerings to him and will listen for his voice there in the walls of his tomb."

"Oh, Kachou, you cannot escape your marriage," Izza whispered sleepily. She stroked Kachou's long, luminous black hair, which, unbound for the night, served to cloak her face and shoulders against the dry coolness of morning. "You will only bring *hushuma*, shame, down on Baba El Husein, Mother Itto, Aunt Rhaba, all of us."

"No, I will go to the saint of my own blood. I will find an answer in his presence. And what should I bring to the shrine? Fresh eggs of course. A wax candle? Dried sage grass? The scarce bright flowers? The women offer hair from their head and hair from their sex, but that is to make them swell with child, and I do not wish that."

"You could ask that old Fatima down in one of those tents, the one who reads hands. She would know what to bring to the marabout. But it is all wrong to try to change these things, to break a marriage contract." Even at eleven years, Izza, as all girls of the high plateau, had a grown woman's understanding of the relationships which bound their clan together for the common good. She knew as well the rhythms of planting, grazing, birth and death; the days of the cold wind, the times of scorching sun and meager rain; the times of ritual and ceremony that reinforced the codes, the familiar routines, that adhered to them fast like the henna tattoos on their hands and foreheads.

"But I must do this, must leave this place. My own mother did not wish this for me. She intended that I escape, be free as the hawk that sails down the corridors of these mountains. Ben Moha will not have me for his bed and compound. My own mother did not wish it so, you see."

"You speak so strangely, sister. How do you know what your dead mother wished? Girls, women, they do not talk like you; they don't say such awful things. I think you have the tongue of those night djins in your head now."

Kachou saw it was useless to try to explain further. She slipped on her wool bridal skirt, quickly bound her hair up with the silver pins that had belonged to her mother. She left the shelter with her guardians all mouth-agape in their raucous snoring, and her half-sister's large, black agate eyes streaming tears.

***** ***** ***** ***** ***** ***** *****

Khadija Alandalouse Bennani stepped into her Parisian designer exercise costume for her half hour morning bout on the stationary bicycle in her dressing room. She and her husband lived mostly in a private four room suite in the walled villa of the exclusive Souissi district. This was not their own residence of course, that was in Fez, and, as well, the Bennani's had the mountain chalet at Ifrane and various other beach and farm properties to which they could retreat. The large, modern villa was provided by the State as befitting one of Ministerial rank. She heard her husband, Ahmed, rummaging about in his room next door. He hadn't come to her bed last night, which was hardly unusual, but had returned in his Mercedes about one in the morning after being with his mistress, Madame Rakki. Her daughter Jamila already had the stereo in the children's wing going full blast with noisy Anglo-American music which would certainly numb all her senses by the time she turned nineteen, in one year only. In the courtyard, Rachid, her seventeen year old, began gunning his new Yamaha moto which they had been pressured relentlessly into purchasing, given that the motorcycle craze afflicted most teen age boys of their class. She was positive her sweet, beautiful Kareem, her youngest, sat behind Rachid on the black saddle as he spun the machine up and down the long drive. She prayed that their outside man, Marti, was there watching, assuring they both wore their helmets. She imagined them always careening out of control, being hurled into some massive camion or onto the hard paved drives of their otherwise secure compound. But it was impossible, even in this comparatively calm, orderly capital city to do much to control the recklessness of boys. If she tried to supervise the films they watched, they would go seek out the most depraved video cassette. If you told them what to wear, they would find rags. She should be thankful, her friends said. There were no drugs, no diseases, no simple medina girls claiming Rachid had impregnated them.

She mounted her chrome-plated machine and began her tedious pedaling. This effort had to be taken seriously when one reached the middle years. They would never say in the meeting halls, the galleries of government, nor at the swim clubs and beaches that Khadija Bennani had given up, had lost her youthful beauty, had become just another plump matron forced to wear figure-disguising caftans. Finally, she felt the pulling in her legs, and the perspiration. She had to pay for her little sins. Last evening she had to, out of *politesse*, eat several of those delicious *amuse gueules*, and two *cornes de gazelle* pastries from her hostess's abundant table. But at the meeting, she did make progress. With persistence, she managed to nominate an agenda committee for the program the government would launch, per its agreement in the United Nations, to honor the Decade on Women. And triumphantly she had steered through the election of Zoubida Belmatti as agenda chairperson, and she had cajoled the Minister of Health's wife, Fereda Boujid, who never lifted a finger except to get it lacquered, into preparing the paper on family planning. All in all a very successful three hours, and she pumped all the harder, feeling the almond, sugar and honey excesses of last evening draining from her once ballerina-taut body.

"I trust all is well with you, Khadija." Her husband appeared in her dressing room at an inopportune moment when her hair was matted with sweat and she puffed for breath, racing faster for the wind up of her ordeal. He didn't look his best either, and this didn't all derive from his preoccupations at the Ministry trying to stamp out another one of the misguided student demonstrations. He was just another fifty year old man trying to prove something in the arms of a woman twenty years his junior. Her dear friend, Anissa Benjelloun, confided in her as they were driving home from the meeting last evening, that at least Madame Rakki was not the social climbing trollop her own husband had acquired to accommodate those ridiculous masculine vanities. Such faint praise for Madame Rakki, but indeed the young widow came from some means, and her husband had been a Captain in the Royal Household Guard before that cruel mishap on the auto route.

"What should I say to you, Sidi, that all is just perfectly well?" She worked the pedals of her machine with more furious determination. "You hear Jamila there already with her stereo blasting, and Rachid and Kareem ready to do great harm to themselves on that awful motorcycle. You know that I am busy day and night preparing for the meetings in New York at the General Assembly. So, you see how well things go, Sidi."

"The Prime Minister's office called me today to say that Fatima Benchekroun would also be named to your delegation."

"Yes, I've heard that is to be. I take it your colleagues, our own cousins even, no longer trust me." She dismounted the bicycle and began stripping off her sweat suit. "Have I become so radical that you will send as my alternative a woman who doesn't even hold a *Lycée bac*?" She flung her clothing aside, and, naked before her husband stepped behind the opaque, tempered glass door of the shower.

"We have to be mindful of different points of view, you understand." Ahmed sat on the low banquette in his wife's dressing room. The second maid entered with a tray of *café filtre* and fresh croissants, delivered each morning from their favorite bakery. "You have a right to be upset, but we have to watch the balance in these matters, project the proper image to some of the conservative factions. It will work out. You will achieve your objectives at the meeting."

"Is that what you predict, Sidi?" She would feel the pressure in New York to make equivocal, empty statements, to not push for closure. Well, at least there was some victory in losing half a kilo this week. Her stomach appeared almost as flat as it did twenty-five years ago when she was the rare female student from her country at the Faculty of Law in Paris. She should remind her husband how the artists and photographers sought her out to capture her Moorish beauty; how some of the best families in Paris plied her with invitations; how she brushed aside

THE BRIDES' FAIR

the hordes of men who would have her as their prize. And in her mid-forties she could still turn more heads than 30 year old Madame Rakki.

Her husband shouted over the steamy blast of water, as hot as could be tolerated, reminding her that he would be off to that mountain fair of the young Berber fiancees at mid-morning by military helicopter and that the American Ambassador would be in his party. As she had done yesterday she told him that the ritual was barbaric, a crime against nature to marry off girls of 14 and 15. She retreated from the shower, her tan skin now blood red.

"We do not travel to these fairs to necessarily bless the local customs, but to underpin national solidarity. The state, as you well know, Madam, does not condone early marriages, forced unions or polygamy, but we can't be heavy handed about these things; we can't simply force change, wave a UN agreement at people who have been following their traditions for centuries, and expect them to change their ways at once."

She shrugged for it was little use to reason with him. How could he go on so early in the morning with his booming, official voice that did not fit that small, boyish body? What could Madame Rakki possibly see in him? Prestige? The continued alliance with power? He certainly had few skills as a lover; a few squirming minutes at best, the way of many husbands she gathered from the candid admissions of her friends. "I understand there will be several thousand spectators, half the diplomats of the city, and you thought my going with you might take some edge off my image, might soften the criticism of me?" Khadija wrapped herself in a soft, terry cloth robe and proceeded to sit with her husband at the worked brass platter on which the maid had set the coffee and croissants. "I will not further insult those mountain girls by my presence, nor should you nor the American Ambassador." She was still her nation's Ambassador to the UN for Women's Rights and how out of place she would be under the hot, ceremonial tents picking at the mountains of country food, squeezed in between the caids, the imams, the whole local lot, having to applaud the communal wedding ceremony. "Have you asked Jamila?"

"I thought you had already asked her."

"No, Sidi, I left that pleasure for you."

He went to the children's wing with that painful expression of his, like when they had to make the monthly visit to his mother-in-law, or when it was his task to fire a servant. No, Jamila should go, be the female representative of the Bennani's, and the obligations of the family would be served. His daughter carried no symbols, none of the political trappings of her mother and father, and could be herself and her own judge of the Brides' Fair. Besides, this would be a rare opportunity for the father and daughter to be together. Khadija would be off to university in America next year, and mostly lost to them both forever.

"Mother, did Baba tell you? He wants me to go with him to some ceremony in the mountains this morning." Jamila padded into her parent's apartment in bare feet, wearing too tight jeans and a sloganed T shirt also stretched to bursting. "Talk to him, please. I just can't go," the girl pleaded. "There's cousin Latifa's birthday party at their beach house this afternoon."

"But you can do both," Khadija tried her best to be upbeat. "Your father should be back by late afternoon. And it will be very interesting for you. You'll have something to tell your friends. I'm certain none of them have ever attended a mountain fair; few of them know that such things exist in their own country." Her daughter sat with her mother on the dressing bench, pouting, sure that it would not work out. The beach party, the last of the season, was important to her. Khadija gathered that Colonel Ahmed Alaoui's son, the latest boy friend, would be there. He had just started his first year in the medical faculty, and how Jamila's scientific vocabulary had improved. "You can wear that blue velvet caftan. It is appropriately dignified, and you can bring along your beach clothes so the chauffeur can run you out to Sable d'Or directly from the air station."

Her daughter, now fancying herself in the mirror and fluffing up her long eye lashes, would go with her father. It was inconceivable that she would deny his request. Over and above duty and respect it appeared to be an important occasion; a ride in one of those big helicopters with Ambassadors and other dignitaries. Jamila would be in the very center of things. Since it was the weekend, Latifa's beach party would go on until late evening Mother and daughter were a striking pair in the dressing mirror. She would command a portrait of the two of them, from Joudia Slimani, her artist friend. She knew how to capture the North African light, the depth of character, the subtleties of mood, the interweave of blood, of Spanish Moor, Berber, Semite. Joudia had none of the biting didacticism of some modern painters today, for she herself was forged in the Granada palaces, the Fez medinas, the labyrinthine Jewish quarters. They must do the painting soon, within the year, before she could no longer fight back the thickening of her body, before Jamila went off to America. They would hang the portrait in the gallery of their main residence, among all the bearded male ancestors. Khadija and Jamila would be there for all times. The door of her husband's Mercedes slammed shut. Her son Rachid gunned his Yamaha as if preparing to provide escort. She found herself shaking, and clenched her fists for control.

"Mother, what is it?" Jamila ceased her narcissistic primping.

She could not explain to her daughter, could not exhibit her rage. That there was some talk of her husband's affair with Madame Rakki was one matter. They like the French could accommodate mistresses; they did not agonize over it like the British and the Americans. No, it was not her husband love of another woman that caused the fury in her to well up so. It was that she was no longer trusted; that the authorities had nominated that semi-literate woman to accompany her to the New York meetings, to serve as a counterfoil to her anticipated extremes, to maintain the status quo. That was the cruelest insult and from those cousins of her own blood who sat in the offices of state.

"Mother, why are you crying so?"

"It is nothing, my daughter. It is only your beauty and my joy for you. Your father will be so proud to have you with him today. But remember who you are, and make it known to everyone that you don't approve of girls marrying so very young, too young to know their own dreams."

"Yes, mother, but I will throw a fit if Baba doesn't get me back to the beach party on time. I will be absolutely devastated if that happens."

***** ***** ***** ***** ***** ***** *****

Stu Connors on the radio in the van sounded too cheery for seven in the morning. "I'm out of my funk, Old Boy. Changing my destructive ways—read giving up the gin; even thinking of falling in love. I'll tell you all about it, when you get back to beautiful downtown Rabat, where he's still sitting on a fence of broken glass." Ambassador Crane still hadn't made up his mind about going to the fair, driving everyone in the front office mad undoubtedly. There was not much news of a definitive nature to report, except random gun fire being heard late last evening in the business district of 'Ricks Place,' or Dar Bida, otherwise Casablanca. And, oh yes, some poor young soul hung about trying to crash the party last night, but the bouncers at the door persuaded him to get lost. Someone casing the Embassy, probably. Did they drag him into the vermin-infested dungeon for a brow or butt beating? Or did they just tell him to 'hop it' as the Brits would say? Eric wouldn't mention that neither Dr. McMannus nor Monique Addleman had been seen since dinner last evening. Even Stu Connors couldn't keep that confidential. Between the secretaries and the communications clerks it would out in the tight American community; hot romance between professor and teacher. Jess Williams thought they must be somewhere in the camping area. "There was a lot of action last night. Some folks really into partying. They're probably sleeping it off."

Just as they started off on their search, a tall, large frame man approached them. Late 20's and very American looking, his usually broad, welcoming features now were wrapped with concern.

"What's up Chris? It's Monique, isn't it?" He recalled how Chris had paced before his desk at the Embassy, pleading for a demarche on the new school director, pleading for someone with clout to stand up for Monique.

"She's shaken up about something, but not really hurt or anything," Chris Reily said. "She asked for you though; wants you to come as soon as you can."

Monique seemed to be perpetually shaken up about something. Stu Connors had just told him he had nothing new on the teacher, other than she was clean as the last security report on her concluded. As for McMannus, the CIA Station Chief, Bob Steiner, stuck to his guns, saying the Professor wasn't one of theirs, but added there just might be several guys in North Africa, working for some special branch under deep cover. "You can't open up this can too far. The worms can be real snakes, you know. Steiner seemed more exercised about the Ambassador's visit to the Fair. "How tight is security up there? Does Dalton say?"

Chris had one of those fancy six man tents employing collapsible aluminum poles, the kind of tent that rolled up tight into an impossibly small package a child could carry. Having led Eric to the tent with little further comment, he went off quickly through the maze of other tents and camping gear, saying only that he had to find the kids who had come with him. "They're off buying tourist trinkets or trying to find some far out pot, I suppose."

Through the door flaps and netted window openings, slits of sunlight flashed on and off in the shadows. She lay face up on the bunk, her hands folded below her breasts. The caftan which she had purchased at the lower valley fair was dirty and torn at the neck line, but otherwise encased her long, slight body. She was as still as a corpse on some medieval bier imagined by a Rosetti painting. She lacked only a bouquet of flowers or a garland in her auburn hair which was flared out about her head. Was she playing the victim again? These histrionics of hers, these grand gestures were becoming tiresome.

She elbowed herself up. "I've been such a nuisance, I know. I probably called you away from your breakfast, but I needed to talk to you right away." She could see that the oh-so-correct man looked as if he had it with her. They all seemed put off by her, thought she was some freak, some soulless spore that would infect them with a deadly disease. But he had stood up for her with her nervous, up tight director, who Fiona her British teacher friend called "that wee man." And he had done his best to comfort her after that business in the forest. But now he really seemed annoyed. Even her best friend, Chris, didn't know what to do or say when she stumbled into the tent at some ungodly hour this morning ashamed and angry. She thought they had a special bond after that pot-drunk night. He used to give her good long hugs when she was down, fed up with work, with the sameness of life, but lately he seemed more distant, which was just as well she supposed. They were teaching colleagues after all, and it was best not to be too close.

She wanted to confide in Mr. Dalton and say 'I treasure the calendar my father sent me in his 'care package. I look at it every morning, first thing. It has beautiful shots of the Rockies, the Kansas wheat fields, the Maine coast line. My father sent it to me to make me homesick, to tell me I should give up playing the exile, that the world had become too dangerous. 'But Max, Baby, your daughter is safer here among these shifty, jihad-crazed Arabs than she is on the streets of LA, or New York.' I tick off the days. I've been here three months shy of three years and in Africa for seven. Can you believe it? In a year I'll be thirty and supposedly grown up, worldly wise and all that stuff."

But she couldn't indulge herself with him like this. She had to tell him straight out. "I saw those same eyes, blurred in the shadows, and heard the same crunching of someone near, looking at me. It wasn't an animal, back there in the woods either. It was some weirdo, you know, who else would watch a woman squat down to pee? Or someone looking out for me, wanting to help me. "Was it the Corporal trying to help me? Was it you?" How could she best explain it without making herself more foolish, more of a kook? And someone was watching them when they were on the ridge far above the great field when the sputtering propane lights, the glow of the braziers below them seemed to mirror the profusion of stars. The field rippled like the sea. The many tents were the bumps and peaks of the waves and the reflected stars rode them up and down. But there was no soothing, no serenity. Rachid insisted on trying to make out right in the open, his hand on fire under her caftan which he had unpinned, the fibula in his hand, and pulled down about her cold, bare shoulders. She could really shock this Mr. Dalton who already thought she was from outer space. She had guys she hardly knew on beaches in Malibu, and sure, in cars like everyone else. That was teen age stuff though. This was about being grown up, about ending a real relationship. She had been taken in by his smooth intensity and had been hurt, been just his American conquest, his American slut. She just knew his family had some Maghrebi princess all picked out and waiting for him as soon as he screwed his quota of dumb, fawning women. She said as firmly as possible over and over that he should stop, but Rachid kept trying to get her going, swearing that he needed her, that he wanted her help at the Fair. But this time she wasn't going to be pulled under by this guy and she yanked his hands away from probing her body and said she would scream bloody murder if he didn't let her go right then and there. She felt so cold, uncomfortable, the hundreds of lights below just a dizzy swirl. There was a noise behind them. Stones slid and grated as a shoe stumbled down hard. A man had been watching them, listening nearby behind an outcropping of rock.

"You know that man we picked up, the one traveling with the French family whose car ran off the road?" she said, forcing herself to be calm, to tell Mr. Dalton only that which was pertinent.

"Yes, the film technician. Very polite. What is his name? Ali Kadiri, isn't it?"

"He's no film technician, and his real name is Rachid Lahloui. He was getting a law degree, but dropped out of the University last year. He was also in one of my English classes at the language school. We became good friends, lovers. He would go away for weeks at a time, looking after family business he said; almonds, and citrus down in the southwest, in the Souss and the Maas, but that was just lies, I'm sure, like most of what he told me about himself. He found me after the folk dancing had finished and insisted we talk, that he needed my help. It was over between us, really over, but he insisted. He was making such a scene that I went with him."

"And the person you heard or saw watching you, what happened to him?"

"I don't know. I really don't. Rachid went scrambling down the rocks after him and they both ran off into the night." She did not break down as she had in the forest yesterday. There were no tears, and she felt relieved that she had done what she had to. Should she feel guilty that she had betrayed Rachid, or congratulate herself? He was obviously up to something, pretending he was somebody he wasn't, pleading for her help, trying to get her all fuzzy with his kisses on her neck and his long fingers massaging her breasts. She once so ached with love for him. He once embodied all she felt about this country and its dark eyed, beautiful people. "I told Chris about Rachid being here and what he tried to pull. They knew each other from the school, and Chris said he would go and try to find him, try to talk some sense into him."

She agreed to go with Mr. Dalton to change, to shower, to cleanse away the feel of him still on her. She draped Chris's rain cape over her dirty caftan, and he gave her one of those huge, all-encompassing hugs she so needed. She wanted to tell him more, but that had to wait, for the usually patient, unflappable Mr. Dalton was suddenly in a hurry.

****

THE BRIDES' FAIR

Maleka did not hear him leave. They had lain together all evening in the private place the merchant had made for them behind the stacks of rolled carpets. The voices of the first customers of the morning woke her. Outside under the awning, the merchant's helpers prepared the tea service and another long session of bargaining would begin with the usual theatrics of the seller and the long unflinching silence of savvy buyers. The merchant's women in the adjoining tent would soon come for her. She would be dressed in the costume of the local people and designs in henna would be sketched on her face and hands. Such irony. Neither she nor her mother, both raised in the big coastal city, had ever covered themselves with the marks of old ritual and superstition. Ironic too that the dress of a Berber bride would come after not before the nuptial night.

Her shoulder wound now acted up again, but it had been set off by the night's love making. The pills the nurse had given her at the UN camp would help ease the pain. She had to be strong and do her part as sworn. The night had changed much but resolved little. Hidden out together so with no sign of Rachid or Ali, it was inevitable even though they had promised each other over and over during their two year friendship to abstain; and even after all the solemn pledges they had made in training about celibacy and duty. The noises of the night had cloaked them as had the carpets piled up around them; as had the music of drum, fife and ouad; the snorting and huffing of a thousand animals; the cries of infants, and the snoring and muffled voices from the hundreds of tents. Their desperation had weakened their will. He held her desperately tight, so consumed with guilt for the man he had killed, fearing a terrible outcome with more senseless death, wavering between standing resolute and wanting to escape in the night while they had the chance. They must finish what they had started, she had said firmly to him. There could be no running away.

He had become weak and thus she had not expected to feel any pleasure. Now in the morning after so little sleep, she recalled it all too vividly, and with the breaking of promises became confused. The tent roof above her billowed black like the March clouds bringing sooty, cold rain to Paris where she had studied Science Pol for a year. There the seasons changed with drama and applause. Here in the North African *bled* all remained dusty brown with occasional patches of dark green forest. Not three hours away by jet plane, she heard the thunder of the dark rains. She could see faces from the window of her room in the student *pension* and through the streaking glass of the *bibliotech*. She saw her professors, her few friends, the cold, bleached faces on the Metro. Then, suddenly the bright sun light of Casablanca startled her, and there was her father in the apartment where she had been raised. His proud mustache, that of a *petit officier* in the Custom's Service, hid his scowl. His words stung like the winter sleet of Paris.

"There is no more forgiveness here, no more trust and compassion. You have brought *hushuma* to my house, much shame. And, as well, you have endangered me your two brothers and sister. Oh, but I do know it all. I am not a perfect man. I do occasionally profit by speeding up the bureaucratic formalities. But this helpfulness has kept you in decent clothes, has paid your school fees. It has indeed kept you too long at those godless universities. I know you are seen about the city with other ungrateful children of humble families. I know you help them manufacture frightful words on pamphlets, words that can only bring our ruin. I am not blind and foolish. I can se the infection in this house, how your brother, Achmed, worships your words and devours your pamphlets. I once had a fool's trust in my eldest daughter. They said you did so well with books and ideas. They all said it would be I who would regret not letting you go to university. I once accepted that the old ways must change, that life should not remain forever the same. But look what has come of that. I have now returned to the old verities. Nonsense fills the heads of women. They can not see the practical. Their nature catches them up in unstable emotions."

"It is the quality of the knots," the merchant said from outside the tent where he showed his wares. "Four hundred to the square. And the dyes, they are from the plants and herbs found in the lower valleys, and are not made from chemicals. They are particular to one *duoar*, to one extended family. These are their unique symbols, their interpretation of life's mysteries. Not only will I guarantee that this carpet will return five times the very modest price you pay, but I aver that these symbols in the weave will forever protect your household from misfortune."

Through the night their bodies had intertwined like eels, and he had cried real tears. He had taken her to her first meeting of the MPLM in the secret cell at the university in Casablanca. There she heard all the impassioned talk of those who would achieve a redistribution of wealth. Most students shunned even the more open debates critical of the regime and the status quo. They went sheep-like to the lecture halls and filled their *cahiers* with neat, word-for-word transcriptions. But Maleka had four years of filling notebooks in Casa and in Paris. She had all those restless hours in lectures listening to the sonorous *eminences grises*, and lonely nights in libraries not feeling it right to go out to café hangouts with the more daring students. Moustapha, an advanced degree candidate in economics, found her staring off in the great, dank reading room, numbed by the dryness of her text.

THE BRIDES' FAIR

"You think you are preparing for life sitting here among all this rotting, ancient paper, reading the convoluted nonsense of bloodless intellectuals? Are you afraid of me?" He had the way of one raised in a big villa with servants where he had everything he wanted. He was somewhat cocky, but handsome, and said she had a hauntingly beautiful quality. Only her mother had ever described her so, for she had never dared to keep company with a man.

"You let that Moustapha turn you around with all his talk of revolution?" It was Sabah up in the shifting folds of the tent. She had known her since the *lycée* and she had begged her to come for a coffee in one of those noisy student cafes on the edge of campus. "*Soit prudente, ma belle Maleka,*" Sabah cautioned. She dressed not in the standard jeans or caftan, but in inexpensive knock-offs of the latest from Paris. "I know men like that. He's rich and full of himself, and he goes around the university preying on naïve girls like you, talking about revolution and power to the people. In ten years he'll grow up and become a banker and wont have anything to do with a petty official's daughter and certainly nothing more to do with the poor and downtrodden. So put your hands over your ears Maleka. You can't handle him, and you don't understand what he's talking about."

But Maleka did understand. She and Moustapha had a real purpose to their lives unlike Sabah who thought mostly of clothes, going to Europe to work and marrying someone above her class who could give her the easy life. She had comforted him all during the night, told him what they must do and assured him that they would succeed. She got to her feet. The medicine began working and she felt the strength flow through her.

"You want 2,000 for this? Why that's outright robbery. I could get this same carpet back in the city for a third of the price. If you want to be serious….."

"No, do not walk away. For those of you who are not tourists but diplomats who live and work in my country, I will practically give away this fine carpet, practically give you a *cadeaux.*"

They had gone over it again and again last evening as they dined with the merchant on lamb tajine, couscous and almond pastries. The Instructor had joined them, slipping quietly into the tent through the shadows made by the brazier and the butane lamp. He had to now be with them since he claimed he knew the weapon Ali had been trained to use. Ali, they were certain, had been captured or had abandoned the mission to save himself. And what of Rachid, the boastful and swaggering? Had his over-confidence led him right into the arms of the authorities? His luck was such, however, that he might just appear at the last critical moment.

It had been agreed that the merchant would deliver the weapons which were rolled up in his carpets. He would bring them by donkey before dawn when a number of the stockmen would be about tending to their animals. Everyone knew their part. They would escape in all the confusion. 'Avoid bringing harm to the innocent.' 'Keep casualties to a minimum.' 'Escape as planned.' 'No martyrs, no suicidal strikes.'

The Instructor had been precise, and if Moustapha believed his leadership of the mission had been usurped, he did not show it. "There is something about him I don't trust,' she had said to Moustapha as they lay together during the night.

"We should be ever thankful that he has come to us, for we desperately need his help."

She heard the women in the neighboring tent getting things ready for her. There had to be a bath, a bath of purification, before the henna tattoos were applied and she was dressed as a bride. She did not believe the disguise would help. They had seen through all the others and were now everywhere searching for them. The probability of her escaping from this madness seemed so remote, but she would do her part. She repeated the instructions to herself in the words of their new collaborator. She saw herself moving about the fair grounds like a stiff, inhuman robot. Had she become as her father warned only a puppet, a mindless monster let loose in the world? She had never once seen the witch Aiycha Kandisha, her gold teeth flashing, her snarled tangled hair tipped with fire. She of the city did not know the secrets of women of the rural *bled* who glimpsed the witch by the wells and in the mountain shadows. They said that the wind could carry her spores from these places right into the great port city. They could penetrate the concrete, the glass and the steel doors. They could confuse the brain and make women do stupid things, and so, perhaps, she had been infected. But that was such nonsense for one who had passed all her baccalaureate examinations, had her diploma from the university, had studied a year in Paris itself. She had come to the MPLM, to the training camp, to this fair soberly and with open eyes. She could not blame Moustapha, the Instructor, nor the witch who plagued foolish women.

"It is you who have brought me good fortune already today. I have sold several of my carpets at good prices, and the day is just beginning." The merchant with his trim, pointed beard and his richly embroidered djellaba offered her a breakfast of bread, cheese and strong tea. "I have added a special herb to it for my daughter. This will restore you more quickly than the foreign medicine."

She drank the tea. The sugar could not mask the bitterness of the herbs.

"They will soon gather on the great field. They will wait long for the dignitaries, the important people who rule our lives at their whim and fancy and take our money so they can live in splendor," the merchant said adding that he had done his part before dawn, before the call to prayer.

"And I must do mine," she said. "And accept the consequences, as well."

***** ***** ***** ***** ***** ***** *****

Captain Cherkaoui, the Chief of Security for the Fair, and Army Lieutenant Berrada, who had arrived moments ago with his corporal and driver, listened intently to the foreign diplomat. Cherkaoui stroked his imposing bush of a mustache and his smooth chin, both of which had been neatly barbered earlier this morning by a man in his unit so skilled in these matters that he accompanied him on all his missions. The Captain wanted to believe that the American was being an alarmist, that somehow the nuances did not come through in his use of French, that this was only some matter of the heart, a love triangle. Two men fighting over a woman. The young had such hot tempers. He would never fight over a mere woman, no matter how attractive. Two men fought over this woman and now are ashamed to show their faces and are brooding somewhere in the encampment.

Lieutenant Berrada, however, questioned the American extensively about the film technician. "We assumed he was an acquaintance of Pierre Deschamps and had been riding with him from Rabat," Eric said. "Along the way we were cautioned about picking up people on the road, hitch hikers, but he seemed very much a member of the French group."

Captain Cehrkaoui sent out one of his men to verify that the Tourist Board had made a promotional film of the Fair last year, and had employed no film crew whatsoever this year. Outside the French Embassy tent, the yawning, hung over and somewhat bewildered host of last evening's aperitif explained, "He seemed such a decent type, seemed to know all my contacts at the Ministry of Culture and Tourism. It was in Azrou at the petrol station. He said his car had broken down and he needed to get to the Fair. We had room in my old Peugeot."

Deschamps wistfully recalled his wrecked car and imagined it being stripped for parts by the human vultures near the very crest of the mountain pass.

"And you have a member of your traveling party, this technical advisor who is also missing," the Lieutenant asked. He had the controlled, inscrutable demeanor of someone who commanded men and firmly kept himself and those subordinates focused on the objectives of his mission. "There is some connection between them, perhaps; perhaps it is only the woman, as the Captain wishes to believe." Although he had had only two hours sleep, he remained charged with energy, certain that his success so far in preventing a serious mishap on the bridge near the old French watch tower and in intercepting one of the band of assassins would continue. He would bring honor on his father's house, and move quickly up the promotion ladder to colonel. The Chief of Security, however, being preoccupied with the protocol aspects of the ceremony, and by the comfort of the important dignitaries, hesitated to believe the worst of it. He reached for simple solutions. The supposed film technician had employed ruses and disguises only to approach this flamboyant American woman. Being spurned by her he had retreated back to the city in one of the grand taxis.

The American diplomat was unaware of the incident yesterday afternoon, when the Lieutenant had raced from the old French watch tower to the bridge over the last ravine to the high plateau. He had possibly-and it was still only a possibility until all the facts were known-prevented an assassin in a Renault sedan from ramming the U.S. Embassy van and sending it plunging 100 meters down into the mouth of the abyss. He did not embellish his role in the matter, but the American recalled being waved across the bridge by two of the military and being told that all was in order and they could proceed in all safety up the road to the fair. "We must be direct with one another," the Lieutenant said. "It is very possible that the missing American of yours suspected this Rachid and knew of his affair with the teacher. It is also possible that the one in the Renault who seemed on track run you off the bridge, also knew of your missing American's suspicions and knew that he journeyed with you. If he had succeeded, he would have given the others in his band more freedom to carry out their mission. Is that not a plausible assumption?"

"Up to a point," Eric replied after a long pause. Somewhat shaken, he replayed the scene on the bridge over in his mind. If the Lieutenant had not been so alert and intervened as he had, he and all of his companions would not probably be alive. The car would have pushed them over the edge, or was it wired to explode on impact? They would be flung over the low guard rail, would be careening about in that metal box for an eternity, would be screaming or expelling nothing but fear-constricted air. Would they have felt the finality, the pain as the van crashed onto the rocks and their bloody remains spewed out in one short burst?

Eric recovered for the Lieutenant grew impatient to get on with his program. He told the man that he didn't quite see the connection between the one who crashed off the span to McMannus and Rachid or whoever he was. The latter two seem more clever and determined rather than obsessed with wasting life without having fulfilled their goal. Although he had few of the facts, he believed the two matters were coincidental at best and that the would-be martyr on the bridge, had, in all probability acted independently.

"He is of you CIA then?" the Lieutenant asked.

"He's a Technical Advisor, a Professor of Horticulture," Eric responded.

"Don't these spies of yours always pose as missionaries, archaeologists, technical advisors?" the Lieutenant asked rhetorically. " But first things first. We have to find this Rachid, now, as soon as possible He is very possibly one of the three remaining assassins, and we know from interrogating the one we recently captured down on the south road, that they had a plan to cause serious trouble at this fair. The American agent is of less importance to us."

"But one may lead us to the other," Eric offered.

"Possibly," the Lieutenant said

"But you, the French man, the American woman can identify him," the Captain said. "Doesn't she know him best of all, his particular walk, his profile? But she may be reluctant to help us, since I gather from you, M'sieu Dalton, that she was more than a casual acquaintance."

"She's prepared to help, we all are, and I agree; finding Rachid should be the first priority."

The Lieutenant thought it just too coincidental. An American nurse at the big refugee camp near Zagora had treated one of the assassins for gunshot wounds. Another, a so-called American professor, appears to have had a run in with this Rachid. The driver of the old Renault had intended to ram the American van killing its occupants. The Americans seemed to be at every juncture meddling in the internal affairs of his country, making matters worse than they really were. Being suspicious of the intent of all foreigners, he knew he should take anything the American diplomat told him with a grain of salt.

***** ***** ***** ***** ***** ***** *****

Kachou would not parade with her kin on the central ground this morning. Dressed in her fête costume, the only clothes she had brought with her from the ksar, she found herself pulled to the outer edge of the great field towards the periphery of tents near where the mosque and the marabout shrine stood. The 'Europeans', *les blancs*, with their cameras cried after her for she was the only bride out and about at this hour. Some of the ignorant and old, like Granny Melouda thought those dark lenses a pot boil of sheep's eyes, evil eyes to snatch your spirit and take it off to some foreign place, or transform you into something you were not. Kachou knew better. The glass eyes of those devices held no real magic. They could not violate you. She tried to explain that to Granny Melouda and showed her the photos that her cousin, Abdou, who worked in France had taken of them, but it was no use; some in these mountains would cling to these old beliefs, even with the proof there before them.

Even though she herself knew these things, knew numbers and word, saw the images of the world on the battery powered television box, a present from her cousin, Abdou, she was still pulled to the tent of the old, half *Afarika* woman. She sat in the dark without candle or gas lamp among the strange smells of her herbs and potions. Kachou answered only one or two of her simple questions, and the old woman startled her saying, "Your mother has been dead a long time. She is not here to see her daughter's marriage this day. She died some 14 or 15 springs ago birthing you." She stared at her with empty, yellow, fly damaged eyes. The herbs and scents set out in disarray on a flimsy wooden chest intoxicated her.

Kachou had heard about these seers from her step mother and aunts who went to them for advice about the marriage bed, bad blood between the ksars, the rivalry between wives. This date-brown old priestess wandered all the souks of the high plateau and neighboring valleys, peddling her wisdom and medicines for a few coins, picking up at the same time from her patients their deepest thoughts as well as detailed gossip to assist her in her next consultations. But Kachou had little in the way of grown women's tales for her, insisting only that she was not destined to marry Ben Moha, to whom she had been promised in her infancy. The woman pressed a stiff, arthritic brown finger to Kachou's forehead, on her very tattoos and then to the spot above her ear which ached so in the cold winds.

The woman quickly drew back her finger as if it had been singed by a candle. "Yes, you are of the marabout through your dead mother's blood. You are of this saint, Ben Yassi, who led his clan here through the passes when the cedar and oak grew higher up the ridges than they now do; when there were the long horned sheep and the black mane lion in abundance. Why do you who have such strong power, such *baraka* come to me? There is little I can do for a force that scalds my fingers and sets me trembling."

Was it only a clever act for Kachou could feel no such power and repeated her complaint about her marriage contract to Ben Moha.

"But the sugar has been offered and accepted. The dates and milk drunk and the two households agreed. I do more than a meager business with the brides of this tribe. You are not the only one." She pulled aside the tent flap. There were four bead-fidgeting girls squatting in the shadow of the tent waiting their turn with the seer. "And if I told you, Kachou, the obvious, that you are bound by honor to the marriage contract, that you must not shame your father's house; and if I gave you potions to control Ben Moha's brutishness, to make you less fearful of him straddling you, that would not be enough, am I correct? You are not like the others who wait. You believe you are special. And I believe that as well." The old woman reached into the folds of several caftans she had layered over her ample body and produced a large brown seed pod of the type no longer seen in these mountains. It was strung with a leather thong like an amulet. "You take this daughter, it may help your in you journey from this place. I do not want your coins. Just go."

The white, domed shrine stood near the crenellated wall of the old abandoned villa. Its plaster had been patched and repatched year after year for the Fair, and, with its new coat of paint, it remained, at a respectful distance from the marred surface, a solid, immutable relic connecting the people of plateau with the glories of their past. Even yesterday, after the brides' march, she never felt free to come close to the marabout, her cousins pulling at her, her Other Mother, Itto, calling her back, afraid of the hold of the shrine on her step-daughter. But now she was alone and free to fall on her knees on the white steps, finding only the barest space between the many offerings of sugar, dates, pubic hair, almond cakes, even a bracelet of silver from some desperate girl. As intently as she prayed, her eyes squeezed tight, her hands balled into fists, she neither heard nor felt anything. To hear his voice at last, she must offer something as well. The amulet of the brown seer? That didn't seem right. It was of the old woman, and intended to give Kachou herself protection. There were a few precious sprays of flowers about the steps and up against the sealed door. She knew where to find such flowers, and, with the photo of herself which rested wrapped in plastic, down among the coins and private things in her wool pouch, it would make a beautiful offering, one that would speak to her kinship with the marabout.

Nearby behind the wall and in the courtyard of the old villa she saw familiar flowers. They were blue and gold and grew among the tall weeds and grasses.

They were the last such gifts of nature before the onset of the cold and howling nights.Stepping over the stones and rubble, through a half fallen archway, she felt like a thief, an intruder and believed she would be so-hailed by the occupants of this place. There was no one, no herders out on the west trail, no foreigners poking about the ruins with their cameras. In the tall grasses which almost choked her precious stand of flowers, there was a metallic glint of something. Bending down to pick up the dirty thing, stained with a muddy red substance, she recognized it as a fibula, an elaborate, large pin which joined the folds of a woman's garment around the upper torso. Cleaned, polished, its white opals gleaming, it too could be an offering, and she believed it had been so destined, until saw stretching out for it deep in the grass a large hand, a man's hand reaching out for the pin but very still.

***** ***** ***** ***** ***** ***** *****

As Uncle Eric and her mother suspected, Karen Dennis had not skipped breakfast to go off to the bazaars which had opened early that morning. Karen, born in Manila and dragged by her always curious mother through the shops and markets all over the world, was no longer charmed by fine embroidery, worked brass and silver, and carpets, always mountains of carpets. Horses held far more fascination for her than even the tattooed and gussied up brides, girls mostly younger than she, who would soon assemble for their last parade as available unmarrieds. In the early morning she was a lone spectator watching the riders from the various regional teams competing in the fantasia, exercising their mounts, examining hooves for loose shoes and pebbles, verifying the fastness of harness and rivets. She at first wandered freely, no one paying her much attention. She patted the muzzles of the exquisite Arabian pure breeds, brought up to the Fair for show not competition. She stroked the powerful flanks of the war and draft horses, mixtures of Belgian and Shire.

Some believed her love of horses a female thing, different from that of men who still romanticized about barbaric 19th Century cavalry charges; of hunters looking ridiculous in their bright red jackets going after some unfortunate poor fox or hare; of the whipped up bolting of two year old fillies from the starting gates; of the violent clash of mallets and flanks on polo fields. All of this had to do either with killing or winning or both, and the Berber horsemen would bring all this together on the great field this afternoon after the last ceremony of the brides, the marriage ceremony.

By 14 she had mastered all the equestrian drills, had won a mantle full of ribbons on her horse, her grandparents' present, Bright Star. To her the horse was beauty itself, and the sport the fusion of human and animal in a gentle, non-violent act of skill and common trust. In their weird way, some guys would tell you that the joining of woman to horse was all about sex. Wasn't everything in their way of thinking? Thighs gripping muscular flanks, fleshy ladies being carried off by snorting bulls, by gigantic swans, by leering centaurs. It was all a bit much. Dressage was just skill, control, a bond of trust between you and the animal, and just plain, sweaty work, like any tough sport. You got knocked about in lacrosse, and kicked in the wrong places in soccer, all the hurts and sensations of playing hard.

She had as her breakfast a sinfully hot oil fried beignet, from a vendor's stall. Although she didn't have to worry about her weight like some girls, she was except for holidays, birthdays and events like the Fair, usually the health nut. It was always juice and dry whole wheat toast in the morning, if she ate anything at all, tearing out the house for eight o'clock classes. At this very moment in the restaurant tent, at the table the waiters called *Sifara Amerika*, she could see Cynthia, Uncle Eric and the rest indulging on *café filtre*, butter-loaded croissants, honey and jam, and missing her, but knowing she could take care of herself almost anywhere in the world.

A troupe from an apparently prosperous clan assembled to feed, water and exercise their horses. Unlike the rough, work clothes of other teams, they wore sporty, new running suits ordered up from the city for the occasion. Grooms and riders began strapping on bridles and harness. Some were of embroidered wool and silk in vivid geometric patterns like the tattoos of the young brides. Some were leather embossed with intricate designs of silver. Many of those who fielded such teams counted all of their accumulated wealth, except for their sheep and the jewelry of their wives, in these horses and harnesses.

She learned from one of the grooms who spoke a primitive, sing-song French, that the competition would take place in the early afternoon whenever the authorities so determined. At any rate it would be before the communal marriage and final grand parade of the brides. Throughout the morning riders would keep their impatient, high-strung animals at the ready, on the edge by galloping them up and down the small field where they had assembled or up and down the less rocky and more traveled mountain trails.

She stroked the muzzle of a magnificent Arabian, talking to it the way one does to reassure, to forge a bond. A man, obviously the horse's master came up to her. In his early twenties, he had no weather-etched face, no tobacco and sugar stained teeth like most of the others. In fact he had the soft handsomeness of a man of the city. Some of the girls in the private, French-style *lycée* she attended might describe him, with his small, sharply planed nose, his luxurious wavy black hair, his deep set black eyes as a real throb. "You know about horses, I can tell Mademoiselle, by the your touch and how he reacts to you," he said in educated French.

He put it on thick, and she supposed she should get used to guys trying to hustle her; that was part of being a woman, being almost 18. Last night at the funky dancing in the camping area, one guy, a guy from her *lycée*, Jean Claude, really surprised the hell out of her by inviting her to spend the night in his brand new, American sleeping bag, thinking, she supposed,because it was American and new she'd say yes. "Yes, I used to ride, do drills and dressage." Only last month she had swept the photos and the ribbons from the walls and bookcases of her room and packed them away in a box. They had become childish things. Good-bye Bright Star, her roan five gaiter, languishing in a Virginia boarding stable. Good-bye stupid looking child, cheeks all jowly with baby fat, her riding casque shadowing the determination. Images from three years ago, an eternity it seemed.

He asked the usual things, where she was from, whether she was enjoying the Fair, who she came with. Not properly washed, with her denim skirt still dusty from yesterday's awfully long drive she must have seemed the grungy back packer on the road to Marrakech. She didn't explain about being with the American Embassy; that often put people off. With her French and blondness, people took her for European, Swiss or Alsatian. It provided a certain mystery for guys like him. Perfectly charming, he went on about the Fantasia. Her mother Cynthia should be here, but she knew most of it already, how chieftains in these mountains used the sport to form unruly tribal horsemen into disciplined fighting units; how the contest may have had its origins in the medieval jousting matches brought back by the first wave of Spanish moors sometime in the 8th Century. He went on about the horsemen of Afghanistan, and polo among the Manipur of India. He studied her closely as they talked, not in that sneaky way of some guys, but admiringly as if he were sizing up a fine thoroughbred. She bet he would tell her how attractive she was, and she hated it when guys did that. The outer skin and bones were about the genes you were born with, but what was inside really mattered, and that,he, no one could really see.

"So, you must be here with the *Corps Diplomatique*. Your father is of course the Ambassador from, let me guess...."

THE BRIDES' FAIR

"I have no father. He died when I was young." She'd been saying this all her life, and it had ceased to tug at her throat. "My mother is a consular officer."

"But you must ride, then, you must ride the horse you have befriended."

"I can't take your horse." It was never accept gifts from strangers, there's no free lunch. The guy would certainly expect something in return, but it wasn't like he was going to phone her for a date, was he? And if that was it, she'd be cool, but then she probably wouldn't hang up on him. She could see he was far more interesting than those awkward boys she always got stuck with?

"Mademoiselle, don't worry so. I am Mohamed ben Tassen, and we are well known here to all the people, to all the authorities, and I myself have been to Europe for my studies, and I know what you must be thinking. But do not worry yourself so. I am not about to abduct you and imprison you in my harem. I am a modern person and have no harem of course," he laughed at his silly joke. "And besides the horse is not for the Fantasia, but for the ceremony late in the afternoon, so you have almost all day if you so wish." He snapped his fingers and a groom had a saddle of black leather, embossed with silver about the horn on the mount in seconds it seemed.

She swung up, effortlessly, watched by all the riders and grooms. "I'll just take a quick ride around, thank you. I'll be back in a half hour, no more." She rode off, reigning the spirited animal into a trot. She scanned the field and the alleys made by the tents, looking for someone from her group. Finally she saw the Bakers, and Doug Baker shouted out that he wanted to get her picture against the back drop of the tents. She rode off pretending not to hear, knowing that he'd be sure to tell her mother and Uncle Eric. She eased out the reigns and the horse shot off around the upper field, its iron shoes sparking and clattering against the rocky terrain. She rode some Saturday afternoons still at the Club Royale, but that had become so sedate, the same jumps and fences, few opportunities to race, to run free. He hair whipped about loose, but the animal seemed to hardly exert itself as they circled the field for a second time. The handsome owner had mentioned that he often rode down the wide West Trail. It was up behind the ruin at the end of the lower great field. She could see that it wound down for about five or six kilometers from the plateau, down to a valley with plots of maize, broad beans and the stubble from the barley harvest. She hesitated by the crumbled ruin of an archway, thinking that the ride down and back would take too long. She had promised she would be gone only a half hour, and she had already used up ten minutes racing around the upper field. That would make her really beholden to this Ben Tassen guy. But of course he wouldn't mind.

While she deliberated and the high strung filly shifted back and forth demanding to continue, one of the costumed brides came slowly towards her through the rubble of the archway. Her rouged face streaked with the black khol of her eye makeup. She cried and stumbled forward in shock. Karen dismounted and tried speaking with her in French softly, gently so as not to frighten her. She opened her arms offering to embrace her. She seemed to understand, and pointed back to the tall grass and profusion of wild flowers growing in the inner court where once, decades ago, there had been a proper garden of some kind. Karen hitched the horse to an old iron ring pinioned for that purpose into the stone and mortar wall. She walked nervously toward the overgrown patch in the middle of the inner court, and soon found herself fixed for long minutes at the outstretched arm and hand. Someone had covered the rest of the body with grasses, yanked out by the roots. Her heart racing, but her hand determinedly steady, she brushed back the covering to be greeted by the back of a head, the swarm of flies on the blood of the man's temple. She walked steadily back towards the gate, and looked down the serpentine trail and then towards the mosque, the shrine and the great field. The Berber girl had disappeared and all about her, even the spirited horse, was calm and still.

Chapter IX

Looking like young witches in their black wool capes, their peaked caps and their exotic make-up, over one hundred brides began their final parade as unmarried women. None of them appeared over 16, but an untutored observer would be hard-pressed to discern their proper ages. Poor nutrition and years of inbreeding contributed to the below-average height of some. There were, however, exceptions and anomalies. What appeared to be a small bundled up prepubescent child, could indeed be a mature teenager, and, inversely, a rangy young woman of normal carriage on close inspection could turn out to be only a youngster of 15. Also confusing, a number of divorcees and widows, mostly young women seeking new husbands, marched and intermingled with the virgin brides. Wearing flat instead of peaked caps, their costumes and makeup were otherwise indistinguishable. Older, stoop-labor bent and withered women, whose true ages would also be difficult to guess, wore similar, mother-daughter, festival dress, but hovered on the sidelines scrutinizing the progress and decorum of their wards. The men and boys, turbaned and robed in new white djellabas, some worn over European cut jackets and trousers, also made their way through the ceremonial grounds in a circuit which appeared meandering, but was most likely well-calculated.

Four women from the American Embassy group stood together among the gathering crowd of spectators. Pam Crane, freshly showered with every hair spray gelled in place, looked on bemused, not knowing whether to empathize with the universality of women and brides or to dismiss the quaintness of the ritual. Mai Donatelli, her bruised lip causing a perpetual snarl, managed rapid representations on her sketch pad, capturing precisely the sharp hawk noses, the highlighted eyes, the gesticulation of the hands. Wearing a flowing granny dress to minimize her ample figure and sporting a visored tennis hat to shield her from the brilliant sun, Edna Baker and her Nikon were intently focused on compiling yet another album of her travels, mostly to prove to skeptical relatives that she, an unlikely adventurer, had indeed been to strange and distant places. Cynthia, her typical enthusiasm and relish for detail somewhat muted this morning, nevertheless pointed out for her companions the significance of the head dress and her interpretation of the hand and eye gestures "Now ladies, as I'm sure you know by now, the girls wearing the peaked caps are virgins, never married, and those wearing the flatter scarf-like affair with the spangles have been married before, are widowed, or are going around again, divorcing and trying to find another man. Shouldn't we envious, ladies? See how easy it is to find a new man.

Pam Crane said, " But I thought all through this part of the world it was the man who did the divorcing by simply saying 'I divorce thee' three times, over and done with, neat and simple, the wife out in the cold with nothing but the clothes on their back as it often happens."

"But that's what makes this isolated spot in these mountains so special. It's the women, not the men who do the divorcing. You see they marry very young and usually at this fair. They take their husband on trial, so to speak. If they're not happy, if the guy's a pig, if they are made unwelcome by the women in their new ksar, they come back to the Fair to find a replacement. Here the women decide, and that, ladies, makes it very special."

"That a very good thing," Mai Donatelli commented. " Everyone say have to stay with man because that's the way it was with parents, and their parents. But that not always good. You change, you grow. It not like it was when you 17 or 18 and man comes along promising to protect you, take you away from bad things. Woman should decide when things not working."

"Right on, sister," Pam Crane said. "A gal has to look out for herself and her own needs. Nobody else gives a damn. In spite of all this crap about the new women, political correctness, you name it, you can't be too uppity, can't be too smart, can't be too original, too free."

"I should explain that for them finding a man doesn't come down to just having a warm bed for the winter. It's not so matter-of-fact. There are pressures from the respective families; there's the duty to carry the traditions of the plateau forward, the need to protect the children."

"Did you see that?" Edna Baker said as she clicked away on her Nikon. "That girl with all the silver bracelets just jabbed that boy in the ass. I think I shot her fierce little grin. She's a wild one. She'll tear that boy to pieces when she gets him alone."

"We'll never understand what's really going on here. That may be her brother, or a cousin, or it could be her fiancé. I read somewhere that what you see is not always accidental, or always love at first sight. It's often pre-arranged, the marriage contracts made well before the Fair, and what we're witnessing may only be a reaffirmation. Sometimes these contracts are made at infancy, the parents concerned with keeping their wealth within the extended family, or with infusing the clan with much-needed new blood. But at any rate, if these arranged marriages don't work out, they can freely separate and try out a new mate."

"Did you know that some of these girls are selling their wool capes right off their backs?" Edna Baker said. "Cynthia's has got us all starry-eyed, but just watch those young creatures. They hand their capes over to some of our dear diplomatic colleagues, quickly palm the filthy money, and run down one of those alleys to a tent where they get another. The little hustlers. It's very clear what's going on here, Cynthia dear. The sweet little virgin brides will sell you their capes, hats, snoods and themselves for a price I bet."

"No, not themselves, Edna. Their families would have their blood. Have you noticed the intricate tattoos? For every clan and each girl there are subtle differences, special patterns passed down for generations. See how they dip their eyes at the boys? They roll their eyes, tug quickly at the boy's sleeve—have you got that shot Edna?—wheel about and start down the field again."

"Sure, sure," Edna said. "But you better believe there's a lot of buying and selling going on, Cynthia: horses, donkeys, sheep, virgin girls, the clothes off their backs. Like everywhere else in the real world, it's who's hustling whom."

"Well, yes, for some it's the only opportunity all year to make some money. But it's also a time of hope and joy for these girl, and boys too. Look how carefully dressed they are, the costumes, the jewelry, their hair. Think of all the time and care that went into making the clothes, weaving some themselves, applying the henna, making all the arrangements just to be here, to come through all those difficult mountain passes and trails at the right time. No, it's a time of celebration and happiness, at least for most of them."

"Of course it is. Edna's just trying to get your goat, Cynthia," Pam said. "They have their traditions, romance and all the myths of love and honor, just like we do. It has to be that way, or we'd all be just back in the trees with the chimps giving whomever we took a fancy to a 30 second screwing. But then too, the chimps may have it all over us; none of this fabrication, anxiety and guilt."

"These kids don't understand any of that, they're mostly children," Edna said. "And here we are representatives of the U.S. of A, so ga ga about 15 year olds marrying. We'd be fined for child abuse back home."

"Haven't we become a little too self-righteous about the age issue? Think back 50, 100 years ago in rural America especially. Weren't some girls married off at 15 or 16 ? Life was short and hard and having lots of children as soon as possible an imperative. Isn't it the same for these mountain people, most of whom become old and gnarled by their forties? I was twenty when I rushed, or was rushed into marriage. I thought, and still think that was too young for me, personally. But here in these mountains you're back in time: marry young, have lots of children, and die before sixty. Just look around you, look at all the flirting, the quick touching, the showing off. This is a happy time for them; you can see it in most of their black agate eyes."

"Oh, you bet there's a lot of interesting foreplay here," Pam Crane said. "But do you know anything about the actual love making, Cynthia? I think the girl must start it. These men seem afraid of their women. But down deep most of our men are that way too."

It was just like Pam to get right down to the basics She really had it on the brain, and Cynthia wondered when was the last time she had slept with Harlan, but it was hard to imagine her or anyone sleeping with that awful man. Three of them Pam, herself and Mai, were in their late thirties or early forties, a difficult reflective time, and this Fair and weddings anywhere could do that to you, could bring out those very private thoughts about how the mind and blood conspired to bring a man and woman together, and make you wish you could be for one transcending moment that young bride, passionate in the secret night. "I don't know those details, Pam. I don't know if the young, inexperienced men and women develop a loving intimacy or is it quick, matter-of-fact, obligatory. I would say with young people like these it has to be the former. But you're on to something, Pam. Some men fear their women, are terrified by a woman's potential for passion. Look at the veil, the chador, covering the female form from head to toe, denying that women are beings of nature. Here in these mountains there are no veils, the makeup and dress are vibrant with color, the ritual of attracting a mate public, and with the freedom to divorce I think there's a big difference here on how women are perceived and treated."

"Well, I hope at least she really enjoys herself in the sack while she can," Pam Crane said. "Why, Mai, dear, you've captured that gorgeous young bride resting on that bale of straw perfectly, don't you agree ladies? The tattoos, the small beak of a nose, the hand doing the rosary with her amber beads, her expectant look. I like it very much. I'll buy from you if it's not already promised. Just name your price."

***** ***** ***** ***** ***** ***** *****

THE BRIDES' FAIR

Minister of Interior, Ahmed Bennani, entered into the velour plush of his official Mercedes, bussed his awaiting daughter, and quickly thumbed through the older of papers assembled by his principal office factotum and secretary, Madame Sebti. He had extensively edited his remarks for the ceremony at the fair. His young assistants, unfortunately, knew little of the rural *bled* or how to stir the passions of mountain people, and the always efficient Madame Sebti managed to edit his scrawls and wedged in rewrites and produce a clean version in less than thirty minutes. When she handed him his folder, he noticed how red her eyes had become. Those infernal computer monitors caused that, or perhaps it was an allergy. At any rate she, above all, needed to be ordered to take a week or two off. He made a quick note in his pocket diary to that effect. They started off to the air station through the crowded late morning streets of the city. Hassan, the wizened chauffeur, well beyond retirement age, maintained the quick-reflex alertness that assured him continued employment. He had driven for French colonial administrators when Ahmed himself was a boy. Driving men of power amused him and filled his day, but, Ahmed knew, that the elderly man, in his own right had accumulated wealth, controlling his clan's vast citrus and almond groves in the southern valleys and owning a choice block of flats and shops in the city.

The Minister's daughter, Jamila, correctly robed in a velvet caftan, and with a simple gold chain necklace, stared blankly out the window, eschewing in these first awkward moments alone with her father, all but the most perfunctory conversation, thinking no doubt of her many friends who would be congregating later in the day at Anissa Alaoui's beach villa. Ahmed Bennani tried earnestly to understand his daughter and her generation, for in spite of those who would try to cling on passed their time, it was Jamila and her friends who would inherit the country in a very few years. She could be petulant and insistent about going to these beach parties, about staying on her private telephone for hours with friends, male friends at that. And how these days could you keep them from running all over the city with the wrong types, from associating outside the circle of closely intertwined families? But although she had her frivolous side and could be as temperamental as her mother, she managed exceptionally well in her studies.

It was a different time, of course, but in his own youth, the sexes only mixed *en famille*. His sisters and his female cousins went veiled outside the compound walls on their errands or to assist at women's teas. The changes had been too rapid, too headlong. Daughters of the very best households thought little of revealing most of themselves on the public beaches and could be seen doing the most explicit dances to Western music in the old, high-ceiling salons that had, only a few years back, been the sanctuaries of men. All around him they clamored for progress, their proper place in the modern world, and fathers were expected to acquiesce.

He did recognize the need for change, but it had to be change well-paced and well-monitored. For this reason, he wanted his daughter near him, not off in America. He had tried to make his case, had often said that Jamila should go to the national university which had seen an explosion in female enrollment in the past decade Wasn't it adequate for her needs? Hadn't the State invested millions in upgrading its capacity? Shouldn't they, the Bennani family, give the University their personal endorsement?

'Yes, we should and we will, but Jamila should not be denied her dreams. My family dared to let me go off to the Sorbonne in the late 1960s when the students of the new bourgeoisie were chanting communist rhetoric in the Parisian streets and lecture halls; where the cult of free love and drugs was everywhere. But I returned to North Africa, and you took me to the marriage bed a virgin, husband, if you indeed remember that."

'I am not a dry, desert stone, Lahla. I do remember our nuptials, and, although you persist in not believing me, I envy your courage and your vision. But the times are now very different. The world is even more mad than when you and I were students exposed to the strange behavior of Europeans and Americans. I am preoccupied with the terrorists and the assassins who would ruin our world. I see Jamila, who like you, Lahla, is headstrong, too intelligent, too beautiful, being pulled down be this awful tide. I fear we will lose her. I fear that she will never come back to our house.'

'Too intelligent and too beautiful? You don't make sense, husband. Should we only send dull, ugly daughters off to seize the special knowledge of the United States?'

But it was futile arguing with Khadija. She had become mesmerized by the idealistic pronouncements of United Nations resolutions.

"You're thinking of medicine now, your mother tells me," he said to his daughter. White gloved policemen from the protocol unit had been stationed along the route at the various intersections to ease the passage of himself and the American Ambassador as well as to assure security. So many uniformed men at the medina markets, the bus and train depots, the university and *lycée* campuses could only make the citizenry apprehensive, could only fan the gossip in the tea rooms and public baths. But the Defense Council, of which he was vice chairman, so ordered it against his plea for lower visibility and restraint. "Medicine in the United States will take more than eight years of your life. The system there is different than here or in France. It will take a resolute commitment to go through those years of schooling. You do not need to put yourself through that. Here, you could achieve your medical degree more quickly and intensively with fewer problems."

The pouts and frowns evaporated and she became thoughtful. " I could breeze through the medical faculty here, at least I believe I could. My baccalaureate results in science will probably be good. That's what my professors tell me. But I don't want to take the easy way, and perhaps it wont be medicine after all. It's so difficult to decide when you're eighteen. That's what you do during your first year or two at the university in America. You don't rush into a program of study. You consider your choices. Perhaps I will be an engineer and build beautiful buildings and bridges."

Jamila presented her case well. She talked about the high standards her mother and he had set, and how she was determined to continue the Bennani tradition of excellence and public responsibility. She might become a surgeon, not the first, for Sabha Bidraoui would be finishing her internship in general surgery at Montpeillier next year. Or she would be the first woman professor of civil engineering. There were several other possibilities, all aimed high at the stars. She was perhaps too driven. Careful breeding even through all the Hispano-Moorish strife, through the rampages of conquerors, the tribal blood-letting and intrigue had produced Jamila the brilliant and beautiful. While he should be proud, he could only fear for her future.

"With the pocket phone, the e-mail and the airplane we will remain almost as close as if I were off at the medical faculty in Casablanca, you will see, Baba." Her eyes watered when she realized he had finally softened and she leaned to kiss him on the cheek.

"Perhaps your brother, Rachid should also prepare to do his university in the United Statesl, and Kareem as well. I am only thinking out loud, but perhaps we might invest in an apartment there, a *pied a terre*. Your mother will go more often to New York to the UN, and I, well, I should find more time to travel." She glowed at his plan, and the more he thought about it the more appropriate it became. It wasn't so thinkable to establish a life in a relatively safe, untroubled country as the United States, even though one had to resist its culture's worse elements. There was unrest all through the Middle East and Africa, and he must think beyond his country's well-being and security to that of his family's. The Defense Council had become vocally critical of his stand that they be less heavy-handed with the population, that they go easy in rounding up the fanatics and the student rabble rousers. "We will only drive them into the waiting arms of the

MPLM if we are not more prudent." No they wanted him to be a fire brand, to lead the charge, but that was not his nature. He would soon begin to receive hints, he suspected, hints that he quietly step down. They, in turn, would likely offer him an Ambassadorship, and he would hold out for Washington, or at least Canada. That would not be too terrible an outcome. Jamila had unwittingly arrived at the need to create a safe haven for the Bennani family in America.

The honor guard came to as Hassan slowed the Mercedes before the gates of the Second Central Military District Air Station. The guards' white tunics and pantaloons shone pure and bright under the cloudless rich blue sky. An older refitted Sikorsky helicopter stood at rest on the tarmac like a giant gray beetle, its long appendage-like rotors dipped towards the ground and shuddered from the stiff ocean breezes coming across the flat delta. Those in his party, Larbi Benchekroun, Deputy Minister of Culture and Tourism, and his well-reputed young assistant, Achmed Benabdelssalam, had arrived in advance. Ahmed Bennani embraced the two men, and Jamila received a kiss on both cheeks from Achmed, for he was a cousin twice removed on her mother's side. There had been some talk last year about the possibility of marriage, for Jamila herself did not seem disinterested in the man, but Khadija quickly ruled this out. Jamila would go to university as planned, and Achmed, a young man of twenty-seven with great prospects and sought after by many could not be expected to remain a bachelor waiting until Jamila finished her studies.

The American Ambassador's large, boxy black sedan, flags on either side of the hood flying, moved down the access road toward the helicopter. It was followed by two more modest sedans of U.S. manufacture. The tall man unwound himself from his car and paced slowly down the honor guard line toward the welcoming hand of the Minister of Interior. He wore a light tan summer weight suit of custom tailoring. The breast pocket of his jacket flounced a silk foulard, a deep maroon, a splash of muted color against the simple tan suit. They said in the biographical data that circulated the upper echelons of government that he had been a vigorous, sportive man. Today, however, he appeared particularly haggard, with a baggy darkness about the eyes as if he lacked sleep or had indulged himself with too much drink last evening. The U.S. Ambassador, would be traveling with his body guard, Hamidou, an appropriately muscular man, in an over-sized gray business suit which fairly well disguised his bulk and build.

"Mr. Minister," Harlan Crane said. "I've heard about that invasion down in the southeast. Terrible news. My people at this brides' fair, think we should cancel our trip."

"Invasion? We have had an incident involving a small band of infiltrators or drug runners. And, Mr. Ambassador, we are rounding them up with little difficulty. I assure you everything at the Fair, is *comme il faut*, quite secure." Ahmed could envision the inflammatory cable from the American Embassy already circulating in the halls of the State Department. Next the media would be flapping about like vultures after carrion. They had to continue on as planned. It had to be business as usual.

"You know, Mr. Minister, we want to show the world that we're solidly behind you. I can get on the phone to the White House and to our Naval Command people over in Italy, and get out a platoon of Marines, get them here within forty-eight hours. You know get them here on a training exercise, just to give off the right signals."

'Marines?' Had Ahmed Bennani heard the man correctly? Wouldn't the American President and the Pentagon have to weigh such an action? Wouldn't this agitate the United States Congress, particularly that nettlesome Congressman Joe Farrell? If getting state-of-the-art electronic surveillance equipment was proving so politically difficult for the Americans, he could imagine the furor sending in the Marines would raise. "That would be a significant gesture on the part of the American Government, Mr. Ambassador, and I will take it up with our Defense Council immediately upon our return." Even if the Americans could deliver which was highly unlikely, the reaction would not be favorable. Major General Taeb Salim, who chaired the Council and who had received a year of war fighter training in the United States, would shy away from having even a small unobtrusive platoon of U.S. Marines, more from pride in national self-reliance than from fear of awakening any latent anti-American sentiment. "We should be going, Mr. Ambassador. If all goes well, we should be back at this air station within four hours. If not my dear daughter will be very upset.

At a little passed 11:00 am, the flaccid rotors of the converted military helicopter responded to the engine's whine, and the party of six was ushered aboard. Jamila Bennani laughed aloud as the rotors' wind mussed her long black hair.

***** ***** ***** ***** ***** ***** *****

Earlier that day, Eric Dalton sat with the Marine corporal in the front of the Embassy van parked behind the hotel tents along with several hundred other vehicles. "There may be a couple of dark angels flitting about in the deep shadows. We shouldn't take chances with spirited things we can't see, "he said to Stu Connors over the radio phone. Before it got back to the Embassy, he revealed elliptically that Johnathan McMannus had gone missing and presumably had gotten into a fight with the red-headed language teacher's lover, whom they suspected of being an MPLM rebel. Stu sat at Eric's desk, getting the call patched in from the Communications Center. Eric imagined his colleague intently listening, mulling over how to approach the Ambassador, to warn him, to advise him to cancel his trip with Minister Bennani. Eric saw clearly in his office as well the familiar, comforting photos and memorabilia, the stack of yet-to-read cables and faxes, and over the drumming from the center field, the phones were ringing in the outer office, appointments being made, every hour of the day and early evening blocked out for him, the briefing papers for each appointment being churned out on the printer. Minutes passed while Stu went next door to confront the Ambassador quickly and directly. 'He's not going to give me ulcers.'

"He says you need more than spirits, Old Buddy. He now seems quite determined to sally forth if only to spite our counsel. The die is cast He's about to cross the Rubicon. Packing his shield and breast plate right now."

The man's wit and *bon hommie* had survived even though Harlan Crane must have exploded at the thought of changing his plans at the last minute. Political Counselor Connors signed off with regrets that he hadn't been able to turn matters around, regrets that the fire dragon would be disrupting his good time. 'What good time, Old Buddy?' he wanted to add "Besides protecting the Ambassador is what we get paid for, like it or not; saving the good old U.S.A. from shame and misfortune." But beyond giving Harlan Crane advice and counsel, warning him as he had done, there was little more Eric could do to protect the man. He had no levers, no authority up on this mountain plateau. At the Embassy he could put security plans into play at the touch of a button; voice communications could be monitored; electronic sweeps could be made of all vehicles and parcels; the controls on building passes reviewed. Here the responsibility for protecting dignitaries, for ferreting out any MPLM rebels hell-bent on planting explosives, taking hostages or whatever, belonged to Captain Cherkaoui and Lieutenant Berrada.

'You've got to believe me, Mr. Dalton.' Monique Addleman went over her story again at his urging. They were in the American tent, and she had changed into a skirt and blouse she had borrowed from Cynthia Dennis. The clothing subdued her, took away that startling flamboyance. 'He swore that he had traveled all the way to the Mid Atlas just to be with me. He wanted me to stay with him, be close to him. He said he needed me. But it was the same old, same old business like when he'd go away for weeks, and unannounced he'd be there banging on my door saying he needed me. That's what guys always say when they just want you know what. What about needing you as a real friend, someone to get you through the blahs, someone with whom you can spin and weave the future? No, he never mentioned the MPLM. Once, he seemed to let me inside his real self. Once, back in the city, he got all worked up about the rich and the poor, about his friends from the university with good degrees in science and engineering who couldn't find jobs, about the need for change. But I've heard lots of people talk like that. You know how student types want to change the world.'

Eric knew. In his twenties, into law school, that's when the guilt trip started. Confidence in intellectual skills came with confidence in women, not to the point of being the Lothario of Back Bay, he was hardly the type, but being able to get through an evening of serious conversation and friendship without being driven to prove his virility. Confidence also meant being able to think for the first time beyond his own needs cutting egocentricity loose. He could reach beyond himself and see himself among all others at the same time. He could see the disparity, the oceans of the poor. 'The poor will always be with you' they told him. But screw the cynicism, the status quo; determination and political will can surely change things. He went on that tortuous guilt trip like half his friends. They would teach in the community; bombard Congress with letters to push forward the Great Society; even take a year or two off from studying law and diplomacy to work with VISTA or the Peace Corps.

And there was Rachid, mid 20's a smoldering North African Moslem, going through his own guilt trip,wanting to ennoble himself and make the tangible difference everyone in their twenties thinks they can make. He appeared to come from the solid *bourgeoisie* of the country, not its super elite, but among the small minority of the privileged, nevertheless. "It seemed possible last year, possible that he was serious about me," Monique related. "He promised to invite me to tea with his mother, sister and aunt. Real elegant. Impress the rough cut American. The service would be silver, the villa huge but like a dozen others in the residential park. The women would be ever-so polite, and hide their disapproval. It never happened of course. There was excuse after excuse, and I never got near any of his relatives, or friends for that matter."

"It is obvious he is one of the four," Captain Cherkaoui said after he had walked Monique up to one of the large Caidal tents where in the back half behind a muslin partition, Security had made its headquarters. The black *appliqué* silhouettes of oil lamps festooned on the side walls of the tent signified the power and the light of the low land sultans. There was an irony in this as men clamored at the Captain for instructions, or tried to report the results of their searches of vendors, herders, waiters and porters. Disorder rather than light appeared to reign, yet the Captain remained calm, masking well the panic that must be churning within.

"Why does he pretend he is a film technician? And why is your CIA man following him? Why do they both just melt away?" the Captain asked after calling for quiet, rattling off new instructions and then dismissing the half dozen aides surrounding him. "There were four at the El Mahmid check point. There were three at the UN refugee camp. Lieutenant Berrada arrested one just sixty kilometers south at the cross roads, a man who has revealed little after harsh interrogation. Ergo, there are three unaccounted for, and this Rachid, or whoever he is, is a prime subject for being one of them."

Eric had always challenged pat assumptions, conventional wisdom. While his colleagues back in the Mogadishu debacle were obsessed with taking out the two rival war lords, he argued that this would only ensure their martyrdom, that the random violence via the 'technicals' would not go away, that from the complex Somali clan structure successors would emerge. And although he was fairly certain Captain Cherkaoui was right, he offered that Rachid may not be a MPLM infiltrator. "If he were really skilled and methodical, he would keep himself hidden in the shadows, and not show himself to anyone, especially his former lover." But Eric added that if Rachid did indeed belong to the MPLM band and was here with his other two colleagues to do harm, there might be other accomplices at the Fair as well to assist and make sure their mission's success. And it was just remotely possible he wanted to add that if Jonathan McMannus was truly a straight arrow intelligence officer, perhaps he was chasing after the wrong person or not all the right ones. The CIA had a reputation for overreaching, for not being able to always sort out the harmless from the real trouble makers, for misreading the tea leaves. Look at Vietnam, Central America, Iran, Somalia. They had so steeped themselves in the Cold War antics of Eastern Europe, they had difficulty dealing with the particular vagaries of the Third World, particularly the Arab world, had difficulty in dealing with browns and blacks. Unfortunately, both Cherkaoui and Berrada had a misty-eyed awe of the CIA's invincibility, and even if Eric dared to take the folks from Langley down a peg, they would be convinced he was playing games with them. There was another possibility, another one he dared not raise. McMannus or someone knew exactly what he was doing, who all the players were, but he was single-mindedly playing a different, more devious game.

THE BRIDES' FAIR

"There will always be another side of the coin," Captain Cherkaoui said. "But you agree, do you not, that we have no other suspect? And in this country men of Rachid's generation and class would not come to a rural fair unless he had some business or mission. And for a man like that to make this long difficult trip only for an affair of the heart, well, I doubt it We will look for young men with long, clean fingernails and all their own teeth," Cherkaoui had said. "The sure mark of a bourgeois."

Eric left Monique there with Cherkaoui to sit in the shadows of the tent while they dragged in frightened or enraged bridegrooms returned from work in Europe to find a wife; carpet vendors up from the cities, and even a doctor from the Ministry of Health here to do a promotion on good nutrition. And Monique, with her auburn hair tucked under one of Jess Williams' Marine Corps fatigue caps and attired in Cynthia's country weekend outfit, sat subdued and silent, shaking her head 'no' at each hapless suspect, but preparing herself for the possibility that the next one dragged in would be him, and she would have to betray him.

The drumming and the chanting from the central field abruptly stopped. The fiancée's and the spectators dispersed for their midday meal. Jess Williams started in to shut down the radio and exit the van. The usually controlled, coordinated marine fumbled putting the microphone back on its hook. Something was not right. They had been confined in the van for over ten hours yesterday, and the body odors, the funk and perfumes of that confinement still lingered. Had it all been imagined last evening, the erratic movement of the big van? Eric's mind had been spinning, but not only from the Frenchman's champagne and brandy. The dancers had stopped their subtle swaying; the goat skin drums were put aside for the evening. Twenty years of marriage to Hillary flashed on the night black mountains. And how could he sort out Manila for Cynthia? And Monique too pulled at his desires. He usually prided himself in pushing back the peripheral matters while he concentrated everything on the crisis at hand.

"Corporal." The young man came too automatically to attention. "Please find the Gunny Sergeant. You and he together need to also try to find Chris Reily, the American friend of Ms Addleman's and get his help in quietly searching every van, every 4 X 4, tent and sleeping bag down in the Camping Sauvage." Lieutenant Berrada and his detail had already made such a search earlier this morning, but while they might harass and intimidate their own countrymen, they would be too cursory and polite with the "Europeans."

While giving instructions to Sergeant Donatelli, shaven, cleaned up, but snapping out his 'yes sirs' with an edge of anger, Cynthia found him and presented him with a new crisis. "It's not unlike her to be gone for so long without letting me know. We've always left a note on the fridge, a message on the answering machine." She bit her lower lip as she did those rare times when she could no longer control matters. Last month the Ambassador tried to second guess her when she denied a visa to a well-connected Casablancan businessman's nephew. "The guy's been running drugs, Eric. Interpol has him profiled, and the Ambassador insists it must be a mistake." She bit down so hard her teeth became red with her lipstick mixed with a spot of blood.

"Doug Baker saw her riding a "magnificent horse," as he described it. But that was two or three hours ago." She could have been thrown on one of those rocky trails and be laying somewhere injured and unattended? Neither the Ambassador, the MPLM nor Mcmannus were important any more. He pulled Cynthia to him, and she buried her face in the crook made by his chest and shoulder.

"What have we done wrong, Eric? It was going to be such a great trip. I did all that planning. Everybody seemed to be so up when we started out." She resisted tears, and looked up at him for answers. "Now Dr., Mcmannus is missing. Poor Mai Donatelli has been battered by that awful husband. Edna Baker is playing the bitch again, and Pam Crane is prancing around like the cat who swallowed the cream. Monique's been attacked again, and now Karen. Now Karen," she repeated.

"I'm sure she's all right," he said comforting her and reassuring himself. They headed straight to the upper field where the Fantasia riders had stationed themselves and their horses. It seemed a place preparing for war with smoky fires, the noise of black smiths refitting shoes; men cleaning and polishing long barreled rifles, carefully examining harness and saddle, or brushing down manes and flanks one more time. Cynthia had a two year old wallet photo of Karen. Her daughter's school back in Reston had commissioned a portrait photographer to capture in assembly-line fashion, the class of 15 year olds at their most flattering best. Cynthia had dutifully presented a framed 8 X 10 to the elder Dennises and had bought a dozen snaps for herself. Eric had one among his photo albums along with those of Peter and Susan. Somehow in these stock shots, all the impatience, acne blemishes, shyness and defiance had been air brushed away, leaving what the photographer determined was the youthful ideal.

Eric particularly recalled one of Karen taken five years ago in her riding breeches and black frock coat. Her cheeks still had some pudginess and there was only barest hint of the striking young woman she would become. At that time Eric found himself on the Near East policy staff, weighed down by the never-ending conflicts in the region and by the bright young stars from the White House National Security Council who relished discounting the reports Eric and his colleagues had prepared, calling them unresponsive, overly cautious, bureaucratically fussy. Such put downs were common. Eric was only one senior analyst among so many clogging the system with options and strategies. Nevertheless, assignments in Washington at "Mother State," meant also rediscovering friends, and savoring social events at which he did not have to play the stage manager.

On one of those brilliant, reconfirming May Sundays with its profusion of azaleas everywhere in the sprawling suburban ring, Hillary and he went to see Karen compete in the regional juniors. Cynthia found the sport too aristocratic for her sensibilities, too much of a vestige of Old Europe. Too many of her foreign service friends continued to be awed by these vestiges, by the servant-filled, tea-cup rattling life "in the colonies." She had dared to see up close the extremes of the human condition in Asia and here in North Africa. She had roamed the *bidonvilles* in the heat of day when the smell of human waste and death overwhelmed. But she could not argue with, Bob's parents, the elder Dennises. The horse, lessons, boarding fees and all were their gift to their grand daughter, and Cynthia could not refuse them.

In the trim setting of the exclusive club, spectators applauded earnestly as the boys and girls took their mounts through gates and over fences and moats. In the crowd were those he knew from the Department, men who held Ambassadorial and Senior Service rank, or were slated for such distinction by those in the closed councils of the Department who determined such things.

"Karen, we're so proud, so happy for you," they had all gushed when the twelve year old came down from the judge's stand with her little silver cup for placing second in the juniors. In her sweat stained breeches and rumpled frock coat, all the weeks of practice and being on edge suddenly exploded, rupturing etiquette and decorum.

"But I only got second." She slammed her riding casque to the ground. "Melinda Collins got first, and did you see her brush two of her gates? I did. It's just not fair."

They were embarrassed. Some of their friends and colleagues were staring at the tantrum. They ushered Karen quickly away to the parking lot. That fierce determination, wanting always to be first in everything and having little grace in losing came from her father, although Cynthia would never admit to that. She recoiled at the contemporary buccaneerism which held that winning by whatever means was everything.

At the first station of horsemen, she handed the photo to the outstretched hand of a bearded man, his face deeply etched by sun and wind. He admired it as if it were some rare treasure, paused, and then shook his head. How could he distinguish one 'European' young woman from the dozen who must have passed by this morning? And if he did recognize Karen, why would he want to waste his time with these foreigners and the authorities? However, the bearded man continued to hold on to the photo, and then with the barest of gestures pointed to the farthest group of horses and riders.

They trudged up to the last line of a dozen tethered horses. Two militia men from the security unit shouted angrily at a man in his early twenties. Clean shaven and slight, he was unlike the rough cut, full bearded men in his troupe, who without the niceties of paper contracts, or the chance for wealth and fame, would follow this young man to each contest and would so follow him to battle. "I will go with you if you insist, my brothers," the younger man said calmly while his companions circled behind the apprehensive militia men. "But I fear it will be you who will suffer the consequences for your mistake, not I." The young man fit the description exactly. They could be twins, with this one holding the slight advantage in height and muscularity.

The militia men pulled in from as far away as communities of the Atlantic Plains, went on that they had their orders and now with the horsemen menacing close about began to plead for Ben Tassen's cooperation. The exchange quickly ceased when the Army Lieutenant's jeep drove up. Berrada's dust goggles and binoculars hung from his neck on black leather strapping giving him the air of a military campaigner in the war the British and Germans fought in these neighboring lands a half century past. He dismissed the two militia man with a wave of his hands and apologized to the grandson of Sidi Ben Tassen, telling him that they were hunting down drug runners, for that was the story given out to everyone for the heighten state of security. "Doing one's job too literally as instructed, without deviation or initiative is the way we are trained. It maintains a hierarchy of discipline and control, but it too can misfire."

Cynthia thrust out the photo of her daughter.

"But she was here, and she mentioned you, her mother, so proudly. But I thought she was Swiss, a *Genevoise*, not American. I insisted she take one of the horses for a workout since she seemed so knowledgeable. Time is of little consequence to us here in the mountains, but after almost three hours, I began to think something has gone wrong. I was starting to mount up and go look for her myself, when the two constabulary men came along and insisted I must go with them."

THE BRIDES' FAIR

"Another of your missing Americans?" The Lieutenant said to the senior diplomat. "That is rather odd or careless, don't you agree?" It was all connected he was sure, and he insisted that Eric Dalton and Ahmed Ben Tassen go with him and his driver, more out of suspicion than any concern for the American girl. He also insisted that Mrs. Dennis stay behind and continue her search over by the Fantasia viewing tent where the crowds began to gather.

They drove out of the Fair and down the West Trail where Ben Tassen had suggested she ride. The police recruit at the wheel had never driven in the high mountains, but holding to a fatalism about his own irrelevance and that of his passengers, he continued on where only donkeys, mules and humans dared. They bumped over rocks and ruts, coming within a front axle from sliding off the road into a deep ravine. But Eric remained unmindful of any danger, thinking that he could allow nothing to happen to his God daughter. She had mastered horses, could take them through set piece drills over gates and moats, but she didn't know these pathways, nor could she calculate the shifting rubble, the hoof-trapping crevices.

Ben Tassen, sitting up front finally told the driver to stop on a shelf of rock. "You can see the path winding down to the village below. You can see how steep it is and how it narrows down to where only a mule could squeeze through. I have walked it as a boy many times in the dark and in the snow. It is forbidding." They climbed from the jeep and scanning the hard scrabble piste saw that the semi-circle indentations of the horse's heels led down the path for an imperceptible distance but they also led back up and continued in the direction of the old stone and cement mortared ksar at two kilometers distance.

Chapter X

The mountain people accustomed to these skies, undisturbed but for an occasional hawk plummeting down on prey, saw the speck early on as it darted around the mountains from the west. The drumming and the chanting on the great field began. The black goat hair tents of the merchants of carpets and crafts and the vendors of bread, broiled meats, and sweets emptied of customers. More than two thousand stood around the roped off perimeter of the field. Inside over a hundred men of the various Mid Atlas clans sat on richly harnessed horses, their long-barreled rifles pointing skyward. A white pantalooned and white turbaned honor guard stood motionless, a still portrait from some half-forgotten era. Facing them to form a corridor, fifty of the young brides all wearing their black and white striped hondoros shawls dipped their eyes at the men, and whispered scandalous commentary. The helicopter kicked up tornadoes of dust on the great field, causing the line of brides chosen to be in the arrival ceremony to cringe and scream. The white pantalooned honor guard remained unflinchingly rigid, however. The Minister of Interior stepped first through the hatchway followed by his daughter Jamila Bennani, and then by the Deputy Minister of Tourism and his assistant. The American Ambassador and his body guard, Hamidou, descended the aluminum stairway last, and, at an unseen signal, the teen age brides joined by their mothers and 'cousins' in the crowd let out with a chorus of ululations that pierced the air, reverberated off the mountain walls, and echoed down the lower valleys. The goat skin drummers joined in, and they and the staccato blasting from long tube trumpets tried futilely to overwhelm the greeting cries of the women.

The arriving delegation and the local authorities greeted each other, Minister Bennani embracing with unaccustomed gusto the local caids and several high ranking members of the diplomatic corps. Jamila Bennani brushed her cheek lightly against those of several cousins as well as those of several foreign classmates from her private *lycée* back in the capital. Very much like a celebrity she waved to several she knew outside the tent pressing against the rope barrier. It seemed that almost half of the diplomatic community and a good number of *haut fonctionnaires* and members of their family were either inside the two large viewing tents, or due to lack of space, in an adjacent roped off area . Therefore, flying into this remote almost medieval setting, was little different than attending a ceremony back in the city. The same crowd always seemed to show up. The same crowd circulated at the National Day receptions of the various Embassies; ate, when they ate out at all, at the same restaurants. There was not this day-to-day opportunity for intimate social contact in Rome, London, Paris or Tokyo where the business of international affairs proceeded in a more routinized fashion; and where local officials 'did' lunch but drew the line on closer fraternization with foreign diplomats, unless of course they pursued some multimillion dollar weapons deal, or were intent on espionage. Some preferred the neat business and social demarcations of the bigger, Class One posts. In these smaller missions, everyone seemed to know too much of one's sexual proclivities and capacity for drink, and consequently much time was spent squelching or otherwise spreading such gossip.

The American Ambassador set more than his share of tongues wagging more by his brusque, unpredictable manner rather than by any tendencies at his age to meander through odd bedrooms in small town Rabat. Those who dug deep could find the old musty tales of twenty-five years ago describing a dynamic computer hardware tycoon with a voracious appetite for attractive young women. This seemed hardly the flaccid, mid sixties man who, finally freed from his obligations to press hands and cheeks, said to his wife "Is it always this damn noisy? I'm not going to enjoy this, you know, but I wanted to show these people we're with them on this national unity business."

"Are you all right, Harlan dear? We've had an interesting time of it, a very interesting time," Pam Crane said..

"And where is my by-the-book deputy now that all hell is breaking out? He should be here on deck, don't you think? We have to get the Prime Minister here, and Washington focused on this god damn mess. They've got riots in the city, and you've heard about the invasion, haven't you? They're right near by and headed through these mountains. And then on top of everything else, we've got Congressman Joe Farrell, who thinks these MPLM guerrillas are all noble freedom fighters, right out of Lawrence of Arabia. Well, he's coming here Wednesday. That's all we need."

"Take it easy, Harlan, dear." Pam Crane guided her husband onto the low cushions besides the Minister of Interior. Ahmed Bennani explained to the several other foreign Ambassadors seated nearby, the significance of the marriage fair and the Fantasia they were about to witness. Pam Crane, Doug and Edna Baker already steeped in all the lore by Cynthia Dennis, listened politely, nevertheless, while the American Ambassador, who had been up half the night on the phone to Washington, had much difficulty keeping his eyelids from drifting shut even with all the din of trumpeting, ululating and drumming still going on unabated before the caidal tent. The young brides paraded back and forth before the tent, and security men seemed everywhere among them and in the crowd of spectators. Hamidou, Ambassador Crane's bodyguard, had recruited Jess Williams, and they bounced back and forth behind the seated American contingent, conferring with the North African security men and scanning the crowd which pressed to the left of the tent, behind a wall of local constabulary.

Captain Cherkaoui greeted the Chef de Brigade, Nasiri, when he landed just behind the big Sikorsky helicopter of the great ones from the city, in his small and antiquated Puma II. They embraced for they too were related, tracing a common grand parent back to an industrious cloth merchant in the old medina of Fez. The Chef de Brigade, the only survivor of his border patrol, wore a neck brace and his face sagged from over twenty-four hours without sleep. He had little time for pleasantries and listened impatiently as his cousin explained the tight security. "We have men disguised among the crowds and several score out on the periphery of the grounds. The assassins will be taken, *inchallah*, and may they be shown little mercy."

"One of them is a woman, a young woman. She wore a cap like the others, and it was difficult to tell. Who would think there would be a woman?" Only an hour ago, just as he was about to make the helicopter ascent to the Fair, he had received a message on the radio of his vehicle. "Yes, a woman," the investigator they sent down from the capital said. "The doctor and the American nurse at the camp were not cooperative at first until I threatened to throw the doctor in jail and send the nurse on the first plane back to her country. They had to remove her clothing when they treated her. Her hair is cut short like a man's. She is in her early twenties, medium height, fair, well-featured, they say. Find her. She is as dangerous as the others."

Captain Cherkaoui listened in amazement. Indeed it was ironic that they had been trapped by their own traditions, believing it inconceivable that a woman, a putative Moslem woman of North Africa would espouse rebellion and violence, let alone travel long hard distances unchaperoned and in the company of men. He must change the terms of his search, for his men would pass over any woman, not even dare to approach one, at least one not of their class. But he could not himself abandon the ceremony and the dignitaries, and instead sent runners out to all his assembled detail, including the Army lieutenant. "I must remain here," he explained to his cousin.

"But I have no such obligation," the Chef de Brigade said. "My only duty is to find those who have murdered my men."

The local officials hovering around Minister Bennani explained the proceedings. At the conclusion of the Fantasia meet, the Minister would make his speech underscoring the preservation and integrity of tribal customs, at the same time avowing national solidarity and allegiance to the King. He would stand on a small podium before the tent. Microphones and loud speakers had been installed and tested this morning and security had inspected them yet again, only minutes ago. The Deputy Minister of Tourism and Culture would also speak, extolling the colorful ceremonies such as the Brides' Fair and its attraction to those in the diplomatic community who appreciated the rich folk lore of the region. Minister Bennani would take the microphone again to introduce His Excellency, Harlan Crane, but not before announcing an increase in State appropriations to the mountain commune for road improvement and the construction of a thirty bed hospital at the cross road town in the lower pass. The American Ambassador, then would give a brief message tracing the long friendship between the two nations. Crane after a year and a half at post could manage the speech in halting French, but wanted to add just a brief reference to the dangers of the MPLM rebel movement. As expected Stu Connors had advised against this, as would Eric Dalton But that was their problem. So as not to raise eye brows in Paris for spot lighting the Americans, the French Cultural Attaché, Pierre Deschamps would also give brief remarks, and after the speeches, all three would assist in the awarding of the prizes to the Fantasia team. This event would be followed by the communal marriage ceremony and the blessings of the imams. "Then, *inchallah*, we can depart."

"How long is this supposed to take?" Harlan Crane asked.

"Not more than two hours, all told," Minister Bennani replied. "I have been so assured by the organizers. As you recall I have promised my daughter that there will be no delays. Her beach party later this afternoon in the City takes precedence over regional festivals as well as matters of high state."

The first team of ten horsemen paraded past the caidal tents, and after shouting 'Allah Akbar' and dipping their rifles to the ouizzers and other dignitaries, they rode at a slow uniform trot to the other end of the course. There they came about and at an unseen signal charged perfectly abreast down the field. It was a charge learned long ago from Moorish horsemen who struck fear in the armies of Catholic Spain. Then, riding toward unwieldy pikes and lances they flourished curved, decapitating swords instead of muskets. Horse warrior drills, perfected over the centuries had been also employed against the Portuguese who had once held the south western coastal ports. They were used in the 1930's against the dispirited armies of Generalissimo Franco. Now the traditions of battle were confined to contests of precision rider ship. The first team could have easily trampled all in the row of tents at the end of the field, but on cue, they reined in at an exact ten meters before the spectators, coming to a perfect, all-abreast halt and simultaneously firing off their rifles. This assault to the ears set off more screeching ululations from the women as well as enthusiastic applause.

A second team thundered down the hundred meters of hard, stony ground, and then a third, all coming to a perfect uniform halt at the designated point before the judging tents, and all blasting the air with their muskets. The field swirled with dust, and when the tenth and last team had reined in and set off their rifles, the spectators in the central caidal tent could barely distinguish the horsemen through the dust, nor could they distinguish the explosion of the first mortar shell from that of the horsemen's volley until they felt its shock waves and saw the riders and horses being hurled about. Horses nickered in pain, but otherwise there was a paralysis of silence for a moment before another burst hit closer to the tent, and then a third. Explosions were heard elsewhere on the fair grounds, and wails of screaming echoed through the high plateau. Pam Crane huddled over her husband who slumped against the banquette cushions and struggled for breath.

The local constabulary on the edges of the fair grounds began firing at shadows, specters, rocks that took on human shape. The black oil lamp appliqués on the central tent bled from the shrapnel and bullets which flew about. An enraged Ahmed Bennani intent on stopping the madness, shouting for order and discipline to unseen security men, rushed from the tent and onto the field. Shrouded by the dust, he slumped in pain and staggered to crouch behind one of the writhing horses that had been cut down by the mortar shells. Somewhere up in the direction of the old ruins, the shrine and the mosque, there was more gun fire, then all abruptly ceased. For an apprehensive time there was quiet; no human wailing, the huffy neighing of dying horses, nor the gruff commands of the security forces. Then, when the danger seemed to have passed, the clamoring among the brides, spectators, and horsemen resumed, rumbling in shock waves throughout the fair grounds.

How many had been killed or wounded by stray bullets or shrapnel could not be quickly determined due to the swirls of dust everywhere, and everywhere people racing about to find loved ones, to assess their losses. From the screams and confusion it appeared that many had been injured, but then terror makes a pricked finger a ruptured artery, a puff of night fog a monstrous apparition. Ahmed Bennani would live. His daughter, Jamila, cradled his head in her arms, and the blood running from a crease in his scalp purpled her elegant blue caftan. Still alert, he asked a numb and bewildered Captain Cherkaoui who finally came to help staunch the bleeding for an assessment. The American Ambassador and the seriously wounded would be evacuated immediately; more helicopters were to be flown in along with medical teams, the Minister instructed. He insisted that the ceremony continue, that they go on with the awarding of the prizes to the horsemen, and of course the marriage ceremony must be held without fail. Cherkaoui and his men, stunned, disbelieving, were slow to act. A Red Crescent medical worker, much harassed by cries and commands for aid, was rushed forward through the confusion, permitting Jamila Bennani to wipe her blood damp hands unceremoniously on her robe, and rise to her feet. Now transformed and, no longer preoccupied about missing the beach party at Sable d'Or, she firmly commanded Captain Cherkaoui to heed her father, to alert the people through the microphones that the danger had passed and to request that the dancers and drummers reassemble. The horsemen would gather again and all the fiancées who were able would prepare themselves for the final marriage ceremony.

Gunfire erupted briefly as two injured horses were dispatched and hauled off the field. The crowd again sucked in its breath, and, after a long, waitful pause again raised its cries. There were several dead on the fair grounds including one of the bridegrooms and the second secretary from the Embassy of Spain. There were a score of injured. At least six children and two of the brides had been trampled by the panicking crowds and would need to be evacuated to the regional hospital. A journalist with a cam recorder darted among these victims, creating graphic images which would become but brief, half-regarded flickers on the TVs of cozy pubs and living rooms.

Mai Donatelli squatted on the ground, her hands tight over her ears. Had it been like that 25 years ago in Laos when the mortars, grenades and automatic rifles tore up the jungle path where she, her family and hundreds other fleeing refugees cowered? Above the undergrowth which provided little protection, the great trees whined and sighed as the projectiles hurtled through to shred vegetation and those around her as well. The Frenchman, Henri Petard, who had admired her sketch pad last evening found her and consoled her. Her husband, Jerry, his face apparently bleeding from the attack, shoved and rammed his way back and forth through the crowds, loudly calling her name. If he saw her there down on her haunches, the Frenchman kneeling beside her, he did not acknowledge it.

Cynthia searched frantically for her daughter, but stopped to calm several hysterical women including Edna Baker who went on incoherently about dying far from home and about the high prices for carpets and trinkets.

For his bravery during the attack, Ahmed Bennani's status in the Ministerial Council would be redeemed, and many embellished stories would be told by carpet factory girls in Dar Bida, Fez and Mekness, by tenders of sheep in the Atlas foothills as well as by school girls from Agadir to Oujda, of how Jamila Bennani had walked through bombs and bullets to her father's side, and then how she, her blue caftan stained with her father's blood, calmly directed the shocked and bewildered security men and local authorities to regain order and tend to the injured.

There would be many conflicting reports on what had occurred up in the old Ben Tassen family ruins almost one kilometer distant, and on the number, make up and fate of the rebel force, which had installed itself among the crumbling walls, salons and foyers. Eric Dalton would not set down all the details in his top secret cable to Washington, nor give himself any role in the assault on the old mountain villa, and in the rescue of Karen Dennis. Neither would the local authorities be forthcoming about these details, and would cordon off the compound against the prying of thrill seekers and journalists. They would claim in generalities that they had thwarted the villainous rebels, capturing or killing all, thus preventing further harm to the innocent participants of the mountain fair.

There would of course be claims, counter claims and denials of the events, but Eric recalled them all too vividly. He, Lieutenant Berrada, Mohammed Ben Tassen and several of the security forces doubled back up the West Trail following the tracks of the horse's heels up to the main gate of the ruin. They found the horse grazing in the court yard impervious to any danger, patiently waiting for its rider to return. In the center, an over-grown patch of weeds, wild flowers and determined perennials were the survivors of what had been a well-nurtured formal garden. It was once a rarity of flourishing growth among the rock rubble and the over-grazed esparto and sage grasses of the high plateau.

THE BRIDES' FAIR

While very modest when compared with the Moorish Alhambra in Spain or the lowland palaces, and without the subtle Islamic curves and calligraphy, the compound had once featured a series of reflecting pools and water gardens, the mosaic tile remnants of which emerged here and there from the weeds and grasses. An elaborate network of conduits leading to the ridge line to the south and the mountain aquifers beyond had once supplied the fountains that spilled into the pools. The picturesque ksar which the 18th century English engraver, David Roberts, would have coveted, consisted of three mostly crumbled multi-storied stone and rose mortar structures connected by simple colonnaded passageways. It had been built in the late 1700s by the Ben Tassen clan as an aerie commanding the valley below and as a sentinel against bandits and marauding Tuaregs from the desert, those who would rustle prized rams and abduct young wives and daughters. Later in a more settled time, it became a sumptuous mountain lodge for escaping the summer heat of the lowlands. In its final years, when the young heirs of the clan spent more and more time in the coastal cities and in Europe, the place had been left to the rough hands of herders and squatters.

Before they entered the court yard to begin their search for Karen Dennis, the first of the 60 millimeter mortar rounds whooshed over their heads to explode on the field where the horsemen were displaying their skills. Almost simultaneously with that, they heard two other explosions, one near the platform where the dancers and musicians performed and the other up near the corals of sheep and goats. Rushing headlong into the courtyard, they were met by a burst of automatic weapons fire. Eric tackled the Lieutenant like the football linebacker he had been in college days, pulling him down and scuttling back towards the arched gateway. The Lieutenant was not appreciative, wondering why this American, this *blanc* had risked his life so. Someone, a man from a roof top of the ruin shouted a warning in French and Arabic. If they approached further, the throat of their hostage, a blonde young woman, would be slit like an *Id el Kebir* lamb. A second mortar streaked from the ruins and fell on the fantasia field one kilometers down below them.

"There's a hidden entry around the wall to the rear of the main building," Ben Tassen had informed them as they crouched helplessly outside the gate, waving back a score of security men who had rushed up to assist. A compound as substantial as this would have had some kind of bolt hole, some provision for escape, and Mohammed Ben Tassen pointed to the weeds and grasses which covered the rocks and wood plank cover of what could have been a water well, but which led down to a narrow passageway. It ran under the wall, under what had once been a kitchen garden for herbs and root vegetables, and into the main building of the complex. Ben Tassen senior had revealed it to his young son ten years ago as a place where he himself had played as a boy. He and the Lieutenant squeezed in after Ben Tassen, crawling single file on their bellies, their lungs filling with the rank odors of the abandoned nests of rodents and of mold from the seepage of snow melt and rain. Some of Eric's colleagues back in the Department would find the humor in it. "Groveling on your belly again, Dalton? An appropriate diplomatic posture."

After ten meters or so the end was reached, and through a removable floor panel they found themselves in a small storage room off the main salon. The larger room had been layered once in carpets of deep blues and reds. Banquettes of cedar wood with cushions of richly brocaded fabric would have lined the walls. Bright, elaborately etched brass trays on wooden stands would have served as tables for the mounds of sugared mountain couscous and the pungent lamb tagines. But the room had been empty of these amendments for years; the plastered walls were puffed and scabrous from the snows and rains which blew through the now shutterless windows. The room was bare except for two bodies slumped together like exhausted lovers. Only two hours ago, the Lieutenant had sent his corporal, Aboukar, and a man from the regional militia to make another final search of these ruins. They had been shot in the back of the head at point blank range. The Lieutenant exhibited no emotion. Grief for his comrades, his 'brothers' would have to wait.

A stone staircase led up to the second and top story, which except for ax hewn oak beams, had lost some of its roof. A cloudless, blue sky was above them, immutable except for the trail of a third mortar round which thumped off from the clay tile deck of the adjoining passageway. Then there were angry shouts, quickly silenced by gun fire, and as Eric rushed up the stone stairs, he feared he was too late.

One man slumped back from the mortar tube, and a pistol was frozen in his hand. He as the other man who lay atop Karen Dennis wore black robes, their heads wrapped in scarves of the kind the desert nomads wore. Eric rushed to Karen who lay gagged and bound under the smaller of the two men, who groaned from his wounds as he pushed him aside. Her blue eyes danced wildly as they greeted his. Unharmed, and free of her bonds, she stood and tried to appear matter-of-fact about her ordeal, more for the benefit of the concerned and solicitous Mohamed Ben Tassen than for her near frantic God Father who nevertheless rubbed her wrists where the cords had slowed her circulation, and wiped away the perspiration that in the cool mountain air could have only been induced by fear. When the confusion died down, she explained how she came back up the West Trail on the wonderful horse, and saw a frightened Berber girl in the courtyard. She had dismounted and gone to look for the girl thinking she could be of help. She could not find her, but saw the dead body in the grass and the two in the salon, and could sense the danger around her. Before she could get back to the horse and out of the courtyard someone grabbed her from behind. She never saw his face, but assumed it was the bigger man.

Several meters distant on the adjoining roof a black hooded djellaba or robe lay bunched up beside an AK47 and a remote control device. Orders were given to spare no effort in searching the ruins and the surrounding area for the missing terrorist, or indeed terrorists. Pulling the scarf from the face of the dead man at the mortar, Eric Dalton had full expected to discover Professor Jonathan McMannus, but the man with the frozen stare and the twisted, agape mouth belonged to the big, affable Chris Reilly, the instructor at the language school. The Lieutenant also shook his head in disbelief. "This is not your missing American. It is the man I stopped on the road yesterday. He was driving an expensive jeep. There were others with him, and I asked questions of one of them, a young woman of our country. She didn't appear to belong with the others in the vehicle, and, frankly, Mr. Dalton, I did not like the sight of one of our daughters camping out unchaperoned with a group of 'anglos.' They all are most likely mixed up in this awful affair."

Eric suggested that the woman seated next to Reilly in the jeep was probably the one who received treatment at the UN Refugee camp, and the one who had been positioned on the nearby roof. Neither the official government report nor his own would credit the rebel woman with killing the American sympathizer or spy, although it was apparent from the position of Reilly's wounds what had happened. He had shot the other man, Moustapha, who was apparently trying to save Karen, and was in turn was cut down by the rebel woman. It also appeared that Reilly was intent on killing all up on the roof, before he made his escape and blended back in the crowd as just another 'European.' The honors for the for the capture of Ali, Moustapha and the killing of Rachid, and a fourth, unnamed terrorist would go to Lieutenant Berrada. Even over his modest disclaimers, he would be cited with bravery, raised up to Colonel in rank, and presented with the country's highest decorations. The autopsy report, the ballistic analysis, and the interrogation records confirming who had killed Rachid and the fourth man, would be hastily boxed up, shipped to a secret government storage facility, and quickly forgotten.

In the immediate aftermath of the assault, Lieutenant Berrada exerted his control over the largely undisciplined security men who turned over every stone and every bit of rubble inside the compound as well as all about the perimeter, believing as the rumors flew about, that there had to be a full company of MPLM rebels about not merely the three on the roof. But their only find was the body of Rachid in the weeds of the courtyard and one of the Berber brides. "Sidi," a security guard said to the Lieutenant. "She was hiding in the shrine there." He pointed to the domed structure a hundred meters away in the direction of the fair. "Only disbelievers and bandits dare to enter and disturb the spirit of the marabout." The young girl wailed hysterically. The black kohl which had outlined her lids and lashes streaked down her cheeks defacing the intricate henna signs and portents. Her hair so carefully arranged had loosened from pins of pure silver.

The Lieutenant did not believe this mountain girl, this mere child, this peasant was anyway involved in this mayhem. With her sharp nose and high cheek bones she was not the stylish young woman who had been riding in the American sympathizer's jeep. It seemed clear cut. Frighten by the explosions and gunfire, she had hidden in the marabout, but he summoned the Americans, nevertheless, asking the young blond if this was the girl she had seen earlier running from the ruins. She slowly scrutinized the terrified Berber bride. "No, definitely. She's definitely not the one I saw. The other was much shorter," Karen Dennis lied.

On examining Rachid's body, they saw the bullet wound to the temple which had killed him, but there were other signs of trauma as well. A lesser wound to the head caused by a blunt instrument or a rock, and several bruises to the face and nose indicating that there had been a scuffle of some kind. "A shot to the temple, but before he died he fought with his assailant."

"Or with someone else, with McMannus," Eric speculated. He and the Lieutenant concurred that this slight girl of a little more than 100 pounds by Western measure, would not have the strength to fight with the man, nor would she know anything about hand guns. But why would Reilly do this? Eric asked. He would need Rachid and all the help he could get.

The girl was then let free, with admonishments to return immediately to her relatives down at the fair grounds. White djelabas were found for the bodies of the two soldiers, but those of Reilly and Rachid lay uncovered for the remains of the day, with Chef de Brigade Nasiri passing the latter by on at least two occasions to spit upon the corpse. Moustapha's wounds were attended to by medics from the security detail. Although he would live, his interrogation would be such that he would wish it had all come to and end in the ruins.

Within the hour, the human wailing, the huffy neighing, and the shouts and gruff commands ceased. The horse warriors, the tattooed brides and most of the several thousand spectators cautiously reassembled.

At a police check point on the road down from the fair grounds, an efficient regular of the police, not one of the meek, accepting militia, spotted an 'anglo', Professor McMannus, jammed into a grand taxi with venders and their unsold wares. He tried to cover his face with the scarf he had used to combat the road dust on the trip up.

The man, a cut on his face, his wind breaker shredded by something sharp, admitted that it was he who had seen Monique and Rachid last night. "You can call me anything you want, pervert, weirdo, but I was only concerned for her. We had been together for a little while at the evening folk festival, and I wondered why she had just disappeared. I was only looking out for her, you see?" The Professor sat on the banquette, trembling, his head in his hands. "In the woods back there and last night I didn't want to look up her dress or anything like that. She's special, but she can't take care of herself very well. You can see that Dalton. It's not some fantasy of mine."

Captain Cherkoui offered that if McMannus had killed Rachid last night he had done them a favor, but he would be under investigation, nevertheless.

"It was so dark with most of the night fires extinguished, with even the hundreds of animals above the great field silent. He heard me behind them up by the old walls near that ruin, and we fought. I'm not a fighter, but I work out and I had about fifty pounds on him even though he was wiry and strong himself. Monique ran away, and I managed to get the better of him, get in a few good licks, before he took off through the alleys of the ruins. I followed him. That's when he stopped about 10 feet away behind an old wall, turned and said "I have a gun, and I have to kill you." I froze in the darkness, picked up one of the many bricks scattered about in the ruins. I've never hurt anyone, believe me. But I guess instinct for self preservation takes over. I threw hard at him, but even if I managed to hit him from that distance it couldn't have killed him, only stunned him a little, but not killed him. I got away fast and went looking for Monique. I don't know what happened really; why we had to get into such a fight, but I could see his hands all over her and she was beating at him to stop, to let her go."

Eric could picture the usually calm Professor enraged, struggling with Rachid, unfazed by the slashing of the fibula, obsessed with his mission to protect Monique. The man became less coherent as the police hammered questions at him, and it was then that he acknowledged that he wasn't some crazy stalker. He had dated Monique, once only he admitted, back in the capital, just two weeks ago. It was a dinner date, a pleasant time, he believed. There was no sex, and he had not pressed himself on her for any. They took him off for further questioning, more concerned about any connection he may have had to Rachid and the MPLM than the murder of Rachid itself. They would let him go soon, within the hour and call it self defense, a fight among rivals for a woman, and here as in much of Europe, few were prosecuted for such crimes of the heart.

"We have ordered the helicopter back to the field, Excellency," Captain Cherkaoui said to Eric Dalton. The man had recovered his wits somewhat and was no longer the stunned immobile man who had to be challenged to act by a woman, a girl only. "Your Ambassador will be put on board immediately along with the Minister. It would be unfortunate if he were to die here in this mountain commune."

Thankfully, the Red Crescent had an oxygen mask which they rushed up from the mobile infirmary van to the caidal tent where Harlan Crane lay. It would prove to be of only temporary relief to a man who had battled several coronaries. His wife, Pam, who sat quietly by him holding his limp hand, knew well that he would not have outlived his term of office even if he had been able to enjoy the quiet dinner parties and the afternoon of slow-paced golf associated and indeed promised for this once trouble-free, Class Two diplomatic post. Eric and the authorities saluted when they loaded the stretcher. Hamidou, the bodyguard, anxiously supervised the maneuver, worrying about the tightness of the mask over the distorted face. Pamela Crane shivered against Eric in her good-bye. "I really need him to be there to pick me up at times, and he would understand, you see., understand like a kind father would."

Eric could only offer up the standard pap. It would all work out for the best. Casablanca University Hospital had a world class coronary unit. They both knew better. On the nod from Captain Cherkaoui, she managed to compose herself and receive the embraces from Cynthia, Mai Donatelli and Monique Addleman with grace. She clasped Eric's hand tightly in her good bye and searched his face for a blessing. As she disappeared into the hull of the helicopter, he debated what would become of her. Was it to be so predictable? Would she play the rich widow frequenting secluded spas and resorts to recruit the tennis pros for her bed? Or would there be shrines to her husband and the establishment of the

Crane Charitable Trust to preoccupy her? Would she fill her evenings with pro bono activities and self-improvement lectures?

Ahmed Bennani insisted on walking to the helicopter. He leaned, however, heavily on his daughter, who, a full foot taller than her father, carried herself with dignity, mindful, as photographers crowded about, of her new prominence. The Minister managed to embrace the Caids of the mountain commune, the civil authorities, and Eric Dalton as well. *"M'sieu le Chargé,"* he said. "They told me an American was found dead among the rebels, and that you were very helpful to us as well as courageous. We must stay in touch over the next few days certainly. We should coordinate our response to the outside world. As you know well the aftermath of terrorism is always more difficult to manage than response to the act itself."

The helicopter lofted up as a second appeared over the wall of mountains and arrived to begin a shuttle for the evacuation of the wounded and the distressed. Eric thanked Captain Cherkaoui for his many efforts on behalf of the safety of the American party.

"I appreciate that, but they will hold me accountable for letting this happen. I will face the tribunal and be blamed. The need for a scapegoat will be great, you see? Don't look so alarmed, M'sieu. They won't put me up against a wall, only relegate me to obscurity. But that is fate, *n'est-ce pas?"* Aides rushed up with urgent matters. "There is no time to dwell on these outcomes. We both are only servants of our respective countries, ruled by codes, traditions and by what is in the common interest. Our individuality is quite secondary to these considerations."

Most of the American party was too numb to watch the communal marriage ceremony. Over one hundred virgin brides and a score of the once-married gathered on the central field together with their prospective husbands who all wore white djellabas, bright and reflective of the late afternoon sun. But the young fiancées were not transformed by the solemnity of the moment. Some looked about nervously not reassured that order had been restored and fearing they soon would be obliterated by a mortar bomb or bullet. Even for all the pageantry and color, few stood behind the roped fences as witness or heard the droning of the imam. As a great mobile circus in its final performance before moving on, hundreds began pulling down tents and packing equipment in trucks and carts. The main caidal tent where the VIPs had sat during the aborted Fantasia, lay flattened except for its main poles. Trucks, carts, animals and diplomatic plated vehicles began causing a jam at the ceremonial horse shoe arch.

"Do you think they'll come again next year to barter their animals, trade their goods, and marry off their daughters before winter closes all the passes?" Eric asked.

"I imagine nothing will change. They will come next year, more apprehensively perhaps, but they will come as they have for many years. These traditions seem to be immutable, "Cynthia said. A shot rang out in the upper field and people everywhere cringed down.

"They've just killed the last of the wounded horses," Karen said, crying unashamedly.

Captain Cherkaoui came to request that all the Americans except the Marine van drivers leave on the next helicopter. Eric protested saying that the wounded should have priority. Another med evac helicopters is en route from Dar Bida, the Captain explained, adding that he had orders from the capital to evacuate the remaining official Americans.

"We are already being blamed for this mess, aren't we?" Eric asked, not expecting any answer from the circumspect official.

Getting his instructions for gathering the luggage and driving back, the Marine corporal said, "Tough scene, Sir. Shouldn't have come on this trip, the Sergeant neither, Sir. You're not going to put me on report too, are you, Sir?"

"For what? For being with Mrs. Crane in the van last evening? I think you're going to have to sort that out for yourself. It's of no consequence to me. I don't believe you violated any regulations of my agency."

"Last night I was keeping an eye on her, just doing my job, and she saw me following her and started in with all sorts of stuff."

"I really don't want to hear about it, Corporal," Eric said. Cynthia would undoubtedly tie it all together, reason that the spell of the Brides Fair and Pam's imminent widowhood compelled her to find a new mate, made her the aggressor, caused her to seduce Corporal Williams and not the Dutch man, Hans van Luyten. After all, the Corporal better fit her fantasy of a dark skin young Berber lover. Eric, being more the pragmatist, would try to be kind with Cynthia and her far-fetched notions. It was another one of those ironies, however, that the Ambassador's wife would forever recall in her dairies and day dreams being far up in the Mid Atlas mountains of North Africa wildly making out like a school girl in a big, white U.S. Embassy van, while the Corporal would continue to dread the experience and would always be haunted by the specter of a court marshal or something worse.

As they reached for altitude over the first deep gorge, the helicopter tilting forty-five degrees forward, it was Karen Dennis who first spotted her below them at about three kilometer's distance from the fair grounds running down the serpentine West Trail. It was, she reasoned, very likely the Berber girl who had been lurking about the old ksar and the Marabout shrine. They could see clearly the black and white wool haik of a bride. She had lost her peaked virgin cap and her long black hair had lost its silver pins as well for it streamed behind her like a great hawks sailing wings.

Below Kachou realized that the man-made machine going up the mountain drafts and making such a noise was not after her, but she continued running, nevertheless, the exhilaration pumping through her lungs. Her new, soft leather marriage slippers flew over the hard scrabble and rocks and transferred no pain. The amulet from the old seer, who knew all the scandalous secrets of women, glowed at its place between her breasts. Whether it was the amulet, her own baraka, or the foreign girl's kindness or the help of that woman with the red hair that protected her from the authorities, protected her from being raped by that awful, smelly foreigner, saved her from mating with a man more than twice her age, did not seem to matter any more for she at last knew she was free.

The foreign girl had terrified her at first, trying to ride her down, when Kachou wanted to tell her, in simple French, how she found the man in the tall grass and flowers and how she found the fibula besides him. She who flew up and down these trails like a dark African runner in the mountains of the East, easily escaped the horse rider and doubled back, going up above the ridge line and down to where many fine vehicles of the foreigners were parked. No one was about, for the assaults of the horsemen were about to begin, and everyone had gathered on the fair grounds. The foreign girl with the tawny hair of a lioness went off in the opposite direction, down the West Trail. And then someone saw her as she tried to hide under a big white van, a man older than her fiancé, and a 'European.' He beckoned for her to come out and stand before him. She froze and couldn't run from him, like when she woke sometimes on her mat, her mind functioning, but unable to moved a finger, arm or leg, all prickly, fearful she had some paralytic disease, or was indeed dead. The man smelled of forbidden beer and had much hair sticking through his shirt. He reached to touch her, to hold her chin, to briefly knead her backside like a rude old uncle. There was a strange sadness to him, or was it something she did not understand, something evil? He tried to trace the henna tattoos on her cheeks, forehead and down her throat, but she pushed his hand away. She knew she must have seemed odd to him, a curiosity, even though to her own people, those of her ksar she was normal, pretty even.

There would be much shame upon her household to be seen so, being touched by a foreign man, any man but her fiancé. The girls and women in her compound told terrible stories about men such as this one as well as those from the lowlands of this very country, but just as alien. They had little respect for mountain girls and would think little of forcing themselves on you in the cruelest way. She tried to compose herself, gather her wits and back slowly away . He reached in his pocket for a wad of paper money, far more than her own father had ever gathered in his best years of selling wool and animals. Before she could protest, he stuffed the bills roughly down the folds of her blouse, flung open the door of the van and pushed hard at her back for her to climb inside. This could not happen to her, and her anger grew quickly like a desert storm. His breath came strangely now, and she swung about, the long heavy pin of the fibula positioned through her fingers . She raked the man's sad face and jabbed at his body until the blood came and his arms flailed about. A woman with hair like fire itself appeared from the shadows made by all the many vehicles and the city-made tents. This was surely the djin who had come to save her and save this alien as well, for she would not have stopped poking the fibula into his face and chest if the person or thing with red hair had not yelled something harsh at the man and then, in Kachou's own tongue had more gently advised her to run away up towards the great field. Before she ran away, she held up the fibula with its smears of the man's blood to the strange woman and then dropped it at her feet as an offering.

When all were watching the horsemen of the Fantasia, she crept passed the empty merchants' tents, across the great field and back up to the marabout where a power greater than the winds in the worst months of winter, pulled her through the half-open door and into the darkness. She fell on her knees, reaching out for the spirit of her mother and that of her mother's own lineage, this very saint who had kept the low land sultans from these valleys over many decades. And as she prayed her most fervent best, the world outside exploded; there were terrible sounds and much yelling and screaming. She feared it was she who had caused the madness by daring to enter the shrine, by stabbing the alien man until his blood came, by refusing to wed old Ben Moha .Even her own ancestor sought to punish her and all around her. Certainly, all her family, Other Mother Itto and Aunt Rabah,were now being consumed by the angry fires outside. But soon the militia men swarmed through the door and dragged her from the shrine.

The foreign girl, who must have had much kindness in her spirit, had lied to the government men with such ease, saying that she, Kachou, was not the one up in the old ruins, the one who discovered the dead man among the tall grasses.

THE BRIDES' FAIR

Why had she not told them the truth? She ran watching with a close eye the flying machine pass beyond the mountains. Yes, this terrifying day had demanded all the spirits of her mother and of the marabout, and of the old seer's amulet, and there must have been much special magic in that silver and jeweled fibula as well to protect her from the awful smelling man who would violate her body, which had summoned the djin with the red hair. She who could run without exhaustion up and down these trails, run as swiftly as the long distance runners from the Ethiopian and Kenyan mountains, finally slowed to a walk. Far down below she saw the crossroads town where the buses and the grand taxis came that journeyed down the mountains to the cities on the sea coast. An uncle, her own mother's brother, lived there in Dar Bida and had his own fresh produce stall in the great, new medina. She would find him there, for she now had that paper money for her fare safe down below the amulet, down between her breasts. Having so decided, there was no reason to run so anymore, and she walked with a confident, steady step to a nearby well. There were many who came all this way down the trail for its cool sweet water. At the well a woman kneeled before a plastic basin left for use of passers by. The woman wore the clothing of a bride from her mountain clan, but as she scrubbed her face clean of the henna tattoos and the sweat of her exertions, Kachou saw that she was not a woman of her people. Her hair was short and her nose small like the city women in the magazines. She started to run passed her, afraid that this was another apparition, one who would force her back up the trail to her betrothal obligations.

The woman spoke to her gently in a dialect not of her own people and asked if it was far to the place where the bus came.

Kachou, reassured that the woman was of flesh and blood, and, as frightened as she, asked "Are you too running from your people and the ceremony of marriage?"

"Yes, I am leaving everything behind me," Maleka replied.

Kachou joined the woman at the well, pulled up the goat skin bucket and drank her full. Then, following her new companion's example she washed herself of dirt and blood. She began scrubbing away the black khol around her eyes and erasing the henna symbols on her face, but she believed it wise not to touch the designs on her hands until her journey was completed.

Chapter XI

Alone in his own office at last, behind the formidable walls of the U.S. Embassy, he waited for Bob Steiner, the CIA Station Chief. In this rare private moment since assuming charge, he scanned the familiar objects as a necessary reorientation, as a return to the constant and unchanging: the Korhogo wall hanging with the mystical half-human, half animal figures frozen in their dance; the pictures of former bosses, Ambassadors, Secretaries of State, most well-removed now from the current disorders in the world by death or retirement to obscure, protected hide-a-ways in Maine, New Mexico and Florida; the large framed photo of Hillary and the two children, Peter and Susan, when they were younger and eager to radiate confident beams to the camera lens. He had had little sleep in the past few days, and a sip of rare single malt Scotch from a bottle never before opened made him reel. For a moment he was back on the mountain road lurching, swerving, fearing that the unstable Marine Sergeant at the wheel would get them all killed, would in a flash of madness steer through the flimsy guard rail. The spiral plunge into the deep Mid Atlas gorge was endless; there was ample time to reflect upon failures, accomplishments, loves and regrets.

The past five days since returning from the Brides' Fair had run together. He had had little sleep and had been rubbed raw by the new pressures he faced. There had been the long late night call from Hillary, and twice this day he had led ceremonies of farewell at the airport . First, it was to the airport to see off Chris Reilly's coffin on the early morning flight to Paris, the one that connected with first of the transatlantic flights to the States. There had only been himself Cynthia Dennis, the Consular Officer, Monique Addleman and one of her colleagues, Fiona, from the language school. They were in the air freight shed, not the Salle d'Honneur, as the simple wood coffin was placed in the aluminum container. Cynthia Dennis then wired the bill of lading and the death certificate to a handle and with a plier-like device of her office, clamping them with an official seal. The finality of it set off the traces of tears from Fiona. Monique appeared more bewildered than bereaved as the British girl twisted at a ring of fine filigree gold of Senegalese make. At least the man had not been only a cold, well-programmed machine who followed orders without question, orders never put in writing, but only implied in the briefest of messages from some obscure office in Washington or somewhere even more shadowy. Strangely or appropriately, the corpse had lain along side that of the Ambassador in the small Embassy mortuary refrigerator while the Top Secret cables flew back and forth to Washington. "Killed while on official mission" it would be concluded, for he was considered a technical advisor of the US government. But there would be no burial ceremonies, nothing to the press, of course.

He had gone back to the Embassy with Cynthia in his car with Maphoud, his driver at the wheel. The air freight shed had not been air conditioned and their clothing blotched with sweat and remained so throughout even as Maphoud adjusted the car's temperature to its lowest point. She said little about her own phone call to Hillary only that she promised to talk to him soon. Eric reviewed their long friendship and wondered what was next for both of them, and, not unexpectedly, she brought up that night in Manila.

"I've tried to forget it. It was embarrassing," he said.

"We got very high. At least I did. It happens to the best of people, people with the most honorable intentions, doesn't it? I blame myself," she said.

"It wasn't like that. All these years I wanted to tell you, but it was just too awkward. You were more than very high. You got very sick all over yourself. All that Chinese food, the gin and tonic, the beer just came out in rivers. You should have seen me trying to get you into the shower. You were as loose as a rag doll. You laughed a lot under shower. I got wet too trying to hold you up. I dumped your clothes in the washing machine, and put you dried off and naked as a baby in your bed."

"I only remember your hands on me. I guess that was the towel, and I thought I was making love so slowly, so deeply. Then Karen cried for her 4 am bottle, and I woke up with the worst head, the mother of all headaches, and thought 'Oh God, what did I do?' I remembered vaguely being all over you on the couch and thought the inevitable had happened. I could never look you or Hillary in the eye again, and I wanted to grab Karen and head right to the airport, leave Manila that very morning, I was so ashamed. So that was it; I go sick, very sick and you cleaned me up in the shower?"

"That was it, yes," he said much relieved. They passed through the outer ring of the city with its comparatively new housing for those of modest means. Apartment blocks four and five stories high seem to be fused continuously across the landscape. The flat roofs sprouted thick nests of tall television aerials, most beamed across the thirty miles or so of ocean to Spain and beyond to catch the afternoon romance serials and the soccer matches. All the buildings of cement block and stucco were white by royal decree, and this whiteness was made even more so by the mid-morning sun, and from a distance as they drove along the coastal road into the city, the winding arrays of habitation appeared like bleached spinal columns of monstrous animals.

"That's another one of our little secrets, isn't it? You've always looked out for me, got me into the Consular Office program by badgering the State bureaucracy. You took us into your family, making Karen and I feel we really belonged. And all the time, I thought the glue that held us together was our little secret, not dark or unhappy, but sort of sweetly sad. That was my own fantasy. And how could I have believed you of all people would take advantage of a drunken newly minted widow even when she threw herself at you?" The white apartment blocks were behind them and they were in the city's business district, packed with morning traffic. "You tried to tell me, tell me it had to do with Tom. You extended yourself then because you felt guilty about encouraging him to go on that mission to Mindanao."

"It was more than that. I saw you so differently out on that beach beyond Subic Bay. Sure I felt obligated. You know me, duty and all that stuff, but sitting on the sand with you while you talked out your grief, your uniqueness touched me. You became more than Tom's wife, more than a widow to feel sorry for. You were an exceptional young woman who dared to explore the streets and sites of a strange, new city; who learned Tugaleg, rode the crowded Jeepnees, and didn't just sit around the Embassy club house whining about the heat, the bugs and the thieving Filipino maids." That feeling of admiration and more for her had returned that first night up in the mountains watching the Berber dancers out on the great field. The thoughts of Cynthia and Manila began to absorb him. When he had dried her off with the big terry cloth towel he had sat on the bed beside her, wanting her properly as a wife, wishing the system could allot him two wives as in these countries of North Africa, but knowing that he could not have her in any way.

The black iron gates of the U.S. Embassy compound swung open. The guards scanned the vehicle's undercarriage with their pancake devices, and they entered Fortress America. "Up at the fair," Cynthia said, "I thought of getting myself one of those flat black caps with the spangles the once-married women wear, getting a colorful Berber costume and parading myself three times around you, declaring my intentions."

No, it could not happen now especially after his long talk with Hilary and her wavering about going ahead with the divorce. He had entertained the possibilities with Cynthia often, after all they were much a like and had shared a great deal together, including the recent disastrous events in the mountains. But would it work with Tom Dennis there in the background to haunt them both? They would continue to be close friends, but then in a year or so when the air had cleared, and if they were both truly free…Well, they would keep a rain check on it.

Now was not the time, Cynthia agreed. In their tight little Embassy world, she played by the rules and wouldn't have them calling her a husband stealer, a poacher, even though it went on all the time. She genuinely felt for Hillary. That was another rub. She had tried her best with her. They had been on the phone for over an hour last evening, running up quite a bill, and frustrating Karen, expecting, a call from that Mohammed Ben Tassen, half to death. She hadn't brought up the Philippines, but told Hillary how courageous Eric had been when the bombs went off, when everyone panicked. Eric was under more pressure than ever before and needed someone, Hillary, standing beside him.

"But that's just it," Hillary said. "He lives for pressure. He's so wound up in it, he can't feel anymore. I need somebody who's flesh and blood, not some diplomatic robot, and I need neighbors and friends who don't go off every three or four years and become just yearly Christmas cards."

Cynthia had listened, but didn't mention sitting with him, infusing the night mountain air at the Brides' Fair, or tell of the other women in their party who found him very human.

Bob Steiner entered Eric's office after a quick tap on the door. He sat on the stout, brown naugahide couch, a relic from a time when almost every senior official's office in Washington and in scattered Embassies abroad contained the same ponderous furniture as testimonial to the status of the occupants. No matter that for all of its firm cushioned heft these couches were clad in synthetic leather not the real stuff, they were more comfortably supportive than the hard edged contemporary issue one could order on a free choice basis from a government approved catalog. Both he and Steiner had been kicking around long enough to be attached to good, old fashioned naugahide rather than modern Scandinavian, and perhaps they being in their mid-forties and mid career, were already relics themselves.

Steiner, tried to appear at ease, collegial. He had seen all the traffic, knew that Eric had been bombarded with Top Secret cables, emails, secure line phone calls and told by one under secretary, two assistant secretaries and the office director for North Africa of Washington's preferred position. But Eric hadn't caved as expected, at least not yet, and being now in charge, without Crane or anyone hovering over him, had repeated in terse response to all the clamor from Washington, "The Embassy does not concur in your assessment."

"You're up there in La La Land. Come down to earth Old Buddy, "Steiner said. "Reilly was just another misguided rich kid playing poor, extending himself to the oppressed and rebellious."

They didn't agree on most of it except that Reilly got to know his students, Moustapha, Rachid and Maleka very well. He was, or 'acted' as Eric maintained, their helpful friend; gave them rides home and on Sundays drove them out to the Atlantic beaches; made them presents of Embassy commissary cigarettes. "He was deep cover, a guy who lived on the land and needed little support." Eric had questioned Chris Reilly's role as an English teacher. "A big, self-assured athletic thirty year old with an expensive 4X4. It didn't make sense. A teacher? No. A fast-talking lawyer or stock broker, or an under cover operative? Yes."

Steiner rose from the brown, naugahide sofa. His fleshy, Falstaffian face, two big for his body showed for all its malleability nothing. "Wouldn't I have known, Eric? Even if I was only a mail drop I would have known something."

Not necessarily. Washington was mucking things up in the best traditions of El Salvador, Angola; obscure offices at Langley and at State playing the entrepreneur, fighting private wars. They didn't need to clue in their official man in Rabat, and certainly the Embassy itself didn't need to know. He and Steiner were only checkers of messages and pushers of paper, after all.

"Where is all this fantasy, this speculation going to get you, Eric?" he heard himself say. "I would advise you to go along with the program, or you're going to be on a lot of shit lists back Washington. You want to make Ambassador, don't you? That's the ultra for you, isn't it? You can kiss that good-bye if you continue like this."

Any thoughts Eric had about an Ambassadorship and staying in the service for the long haul seemed secondary to sorting out all the interweave of those who journeyed up to the high Mid Atlas plateau, both those who bungled and terrorized and those he held dear. "How did Reilly think he could get away with it? This country's one of the few real friends we have in this part of the world, and our deep cover operative, Washington's puppet on a short string, stupidly ruined that relationship; at the very least he seriously damaged it. How can I look Ahmed Bennani and the rest of them in the eye anymore?"

Two hour after the plane carrying Chris Reilly's body in its cargo hold left on its hop to Paris, Eric had to return to the airport along with a host of others to meet the U.S. Air Force Hercules protocol flight. He waited with Stu Connor for the host government delegation to arrive. Even for a somber ceremony the man was uncharacteristically dapper, with a new bow tie and pants that were sharply creased. The secretary in the ECON section, Ellen Whitaker had worked wonders. He no longer lacked hope or purpose.

Pam Crane sat near at hand by the flag-draped aluminum coffin container. She wore no veil, that would be a bit much, but had on a broad brim black hat which shadowed her face appropriately, and a mid-calf black dress of the sheath type, cinched by a simple cloth belt. What would she do next? He didn't see her as some gay, liberated 40 something widow cavorting with all the pretty men in foreign spas, having numerous open flings while her looks and energy endured. She had more to her than that, and would return quickly to her charity work, would serve as a mover and shaker, not a mere token, on the boards of worthy non-profit organizations. She would not disgrace herself or the Crane name and would guide her son, Jason, dutifully into manhood. Surely, she would have discrete affairs, perhaps a lasting one, out of the public glare. After all she was as human as the next person, and needed such companionship for her survival.

The Marine Corps honor guard of four from the eight man Embassy contingent, included Lance Corporal, Jess Williams, but not the Gunny Sergeant, who with his lacerated face was declared unfit for duty and ordered by the Chargé d'Affairs, Eric Dalton, to leave post within 72 hours. The Marines were appropriately in their dress blues, white gloved and unmoving in the red carpeted waiting room.

"I don't know, Old Friend," Stu Connor said while they waited for the ceremony to begin. "But those people just don't act alone anymore, certainly not after all their problems with macho mavericks in Central America, with bungling in the Middle East, with misreading terrorist threats to the U S of A itself. Somebody gave him instructions to come out of his hole and do the necessary."

"Not Bob Steiner."

"No, he's just a reporter out here like the rest of us. He didn't real know what his man was up to. Probably never met him face to face. Just passed occasional messages, if that. No, something came directly from Washington, certainly not through any official channels."

"You've checked the phone logs of the Ambassador? I bet they'll tell a story."

"I have them in my safe already; numbers dialed, parties actually talked to unclear, but I did note one or two to a local number, perhaps one of Chris Reilly's safe phones. At any rate most of those folk back in Washington will deny having talked to His Nibs about anything but the fine Moroccan weather. Believe me, my friend, we're all playing by different rules these days. The knight becomes the bishop, and the bishop the pawn, and there's no master plan, only opportunity, and no one claims responsibility for anything. Not in their job description."

On behalf of the host government, Minister of the Interior, Ahmed Bennani, wearing a hat to cover the wound to his scalp, and the Deputy Minister of Foreign Affairs gave brief, unemotional statements and placed a wreath of wine red roses grown in the valleys beyond Marrakech, on the bier. Peter Burton of the British High Commission, and Dean of the Diplomatic Corps, as the Ambassador with the longest tenure, spoke on behalf of that community. He decried terrorism, went on about the diplomat abroad as an endangered species, but paid only passing tribute to Harlan Crane. The man had not endeared himself neither to his colleagues nor to the profession. Pamela Crane with fitting solemnity, without exchanging words shook the hands of the officials, lingered a moment longer in a farewell embrace with Eric Dalton, and, then, following the gurney wheeled by the Marines to the waiting plane, tried in vain to catch the eye of the Afro-American Lance Corporal.

The special U.S. Air Force flight finally lifted off the east-west runway, becoming soon a black smudge of engine exhaust against the perfect blue of the North African sky. The messages in from Washington, informed that Harlan Crane would be buried at Arlington National Cemetery with full honors, as was only fitting. He had been both a serving Ambassador and a veteran, having been Captain of Infantry in an Ohio National Guard Unit that had seen duty in Vietnam. The Embassy would be expected to be represented. Would it be the Chargé d'Affaires himself? Without question, more for Pam Crane's sake than anything else. He could use the occasion to have it out with the Department, since the air would have cleared by then, and the death of Crane and others largely forgotten as they all became absorbed in containing the next brush fire. He would take ample leave time to look into his personal business as well, as Cynthia, Stu Connors and others advised.

THE BRIDES' FAIR

They quickly cleared the sale d'honneur of the funerary wreathes and sprays of deep red roses. Most appreciated that they only had to wait twenty minutes between planes for the arrival of the American Congressional delegation. The Americans today dominated the events, taxing the airport services, and feeding more speculation and rumor. The Moroccan gendarmes kept the sale d'honneur free of the media. They waited outside with their mini cams, cameras and recorders. Their press credentials, photo ids and other tokens of official status hung about their necks, swaying with them first this way and then that in ballet unison as another diplomatic limo quickly discharged another someone of newsworthy or so-so importance. All of them had received the Embassy's several press releases, heavily edited by Washington and less informative than the reports in *Maroc Soir*, CNN, the BBC and the AFP. They all clamored for exclusives, but not even those several they truly trusted, not even the AP stringer Arlene Roth, wife of the US AID Director, of the Embassy's senior team, could get in the door on this one.

As Chargé d'Affaires he could had to stick to scripted responses, first having tried to avoid, evade and otherwise refuse all requests for interviews. He had a copy of the talking points in the breast pocket of his suit jacket, but like the Press Releases, it was generalized pap which would only spark more questions which would only lead to more "I'm not at liberty to answer that."

"We'll have to let the press in for Farrell," Eric said to Stu Connors. "He'd be surprised and a little bit upset that his visit draws no attention."

Ahmed Bennani and his party also waited for the arrival of the Congressman sitting on overstuffed chairs and divans of fine, supple Moroccan leather. The diminutive Minister of Interior appeared almost swallowed by his cushion and held to the arms of the chair as if to avoid drowning.

"Believe me when I say how ashamed and disgusted I am by this whole business, by the pain and trouble we Americans have caused you." Eric had tried several times to get through to Bennani by telephone, but had been given the run around by an imperious secretary. He certainly understood why the man would want to avoid him.

"I accept that, M'sieu. I know of your good will and professionalism," Bennani said wearily, but without a trace of rancor. "We are always at airports these days, *n'est-ce pas* ? Tomorrow I will come again with my daughter, the one you met at the fair, and my sons. We'll be seeing Madam Bennani off to New York where she'll be representing us at the United Nations women's rights session. I may try to join her there in several weeks. We plan to take a little holiday, our first holiday together in some time, you see?"

When the Air France Airbus hit the runway, the Minister changed his tone. "Your Congressman, being on your Human Rights Committee, will want to know about the treatment of the two prisoners of that misguided band of terrorists. They have already become a symbol for some of your Western media, and some of our more militant youth here, I must admit. Nevertheless, I will remind your Congress that four national police officers were killed by them, three in cold blood. They have become our martyrs as well as those six innocent spectators who were trampled to death in the panic they caused. No, we will not put on a public circus trial for your people or your journalists. If your Congressman fails to understand our position, fails to understand my feeble English, I trust you will tell him that there is absolutely no room for negotiation or compromise on this."

"No questions. No questions," the Congressman said to the small cluster of Western media stringers who were permitted into the salle d'honneur. "But may I say to you all very simply that I, my staff and indeed all of my Congressional colleagues are deeply saddened by the tragic loss of Ambassador Harlan Crane. To those of the United States Mission assembled here, let me say briefly that all of us are greatly indebted to you for your perseverance, your professionalism and for the difficult role you play in representing us abroad." After he had shaken the hands of Minister Bennani, the Deputy Foreign Minister, all the lesser officials, and the dozen of senior and junior officers that had been trouped out from the Embassy, he turned to Eric. "It's unfortunate timing on my part isn't it? Or it's fortuitous. An Ambassador dead; one of our popular technical advisors, the teacher, as well. Yes, they gave me a thorough briefing in Washington, although I'm still not sure what really happened up in those mountains. My Committee will expect my personal, off-the-record report on what the devil went on here. So I expect you will level with me."

The Congressman had large, prematurely gray shocks for eyebrows that hung over his lids like visors. His hair was equally gray and bushy, and if he did visit an 'in' Washington salon, they were artful in maintaining the man's unkempt, harried image. "But why would the rebels waste precious capital in hitting a rural fair far up in the mountains? The pattern of most of these revolutionaries is to embarrass the military through well-planned ambushes, or to display their daring by infiltrating major population centers. But to mow down a few horses and some sheep herders, what's the political gain?"

THE BRIDES' FAIR

They now sat in the plastic bubble, the classified, bug proof conference room, futuristic and unreal to most. The Congressman remained alert in spite of the all night flight to Paris, the two hour wait at Charles De Gaulle, and another two hours down to North Africa. At first Eric repeated much of the two long reporting cables that he and Stu Connors had ground out that Sunday when he had returned to the city by helicopter. " Remember we had half the diplomatic corps there, a high level Moroccan delegation, and a few Western journalists, covering this major folk spectacle. What better way to embarrass the authorities and get the attention of the international community ? What better way to demonstrate that they could reach one of the most isolated regions of the country, to elude the police and the militia, slip through the check points, and perhaps win some support from the mountain clans? One thing the MPLM didn't count on in all probability was the presence of the American Ambassador and the Minister of the Interior. They didn't count on all the increased security. That was a last minute decision of the central authorities, who wanted to show the flag at this important rural fair, having some justifiable concerns about national solidarity. That same day, as we reported, they tried without success to stage a riot in Casablanca, hoping the marching trade unionists and the student groups would join in. They tried too to blow up the main railroad bridge on the southern line but were caught by a sharp-eyed Pioneer scout unit. They managed to cause some minor damage as we hear it from the government, to a military microwave communications installation. So it wasn't a good show by any account, you see? They bungled, but killed unnecessarily, killed the innocent, and, in the bargain, we, the U.S., are being made the heavy."

"Well, you got a few columns in some of the papers back home. Moved the domestic violence and sex off the front pages for a hot minute. A few are even passing right over any hint of dirty tricks by the boys in Langley, saying it was a calculated assassination attempt on the American Ambassador."

"Of course, neither you nor I believe that," Eric said. The Congressman had been told that the media was hounding the Embassy, accusing it of a cover up and looking under the rocks for that smoking gun. "We believe that the original mission of that small band was simply to fire off a few mortar rounds, try not to hurt anyone, and engage in a brief fire fight with the lightly armed security forces as they slipped down out of the mountains in their escape back to their desert camp. But something went wrong. One was captured before he even got half way up the mountain to the fair. The other young man in the band was found dead in an old ruin near the fair grounds after having had a fight with our mild mannered professor of horticulture. That left, two of the original group plus

Reilly who came to the rescue so it seems. But there's some evidence he planned to join up with them all along, and it's almost certain that he planned to gun them all down, including his hostage, my God Daughter, in trying to make his escape."

"Theories, conjecture. Nothing hard, Dalton. And whether you're right or not," Joe Farell said, "it's of no consequence. In the final analysis, my committee's sticking with the story that Crane, our American Ambassador, was somehow a target in all of this. Yes, I know he had a weak heart and was an unremitting alarmist to boot, and I know that he was after us day and night to supply this government with fancy hardware to repress a grass roots rebellion for which we, I at least, have some sympathies. You've heard the story many times, probably played some part in them yourself: Super power America trying to plug up all the leaks in every blasted corner of the world; getting itself into messes where it has absolutely no business; seeking political and economic stability even if it means siding with totalitarianism, with the dictator *du jour*."

Eric interrupted the Congressman to agree that they had again stupidly insinuated themselves in the business of another country, a country that had been one of our closest allies .

"Sure, sure Dalton, but the MPLM has no voice in any of this, no political representation, right? They're outlaws to some and freedom fighters to others. My committee has several petitions on their behalf. The press is already having a field day with this. Freedom fighters cut down, and a U.S. Ambassador killed in the line of duty."

"A US intelligence operative orchestrating events, " Eric added.

"All people know so far, is that an American technical advisor, a humble English teacher, for God's sake, died heroically up in those ruins trying to stop the bloodshed. Nobody is going to budge on that one Dalton, no matter how many people cook up conspiracy and double agent plots."

"We have another problem, Joe," Marsha Lipkin said to the Congressman with accustomed informality. " We need confirmation that the authorities have indeed captured, the woman, Maleka Diouri, I believe. Aren't they holding her with that other one, without counsel. I see torture, summary execution, all in violation of numerous Geneva conventions. And wasn't it this Maleka who actually stopped the others from firing off those bombs, and wasn't she who really saved your Karen Dennis's life?" Marsh Lipkin's glasses slipped down to the bridge of her nose while both elbows rested like clubs poised for combat on the blond oak conference table. The air conditioning hissed bringing filtered air into the plastic bubble conference room of the Embassy, the room presumably immune to the most advanced electronic listening gear, the room from which no secrets could escape.

Eric had Bob Steiner working all his strings with the local security agencies, and had nothing not even a hint or a rumor of any capture of the woman MPLM rebel. There was only a biographical sketch of her and the others. It seemed too that the woman's younger brother had been killed in an accident on a mountain road near the fair, either traveling to join up with the group, or bent on becoming a martyr by sending the Embassy van crashing off a span over a ravine. As far as where the two men were being held and there ultimate fate, well, there was nothing, for most of their best contacts had become like the deep Atlas canyons, only echoing back one's repeated questions. Of all the other MPLM units active over the long weekend of rallies and fairs, the authorities claimed to have killed six and captured eleven. Also, more than one hundred suspected sympathizers had been rounded up, including one from the Mid Atlas Brides' Fair, a merchant of fine carpets from Casablanca. " Depending on your sympathies, Congressman, this was not a poor accounting for a government which did not appear, to our late Ambassador, at least, to take the MPLM threat seriously."

"That begs the question," Marsha Lipkin said. "We want to make sure they all will get a fair trial."

"We want you to arrange that we talk to them," Joe Farrell added. "We have leverage in this country, don't we Dalton? We give them all this foreign aid and military hardware."

"Not as much as you think, Congressman." Eric knew the request would be coming. It was a non-starter at best, although the Embassy would try and catalog all the polite and harsh refusals. "We very may well have lost any influence we had now that the fingers are pointing at us, pointing at Reilly and possibly the Ambassador himself." There was a special irony to have presided over the send off of two bodies who were very possibly co-conspirators in this whole damn affair. The irony of them sharing the same refrigerated crypt for three days was even grimmer. Ambassador Crane had been going on for several weeks about how the host government didn't take the MPLM seriously. For weeks he cornered people at cocktail receptions about the threat. He was on the phone every night to Washington and apparently had direct talks with Reilly as well.

"Harlan Crane? No one took him seriously in Washington, except that he was a big contributor to the party and had a very attractive wife. But Washington will now praise to the heavens and tell the world he died in the line of duty, an American hero."

" My political advisor, Mr. Connors, has had his telephone log analyzed, and we have a number of confirmed calls to political friends, to the National Security Council, to perhaps our teacher, Chris Reilly and we found six or seven calls to the chief cook and bottle washer at Langley, himself."

"Can I accept that?" Joe Fared asked. " And aren't you on the wrong side of this? I hear you blaming us, Crane, this teacher, Reilly, and the MPLM. What about the government here? If they had the right set of policies, they wouldn't have a restless young population and high unemployment. They wouldn't have the MPLM."

"I'm not in the blame game, Congressman," Eric said. "I'm just looking for the truth."

"Search away, and when you find it let me know," the Congressman said with his first smile of the meeting. "And if you're right about, Crane, and you probably are, think of the pain back in Washington; think of the pain to his wife, and he has a son, doesn't he, studying medicine or something?"

"I've thought about it. I thought about it long and hard."

"Now getting back to Maleka Diouri and the others," Marsha Lipkin said.

"There are principles here," the Congressman said as they went round and round with each other in the plastic bubble. "Justice, fairness, human rights, transparency. I've got to stick by those."

"And I by my principles as well, Congressman."

Chapter XII

At dusk in the old medina of the city, the electronic amplifiers carried the muezzin's voice from the central mesjid tower. "Allah Akbar. Allah is the One, the compassionate." The sound reached up over the blinding white billows of drying sheets on the flat roof tops; soared over the great delta near the old Roman port of Sallaca; drowned out the crashing of the ocean surf, and raced out over the blue-black Atlantic. Muted and distorted by the winds, it would somehow float on for more than four thousand miles to America's Carolina coast where in a parking lot of an expansive shopping mall, someone would look to the sky and hear faintly something that was neither avian nor airplane. The charcoal fires combined with the exhaust of the evening's rush hour vehicles, refracted the residual light of the sun, softening the rectangular, white-washed medina structures. Then, the dusk haze joined with the spume of the ocean waves to make the city, even the steel and glass towers of the new business district, appear lost and indefinite as in a Turner landscape.

Eric had arrived early, and while waiting for the others, Monique Addleman offered him a glass of sauvignon blanc, made from grapes grown on the terraced vineyards near Meknes where there had been such vineyards since the time of the great Roman-Berber ruler, Juba II, two thousand years ago. The chilled bottle sweat with moisture in the early autumn heat of North Africa. They sat together for a moment in the wrought iron chairs that a medina *forgeron* had made from a design she had found in a magazine. She rose, placed a hand on Eric Dalton's shoulder, and then removed herself to her small, well-equipped kitchen to help the housekeeper, Mina, with the *amuses gueules* and the feast of saffron chicken and vegetable couscous. "Sort of a thanksgiving, and a welcoming too." She sung sometimes in French, sometimes in Arabic to cheer on her culinary skills, quite basic when compared to Mina's, but she dared to improve. In recent days, since their return from the mountain fair, she had become obsessed with spices, sauces, mincing those awful onions, and had even tried her hands a baking, as if suddenly after all that terrible business these things mattered. Her guests would learn this and be surprised by her almond crusted torte, all hers to the very whipping of the eggs, in spite of Mina's efforts to help.

The others would arrive any minute. Doug Baker about now would be on the dangerously fast auto route from the Casablanca airport, having retrieved Max Addleman, Monique's father, as he insisted on doing. Their talk would be of locations, the evaluations of local film crews, whether *primes d'encouragements,* or bribes, were required for government permits, and especially, given the events of five days ago, the risks of sinking big bucks into any film project. Doug's wife, Edna Baker, still feeling more on edge than normal even with the strong sedatives prescribed by the helpful Embassy nurse, had told Monique 'perhaps just for desert,' which meant she would appear with a flourish, but late. Lance Corporal Williams asked if he could bring his girl friend, Zoubida, and similarly the hostess encouraged Mae Donatelli to come with her *trés sympa ami* from the French Embassy. Cynthia would be here soon with flowers from that florist in the old souk, not the rich, chocolate desert she offered, for she and Monique had gone on some time over the phone about baking and daring to bake an almond crusted torte. Jonathon McMannus would also be here, and there had been much back and forth with Monique two nights ago about the wisdom of inviting him.

Monique had called Eric at the Embassy several times, catching him at last. She had her dinner party on her mind and wanted to know his schedule. Her father was coming, and she needed to do something special as well as show off all her new friends. At the airport that morning as they watched Chris Reilly's coffin in its aluminum container move out on the baggage cart to the waiting flight to Paris, she had been appropriately silent only nodding a good bye to him and Cynthia Dennis when they had finished and turned to leave for their cars. Within the week Monique had lost a lover whom she had grown to fear if not despise, and a teaching colleague who she believed she could trust, lean on, hug when she had the blahs. She had lost them both within hours of each other.

On the phone, she sounded recovered and getting on with her life, but he asked if it wouldn't be too much for to have a dinner party so soon. Wait a week or two, he advised. "No, it'll be all right, " she had said. "I'm tougher than I seem. But if you could drop by for a bit, I'd like to go over the planning, you know, who to invite and all. Also, we could talk about what exactly went on at the Brides' Fair. I'm still confused."

THE BRIDES' FAIR

He had only an hour or so to spare before he had to be at the Ambassador's residence, *Dar America* as some labeled it, to host a reception for Congressman Farrell, who, thankfully, would be leaving on a morning plane, going up the line to Algeria, Tunisia, and ending up in Egypt. Over sixty guests had been invited, but Eric didn't expect too many from the host government after Farrell had pounded too many conference tables and asked too many questions that could not be answered. Ahmed Bennani had already sent his regrets claiming he'd be hosting a small dinner party, *en famille*, for his wife on the eve of her departure to New York and the UN women's conference. The Deputy Foreign Minister had been assigned to put in an appearance, a brief one Eric was sure, and of course there would be the usually band of suspects from the Diplomatic Corps, coming to lap up the latest rumors and the free booze.

At her entry way, an intricately carved arch framing an antique oak door with a rich linseed oil patina, they embraced for a time but did not kiss beyond the brief European presses to each cheek. What did she really want to say? Thank you for standing up to my director at the school; for comforting me in those woods when I was so frightened; for not believing I was mixed up in that awful business with Rachid and Chris; for not thinking me a flake?

He had had his fantasies, one when he woke just that morning in the empty upper floor of his residence, hearing the first stirrings of the maid, Rachida, and the houseman, Mohamed, as they fussed about to make his simple breakfast of toasted baguette with cheese, coffee, and freshly squeezed orange juice. It would be something extraordinary to just pack it in, go back to the States with her, the two of them sitting close, nuzzling each other playfully on the seven hours across the Atlantic to Washington. He would chuck it in, tell 'Mother State' finally where to get off. He'd find a teaching job without too much trouble at some quiet New England college, not one of those overwhelming state universities, or over-precious Ivies. He'd be excellent at explaining the intricacies and the illusions of international relations. She'd fit right in as an instructor of French and Arabic. Her classes would be over-subscribed. They would have two children and live just off campus in one of those old, sprawling country cottages. They would eschew signing up for guided learning tours to foreign places, and would reject any notion of themselves serving as tour leaders.

That evening Monique showed him about her jewel of an apartment, the thick masonry walls, the carved wood wainscoting and door and window frames and the rustic glazed floor tile suggesting the inner sanctum of some medieval castle, the terrace looking out to the river delta, a balcony above a defensive moat. For her part, Monique also had envisioned Eric Dalton as a lover, seeing them together in her stout bed. The bed would hum from the pleasure of it; the thick walls would echo their cries. He would be the one to bring good, lasting baraka to it as the medina craftsman had foretold. The squiggles and curlicues cut deep into the oak would become reconfigured with their new blessings. They would endure beyond one night and beyond a lazy weekend with too much good wine. They would outlast the confusion of embassies and politics, and the children they produced on that sturdy bed would be too clever and too beautiful for words. It wouldn't happen with Eric Dalton, she knew. He had rushed to her apartment not to offer himself to her, but to bring some closure to his role of guide and mentor to those who had journeyed with him to the mountain fair.

She had fetched a school cahier in which she had written her proposed guest list. "Do you think I should invite Dr. McMannus?" she asked

"Yes, I definitely would," he had replied.

She told Eric that Dr. McMannus had sent a note to her school that morning. Was he too embarrassed to come by personally? He should be for all the freaky stuff he pulled. He mentioned the fibula and asked in his note didn't they still have that date to take it to that expert to look at? Date? That was far out, although they had a date for dinner at the Alhambra a month ago The food was marvelous; they had some things in common, the languages, roaming around Africa. He behaved himself, but she had never thanked him. Well, someone should look at the caftan pin. It had been in the middle of a lot of really bad stuff. "Isn't he a little weird?" she had asked Eric.

"I thought so, but when you sort it all out, I believe he was really concerned about you."

"Trying to see me take a pee? And didn't he go to extremes with Rachid? I wanted to get away from the guy, sure, but he didn't have to go and kill him."

" McMannus didn't kill him. Reilly did; probably thought he was too impetuous, making such a scene with you; thought he would screw things up. And in the forest, I think, too, McMannus was concerned about your safety, not playing the Peeping Tom."

Eric, half-dozing on Monique's terrace, heard the women talking and laughing in the kitchen; caught the aromas of cumin, saffron, stewing meats and vegetables, and witnessed how the electric lights sprinkled themselves along the far banks of the delta. His anger had subsided somewhat. As he and Congressman Farrell had argued, who was to blame for the senseless killings?

THE BRIDES' FAIR

Had anyone, the government here, the MPLM rebel faction, the US gained anything by it? The big buzz in the city didn't have anything to do with blame, culpability, and the screw ups of the one and only Super Power, but with two attractive young women, Jamila Bennani and Maleka Diouri. From different worlds and destinies, the popular press splashed their pictures across the front page together with the gushy, wildly imaginative stories. Perhaps, those who reached behind the sensationalism would find the answers.

Although, Eric Dalton was on just a few shit lists back in Washington, and with his career, his marriage and any thoughts of repairing old or finding new relationships up in the air, he felt relieved that everyone who had traveled with him to the Brides' Fair had returned in one piece to the capital, for which he gave thanks to all the real and unreal forces that had intervened on their behalf. Some were physically scarred, and most emotionally so. All would be here tonight, except the Gunny Sergeant and Pamela Crane. On different flights they both now had landed in Washington, with the Ambassador's wife and her husband's coffin met with ceremony, by the Secretary of State himself perhaps. Eric hoped the Sergeant had not been met by 23 year old kids from Quantico wearing SP arm bands, but by someone from Navy medical. He had advised in his message to Washington, that "Sergeant Donatelli had served with distinction as Guard Commander during most of his tour; however, during the last several months at post he had become unstable, at times violent, and was in urgent need of observation and counseling."

Lance Corporal Jess Williams pulling his shy friend, Zoubida along burst through the arched door way. He was all 'hi guys' and hugs. Cynthia followed shortly thereafter holding out a large arrangement of yellow roses, sweat peas and baby's breath. She went on about the long lines for visas at the Embassy and getting to the florist only seconds before closing time, when they were rolling down the metal shutters for the night. Karen would be arriving soon with that nice and so helpful Mohamed Ben Tassen. Astonished by the view from Monique's terrace, Cynthia, as usual, dug up facts on the historic significance of the structure, built along the river in the 17th century as a fortified palace. She couldn't recall the original architect's name, an Andalusian Moor she assumed, but the well-known architect, Ben Abdelatif responsible for the renovation, had been sent by the Embassy on a lecture tour in the United States. "You remember him, Eric. It was just last year." Eric didn't remember the man. There were so many comings and goings through the Embassy's revolving doors, he could no longer keep up.

The oak door, an antique Cynthia surmised, salvaged from the original construction, remained open as with welcoming dinner parties everywhere in the world. Jonathan McMannus hesitated a moment in the archway, looking for the hostess, his discomfort apparent. He had trimmed his beard to a less hirsute Van Dyke style, and wore a bandage on his cheek. Eric never realized how tall and trim the man was, for on the trip to the Fair he had been bundled up in bulky travel clothes and wore those heavy hiking boots that had become fashionable in America, but were a necessity to those who tramped about tilled fields and dense orchards. After greeting the few who had already arrived, the hostess did her best to make him feel at home by bussing him warmly on both cheeks and accepting his bottle of fine champagne with a cry of appreciation. "The pin? Yes, the fibula. I have it safely tucked away in my bed room. We should definitely go together to get it appraised. It has been through a lot, don't you agree?"

They all stood on the terrace sipping their drinks and waiting for the others to arrive. It would be a great party, a great reunion and Monique had done wonders in getting everyone together. They looked out over the darkening roof tops with their drying clothes, their forest of TV antennas and their profusion of geranium pots. The contiguous buildings of the old medina stepped down to the banks of the river delta. Across the delta similar buildings of the twin city, Salé reached out as if to form a bridge. The good friends clicked glasses, freshly chilled and fogged and sweating in the North African night. "That was the Roman port of Sallaca as you know. But in the 17th and 18th centuries," Cynthia explained. "Pirates, many of them English used to harbor there. They were known as the Sale Rovers. There's a folk song; you may know it. It goes like…….." Even Cynthia had to laugh at herself and at this bit of history which seemed so insignificant compared to all they had been through.

THE END